D0842553

THE PEARL THAT BROKE ITS SHELL

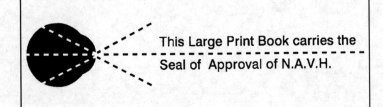

This Large Print Book carries the
Seal of Approval of N.A.V.H.

THE PEARL THAT BROKE ITS SHELL

NADIA HASHIMI

THORNDIKE PRESS
A part of Gale, Cengage Learning

GALE
CENGAGE Learning·

Farmington Hills, Mich • San Francisco • New York • Waterville, Maine
Meriden, Conn • Mason, Ohio • Chicago

GALE
CENGAGE Learning®

Thorndike Press® Large Print Peer Picks.
The text of this Large Print edition is unabridged.
Other aspects of the book may vary from the original edition.
Set in 16 pt. Plantin.

LIBRARY OF CONGRESS CATALOGING-IN-PUBLICATION DATA

Names: Hashimi, Nadia, author.
Title: The pearl that broke its shell / by Nadia Hashimi.
Description: Large print edition. | Waterville, Maine : Thorndike Press, 2016. | Series: Thorndike Press large print peer picks
Identifiers: LCCN 2016024672| ISBN 9781410493934 (hardcover) | ISBN 1410493938 (hardcover)
Subjects: LCSH: Large type books. | Women—Afghanistan—Fiction.
Classification: LCC PS3608.A78975 P43 2016 | DDC 813/.6—dc23
LC record available at https://lccn.loc.gov/2016024672

Published in 2016 by arrangement with William Morrow, an imprint of HarperCollins Publishers

Printed in Mexico
1 2 3 4 5 6 7 20 19 18 17 16

To my precious daughter, Zayla.
To our precious daughters.

Seawater begs the pearl
To break its shell
— FROM THE ECSTATIC POEM
"SOME KISS WE WANT,"
BY JALAL AD-DIN MOHAMMAD RUMI,
THIRTEENTH-CENTURY PERSIAN POET

CHAPTER 1
RAHIMA

Shahla stood by our front door, the bright green metal rusting on the edges. She craned her neck. Parwin and I rounded the corner and saw the relief in her eyes. We couldn't be late again.

Parwin shot me a look and we picked up our hurried pace. We did the best we could without running. Rubber soles slapped against the road and raised puffs of dusty smoke. The hems of our skirts flapped against our ankles. My head scarf clung to beads of sweat on my forehead. I guessed Parwin's was doing the same, since it hadn't yet blown away.

Damn them. It was their fault! Those boys with their shameless grins and tattered pants! This wasn't the first time they'd made us late.

We ran past the doors, blue, purple, burgundy. Spots of color on a clay canvas.

Shahla waved us toward her.

"Hurry!" she hissed frantically.

Panting, we followed her through the front

door. Metal clanged against the door frame.

"Parwin! What did you do that for?"

"Sorry, sorry! I didn't think it would be that loud."

Shahla rolled her eyes, as did I. Parwin always let the door slam.

"What took you so long? Didn't you take the street behind the bakery?"

"We couldn't, Shahla! That's where he was standing!"

We had gone the long way around the marketplace, avoiding the bakery where the boys loitered, their shoulders hunched and their eyes scouting the khaki jungle that was our village.

Besides pickup games of street soccer, this was the main sport for school-age boys — watching girls. They hung around waiting for us to come out of our classrooms. Once off school grounds, a boy might dart between cars and pedestrians to tail the girl who'd caught his eye. Following her helped him stake his claim. *This is my girl,* it told the others, *and there's only room for one shadow here.* Today, my twelve-year-old sister, Shahla, was the magnet for unwanted attention.

The boys meant it to be flattering. But it frightened the girl since people would have loved to assume that she'd sought out the attention. There just weren't many ways for the boys to entertain themselves.

"Shahla, where is Rohila?" I whispered. My

10

heart was pounding as we tiptoed around to the back of the house.

"She's taken some food to the neighbor's house. Madar-*jan* cooked some eggplant for them. I think someone died."

Died? My stomach tightened and I turned my attention back to following Shahla's footsteps.

"Where's Madar-*jan*?" Parwin said, her voice a nervous hush.

"She's putting the baby to sleep," Shahla said, turning toward us. "So you better not make too much noise or she'll know you're just coming home now."

Parwin and I froze. Shahla's face fell as she looked at our widened eyes. She whipped around to see Madar-*jan* standing behind her. She had come out of the back door and was standing in the small paved courtyard behind the house.

"Your mother is very much aware of exactly when you girls have gotten home and she is also very much aware of what kind of example your older sister is setting for you." Her arms were folded tightly across her chest.

Shahla's head hung in shame. Parwin and I tried to avoid Madar-*jan*'s glare.

"Where have you been?"

How badly I wanted to tell her the truth!

A boy, lucky enough to have a bicycle, had followed Shahla, riding past us and then circling back and forth. Shahla paid no attention to him. When I whispered that he was looking at her, she hushed me, as if speaking it would make it true. On his third pass, he got too close.

He looped ahead of us and came back in our direction. He raced down the dirt street, slowing down as he neared us. Shahla kept her eyes averted and tried to look angry.

"Parwin, watch out!"

Before I could push her out of the way, the cycling stalker's front wheel rolled over a metal can in the street; he veered left and right, then swerved to avoid a stray dog. The bicycle came straight at us. The boy's eyebrows were raised, his mouth open as he struggled to regain balance. He swiped Parwin before toppling over on the front steps of a dried-goods shop.

"Oh my God," Parwin exclaimed, her voice loud and giddy. "Look at him! Knocked off his feet!"

"Do you think he's hurt?" Shahla said. She had her hand over her mouth, as if she had never seen a sight so tragic.

"Parwin, your skirt!" My eyes had moved from Shahla's concerned face to the torn hem of Parwin's skirt. The jagged wires holding the spokes of the bicycle together had snagged Parwin's dress.

It was her new school uniform and instantly Parwin began to weep. We knew if Madar-*jan* told our father, he would keep us home instead of sending us to school. It had happened before.

"Why are you all silent only when I ask you something? Do you have nothing to say for yourselves? You come home late and look like you were chasing dogs in the street!"

Shahla had spoken on our behalf plenty of times and looked exasperated. Parwin was a basket of nerves, always, and could do nothing but fidget. I heard my voice before I knew what I was saying.

"Madar-*jan,* it wasn't our fault! There was this boy on a bicycle and we ignored him but he kept coming back and I even yelled at him. I told him he was an idiot if he didn't know his way home."

Parwin let out an inadvertent giggle. Madar-*jan* shot her a look.

"Did he come near you?" she asked, turning to Shahla.

"No, Madar-*jan.* I mean, he was a few meters behind us. He didn't say anything."

Madar-*jan* sighed and brought her hands to her temples.

"Fine. Get inside and start your homework assignments. Let's see what your father says about this."

"You're going to tell him?" I cried out.

"Of course I am going to tell him," she answered, and spanked my backside as I walked past her into the house. "We are not

13

in the habit of keeping things from your father!"

We whispered about what Padar-*jan* would say when he came home while we dug our pencils into our notebooks. Parwin had some ideas.

"I think we should tell Padar that our teachers know about those boys and that they have already gotten in trouble so they won't be bothering us anymore," Parwin suggested eagerly.

"Parwin, that's not going to work. What are you going to say when Madar asks Khanum Behduri about it?" Shahla, the voice of reason.

"Well, then we could tell him that the boy said he was sorry and promised not to bother us again. Or that we are going to find another way to get to school."

"Fine, Parwin. You tell him. I'm tired of talking for all of you anyway."

"Parwin's not going to say anything. She only talks when no one's listening," I said.

"Very funny, Rahima. You're so brave, aren't you? Let's see how brave you are when Padar-*jan* comes home," Parwin said, pouting.

Granted, I wasn't a very brave nine-year-old when it came time to face Padar-*jan*. I kept my thoughts bottled behind my pursed lips. In the end, Padar-*jan* decided to pull us out of school again.

We begged and pleaded with Padar-*jan* to

14

let us return to school. One of Parwin's teachers, a childhood friend of Madar-*jan,* even showed up at the house and tried to reason with our parents. Padar-*jan* had relented in the past but this time was different. He wanted us to go to school but struggled with how to make that happen safely. How would it look for his daughters to be chased by local boys for all to see? Awful.

"If I had a son this would not be happening! Goddamn it! Why do we have a house full of girls! Not one, not two — but five of them!" he would yell. Madar-*jan* would busy herself with housework, feeling the weight of disappointment on her shoulders.

His temper was worse these days. Madar-*jan* would tell us to hush and be respectful. She told us too many bad things had happened to Padar-*jan* and it had made him an angry man. She said if we all behaved then he would go back to being his normal self soon. But it was getting harder and harder to remember a time when Padar-*jan* wasn't angry and loud.

Now that we were home, I was given the extra chore of bringing the groceries from the store. My older sisters were quarantined since they were older and noticeable. I was, thus far, invisible to boys and not a risk.

Every two days I stuffed a few bills from Madar-*jan* in the pouch that she had sewn into my dress pocket so I would have no excuse for losing them. I would wind my way through the narrow streets and walk thirty minutes to reach the market I loved. The stores were bustling with activity. Women looked different now than they had a few years ago. Some wore long blue *burqas* and others wore long skirts and modest head scarves. The men all dressed like my father, long tunics with billowing pantaloons — colors as drab as our landscape. Little boys wore ornate caps with small round mirrors and gold scrolling. By the time I got there, my shoes were again dusty and I would resort to using my head scarf as a filter for the clouds of dirt the hundreds of cars left in their wake. It was as if the khaki-colored landscape were dissolving into the air of our village.

Two weeks into our expulsion from school, the shop owners had gotten to know me. There were not many nine-year-old girls who would walk determinedly from shop to shop. And having watched my parents haggle prices down, I thought I could do the same. I would argue with the baker who tried to charge me double what I had seen him charge my mother. I bickered with the grocer trying to tell me that the flour I wanted was imported and, thus, subject to a surcharge. I pointed out that I could just as easily buy the same fancy flour from Agha Mirwais down the block and scoffed at the price he quoted. He gritted his teeth and put the flour in the bag along with the other groceries, muttering words under his breath that no child should hear.

Madar-*jan* was pleased to have my help with the market. She was busy enough with Sitara, who was just taking her first steps. Madar-*jan* had Parwin look after Sitara while she and Shahla took care of the household chores of dusting, sweeping and preparing the night's meal. In the afternoons, Madar-*jan* made us all sit down with our books and notebooks and complete the homework she assigned us.

For Shahla, the days were isolating and difficult. She longed to see her friends and talk with her teachers. Shahla's strengths were her intuition and her intelligence. She wasn't at the very top of her class, but she usually charmed her teachers just enough to push her onto the short list of star pupils. She was average looking but put extra care into her appearance. She would spend at least five minutes brushing her hair every night, since someone told her it would make her locks grow longer. Shahla's face was what people would call pleasant, not beautiful or memorable. But her personality made her glow. People looked at her and couldn't help but smile. Polite and proper, she was a favorite in school. She had a way of looking at you and making you feel important. In front of family

17

and friends, Shahla made Madar-*jan* proud as she would speak maturely and inquire after each member of the family.

"How is Farzana-*jan* doing? It's been so long since I've seen her! Please do tell her that I was asking about her," she would say. Grandmothers would nod in approval, praising Madar-*jan* for raising such a respectable girl.

Parwin was another story. She was striking. Her eyes were not the mud-brown color the rest of us had. Instead, hers were a hazel-gray blend that made you forget what it was that you were going to say. Her hair hung around her face in wavy locks with a natural luster. She was undeniably the best-looking girl in our whole extended family.

But she was completely lacking in social skills. If Madar-*jan*'s friends stopped by, Parwin would shrink into a corner, busying herself with folding and refolding a tablecloth. If she could manage to escape before company made it into the room, even better. Nothing was more of a relief to her than avoiding the traditional three-kiss greeting. She kept her answers brief and all the while kept her eyes on the nearest escape route.

"Parwin, please! Khala Lailoma is asking you a question. Can you please turn around? Those plants do not need to be watered at this very moment!"

What Parwin lacked in social skill, she more

18

than made up for in artistic ability. She was masterful with pencil and paper. Graphite turned into visual energy in her hands. Wrinkled faces, an injured dog, a house too damaged to repair. She had a gift, an ability to show you what you did not see, even though your eyes graced the same sights as hers. She could sketch a masterpiece in minutes but washing the dishes could take hours.

"Parwin is from another world," Madar-*jan* would say. "She is a different kind of girl."

"What good is that going to do her? She's going to have to survive and make her way through this world," Padar-*jan* would retort, but he loved her drawings and kept a pile of them at his bedside to flip through from time to time.

The other problem with Parwin was that she'd been born with a bad hip. Someone had told Madar-*jan* she must have been lying on her side too much when she was pregnant. From the time Parwin started to crawl, it was obvious something was off. It took her much longer to learn to walk and to this day she hasn't lost her limp. Padar-*jan* had taken her to a doctor when she was five or six but they said it was too late.

Then there was me. I didn't mind the expulsion as much as my sisters. I suppose this was because it gave me opportunity to venture out on my own, without two older

19

sisters to chastise me or insist I hold their hands as we crossed the street. Finally, I had freedom — even more than my sisters!

Madar-*jan* needed help with the errands and lately it was impossible to depend on Padar-*jan* for anything. She would ask him to pick up some things from the market on his way home and inevitably he would forget, then curse her for having an empty pantry. But if she went to the bazaar by herself, he went into an even worse rage. From time to time, Madar-*jan* asked the neighbors to pick up an item or two for her but she tried not to do that too often, knowing they already whispered about the peculiar way Padar-*jan* had of walking up and down our small street, his hands gesturing wildly as he explained something to the birds. My sisters and I wondered about his behavior too, but Madar-*jan* told us our father needed to take a special medicine and that was why he sometimes acted strangely.

At home, I could not help but talk about my adventures in the outside world. It bothered Shahla more than Parwin, who was content with her pencils and paper.

"I think tomorrow I'll pick up some roasted chickpeas from the market. I have a few coins. If you like, I could bring you some, Shahla."

Shahla sighed and shifted Sitara from one hip to another. She looked like a young exasperated mother.

"Forget it. I don't want any. Just go and finish the chores, Rahima. I'm sure you're just dawdling out there. In no rush to come home, I bet."

"I'm not *dawdling.* I go and do the errands that Madar-*jan tells* me to do. But never mind. I'll see you later."

It wasn't so much that I wanted my sisters to be envious. It was more that I wanted to celebrate my new privileges to come and go, to wander through the shops without my sister's supervision. If I had a little more tact, I would have found another way to express myself. But my loud mouth caught Khala Shaima's attention. Maybe there was a higher purpose to my insensitivity.

Khala Shaima was my mother's sister — her older sister. Madar-*jan* was closer to her than anyone else in her family and we saw her often. Had we not grown up around her, we probably would have been frightened by her appearance. Khala Shaima was born with a crooked spine that wiggled through her back like a snake. Although our grandparents had hoped to find a suitor before her shape became too obvious, she was passed over time and again. Families would come to ask about my mother or Khala Zeba, the youngest of the sisters, but no one wanted Khala Shaima with her hunched back and one raised shoulder.

21

She understood early in life that she would not catch anyone's eye and decided not to bother fussing with appearances at all. She let her eyebrows grow in, left those few stray chin hairs and dressed in the same drab clothing day in and day out.

Instead, she focused her energies on her nieces and nephews and taking care of my grandparents as they aged. Khala Shaima supervised everything — making sure we were doing satisfactorily in school, that we had proper clothing for the winter and that lice hadn't nested in our hair. She was a safety net for anything our parents might not have been able to do for us and she was one of the few people who could stand being around Padar-*jan*.

But you had to know Khala Shaima to *get* her. I mean to really *get* her. If you didn't know that she had the best intentions at heart, you could be put off by the lack of pleasantries in her conversation, by her sharp criticisms or by the doubtful squint in her eyes while she listened to you talk. But if you knew how she'd been spoken to her whole life, by strangers and family, you wouldn't be surprised.

She was good to us girls and always came with candy-laden pockets. Padar-*jan* would comment snidely that her pockets were the only sweet thing about Khala Shaima. My sisters and I would feign patience while we waited for the rustle of chocolate wrappers. When she arrived, I had just returned from the market, and in plenty of time to get my share of the sweets.

"Shaima, honest to God, you're spoiling these girls! Where are you getting chocolates like these from these days! They can't be cheap!"

"Don't stop a donkey that's not yours," she fired back. That was another thing about Khala Shaima. Everyone used those old Afghan proverbs, but Khala Shaima could hardly speak without them. It made conversations with her as circuitous as her spine. "Stay out of it and let's let the girls get back to their homework."

"We're done with our homework, Khala Shaima-*jan,*" Shahla said. "We've been working on it all morning."

"All morning? Didn't you go to school today?" Shaima's eyebrows furrowed.

"No, Khala Shaima. We don't go to school anymore," Shahla said, averting her eyes since she knew she was throwing Madar-*jan* into the fire.

"What does that mean? Raisa! Why aren't the girls in school?"

Madar-*jan* lifted her head from the teapot reluctantly.

"We had to take them out again."

"In God's name, what ridiculous excuse did you come up with this time to keep them

23

from their studies? Did a dog bark at them in the street?"

"No, Shaima. Don't you think I would much rather have them going to school? It's just that they're running into foolishness in the streets. You know how boys can be. And, well, their father is just not happy to send them out so they can be toyed with by the neighborhood boys. I don't blame him, really. You know, it's only been a year that the girls are even able to walk in the street. Maybe it's just too soon."

"Too soon? How about too late! They should have been going to school all this time but they haven't. Imagine how far behind they are and now that they can catch up, you're going to keep them at home to scrub the floors? There will always be idiots in the street saying all kinds of things and giving all kinds of looks. You can believe that. If you hold these girls back for that, you're no better than the Taliban who closed their schools."

Shahla and Parwin shot each other looks.

"Then what am I supposed to do? Arif's cousin Haseeb told him that —"

"Haseeb? That moron who's dumber than a Russian tank? You're making decisions for your children based on something Haseeb said? Sister, I thought more of you."

Madar-*jan* huffed in frustration and rubbed her temples. "Then you stay here till Arif gets home and you tell him yourself what you

24

think we should do!"

"Did I say I was leaving?" Khala Shaima said coolly. She propped a pillow behind her uneven back and leaned against the wall. We braced ourselves. Padar-*jan* hated dealing with Khala Shaima's intrusions and he was just as blunt as she was about it.

"You're a fool to think these girls are better off rotting in this home instead of learning something in school."

"You never went to school and see how well you turned out," Padar-*jan* said facetiously.

"I've got a lot more sense than you, *engineer-sahib.*" A low blow. Padar-*jan* had wanted to major in engineering when he finished high school but his marks didn't make the cut. Instead, he took some general classes for one semester and then dropped out to start working. He had a shop now where he fixed old electronics, and though he was pretty good at what he did, he was still bitter about not making it as an engineer, a highly regarded title for Afghans.

"Damn you, Shaima! Get out of my house! They're my daughters and I don't need to listen to a cripple tell me what I should do with them!"

"Well, this cripple has an idea that may solve your problem — let you keep your precious pride while the girls can get back into school."

"Forget it. Just get out so I don't have to look at your face anymore. Raisa! Where the hell is my food?"

"What is your idea, Shaima?" Madar-*jan* jumped in, eager to hear what she had to say. She did respect her sister, ultimately. More often than not, Shaima was right. She hurriedly fixed a plate of food and brought it over to Padar-*jan,* who was now staring out the window blankly.

"Raisa, don't you remember the story our grandmother told to us? Remember Bibi Shekiba?"

"Oh, her! Yes, but how does that help the girls?"

"She became what her family needed. She became what the king needed."

"The king." Padar-*jan* scoffed. "Your stories get crazier every time you open your ugly mouth."

Khala Shaima ignored his comment. She had heard much worse.

"Do you really think that would work for us too?"

"The girls need a brother."

Madar-*jan* looked away and sighed with disappointment. Her failure to bear a son had been a sore spot since Shahla's birth. She had not anticipated that it would be brought to everyone's attention again tonight. She avoided Padar-*jan*'s eyes.

"That's what you've come here to tell me!

26

That we need a son? Don't you think I know that? If your sister were a better wife, then maybe I would have one!"

"Quit jabbering and let me finish."

But she didn't finish. She only started. That night Khala Shaima started a story of my great-great-grandmother Shekiba, a story that my sisters and I had never before heard. A story that transformed me.

CHAPTER 2
SHEKIBA

Shekiba.

Your name means "gift," my daughter. You are a gift from Allah.

Who could have known that Shekiba would become the name she was given, a gift passed from one hand to another? Shekiba was born at the turn of the twentieth century, in an Afghanistan eyed lasciviously by Russia and Britain. Each would take turns promising to protect the borders they had just invaded, like a pedophile who professes to love his victim.

The borders between Afghanistan and India were drawn and redrawn from time to time, as if only penciled in. People belonged to one country and then the other, nationalities changing as often as the direction of the wind. For Great Britain and the Soviet Union, Afghanistan was the playing field for their "Great Game," the power struggle to control Central Asia. But the game was slowly coming to an end, the Afghan people ferociously resisting outside control. Chests expanded with pride when Afghans talked about their resilience.

But parts of Afghanistan were taken — little by little until its borders shrank in like a wool sweater left in the rain. Areas to the north like Samarkand and Bukhara had been lost to the Russian Empire. Chunks of the south were chipped away and the western front was pushed in over the years.

In that way, Shekiba was Afghanistan. Beginning in her childhood, tragedy and malice chipped away at her until she was just a fragment of the person she should have been. If only Shekiba had been prettier, something at least pleasing for the eye to gaze upon. Maybe then, her father could have hoped to arrange a proper marriage for her when her time came. Maybe people would have looked at her with an ounce of kindness.

But Shekiba's village was unforgiving. To get to Kabul, one had to ride one week, crossing a river and three mountains. Most people spent their entire lives in the village, in the green fields surrounded by mountains, walking the dirt roads that connected one compound to another. Their village was in a valley, dark soil nurtured by the nearby river and tall peaks giving a sense of enclosure, privacy. There were a few dozen clans, extended families who had known each other

29

over generations. Most people were related to each other, somehow, and gossip was one way to keep busy.

Shekiba's parents were second cousins, their marriage arranged by Shekiba's paternal grandmother. Their family, like many others, lived off the land. Each generation splintered the family's land so that people would have a place to build a home, if they decided to leave the clan's main house. Shekiba's father, Ismail Bardari, was the youngest in his home. His older brothers had married before him and filled the compound with their wives and children.

Seeing there was no room for him and his new bride, Shafiqa, Ismail picked up his chisel and set to work. He was lucky though, in that his father bequeathed him a lot with such fertile soil that his share of crops would be guaranteed. He was the hardest working of his brothers and his father wanted to ensure that the land's potential would be realized. There were many hungry mouths to feed and a good yield could bring in extra income from the village. His brothers lacked Ismail's instincts. He had a gift. He knew just the right temperature at which to plant, how often to till the soil and the perfect amount of water to make crops grow. Ismail's brothers resented him for being their father's favorite. They pretended to prefer living in the main home. In the end, he surrounded the house with a wall of mud and stones to give it privacy, as a proper Afghan home needed.

Ismail brought his nervous bride to their new home, surrounded by a small plot of land that bordered his brother's. Standing outside, she could see her in-laws coming and going from the house, their *burqas* blue spots on a khaki landscape. When the women headed in her direction she would hurry inside and cover herself, embarrassed that her belly was swollen with child. But Shafiqa's in-laws found her dull and timid, and over time they took less interest in her and her children. The women sighed heavily when they spoke with her and whispered to her husband when she wasn't near. Had Shekiba's father been like most other men, he might have heeded those whispers and taken a second wife. But Ismail Bardari was unlike some other men and stayed with the one wife he had, however his mother and sisters felt about her.

Shekiba's brothers, Tariq and Munis, were the only real link to the clan. Shafiqa watched over Shekiba and her little sister Aqela, nicknamed "Bulbul" because her light, melodic voice reminded Ismail of the local songbird. Tariq and Munis would come and go between their father's and their grandfather's homes, acting as couriers of clothing, vegetables and news. The boys were well liked by their grandparents and valued as male heirs. Ismail's mother, Bobo Shahgul, often said the two boys were the only good thing to come from Shafiqa. The boys overheard many hateful comments but they knew better than to share everything they heard. Shekiba and Aqela didn't realize how little their father's family cared about them since they spent their days close at their mother's side. Sometimes, too close.

A clumsy two-year-old Shekiba changed her life in the blink of an eye. She woke from a midmorning nap and set off to find her mother. Shekiba heard the familiar sounds of peeling in the kitchen and stumbled into the cooking niche. Her small foot caught on the hem of her dress and her arm flailed into the air, knocking a pot of hot oil from a burner top before her mother could reach her. The oil flew out and melted the left half of Shekiba's cherub face into blistered and ragged flesh.

Shafiqa screamed and doused her daughter's face with cool water but it was too late. It took months to heal, as Shafiqa diligently kept Shekiba's face clean, using a compound the local alchemist had mixed for them. The pain got worse as her skin fought to recover. The itching drove Shekiba mad and her mother was forced to wrap her hands in cloth, especially while she picked away at the dead, blackened skin. Fevers came, so high they made the toddler's body tremble and writhe, and Shafiqa had nothing to offer, nothing she could do but pray at her daughter's side, her body rocking back and forth, and beseech Allah for mercy.

Bobo Shahgul came to see Shekiba when she heard about the incident. Shafiqa anxiously waited to hear any helpful advice her mother-in-law might offer but Bobo Shahgul had none. Before she left, she suggested Shafiqa pay closer attention to her children and muttered thanks that it hadn't been one of the boys.

Shekiba's survival was nothing short of a miracle, another gift from Allah. Though her face healed, she was not the same. From then on, Shekiba was halved. When she laughed, only half her face laughed. When she cried, only half her face cried. But the worst part was the change in people's expressions. People who saw her profile from the right would begin to smile, but as their view turned the corner, beyond her nose, their own faces would change. Every reaction reminded Shekiba that she was ugly, a horror. Some people would step back and cover a gaping mouth with a hand. Others would dare to lean in, eyes squinted, to get a better look. From across the road, people would stop in their tracks and point.

There. Did you see her? There goes the girl with half a face. Didn't I tell you she was horrid

33

looking? God only knows what they did to deserve that.

Even her aunts and uncles would shake their heads and cluck their tongues every time they saw her, as if every time they were freshly disappointed and shocked to see what she looked like. Her cousins came up with twisted names for her. *"Shola* face," as her skin resembled the lumpy soft rice. *"Babaloo,"* or monster. That one she hated more than the others, since she too was afraid of the *babaloo,* the creature that frightened every Afghan child in the night.

Shafiqa tried to keep her sheltered from the comments, the jeers, the stares, but it was too late to save Shekiba's self-esteem, a commodity people didn't value much anyway. She covered Shekiba with a *burqa* when she saw people approaching their home or on the rare occasion when the family ventured into the village.

Remember, "Shekiba" means "a gift." You are our gift, my daughter. No need to let others gawk at you.

Shekiba knew she was horribly disfigured and that she was lucky to even be accepted by her immediate family. In the summers, the *burqa* was hot and stifling but she felt safer within it, protected. She was not exactly happy but was satisfied to stay in the house and out of sight. Her days passed with fewer insults that way. Her parents withdrew even more from the clan, and the resentment toward Shafiqa's aloofness grew.

Tariq and Munis were both energetic, and being just a year apart in age, they could pass for twins. When they were eight and nine, they were helping their father with the field-work and running errands in the village. They usually ignored the comments they heard about their "cursed sister" but Tariq had been known to throw back insults from time to time. On one occasion, Munis came home with scattered bruises and a foul temper. He'd had more than he could take of the local boys pestering him about his half-faced sister. Padar-*jan* had gone to the boy's home to make amends with his parents but he never reprimanded Tariq or Munis for defending their Shekiba.

Aqela, always smiling, would sing nursery rhymes in her sweet *bulbul* voice and kept her mother and Shekiba's spirits lifted as they did the chores. They were happy keeping to themselves. They didn't have much, but they had everything they needed and never felt lonely.

In 1903, a wave of cholera decimated Afghanistan. Children shriveled up within hours and succumbed in their mothers' weak arms. Shekiba's family had no choice but to use the poisoned water that coursed through their village. First Munis, then the others.

35

The illness came quickly and it came strong. The smell was unbearable. Shekiba was stunned. She saw her siblings' faces grow pale and thin in days. Aqela was quiet, her songs reduced to a soft moan. Shafiqa was frantic; Ismail quietly shook his head. Word came from the compound that two children had died, one from each of Shekiba's uncles.

Shekiba and her parents waited for their own bellies to begin cramping. They nervously cared for the others, watching each other and waiting to see who else would become ill. Shekiba saw her father put his arms around his wife's shoulders as she rocked and prayed. Aqela's skin was graying, Tariq's eyes were sunken. Munis was quiet and still.

She was thirteen when she helped her parents wash and wrap Tariq, Munis and Aqela, the songbird, in white cloth, the traditional garb for the deceased. Shekiba sniffled quietly, knowing she would be haunted by the memory of helping her moaning father to dig the graves for her teenage brothers and delicate Aqela, who had just turned ten. Shekiba and her parents were among the survivors.

It was the first time in years that the clan made an appearance. Shekiba watched her uncles and their wives come in and out of the house, paying their obligatory respects before moving on to the next home grieving their dead. It went without saying that they pitied Shekiba's parents, not so much for the loss of their three children, but for the disappointment that Allah could not have spared one of the sons instead of the defective girl. Luckily, Shekiba was numb by then.

Thousands died that year. Her family's losses were notches on the epidemic's belt.

One week after her three children were buried, Shafiqa began to whisper to herself when no one was looking. She asked Tariq to help her with the water pails. She warned Munis to eat all his food so that he would grow up to be as tall as his brother. Her fingers moved through the yarn of the blanket as if she were braiding Aqela's hair.

Then Shafiqa started sitting idly, plucking individual hairs from her head, one by one, until her scalp was bare; then her eyebrows and lashes disappeared. With nothing left to pluck, she resorted to picking at the skin of her arms and legs. She ate her food but gagged on pieces that she had forgotten to chew. Her whispers became louder and Shekiba and her father pretended not to notice. Sometimes she would listen and then giggle with a lightheartedness alien to their household. Shekiba slowly became her mother's mother, making sure she bathed and reminding her to go to sleep at night.

A year later, in the same dismal month of Qows, Shekiba's languishing mother decided not to wake up from sleep. It came as no surprise.

Ismail held his wife's hands and thought how tired they must be from all the wringing they had endured. Shekiba brought her cheek to her mother's and saw that her eyes had lost their desperate glassiness. *Madar*-jan *must have died looking at the face of God,* Shekiba thought. Nothing else could have brought the look of peace so quickly.

The house sighed in relief. Shekiba bathed her mother one last time, taking care to wash her bald head and realizing that her mother had even plucked the hairs from her womanly parts. The weight of sadness lifted. Her corpse was shockingly light.

By the following day, Shekiba and her father were back in the field to open the earth once more. They did not bother to tell the rest of the family. Her father read a prayer over the mound of dirt and they looked at each other, quietly wondering which of them would join the others first.

Shekiba was left with her father. A cousin stopped by to tell them of an upcoming wedding and took back news of the new widower to the rest of the clan. The hawks descended on the house within days, extending their condolences, but only after they advised Shekiba's father that he now had the opportunity to begin again with a new wife. They named a few families with eligible daughters in the village, most of them only a few years older than Shekiba, but her father was so heartbroken and fatigued that his family could not manage to arrange a new wife for him.

Shekiba came of age with only her father to turn to, his sparse words, his lonely eyes. She worked beside him day and night. The more she did, the easier it was for him to forget that she was a girl. He began to think of her as a son, sometimes even slipping and calling her by her brothers' names. The village chattered about them. How could a father and daughter live alone? Sympathy gave way to criticism and Ismail and Shekiba grew even more distant from the outside world. The clan did not want to be associated with them and the village had no interest in a scarred old man and his even more scarred daughter-son.

Over the years, Ismail lulled himself into believing that he had always lived without a wife and that he had always had only one child. He managed by ignoring everything. He was the only person who did not see Shekiba's marred face and did not notice that, as a young woman, she might need some direction from a female. When she bled every month, he pretended not to smell the soiled rags that she would keep soaking and hidden behind a stack of logs in their two-room home. And when he heard her shed tears, he shrugged her sniffles off as a touch of flu.

Shekiba's father took his daughter-son to the fields to help him manage their small plot of land. She hoed, she slaughtered and she chopped as any strong-backed son would do for his father. She made it possible for Ismail to go on believing that life had always been father and son. Shekiba proved to be able-bodied, affirming her father's confidence in her ability to manage the farm. Her arms and shoulders knotted with muscle.

Years passed. Shekiba's features grew coarser; her palms and soles were thick and callused. Every day, Ismail's back hunched more, his eyes saw less and his needs grew. There were days Shekiba was left to run the entire farm and house on her own.

Had Shekiba been any other girl, she probably would have felt lonesome in this solitary life, but her circumstances were different. The children nearby would always point and tease, as would their parents. Her appearance was shocking everywhere, except at home.

People who are beset by tragedy once and twice are sure to grieve again. Fate finds it easier to retrace its treads. Shekiba's father became weaker, his voice raspier, his breaths shallower. One day, as Shekiba watched from the wall of stone and mud, he grabbed his chest, took two steps and crumpled to the ground with a sickle in his grip.

Shekiba was eighteen years old but she knew what to do. She dragged her father's body back to the house on a large cloth, stopping every few steps to adjust her grasp and to wipe away the tears that trickled down the right side of her face. The left side of her face remained stoic.

She laid his body in the living room and sat at his side, repeating the four or five Qur'anic verses that her parents had taught her until the sun came up. In the morning, she began the ceremony she had performed too often in her short life. She undressed her father, careful to keep his private areas hidden beneath a rag. The ritual washing should have been done by a man but Shekiba had no one to call on. She would rather have invited Allah's wrath into her home than turn to those vile people.

She bathed him, turning away as she poured water onto his man parts and blindly wrapping his stiff body in a cloth, as she and her mother had done with her sister. She dragged him back outside and opened the earth one final time to complete her family's interment. Shekiba chewed her lip and debated digging one more spot for herself, thinking there would be no one left to do so when her turn came. Too tired to do anything more, Shekiba said a few prayers and watched her father disappear under clods of earth — disappear like her sister, her brothers and her mother.

She walked back to the hollow house and

sat silently — afraid, angry and calm.
Shekiba was alone.

Chapter 3
Rahima

"We wouldn't be the first. It's been done before."

"You're listening to that lunatic Shaima and that story about your precious grandmother."

"It wasn't my grandmother. It was —"

"I don't care. All I know is that woman makes my head ache."

"Arif-*jan,* I think it would be wise for us to consider this. For everyone's sake."

"And what good will come of it? You see everyone else who has done it? They all have to change back in a few years. It doesn't help anything."

"But, Arif-*jan,* she could *do* things. She could go to the store. She could walk her sisters to school."

"Do what you want. I'm going out."

I listened carefully from the hallway, just a few feet from the bedroom we all shared. Our kitchen was behind the sitting room, a few pots and a gas burner. Our home was spacious, built in a time when my grandfather's family had more. Now these walls were bare and cracking and looked more like those of our neighbors.

When I heard Padar-*jan* strain to get up, I quickly tiptoed off, my bare toes silent on the carpet. When I was sure he was gone, I came back to the living room to find my mother lost in thought.

"Madar-*jan*?"

"Eh? Oh. Yes, *bachem.* What is it?"

"What were you and Padar-*jan* talking about?"

She looked at me and bit her lip.

"Sit down," she said. I sat cross-legged in front of her, careful that the hem of my skirt reached over my knees and covered my calves. "You remember the story your *khala* Shaima told the other night?"

"The one about our great-great-great-great . . ."

"You're worse than your father, sometimes. Yes, that one. I think it is time we change something for you. I think it would be best if we let you be a son to your father."

"A son?"

"It's simple and it's done all the time, Rahima-*jan.* Just think how happy that would make him! And you could do so many things that your sisters wouldn't be able to do."

She knew how to pique my interest. I cocked my head to the side and waited for her to go on.

"We could change your clothes and we'll give you a new name. You'll be able to run to the store any time we need anything. You could go to school without worrying about the boys bothering you. You could play games. How does that sound?"

It sounded like a dream to me! I thought of the neighbors' sons. Jameel. Faheem. Bashir. My eyes widened at the thought of being able to kick a ball around in the street as they did.

Madar-*jan* wasn't thinking of the boys in the street. She was thinking of our empty cupboard. She was thinking of Padar-*jan* and how much he had changed. We were lucky when he brought home some money from an odd job here or there. Every once in a while, his mind focused enough that he was able to tinker with an old engine and breathe life back into it. His small earnings were spent, unevenly, on his medicine and keeping us clothed and fed. The more Madar-*jan* thought about it, the more she realized how desperate our situation was becoming.

"Come with me. There's no reason to delay anything. Your father is taking more and more . . . medicine these days. Your *khala* Shaima is right. We need to do something or we're going to be in real trouble."

We girls were nervous about getting sick. We worried that if we did, we would have to take the same medicine that Padar-*jan* took. It made him do funny things, behave in funny

45

ways. Mostly he just wanted to lie about the house and sleep. Sometimes he said things that didn't make sense. And he never remembered anything we said. It was worse when he didn't take his medicine.

He had broken nearly everything in the house that could be broken. The dishes and glasses survived only because he lacked the energy to pull them from the cabinet. Anything within reach had already been thrown against a wall and smashed to pieces. A ceramic urn. A glass plate that Madar-*jan* had received as a gift. They were casualties of the war inside Padar-*jan*'s head.

Padar-*jan* had fought with the *mujahideen* for years, shooting at the Russian troops that bombarded our town with rockets. When the Soviets finally slinked back to their collapsing country, Padar-*jan* came home and prayed that life would return to normal, though few people could recall such a time. That was 1989.

In that year, he returned home to his parents, who barely recognized him as the seventeen-year-old boy who had left home with a gun slung over his shoulder in the name of God and his country. His mother and father hurriedly arranged a marriage for him. At twenty-four years old, he was long overdue and they thought a wife and children would bring him back to normal, but Padar-*jan,* just like the rest of the country, had

46

forgotten what normal was.

Madar-*jan* was barely eighteen when they were wed. I imagine she must have been as terrified on her wedding night as I was on mine. Sometimes I wonder why she did not warn me, but I suppose those are not things women should speak of.

As the country planned for new beginnings, so did my parents. My sister Shahla came first, followed by Parwin and me. Then came Rohila and Sitara. We were all a year apart and close enough in age that only our mother could tell us apart once we were walking. But with one daughter after another, Madar-*jan* did not become the wife that Padar-*jan* expected. Even more sorely disappointed was my grandmother, who had respectably borne five sons and only one daughter.

Things fell apart at home, just as they did across the country when Russia left. While the Afghan warriors turned their guns and rockets on each other, Padar-*jan* tried to settle into life at home. He tried to work alongside his father as a carpenter but a man who had been taught only to destroy found it hard to create. Loud sounds jarred him. He grew frustrated and drifted back to the warlord, Abdul Khaliq, he had fought under.

Warlords were Afghanistan's new aristocracy. Allegiance to a man with local clout meant a better life. It meant an income when there otherwise would be none. It wasn't long before Padar-*jan* had oiled his machine gun, slung it over his shoulder and gone off to fight again, this time in Abdul Khaliq's name. He returned home every so often. When he returned the first time and found that Madar-*jan* had given birth to yet another girl, me, he walked out again and returned to the killing fields with fresh anger.

Madar-*jan* was left behind with a houseful of girls and only her bitter in-laws to turn to. We lived in a small two-room house, part of the family's compound. War pushed families together. Two of my uncles were killed in the fighting. My uncle's wife died giving birth to her sixth child. Until he could remarry two months later, his children were cared for by my mother and my other aunts. We should have felt like one big family. We should have been kind to each other. But there was resentment. There was anger. There was jealousy. There was, as there would be in the rest of the country, civil war.

Madar-*jan*'s family lived a few kilometers away, but they might as well have been on the other side of the Hindu Kush mountains. They had given their daughter to Padar-*jan* and did not want to interfere in her relationship with her new family. Madar *jan*'s deformed sister, Shaima, was the exception.

Deformities were not easily forgiven, so Khala Shaima steeled herself to resist the name-calling, the ridiculing, the gawking.

Older than Madar-*jan* by nearly ten years, our aunt would tell us things that no one else would say. She would tell us about the war, how the warlords controlled everything and conquered without mercy, even attacking women in the most shameful way of all. Usually Madar-*jan* hushed her older sister with a pleading look. We were young, after all, and it wasn't Khala Shaima who would have to quiet our night terrors. Sometimes Khala Shaima forgot we were children and told us so much that we sat wide-eyed, frightened of our own father.

When Padar-*jan* came home, we cowered. His moods ranged from jubilant to foul but there was no predicting where on the spectrum he would be or when he would make an appearance. Madar-*jan* was lonely and welcomed her sister's visits, even if her mother-in-law griped about them. My grandmother made sure to report to her son just how many times Khala Shaima had come to visit while he was away, clucking her tongue in disapproval and inciting his wrath. It was her way of showing Madar-*jan* that she was in control of our home, even if it sat fifty feet away from the main house.

Everyone wanted control but it was hard to get. The only one who seemed to have any was Abdul Khaliq Khan, the warlord. He and his militia were able to gain control of our town and the neighboring towns, having

49

pushed back their rivals. We were north of Kabul and hadn't seen any fighting in about four years but from what we heard, Kabul was besieged. People in our town shook their heads in dismay at the news but our homes were already pockmarked and turned to rubble. It was time for the privileged in Kabul to taste what we had survived.

Those were ugly times. I can only imagine what my father must have seen from the time he was just a teenage boy. Like so many others, he numbed himself to the ugliness with the "medicine" that Madar-*jan* referred to. He clouded his mind with the opium that Abdul Khaliq kept around, as crucial to his men's ability to wage war as the ammunition strapped to their backs.

Madar-*jan* grew weary of our father but all she could do was look after us girls. Khala Shaima brought her some concoction that she took so she wouldn't have any more children after me. I don't know what the medicine was, but it worked for six years. When Madar-*jan* felt her belly stretch again, she prayed and prayed and did all the things that Khala Shaima told her to do. Nothing worked. Disappointed and fearful, she named our youngest sister Sitara and dreaded the day that Padar-*jan* would come home to find out she had brought yet another daughter into his home.

Then came the Taliban. They were just

another faction in the civil war but they gained in strength and their regime crept across the country. It didn't affect us much until we were pulled out of school, windows were blackened and music was banned. Madar-*jan* sighed but carried on, her daily routine largely unaffected by the new codes.

When word got out that our town had fallen to the Taliban, Abdul Khaliq brought his men home to fight back — and to defend his honor as a warlord. There were weeks of explosions, crying, burying, and then the men came home, victorious. Our town was again our own.

Padar-*jan* stayed home for a few months. He spent time with his brothers, tried to help his father recover some business and even helped some of the neighbors to rebuild their homes. Things were going well until the day that a young boy came knocking on our door with a message for Padar-*jan*. The next morning, Padar-*jan* oiled his machine gun, donned his *pakol* hat and headed back out to rejoin the war.

He came back here and there but his mood swings were worse with each visit. We saw him only two or three days at a time and we were children, too young to understand the rage he brought home. He was not the same person at all. Even Bibi-*jan,* my grandmother, would cry after his visits, saying she had lost another son to the war.

It was my cousin Siddiq who told us about the news. He had heard from our grandfather.

"Amrika. That's who. They came and they're bombing the Taliban. They have the biggest guns, the biggest rockets! And their soldiers are so strong!"

"Why didn't Amrika come before?" Shahla had asked. She was nearly twelve years old then. Wise enough to come up with questions that made us look at her with admiration.

Siddiq was ten but had the confidence of a boy twice his age. His father had been killed years ago and he grew up under our grandfather's wing. He was the man of his house.

"Because the Taliban bombed Amrika. Now they're angry and they're bombing them back."

Our grandfather entered the courtyard and overheard our conversation.

"Siddiq-*jan,* what are you telling your cousins?"

"I was just telling them about Amrika, Boba-*jan.* That they're firing rockets at the Taliban!"

"Padar-*jan,*" Shahla asked timidly, "did the Taliban destroy many homes in Amrika?"

"No, *bachem.* Someone attacked a building in Amrika. Now they are angry and they've come after him and his people."

"Just one building?"

"Yes."

We were silent. It sounded like good news. A big, powerful country had come to our rescue! Our people had an ally in the war against the Taliban!

But Boba-*jan* could see in Shahla's eyes that there was something that puzzled her and he knew just what it was. Why would Amrika be so upset after just one building was attacked? Half our country had crumbled under the Taliban. We were all thinking the same thing.

If only Amrika would have been upset about that too.

CHAPTER 4
SHEKIBA

Shekiba continued to toil in the fields as if her father were at her side. She fed the chicken and the donkey and fixed the plow when the axle snapped on a stone in the field. The house was quiet, somber. Sometimes the silence grated on her nerves and she would try to break it with the sounds of chores, or by talking to the birds perched on the wall. Some days she felt content, almost happy, to be self-sufficient. She hoped her mother liked the small flowers she had planted while she listened to the *bulbul* sing over Aqela's grave.

Some things were difficult. Without her father around, Shekiba had no connection with the village or its resources. She used the cooking oil sparingly and was careful with how much she harvested from their field so that she would not go hungry. She dug a small trench between the house and the wall and buried some potatoes so that she would have a stock for the coming winter months. She picked the beans and ate a few, leaving the rest to dry for later.

Her father's death seemed to usher winter in sooner than usual, by Shekiba's warped sense of time. Shekiba had little reason to care about the month or year. The sun would rise and fall and she continued to do her chores, occasionally bothering to wonder what would come of her. How long would this existence last? More than once she thought of ending her life. Once, she'd pinched her nose and shut her mouth. She felt her chest tighten and tighten until she finally took a breath and continued to live, cursing her weakness.

She again contemplated digging her own plot, beside her father, and lying down in it. Maybe the dark angel Gabriel would see her and reunite her with her family. Shekiba wondered if she would see her mother again. If she did, she prayed it would be the mother who sang while she cooked their meals, not the bald, glassy-eyed woman Shekiba had buried.

Winter came and Shekiba floundered along, subsisting on what she had managed to keep through the fall. Each time she bothered to undress and bathe, she noticed her ribs protruding more. She used her siblings' clothing to cushion her hip bones from the hard floor. She grew weak, her hair brittle and frayed. Her gums bled when she chewed but she barely noticed the taste of blood in her mouth.

Spring came and Shekiba looked forward to the warmth of the sun and the tasks that came with it. But along with spring came a visitor, and the first hint that Shekiba would not be allowed to live like this for long.

She was feeding the chicken when she saw a young boy in the distance, coming toward her home from her grandfather's house. She could not tell who it was but went inside and donned her *burqa*. She paced back and forth, peeking through the door from time to time to confirm that the boy was still coming toward her. Indeed he was, and as he neared, Shekiba could see that he was no more than seven or eight years old. She marveled at how healthy he looked and wondered what her cousins were eating at the main house. Once more, Shekiba was thankful for the ability to hide behind the blue cloak.

"*Salaaaaaam!*" he called out when he was near enough. "I am Hameed! Dear uncle, I want to speak to you!"

Hameed? Who was Hameed? It did not surprise Shekiba that she didn't recognize him. Likely many cousins had been born since she lost contact with the clan. Shekiba wondered how to reply. Should she answer or should she keep quiet? What would invite less inquiry?

"*Salaaaaaaam!* I am Hameed! Dear —"

Shekiba cut him off.

56

"Your uncle is not home. He cannot speak to you now."

There was no answer for a time. She wondered if Hameed had been warned about her. She could imagine the conversation.

But be careful. Your uncle has a daughter, a monster, really. She is terrible to look at, so don't be too frightened. She's insane and may say crazy things.

Shekiba put her ear to the wall, trying to hear if Hameed was still there or if he was walking away.

"Who are you?"

Shekiba did not know how to answer.

"I said who are you?"

"I am . . . I am . . ."

"Are you my uncle's daughter? Are you Shekiba?"

"Yes."

"Where is my uncle? I was told to bring him a message."

"He is not here."

"Where is he then?"

At the edge of the field. Did you see the tree? The one that should be growing apples but grows nothing at all? That's where he is. You walked right past him, along with my mother, my sister and my two brothers. If you have anything to tell him, you can tell him as you make your way back to the house with all the food.

But Shekiba did not say what she was thinking. She had that much sense left in her.

"I said, where is he?"

"He has gone out."

"When will he be back?"

"I do not know."

"Well, tell him that Bobo Shahgul wants to see him. She wants him to come to the house."

Bobo Shahgul was Shekiba's paternal grandmother. Shekiba hadn't seen her since before the cholera took her family. Bobo Shahgul had come over to tell her son about a girl in the village, the daughter of a friend. She had wanted her son to take her on as a second wife, maybe even to have him move back into the family compound with the second wife and keep the first wife at this house. Shekiba remembered watching her mother listen to the conversation with her head bowed, saying nothing.

"Tell Bobo Shahgul that . . . that he is not here now."

She was skirting the truth.

"You will tell my uncle what I have said?"

"I will."

She could hear his footsteps grow distant but waited a full hour before emerging from the wall, just in case. She wasn't the brightest girl, but even Shekiba knew it was just a matter of time before her grandmother sent another message.

Three months passed.

Shekiba was attaching the harness to the donkey to begin tilling the soil when she saw two men walking toward the house. She darted inside and grabbed her *burqa* in a panic. Her heart fluttered as she waited for them to near. She kept her ear against the inner wall, listening for footsteps.

"Ismail! Come out and speak to us! Your brothers are here!"

Her father's brothers? Bobo Shahgul meant business. Shekiba frantically tried to think of something reasonable to say.

"My father is not at home!"

"Enough with the nonsense, Ismail! We know you're here! You're too much of a coward to leave your home! Come on out or we'll barge in there and shake some sense into you!"

"Please, my father is not home!" She could hear her voice cracking. Would they force their way in? It wouldn't take much effort. The door would fold in at their slightest touch.

"Goddamn you, Ismail! What are you doing hiding behind your daughter! Move aside, girl, we are coming in!"

CHAPTER 5
RAHIMA

Madar-*jan* took me behind the house with
Padar-*jan*'s scissors and razor. I sat nervously
while my sisters watched. She pulled my long
hair into a ponytail behind my head, whispered a prayer and slowly began to shear
away. Shahla looked astonished. Rohila
looked entertained and Parwin watched only
for a moment before running back into the
house for her pencils and paper. She sketched
furiously with her back turned to me.

Madar-*jan* cut and trimmed, bending my
ear forward to trim around it. She cut my
bangs short and straight across my forehead.
I looked at the ground around me and saw
hair everywhere. She brushed the loose
strands from my shoulders, blew at my neck
and dusted off my back. My neck felt bare,
exposed. I giggled with nervous excitement.
Only Shahla noticed the single tear that
trickled down Madar-*jan*'s cheek.

The next step was my clothing. Madar-*jan*
asked my uncle's wife for a shirt and pair of

60

pants. My cousin had outgrown them, as had his older brother and my other cousin before him. She sent me inside to get dressed while she and my sisters swept my girl hair from the courtyard.

I slipped one leg in and then the other. They were slimmer and heavier than the usual balloon pants I wore under my dresses. I cinched the strings at the waist and made a knot. I pulled the tunic over my head and realized there was no ponytail to pull through after it. I let my hand run against the back of my head, feeling the short ends.

I looked down and saw my knobby knees through the pantaloons. I folded my arms across my chest and cocked my head, as I'd seen my cousin Siddiq do so many times. I kicked my foot, pretending there was a ball in front of me. Was that it? Was I a boy already?

I thought of Khala Shaima. I wondered what she would say if she were to see me like this. Would she smile? Had she really meant it when she suggested I should be turned into a boy? She told us our great-great-grandmother had worked on the farm like a boy, that she'd been a son to her father. I had waited for her to go on, to get to the part where our great-great-grandmother turned into a boy. Khala Shaima said she would come back and tell us more of the story another day. I hated having to wait.

I smoothed my shirt down and went back out to see what my mother thought.

"Well! Aren't you a handsome young boy!" Madar-*jan* said. Even I could detect the hint of nervous uncertainty in her voice.

"Are you sure, Madar-*jan*? Don't I look odd?"

Shahla covered her mouth with her hand at the sight of me.

"Oh my goodness! You look just like a boy! Madar-*jan,* you can hardly tell it's her!" Madar-*jan* nodded.

"You won't have to get your knots taken out anymore," Rohila said enviously. Getting the knots brushed out of our hair was a painful morning routine. Her hair coiled into a mess of tiny birds' nests that Madar-*jan* struggled to brush out while Rohila winced and squirmed.

"*Bachem,* from now on we're going to call you Rahim instead of Rahima," Madar-*jan* said tenderly. Her eyes looked heavier than they should have at the age of thirty.

"Rahim! We have to call her Rahim?"

"Yes, she is now your brother, Rahim. You will forget about your sister Rahima and welcome your brother. Can you do that, girls? It's very important that you speak only of your brother, Rahim, and never mention that you have another sister."

"Just in case we forget what she looked like, Parwin drew this picture of Rahima." Rohila handed Madar-*jan* the sketch Parwin had done while she was cutting my hair. It was an incredible likeness of me, the old me with long hair and naïve eyes. Madar-*jan* looked at the drawing and whispered something we didn't understand. She folded the paper and placed it on the tabletop.

"Is that it? Just like that? She's a boy?" Shahla looked skeptical.

"Just like that," Madar-*jan* said quietly. "This is how things are done. People will understand. You'll see." She knew my sisters would be the hardest to convince. Everyone else — teachers, aunts, uncles, neighbors — they would accept my mother's new son without reservation. I wasn't the first *bacha posh.* This was a common tradition for families in want of a son. What Madar-*jan* was already dreading was the day they would have to change me back. But that would only be when I began to change into a young woman. That was still a few years away.

"Oh, wow." Parwin had returned to the courtyard to see what happened.

"So just like that. She's a boy."

"Nope, not yet," Parwin said calmly. "She's not a boy yet."

"What do you mean?" Rohila asked.

"She's got to walk under a rainbow."

"A rainbow?"

"What are you talking about?"

"My God, Parwin," Madar-*jan* said, smiling faintly. "I don't remember telling you about that poem. How do you even know about it?"

Parwin shrugged her shoulders. We weren't surprised. Parwin couldn't tell you if she had eaten breakfast but she often knew things that no one expected her to know.

"What is she talking about, Madar-*jan*?" I asked, curious to find out if Parwin was right or if her imagination had gotten the best of her today.

"She's talking about an old poem. I don't know if I can even remember how the story goes but it's about what happens if you pass under a rainbow."

"What happens if you pass under a rainbow?" Rohila asked.

"There's a legend that walking under a rainbow changes girls into boys and boys into girls."

"What? Is that true? Could that really happen?"

This perplexed me. I hadn't walked under a rainbow. I'd never even seen one, for that matter. How was this change supposed to work?

"Tell us the poem, Madar-*jan*. I know you remember it. *We drank in spirits . . .*" Parwin started her off.

Madar-*jan* sighed and went into the living room. We followed. She sat with her back against the wall and looked to the ceiling,

64

trying to recall the details. Her *chador* fell across her shoulders. We sat around her and waited expectantly.

"*Afsaanah, see-saanah . . . ,*" she began. One story, thirty stories. And then she sang the poem.

> We drank in spirits and played in fields
> Enamored of
> Indigos, saffrons and teals
> There was fog in the space
> Between them and I
> Colors reach to touch God in the sky
> I envy the arc, stretched strong and wide
> As one brilliance blends into another
> Colors bow deeply to welcome a brother
> We humble servants, meekly pass under
> Rostam's bow changes girl to boy, makes
>   one the other
> Until the air grows dry and tires of the
>   game
> And the mist opens its arms, colors
>   reclaimed

CHAPTER 6
SHEKIBA

Shekiba sat with her back against the cool wall. It was night and the house was quiet. Snoring came from every direction, some louder than others. By the soft glow of the moon, she could see the kettles and pots she had washed and stacked in the corner to make room for her blanket. Like most nights, her eyes were wide open while everyone else's were closed. This was the hour of night when she would wonder what she could have done differently.

Her uncles had barged into the home that day, refusing to be turned away. Now that she had been reunited with her grandmother, she could hardly blame them for their persistence. No one wanted to disappoint Bobo Shahgul. She was horrid enough when she was satisfied.

It hadn't taken long for Shekiba's uncles to realize that something had happened to her father. The house smelled of rot and loneliness. Shekiba had stopped sweeping the floor and had let the potato peels collect in a corner, too disinterested to take them outside. After a time, she didn't notice the smell. But it wasn't just the house. Shekiba had become apathetic. She hadn't bothered to wash her dress, and for most of the winter, she had curled up in a ball under a blanket, letting her own stench fester. Daylight and warmth had inspired her to wash herself but it would take more than a few baths to undo what had become of her. Her hair was a tangled nest of lice and unbrushable for months.

Shekiba was pale and gaunt. For a moment, her uncles believed they may have been looking at a *djinn,* a spirit. How could living flesh look like that?

They asked for her father, their eyes scouting the room and realizing instantly that he was not there. Shekiba trembled and turned to the side, wanting to hide from them but making sure they were not approaching her. They couldn't see her, but they could smell fear, sweat and blood. They asked again, louder, angrier.

That was when Shekiba left. She heard a scream and a blue ghost ran into the wall that had sheltered her from the view of others — the wall her father had built to guard his family. Another scream, and as she fell to the earth, hands grabbed the ghost, shocked at how easily their fingers circled bones. The ghost wanted to fight back, to run away and escape, but the men had meat on their bones. They gripped her and she let go, allowing them to roll her onto her blanket and carry her back to the family compound in much the same way that she had carried her father to his grave.

As she passed by the tree where her family lay buried, Shekiba moaned and called out to them. She tried to lift her head to see the rounded mounds of earth.

Madar. Padar. Tariq. Munis. Bulbul.

She did not see her uncles look at each other, sharing a realization that the entire family was dead, even their brother Ismail. Shekiba didn't see them bite their tongues, hold back their tears and mutter that they should have been there to wash their brother's body and throw dirt on his grave. Shekiba was the last survivor — the one who should not have survived. They wondered how long this girl had been living alone and shook their heads with the shame of the situation. A girl, by herself! What dishonor this could bring to their family if anyone in the village were to find out!

They laid her in the courtyard of the home while they went to notify Bobo Shahgul. Within minutes, the spry old lady stood over Shekiba, peering down through her cataract-clouded eyes to get a better look at the grandchild she could do without.

"Tell your wives to get her washed up. Warn

68

them that her face will turn their stomachs. And tell them to feed her. We must deal with this creature now if we are to save our good name within the village. May God punish her for keeping her father from us, *my son*! Not even telling us when he left this world! She will pay for this."

Bobo Shahgul proved to be a woman of her word. Since her husband had died two years ago, she had happily taken on the role of the family matriarch. She presided over her sons' brides with her walking stick, though there was nothing at all wrong with her legs. She had earned the right to walk with her head high since she had given her husband six sons and two daughters. Now it was her turn to oversee the roost with the same iron fist she had survived.

Shekiba let herself be undressed and bathed. She found it much easier than resisting. The youngest wives were assigned the formidable task of deconstructing the beast Shekiba had become. Pails of water were brought in. Her hair was sheared, too far gone to salvage. They cursed her for the rank smells of every body recess, their nostrils seared. They put food in her mouth; someone moved her jaw, reminding her to chew.

In a few days, Shekiba's mind returned to her body. She began to hear what people were saying; she began to notice that her belly did not ache with hunger. Her fingers reached up and felt a head scarf covering the ragged edges of her chopped hair.

I must look like one of my cousins, she thought.

Her skin was raw and reddened from the brutal baths she had been given. Her aunts had scrubbed a layer of filth from her with a washcloth too rough for her frail skin. She had some scabs, while other areas stayed red and chafed, her body too malnourished to repair minor damage. At night, she slept on a blanket in the narrow kitchen, her feet often knocking against a pot and waking her up. In the morning, she was moved into one of many rooms where she would be out of the way while the wives prepared breakfast.

I'm tired of lifting her. Get Farrah to help you. My back is aching.

You say the same thing every day! Your back, your back. Surely, it's not from doing anything around here. What has your husband been doing to you! Tell him to go easy.

Giggling.

Shut your mouth and pick up her arms. Ugh. I am queasy enough today. I can't stand to look at her face.

Fine, but we'll put her in your room. My room still has her smell from yesterday and I cannot stand it.

Shekiba let herself be moved around and insulted. At least she was not being asked to

70

participate in this existence. But that would not last. Bobo Shahgul had other plans for her.

The family home had a small kitchen where the wives all helped cook. There was one main family room where everyone sat around during the day, the children played and meals were shared. Surrounding those two main rooms were four or five other rooms, each assigned to one of Bobo Shahgul's sons. Families slept together in one room. Only Bobo Shahgul had a room of her own.

Shekiba was on her side in her uncle's room when she vaguely felt Bobo Shahgul's walking stick jab into her thigh.

"Get up, you insolent girl! Enough of your nonsense. You have been asleep for over a week. You're not going to get away with this kind of behavior in this house. God only knows what craziness your mother allowed."

Shekiba winced. A downside to her recovery was that her body now had the energy to sense pain. Again, the stick poked into her leg. Shekiba rolled onto her side and tried to push herself back, away from her grandmother. Her head was heavy with too much sleep.

"Insolent and lazy! Just like your mother!"

There was no escape from this woman. Shekiba eased herself to a sitting position and managed to focus her eyes on her grandmother.

"Well? Have you nothing to say for yourself? Disrespectful and ungrateful. We have bathed and fed you and you can do nothing more than sit there and stare like an idiot?"

"Salaam . . . ," Shekiba said meekly.

"Sit up straight and watch your legs. Although you may not know it, you are a girl and you should sit like one." Bobo Shahgul snapped her stick against her granddaughter's arm. Shekiba flinched and straightened her back as best she could. Bobo Shahgul leaned in close. Shekiba could see her deep-set wrinkles, the yellow of her eyes.

"I want you to tell me what happened to my son." Each syllable was punctuated by a fine spray of saliva.

Your son? Your son? Shekiba thought, her mind suddenly clear and focused. *Your son was my father. When was the last time you saw him? When was the last time you bothered to send him any food, any oil? You could see him in the field. You could see the pain in his movements. Did you bother to send him anything then? All you cared about was giving him another wife, saving the family name.*

"He was my father." Shekiba left the rest unsaid.

"Your father? And a lot of good that did him! He could have had a decent life. He could have had a wife to look after him, to bear him sons who would grow our clan and

72

work on our land. But you did your very best to keep him secluded, trapped with such a wild creature as yourself that no one would want to come near you or him! First your mother, then you! You killed my son!"

Her stick jabbed Shekiba's breastbone.

"Where is he? What did you do with him?"

"He is with my mother. He is with my brothers and my sister. They are all there together, waiting for me."

Bobo Shahgul fumed at Shekiba's detachment. As she suspected, her son had been buried without her knowledge. Her eyes swelled with rage.

"Waiting for you, eh? Maybe God will see fit that your time come soon," she hissed.

If only, Shekiba thought.

"Zarmina! Come and get this girl! She is to help you with the chores around the house. It is time for her to start earning her stay here. She has caused this family enough grief and she needs to start making up for it."

Zarmina was married to Shekiba's oldest uncle. She had the strength of a mule and the face of one too. Shekiba guessed she was the one who had scrubbed her skin raw. Zarmina walked into the room, wiping her hands on a rag.

"Ahhh, so finally we can stop waiting on this girl hand and foot! About time. God has no use for the lazy. Get up and get into the kitchen. You can start peeling the potatoes.

There is much to be done."

This was the beginning of a new phase in Shekiba's life. She was no stranger to hard work, to lifting and peeling, to scrubbing and hauling. She was assigned the least desirable chores in the house and accepted them without argument. Bobo Shahgul wanted her to pay for her father's death. She made this clear every day, sometimes calling out his name and clucking her tongue.

She would even wail and lament the tragedy of his death.

"He was taken too young. How could he have left his mother to grieve him? How could such a thing happen to our family? Have we not prayed enough? Have we not followed God's word? Oh, my dear son! How could this have happened to you?"

Her daughters-in-law would sit at her side, plead with her to be strong and tell her that Allah would care for him since his own family had not. They would fan her and warn her that she would make herself ill with all this grief. But Bobo Shahgul's sobbing came without tears and turned off just as easily as it turned on. Shekiba continued with the task of brushing the rug. She did not bother to look up.

What happened to you? We heard that they call you shola-*face. Did you put* shola *on your face?*

Her cousins asked the same question over

74

and over again. Shekiba ignored them for the most part. Sometimes people answered for her.

She did not listen to her mother and that's what happened to her. Did you understand what I said? So you had better pay attention to what I say or your face will turn just as hideous as hers!

Shekiba became a very useful instrument for discipline in the house.

Look at what you've done! Clean this up or you will be sleeping with Shekiba tonight!

There was no end.

God has punished Shekiba. That is why she has no mother or father. Now go wash for prayers or else God will do the same to you.

CHAPTER 7
RAHIMA

Madar-*jan* kept me at home for a couple of weeks, wanting me to get used to the idea of being a boy before she let me test the waters outside of our home. She corrected my sisters when they called me Rahima and did the same with my younger cousins who had never before seen a *bacha posh*. They ran into their houses to report the news to their mothers, who smirked. Each had given her husband at least two sons to carry on the family name. They didn't need to make any of their daughters a *bacha posh*.

But Madar-*jan* ignored their looks and went about her chores. Bibi-*jan* hated that anyone in her family was forced to resort to the *bacha posh* tradition.

"We needed a son in the house, Khala-*jan*."

"Hmmph. Would be better if you could just have one as the others did."

Madar-*jan* bit her tongue for the thousandth time.

Padar-*jan* barely seemed to notice the

change. He had been gone for a couple of days and came home exhausted. He sat in the living room and opened an envelope of small pellets. He squeezed them between his fingers and sprinkled the mix into a cigarette casing. He lit one end and sucked on it deeply. Thick, sweet smoke twisted around his face and wrapped around his head. My sisters and I came in from outside to find him sitting there. We stopped short and said hello, our heads bowed.

He looked at us and inhaled deeply. He squinted through the smoke as he noticed that something was different about his three daughters.

"So she's done it then." And that was all he said about the matter.

Khala Shaima was the reassuring voice that Madar-*jan* needed to hear.

"Raisa, what else were you going to do? Your husband is delirious half the time and of no use to you. You can't send the girls to school or even to the market because you're afraid of what will happen. Your in-laws are all too busy talking about each other to help you out. This is your only option. Besides, it'll be better for her, you'll see. What can a girl do in this world, anyway? Rahim will appreciate what you've done for him."

"But my in-laws, I —"

"Forget them! The person who doesn't appreciate the apple doesn't appreciate the

77

orchard. You'll never please them. The sooner you figure that out the better off you'll be."

My first errand as a boy was an exciting one. I was to go to the market for oil and flour. Madar-*jan* nervously handed me a few bills and watched me walk down the street. My sisters poked their faces around either side of her skirt trying to get a look as well. I kept glancing over my shoulder and waved at Madar-*jan* cheerfully, trying to inspire a little confidence in both of us that I could pull this off.

The streets were lined with shops. Copper pots. Baby clothes. Sacks of rice and dried beans. Colorful flags hung from front doors. The shops were two levels, with balconies on the second floor where men sat back and watched the comings and goings of their neighbors. None of the men walked with any urgency. The women, on the other hand, moved purposefully and carefully.

I stepped into the first shop I recognized, a large sign overhead announcing the arrival of a new cooking oil.

"*Agha-sahib,* how much for a kilo of flour?" I asked, remembering to keep my shoulders straight. I couldn't quite bring myself to look the man in the eye so I kept shifting my gaze to the tin cans he had stocked on the shelf behind him.

"Fifteen thousand afghanis," he said, barely

looking up. Not too long ago, a kilo of flour had cost forty afghanis. But money was worthless now that everyone had bags of it.

I bit my lip. This was double what I had seen him charge my mother, which she complained was already too much. I wasn't surprised. I had come to this same man twice before when my mother had reluctantly sent me out to the market and I had been able to bargain him down to half of what he originally demanded.

"That's too much, *agha-sahib*. Not even a king could pay that much. How about six thousand afghanis?"

"You take me for a fool, little boy?"

"No, sir." My chest puffed to hear him call me a boy. "But I know that Agha Kareem has flour for sale too and he charges much less. I didn't want to walk all the way down to his shop, but . . ."

"Ten thousand afghanis. That's it."

"*Agha-sahib,* it's only one kilo I'm asking for. Eight thousand afghanis is all I'll pay."

"Boy! You're wasting my time," he barked, but I knew he had nothing else to do. He'd been picking dirt from under his fingernails when I entered his shop.

"Then I'll pay you twelve thousand afghanis but I'll need a kilo of flour and a kilo of oil to go with it."

"And a kilo of oil? Have you —"

"I'm no fool, *agha-sahib,*" I said, and

forced myself to look him in the eye, as a boy should. He stopped short and his mouth tightened. His eyes narrowed as he took a good look at me. I felt myself shrink under his stare. Maybe I'd gone too far.

Suddenly he let out a guffaw.

"You're a little smart-ass, aren't you?" he said with a smirk. "Whose son are you anyway?"

My shoulders relaxed. He saw the *bacha posh* but it was just as Madar-*jan* had promised — people understood.

"I'm Arif's son. From the other side of the field, past the stream."

"Well done, my boy. Here, take your oil and flour and run off before I come to my senses."

I quickly counted out the bills, took my spoils and hurried back home to show Madar-*jan*. My walk turned to a jog as I realized I didn't have to be demure and proper. I tested an old man walking by. I looked directly at him, meeting his squinted eyes and seeing that he didn't react to my forwardness. Thrilled, I started to run faster. No one gave me a second glance. My legs felt liberated as I ran through the streets without my knees slapping against my skirt and without worrying about chastising eyes. I was a young man and it was in my nature to run through the streets.

Madar-*jan* smiled to see me panting and grinning. I laid the goods before her and

80

proudly showed her how much money I'd returned home with.

"Well, well. Looks like my son bargains better than his mother!" she said.

I started to understand why Madar-*jan* needed a son in the home. Certain chores she had left for my father had not been done in months. Now she could ask me.

When my sister's shoes came undone, the rubber sole flopping like an open mouth, I took them to the old man down the street. With only three fingers on his right hand, he could fix any shoe in any condition. I brought bread from the baker and chased the stray dog down the street. My father would come home, his eyes red and small, and laugh when he saw me.

"*Bachem,* ask your sister to bring me a cup of tea. And tell her to fix me something to eat too," he said, ruffling my hair as he walked lazily to the corner of the living room and stretched out on the floor, his head thumping against the pillow cushion.

I was confused for a moment. Why hadn't he asked me to bring the tea and food? But realization swept over me as I walked into the kitchen. I saw Rohila first.

"Hey, Rohila. Padar-*jan* wants some tea and something to eat. He's in the living room."

"So? Why didn't you put a plate together? You know there's some *korma-katchaloo* in

81

the pot."

"He didn't ask *me.* He said for me to tell my *sister.* That's *you.* Anyway, I'm going out. Don't take all day. He looks like he's hungry," I said cheerfully. Rohila's hazel eyes gave me a look even as she turned to heat up a bowl of potato stew for our father. She was angry and part of me knew I was being a brat, but everything I was experiencing was new and I wanted to enjoy it. I ignored the shadow of guilt and headed out to see if the stray dog had returned for another game of chase.

A month later, school was back in session and my nerves were again rattled. Madar-*jan* trimmed my hair and spoke to me cautiously.

"You'll be in the boys' classroom this year. Pay attention to your teacher and mind your studies," she warned me, trying to make this little talk sound routine. "Remember that your cousin Muneer will be in your class as well. No one, the teacher, the students, no one will ask you about . . . about anything. Just remember that your father has decided to send you to school this year. You are one of the boys and . . . and . . . mind what the teacher tells you."

It would be different, I understood. Khala Shaima's plan had worked well within the confines of our family compound and even in my trips to the bazaar. School would put this charade to the test though, and I could sense my mother's trepidation. My sisters were furious. Padar-*jan* had decided they were to stay home even though I could have accompanied them to school.

Muneer and I walked to school together. He wasn't the brightest of my cousins and I rarely saw him since his mother kept her children away from the rest of us. That probably worked in my favor. He needed to be told only once that I was his cousin Rahim and always had been, and in his mind there never had been a Rahima. I breathed a sigh of relief that I didn't have to worry about his giving me away.

"Salaam, Moallim-sahib," I said when we arrived.

The teacher grunted a reply in return, nodding as each student walked in. I wiped my moist palms on my pants.

I felt the teacher's curious eyes follow the back of my head but it could have been my imagination. I scanned the room and stayed close behind Muneer, noting that none of the boys seemed fazed by me. I kept my head bowed and we made our way to the back of the classroom, where Muneer and I shared a long bench with three other boys. One boy was especially eager to show how much he knew about the teacher.

"Moallim-sahib is very strict. Last year he gave four boys bad marks because their fingernails weren't clean."

"Oh yeah?" his friend whispered. "Then

83

you better keep your finger out of your nose!"

"Boys! Sit up straight and pay attention," the teacher said. He was a rotund man, his shiny bald head rimmed with salt-and-pepper hair. His neatly groomed mustache matched his sparse hairs. "You'll begin by writing your names. Then we'll see what, if anything, you learned in your last class."

I quickly realized the male teachers were just as strict as the women. Class wasn't much different except that there was more whispering and shooting each other looks than I'd ever seen in a girls' classroom. I wrote my name carefully and watched Muneer struggle from the corner of my eye. His letters were awkwardly connected and an extra dot had changed "Muneer" to "Muteer." I debated correcting him but the teacher looked in my direction before I could even begin to whisper. He walked around the room and looked at everyone's names, shaking his head at some and grunting at others. Very few seemed to meet his standards.

He looked over my shoulder and I could hear the air whistle through his nostrils, his belly casting a shadow over my paper. My name got no reaction, which I could take only to mean it had not severely disappointed him. Muneer's notebook, however, made him groan.

"What is your name?" he demanded.

"M-M-Muneer." He stole a glance upward

at the teacher but quickly looked down again.

"*Muneer,*" he said dramatically. "If you come back to this class tomorrow and make a single mistake in your name, I'll send you back to repeat last year's work. Understood?"

"Yes, *Moallim-sahib,*" Muneer whispered. I could feel the heat from his face.

So the boys weren't learning much more than the girls, I realized.

After class, the boys were more interested in racing outside and kicking a ball around than questioning who I was or where I'd come from. Muneer and I walked home with two boys named Ashraf and Abdullah. They were neighbors who lived a half kilometer from our family's house. This was the first time I'd met them, though they knew Muneer and my other boy cousins.

"What's your name again?" Ashraf asked. He was the shorter of the two and had light brown hair and round eyes. He was pretty enough to make me wonder if he was like me, a girl underneath those pants.

"My name is Rahim."

"Yeah, his name is Rahim. He's my cousin," Muneer added. The teacher's warnings had shaken him up but now that we were outside, he was breathing easier.

"Abdullah, have you ever seen Rahim before?"

Abdullah shook his head. He was dark haired, slim and calmer than his neighbor.

85

"No. Are you any good at soccer, Rahim?"

I stole a sidelong glance and shrugged my shoulders.

"Oh, he's really good at soccer," Muneer said emphatically. His reply caught me off guard. "I bet he could beat you."

I looked at Muneer, wondering if he was trying to set me up.

"Oh, yeah?" Abdullah grinned. "Well, he doesn't have to beat me but it would help if he could beat Said Jawad and his friends. They're probably over in the street playing if you want to join them."

"Yeah, let's do it!" Muneer picked up his pace and headed down the side street that led to the makeshift field and away from our house. The field was actually an unused side street, too narrow for a car. The boys were accustomed to meeting there for pickup games.

"Muneer, don't you think we should —"

"C'mon, Rahim. Just for a little while! It'll be fun," Abdullah said, giving my shoulder a light shove.

I suppose I could have been worse. The only thing I knew how to do was to run. Luckily, I did that well enough that the boys didn't notice that my foot never made contact with the ball or that I never shouted for the ball to be passed to me. I ran up and down the street, my shoulders scraping the clay wall of the alley. I kept expecting my mother or father to appear and drag me back home angrily.

I liked feeling the breeze on my face. I liked feeling my legs stretch, trying to catch the others, trying to race ahead of them. My arms swung by my sides, free.

"Over here! Pass it over here!"

"Don't let him get by! Catch him!"

I neared the ball. There were six feet kicking at it, trying to knock it back in their direction. I stuck my foot into the melee. I felt the leather against my sole. I kicked at it, sending it flying in Abdullah's direction. He stopped the ball with his heel and nudged it toward the opposite goal. He was running.

I felt a thrill as I chased after him. I liked being part of the team. I liked the dust kicking up under my feet.

I liked being a boy.

CHAPTER 8
SHEKIBA

Quickly, most of the household work was turned over to Shekiba. Her uncles' wives found that, once she'd recovered, she was quite capable and could manage even the chores that required the combined strength of two women. She could balance three pails of water, instead of just two. She could lift the wood into the stove. They whispered happily to each other when Bobo Shahgul was not listening, not wanting to appear lazy to the matriarch.

She has the strength of a man, but she does the chores of a woman. Could there be any better help for the house? Now we know what it must feel like to live like Bobo Shahgul!

Shekiba heard their comments but it was in her nature to work. She found that sunset came faster if she busied herself, no matter how laborious the task. Her back ached at the end of the day, but she did not let her face show it. She did not want to give them the satisfaction of exhausting her. Nor did she want to risk a beating for not being able to keep up with her work. In this home, there were many ready sticks to teach her that indolence would not be tolerated.

Khala Zarmina, Kaka Freidun's wife, was the worst. Her thick hands came down with a surprising strength even though she claimed to be too old and tired to do any of the more cumbersome tasks in the house. Her temper was short and she seemed to be poised to take Bobo Shahgul's place when Allah finally decided to reclaim the bitter old woman. Bobo Shahgul realized as much and could see through her false flattery but she tolerated it, keeping Zarmina in line with an occasional berating in front of the others.

Khala Samina was by far the mildest. She was wife to Bobo Shahgul's youngest living son, Kaka Zelmai. It took about a week for Shekiba to realize that Samina scolded or hit her only in the presence of the other daughters-in-law. When she raised her hand, Shekiba braced herself. Unnecessarily, she realized. Samina put no more weight into her blows than she would to swat a fly.

She doesn't want to look weak, Shekiba thought. *But now I know she is.*

Shekiba kept to herself, did the work assigned to her and tried to avoid eye contact. She did nothing to invite conversation, although she did provide a good topic for discussions in the house. Summer was a few weeks away when Bobo Shahgul interrupted her scrubbing the floor. Kaka Freidun stood beside her, arms crossed.

Shekiba instinctively pulled her head scarf across her face and turned her shoulders to face the wall.

"Shekiba, when you have finished with cleaning this floor, you are to go into the field and help your uncles with the harvest. I'm sure you will appreciate a chance to get fresh air outside and it seems you are experienced with this kind of work."

"But I still have to prepare the —"

"Then prepare it quickly and get outside. It is about time you helped to grow the food that has fattened your face."

Kaka Freidun smirked in agreement. This was all his idea. He had watched Ismail's land reap a harvest that most others would have thought impossible given last season's pitiful rainfall. It occurred to him that his brother's daughter-son may have inherited his instincts with the earth. Why not make use of her? After all, there were plenty of women to do the housework. Bobo Shahgul had agreed readily. The clan was in need of a good harvest. There were many mouths to feed and for the first time in years, their debts were growing.

Shekiba nodded, knowing that the new assignment would not mean a relief from her current ones. Her days would be longer.

Khala Zarmina was especially angry about the new arrangement but she dared not contest Bobo Shahgul.

"There is more to be done here in the house! Bobo Shahgul has forgotten what it means to take care of the cooking and cleaning. I've left a pile of clothes in need of hemming and darning for Shekiba-*e-shola* but I suppose that will all have to wait if she is going to be out in the field during the day. She had better wake up earlier if she's going to get lunch ready too."

The family had quickly embraced her nickname. In Afghanistan, disabilities defined people. There were many others in the village who had such names. Mariam-*e-lang,* who had walked with a limp since childhood. Saboor-*e-yek dista* was born with one hand. *And if you don't listen to your father, your hand will fall off just like his,* mothers used to warn their sons. Jowshan-*e-siyaa,* or the black, for his dark complexion. Bashir-*e-koor,* the blind, had lost most of his sight in his thirties and despised the children who laughed at his stumbling gait. He knew, too, that their parents joined in the snickers.

Shekiba dried the floor hastily and tightened her head scarf under her chin. She went outside and saw that her uncles were taking a break, leaning against the outside wall and drinking tea that her cousin Hameed had brought out to them. Shekiba turned to as-

91

sess the progress they had made.

From this side of the house she could see her home. It looked small in comparison to the clan's house.

This is how it felt to watch us.

She noticed that there were new pieces of equipment in their field and that her father's tools had been carted over to this side of the land. The house had been emptied. A pile of their belongings lay outside the wall her father had built.

They're taking my home. They wanted our land.

Suddenly, Shekiba realized why it was that Bobo Shahgul had summoned her youngest son after so much time. Her father was tilling the most fertile land the family had and they wanted it. They wanted more than the share of crops he sent over from time to time. They wanted it all. Now there was no one in their way. They were taking her home.

Shekiba thought she would feel nothing but inside, she seethed. No one had thought of her when the house's contents were thrown outside for trash. The few remaining items that had belonged to her mother, her father, her siblings all tossed aside to make way for something new. Was someone going to move into her home? Shekiba realized part of her was still hoping to return to that home, to live there independently as she had before. But, of course, that would never happen.

Shekiba found a container and walked into the field. There was much to be harvested. The onion plants had long yellow leaves and had probably dried up about three weeks ago, given their appearance.

Why haven't they pulled these onions out? Shekiba thought, and leaned over to get a closer look.

"Hey, Freidun! Look what she's doing! Tell her not to touch the onions! They aren't ready yet! This imbecile is going to ruin our lot!" It was Kaka Sheeragha, the skinniest and laziest of the group.

The leaves were brittle in her fingertips. She reached at the base and began to pull the bulbs from the earth.

Almost too late. They're about to rot. No wonder our food tastes the way it does. God knows what they're doing with the rest of the crops.

Kaka Freidun walked over and looked at the three onions she had already unearthed. Shekiba did not turn to look at him. He grunted something and then walked away.

"You didn't say anything to her?" Sheeragha yelled out.

"Enough," Freidun answered. "They're ready."

Sheeragha looked at his elder brother and bit his tongue. The men returned to the fields and grunted instructions at each other. They kept a distance from Shekiba but watched her from the corners of their eyes. She moved nimbly through the rows, her callused fingers weaving between the stems and yanking with just the amount of force needed to bring the bulb to the surface. She stopped only to readjust her head scarf.

But when she had finished one square area, the sun was beginning to set and it was time to prepare dinner. Shekiba resumed her post in the kitchen and was dismayed, but not surprised, to see that nothing had been done for the evening dinner. She quickly started a flame and set some water to boil. Khala Zarmina walked past her and peered into the dim room.

"Oh, there you are! I was just about to boil some rice for dinner but I see that you're here now. I'll leave it up to you, then. I just hope you'll clean your hands well — they're filthy."

Shekiba waited till Zarmina had walked away to let out a heavy sigh. How she wished she would have died on the cold floor of her own home, before her uncles had found her.

Jumaa prayers had just ended. Her uncles were returning home from the small *masjid* in town.

"Children, outside. We are speaking with your grandmother," Kaka Freidun snapped. Shekiba watched her cousins scamper out of the main living room. Kaka Sheeragha looked at her and seemed to be considering something. He followed his brothers into the living room.

Shekiba pretended to walk back into the kitchen with the clothes she had gathered from the clothesline. Before she reached the kitchen, she stopped and sat on the floor to fold the clothes. From there, she could hear some of what her uncles were saying.

"We need to settle this debt. Azizullah is losing patience with us. He says he's waited long enough."

"Hmm. What exactly were his demands?"

"I spoke with him in the village two weeks ago and he told me that he is in need of a wife for his son. He wants one of the girls from this family."

"Is that what he said?"

"Well, he said that there is a debt to settle. And that he was thinking of it more these days because he wants to secure a wife for his son."

"I see." Bobo Shahgul's voice was sharp, matter-of-fact. "How old is his son?"

"His son is ten."

"He still has time."

"Yes, but he wants to arrange the matter now."

I could hear Bobo Shahgul tapping her walking stick on the floor in thought.

"Then we need to arrange a deal with him."

"Zalmai, your girls are the right age. Maybe one of them. The older one. She's eight, isn't she?" Kaka Freidun's voice was unmistakable.

"Sheeragha's daughter is the same age. And your daughter is the same age as Azizullah's son. She would be a good match as well and would settle our debts sufficiently."

"Freidun's got more girls than anyone. It makes sense to give one of —"

"I don't think it is necessary to send one of the girls."

There was a pause as Bobo Shahgul's sons waited for her to explain.

"We will offer Shekiba."

I am not one of the girls.

"Shekiba-*e-shola*? Are you joking? He'll take one look at her and come after us demanding twice what we owe! To offer Shekiba will offend him, for sure!"

Shekiba closed her eyes and pressed the back of her head against the wall.

Your name means "gift," my daughter. You are a gift from Allah.

"Zalmai, I want you to speak to Azizullah and tell him that his son is still young. God willing, he and his father have long lives ahead of them with plenty of time to arrange for a suitable marriage. Tell him it would be more useful for them to have someone who can help them at home now. Tell him a happy wife bears more sons. Then you can offer Shekiba."

"But what if he says no?"

"He won't. Just be sure to tell him that she is very capable. That she has the back of a young man and can manage a household. She is a reasonable cook and she keeps quiet, now that she's been tamed. Tell him that it is an honorable thing to take in an orphan and that Allah will reward him for bringing her into his home. She will be like a second wife without the price."

"And what about the work she's doing here? Who will do that?"

"The same lazy women who were doing it before Shekiba came here!" Bobo Shahgul snapped. "Your wives have been spoiled. They have taken to lying about, drinking tea and making my ears ache with their chatter. It will be good for them to get back on their feet. This is a home, not the royal palace."

The brothers grunted. Would Azizullah really take the offer? they wondered. Better to try than to argue on whose daughter would be given as a bride otherwise.

"Say nothing to your wives now. No need to go stirring the henhouse yet. First let us discuss matters with Azizullah."

Shekiba picked herself up from the floor and hurried into the kitchen before her uncles emerged. She couldn't help but be thankful her parents were not alive to hear this conversation. She felt a tear well in her right eye.

*That is the problem with gifts, Madar-*jan. *They are always given away.*

CHAPTER 9
SHEKIBA

Azizullah took the deal.

Shekiba-*e-shola* packed her two dresses.

"Do not do anything that will bring shame to this family." Her grandmother's farewell to her was unceremonious.

Shekiba did something she never thought she would do. She lifted her *burqa* from her face and spat at her grandmother's wrinkled feet. A wad of saliva landed on her walking stick.

"My father was right to run from you."

Bobo Shahgul's mouth gaped as Shekiba turned and began walking toward her uncle, who was to escort her to Azizullah's home.

She knew it was coming but she did not care.

She also knew Khala Zarmina was watching. And smiling.

The walking stick came down on her shoulders twice before her Kaka Zalmai raised a hand to block his mother's revenge.

"Enough, Madar-*jan,* I cannot take the

beast to Azizullah crippled. Her face is bad enough. If he sees her hobbling surely he will turn us down. Let Allah punish her for her insolence."

Shekiba kept her shoulders up and did not falter. She did not know what lay ahead for her but she knew she could not return to this home. She had closed this door for sure.

"You wretched creature! Allah in all His wisdom has marked your face as a warning to all! There is a monster within! Ungrateful, just like your despicable mother! Do you ever wonder why your entire family is gone, buried under the ground? It is you! You are cursed!"

Shekiba felt something rise within her. She turned slowly and lifted her *burqa* again.

"Yes, I am!" Shekiba smirked and pointed a finger at her grandmother. "And with Allah as my witness, I curse you, Grandmother! May demons haunt your dreams, may your bones shatter as you walk and may your last breaths be painful and bloody!"

Bobo Shahgul gasped. Shekiba could see the fear in her eyes. She stared at her grand-daughter's portentous face and took a nervous step back.

Kaka Zalmai slapped her face with a mighty backhand. Even the deadened nerves on the left side of her face stung with his blow.

Clever, she thought as she tried to catch her balance. *Won't leave a mark there.*

He tightened his fingers around her arm

100

and dragged her away from the house.

"We are leaving. Madar-*jan,* I'll be back when I have gotten rid of this monster. Samina, help my mother back into the house!"

Shekiba had no trouble keeping up with her uncle's pace. She kept two steps behind and played the scene over and over again in her mind. Had she really done that? Had she really said those things?

Her *burqa* hid a lopsided smile.

They walked the four kilometers to Azizullah's home in silence. Kaka Zalmai occasionally looked back and muttered something that Shekiba could not make out. They passed through the village Shekiba had not seen since early childhood. The shops looked more or less the same and there were a handful of people walking about, blue *burqas* following men dressed in loose flowing pants and long shirts.

As they moved further from her family's land, Shekiba wondered if she had done the right thing. What if she found herself alone again? What would she do? But she knew. She would do what she had intended to do months ago.

I will find a way back to our land and bury myself with my family, Shekiba resolved.

Azizullah's home was large in comparison to Bobo Shahgul's. And when she discovered that only Azizullah, his wife and four children lived in it, she was astonished. Azizullah had been given the home by his father, who had been a relatively wealthy man by village standards. Today, Azizullah made his living as a man of commerce. He bought and sold anything that was of any value to anyone. He made trades and loaned money as needed. He knew everyone in the village, but more important, everyone knew him. His family was well connected, with two brothers in the military service.

It was Azizullah himself who answered the outer gate.

The men shook hands and exchanged pleasantries. Shekiba stood just behind her uncle, feeling invisible.

Azizullah was a burly man who looked to be in his thirties. He wore a brown lambskin hat of rippled fur that sat snugly on his head. His eyes were dark and he had a thick but neatly trimmed beard. His clothes and hands looked clean.

He does not look like a working man, thought Shekiba.

"Please come in, Zalmai-*jan.* Join me for a cup of tea."

Kaka Zalmai accepted the invitation and followed Azizullah into his courtyard. Shekiba stood behind, not sure what she should do, until she saw her uncle shoot her a look. She took a step into her new home. The men went into the living room but Shekiba thought it best if she remained outside. She stood with her back to the wall, her shoulders now starting to ache where Bobo Shahgul's walking stick had come down on her earlier. Again, a smile beneath her *burqa.* Nearly twenty minutes passed before she was summoned into the living room by her uncle.

"This is Shekiba, Azizullah-*jan.* You will see that, as we told you, she is a very hard worker and is sure to prove useful in your home. I trust your wife will be pleased with her."

"Zalmai-*jan,* we have lived in this village for many years and Shekiba-*e-shola* is no secret. I had heard of her scars before your brother spoke of it. Now I want to see exactly what it is that I am bringing into my home. Have your niece show her face."

Kaka Zalmai looked in Shekiba's direction and gave her a nod. His eyes warned her against disobeying. Shekiba took a deep breath, lifted her *burqa* and braced herself.

His reaction came slowly. At first, he saw only the right side of her face. Her high cheekbone. Skin with the delicacy and color of an eggshell. Her dark iris and naturally arched brow caught Azizullah by surprise. The infamous monster was half-beautiful.

But as Shekiba turned her face, her left side came into view. She moved slowly, deliberately — anticipating a response. It suddenly occurred to her that Azizullah could be so repulsed as to send her back to her grandmother's house. She held her breath, unsure what to wish for.

Azizullah's brows wove together.

"Impressive. Well, no matter. For our purposes, her face is insignificant."

Insignificant?

"She has no other illnesses? Does she speak?"

"No, Azizullah-*jan*. Aside from her face, she is healthy. She speaks but not enough to pester you. She should be an unobtrusive addition to your household."

Azizullah stroked his beard. He took a moment to contemplate and then made his final decision.

"She will do."

"I am so happy that you see things this way, Azizullah-*jan*. You truly are a very open-minded person, may God grant you a long life."

"And you, my friend."

"I should be on my way then. I trust this will satisfy my family's debt to you. And please know that my mother sends her warmest regards to your wife as well."

Kaka Zalmai spoke so graciously, Shekiba could hardly recognize him as a member of her family.

"Our debts are settled, as long as this girl works as you've said she will."

And she did. Mostly out of fear that she

would be sent back to Bobo Shahgul's house. Soon Shekiba realized that she was much better off here in Azizullah's home anyway. Azizullah called his wife, Marjan, into the living room after Zalmai took his leave.

"This is Shekiba. You should acquaint her with the chores of the house so that she can get to work. Her family speaks highly of her abilities to keep a clean house and manage even heavy tasks. Let us see how she proves herself."

Marjan eyed her carefully, wincing as her eyes fell upon Shekiba's face. She was a good-hearted woman and immediately took pity on Shekiba.

"Allah, dear girl! How terrible!" she exclaimed, wiping her powdery hands on her skirt. She recovered quickly, though. "Well, let me show you around. I was just kneading the dough but it's all done now. Follow me."

Marjan was probably in her late twenties. Shekiba calculated that she must have had her first child at Shekiba's age.

"This is our bedroom. And this is the kitchen area," she said, pointing to a doorway on the left. Shekiba stepped in and looked around. "Oh, for God's sake, look at your hips! How will you squeeze a baby through them?"

Marjan's girth was generous, probably having increased by inches with each new addition to their family.

But Marjan's statement surprised Shekiba. No one had ever mentioned the possibility of her bearing children — not even in jest. She felt a heat rise into the right side of her face and lowered her head.

"Oh, you're embarrassed! That's sweet! Well, let's move on. There are many things to be done while we stand here chatting."

Marjan listed the chores to be done around the house, but she spoke without the bitter condescension of Shekiba's own family. Despite the fact that she'd been brought here as a servant, Shekiba realized Azizullah's home would be a reprieve for her. She caught herself before she broke out into a full smile.

Azizullah and Marjan had four children. Shekiba met the youngest first — Maneeja, a two-year-old girl with soft dark curls that framed her rosy cheeks. Her eyes were thickly lined with kohl, which made the whites glow. Maneeja clung to her mother, her tiny fingers hanging on to her mother's skirt as she eyed the new face warily. Shekiba saw herself and Aqela doing the same with Madar-*jan*. Marjan and Shekiba sat down to finish rolling the dough into thin, long ovals. They would be taken to the baker later to be made into fresh-baked bread.

The eldest child, Fareed, was ten years old. He darted into the kitchen and grabbed a piece of bread before Marjan could chastise him. And before he could take stock of Shekiba's face. Shekiba tried to imagine which of her female cousins would possibly have been arranged as his future bride had her services not been offered instead. It was hard to guess.

Next came eight-year-old Haris and seven-year-old Jawad. They were in a hurry to keep up with their older brother and barely noticed that there was a new person toiling away with their mother in the kitchen. They were energetic boys who froze in their father's presence. But when Azizullah was not around, they quibbled and tackled each other, teaming up against their stronger older brother.

The children seemed to have inherited their parents' attitude toward disfigurement. After their initial surprise and a few bold questions, they no longer seemed to notice.

Within two weeks, Shekiba felt quite at home with Azizullah's family. The boys reminded her of her own brothers, Tariq and Munis. Maneeja had Aqela's dark curly hair. But the resemblance brought Shekiba more pleasure than pain. It was almost as if she was living with her reincarnated siblings.

You did me a favor, Grandmother. The only decent thing you've ever done for me.

Just as she had at Bobo Shahgul's house, Shekiba soon came to manage most of the household on her own. She busied herself with washing the clothes, scrubbing the floors, bringing the water from the well, cooking the meals — just as she had done in the past. Things were considerably easier here, though, since there were only six people to look after. She could tell that Marjan was more pleased with her work than she wanted to show. Azizullah paid her no attention, as long as his wife had no complaints with their new servant.

But when the family took to their beds and the house settled into its night rhythm, Shekiba lay awake as the outsider she would always be. Shekiba had experienced upheaval and change before and each time, she adjusted. She was by now used to the idea that she was not truly part of any home, not truly part of any family. She would be sheltered by these walls only as long as she scrubbed them until her hands bled.

Because she was Shekiba, the gift that could be given away as easily as it had been accepted.

CHAPTER 10
RAHIMA

Khala Shaima told us how Bibi Shekiba adjusted to the changes in her life. Now I had to adjust to the changes in mine. I had to learn how to interact with boys. It was one thing to play soccer with them, running alongside them and bumping elbows or shoulders. It was a whole other to be talking with them as we walked home from school. Abdullah and Ashraf would pat me on the back, sometimes even sling an arm around my neck as a friendly gesture. I would smile meekly and try not to look as uncomfortable as I felt. My instincts were to jerk back, to run away and never look them in the eye again.

My mother would raise an eyebrow if I came home before Muneer.

"Why are you home so early?" she would say, wiping her wet hands on a rag.

"Because," I said vaguely, and tore off a piece of bread.

"Rahim!"

"Sorry, I'm hungry!"

Madar-*jan* bit her tongue and resumed slicing potatoes into round chips with a hint of a smile on her face.

"Listen, Rahim-*jan.* You should be out with the boys, playing. That's what *boys* do — do you understand what I'm saying?"

Madar-*jan* still spoke in circles when it came to talking about my shift from girl to boy. I think she was afraid she would stop believing the charade herself if she spoke of it too directly.

"Yes, Madar-*jan,* but sometimes I just don't want to. They . . . they push each other a lot."

"Then push back."

I was surprised by her advice but the look on her face told me she was serious. Here sat my mother telling me the exact opposite of what she'd always said. I would have to toughen up.

Padar-*jan* had been home for three days and everyone was on edge. Every sound, every smell jarred him, inciting a string of profanities and a few slaps when he mustered the effort. For most of the day, he sat in the living room and smoked his cigarettes. Our heads grew dizzy from the smell and Madar-*jan* had us spend more time in the courtyard. She swaddled Sitara in a blanket and turned her over to Shahla while she did the cooking on her own. Sometimes my uncles would sit with him, smoking and talking about the war, about the neighbors and the Taliban, but none of them smoked as much as Padar-*jan.*

"What do you think it would be like if Kaka Jamaal was our father?" Rohila asked one day. She and Shahla were collecting the laundry from the clothesline. Shahla stopped in her tracks.

"Rohila!"

"What?"

"How could you say such a thing?"

I listened but kept my attention on the marbles in front of me. I flicked my finger and watched one send another off too far to the left. I let out a frustrated huff. Ashraf's aim was much better than mine.

Just pay attention to where you want it to go, Abdullah had said. *You're only looking at the marble in front you. You have to look at the target.*

I froze when he took my hand and showed me how to position my fingers, tucking my pinky under so it wouldn't get in the way. I still wondered what my mother would say if she were to see us. Was this okay too?

Abdullah was right. Once I started looking in the direction I wanted the marble to roll, my shots were better. Marbles tapped against each other and rolled out of the circle. I would have won against Abdullah today. Well, maybe not Abdullah but definitely against Ashraf. My aim was improving.

"It's just a question, Shahla. You don't have to get so upset about it!"

Shahla shot Rohila a chastising look.

"It's not *just* a question. If it were *just* a question, I'd like to see you go and ask it in front of Padar-*jan*. Anyway, Kaka Jamaal always looks like he's mad. Even when he's laughing. Have you noticed the way his eyebrows move?" She cocked her head to the side and turned both her eyebrows inward, leaning toward Rohila, who burst into laughter.

"You can't ask for another father," Parwin interjected. Rohila's chuckles quieted as she turned to hear what Parwin was thinking. "It would throw everything off."

I sat up. My left side had gotten stiff from leaning in one position.

"What are you talking about, Parwin?" I asked.

"You can't just have Kaka Jamaal as your father without making a lot of other changes. That means Khala Rohgul would be your mother and then Saboor and Muneer would be your brothers."

Parwin was Padar-*jan*'s favorite — if he had to pick one, that is. Maybe he'd already suffered enough disappointment by the time she was born that her being a girl hadn't stung him as the other two's had. But more than that, there was something about her temperament and drawings that calmed him. Maybe

112

that's why she was more forgiving of him. Or it could have been the other way around.

"Anyway, you'd better stop before someone hears you," Shahla warned Rohila. Sitara had started to whine and wriggle in her blanket. Shahla bounced her over her shoulder expertly. She was about to enter adolescence, her body no longer an androgynous shape. Rohila, strangely enough, seemed to be two steps ahead of her. Madar-*jan* had started her wearing a bra a year and a half ago when her breasts began to poke through her dresses impertinently.

I had tried her bra on once. Just out of curiosity. Rohila had left it behind in the washroom by accident again. Madar-*jan* had slapped her once for being so indecent. Still, she had forgotten. I laid it out in front of me and tried to make sense of the straps. I stuck my arms through the loops and tried to fasten it in the back, my arms reaching awkwardly, blindly for the clasp. After a few minutes I gave up and looked down at the lumps of cloth hanging loosely over my square chest.

I stuck my chest out, trying to see if I could fill the miniature cups and realizing I didn't want to. Instead, I sat on the ground, cross-legged and comfortable, while my sisters became women.

Later that night, I answered a knock at the door. Padar-*jan* lay in the living room, his loud snores rumbling through his chest.

113

Sometimes he snorted so loudly that Rohila giggled and Shahla's hand instinctively clamped over her sister's mouth to stifle the sound. Parwin would shake her head, disappointed in her sister's behavior. Madar-*jan* shot both girls a warning look; Shahla's eyes widened in a declaration of innocence.

There was a man at the front gate. I recognized him as one of my father's friends. He was gruff and had skin the texture of our plaster walls.

"*Salaam*, Kaka-*jan.*"

"Go and call your father," he said simply.

I nodded and ran back into the house, taking a deep breath before I nudged Padar-*jan*'s shoulder. I called out to him, louder and louder, before his snoring rhythm broke and he fumbled to rub his bloodshot eyes.

"What the hell is wrong with you?"

"Excuse me, Padar-*jan.* Kaka-*jan* is at the gate."

His eyes began to focus. He sat up and scratched his nose.

"Fine, *bachem.* Go and bring me my sandals." I was his son and allowed to wake him up for important matters. I saw Shahla's eyebrows draw upward. She noted the difference too.

I went to the courtyard to listen in on their conversation. I sat away from the gate where they were talking, out of the man's view.

"Abdul Khaliq has summoned everyone.

We'll meet in the morning and then head out. They're bombarding an area north of here and it looks like they'll gain some ground if we don't fend them off. There's a lot of talk about that area. Seems the Americans are going to be sending us some weapons or something."

"The Americans? How do you know that?" Padar-*jan* asked, his back against the gate. His guest had declined his invitation to come in.

"Abdul Khaliq met with one of their men last week. They want those people out of there. They're still looking for that Arab. Whatever the reason, at least they'll be helping out."

"When are we leaving?"

"Sunrise. By the boulder on the road going east."

Padar-*jan* was gone for two months that time but it felt different to me. I felt proud to know my father was fighting alongside a giant like America. My grandfather wasn't so sure it was a good idea. He seemed more suspicious of these Americans but I didn't see why.

Khala Shaima was sitting in our living room when I came home that afternoon. Since my transformation, I had only seen her once, and that was before school had started.

"There you are! I've been aging waiting for

you, *Rahim-jan,*" she said, emphasizing the new twist on my name.

"*Salaam,* Khala Shaima!" I was happy to see her but nervous to hear what she would say about my progress.

"Come sit next to me and tell me exactly what you've been doing. Your mother has obviously failed in getting your sisters to school, despite the fact that we came up with a plan to make everyone, even your intoxicated father, satisfied." She shot Madar-*jan* a look from the corner of her eye. Madar-*jan* sighed and moved Sitara to her left breast to nurse. She looked as if she'd already tired of this conversation.

"I've been going to class and *Moallim-sahib* is giving me good marks, right, Madar-*jan*?" I wanted Khala Shaima to approve, especially since it had been her who had won me these new freedoms.

"Yes, he's been doing well." A small smile. Shahla and Parwin were sitting in the living room, their fingers nimbly sifting through lentils and removing stones. Shahla had done twice as much as Parwin, who had arranged her lentils into piles of different shapes. Rohila had come down with a cold and was sleeping in the next room.

"Well, I'm sorry I wasn't here sooner to check up on you all. My health hasn't been very good. I hate that it keeps me from doing what I want."

116

"Are you feeling better now, Khala-*jan*?" Shahla asked politely.

"Yes, *bachem,* but for how long? My bones are tired and achy and the dust was so bad last month that each breath threw me into a hacking fit. Sometimes I coughed so hard I thought my intestines would fall right out of my body!"

That was Khala Shaima's way of explaining things.

"But anyway, enough talk about old people. You know your sisters aren't as lucky as you, Rahim."

"Shaima! I told you, once things have settled down, I'll be able to send the girls back to school."

"Settled down? Settled down where? In this house or do you mean the whole country? And when do you think that will be, because as far as I can remember these children have been living under rocket fire for their entire lives! For God's sake, I can't even remember a day when this country wasn't at war."

"I know that, Shaima-*jan,* but I don't think you understand my situation. If their father forbids them from —"

"Their father can eat shit."

"Shaima!"

Shahla and Parwin both froze. That was more than we would have expected, even from Khala Shaima.

"You're so defensive about him! Open your

117

eyes, Raisa! Can't you see what he is?"

"What he is, is my husband!" Madar-*jan* yelled, louder than we'd ever heard her before. "And you have to understand that! Please! Don't you think I know better than anyone what he is or isn't? What can I do?"

"Your husband is an idiot. That's why I worry about these girls being around him. Sit with us and you'll be one of us. Sit with a pot and you'll be black."

"Shaima, please!"

Khala Shaima sighed and relented. "Fine. All right then, Raisa. But that's why I keep coming here and harping after these girls. Somebody needs to oppose him."

"And who better than . . ."

"That's right," Khala Shaima said with satisfaction. She turned her attention back to me. Shahla and Parwin resumed their work but at a slower pace, unnerved by Madar-*jan*'s yelling. "So, tell me then. Have you been adjusting well? No troubles with the boys?"

"No, no trouble, Khala-*jan*. I've been play-ing soccer and I'm better than my cousin Muneer, I think."

"And no one's said anything to you?"

"No, Khala-*jan*."

"Good. And what kinds of things are you doing to help your mother?"

"Rahim's been going to the market for me. The store owners give him better prices than they do me."

"Don't forget, Madar-*jan*. I've been working with Agha Barakzai and he's been giving me a little money!"

"I was getting to that, Rahim. You know Agha Barakzai has that little shop in the village. Well, he's been in need of help with errands and I asked Rahim to stop by there and see if he could pick up a bit of work. Agha Barakzai can hardly see anymore with his terrible eyes."

"You're a working boy! Now, that's news!" Khala Shaima clapped her hands together.

"Yup, I go all around town and no one bothers me. I can do anything! I even saw Padar's friend Abdul Khaliq yesterday."

Madar-*jan* stiffened and looked at me.

"Who did you see?"

"Abdul Khaliq," I repeated, quieter this time. Khala Shaima looked as displeased as my mother. I wondered if I'd done something wrong.

"Did he say something to you?"

"Not much. He bought me a snack and told me I was coming along nicely."

Madar-*jan* shot another look at Khala Shaima, who shook her head.

"Raisa, that is not a man to have your children tagging along after. Not even Rahim!"

"You'll stay away from that man, Rahim," Madar-*jan* said, warning me, her eyes wide and serious. "Do you understand me?"

I nodded. My sisters fidgeted in the silence that followed.

"Khala Shaima, could you tell us more about Bibi Shekiba?" Parwin asked.

"Bibi Shekiba? Ah, you want to know more? Well, let me see if I can remember where I left off . . ."

Just as Khala Shaima leaned back and closed her eyes to tell us more of the story, we heard the door open. My grandmother rarely came to visit us but Padar-*jan* had been gone two months and she felt compelled to check up on things, especially when she saw Khala Shaima hobble through the front gate. Khala Shaima treated my grandmother with respect, but it was measured and anything but warm. My grandmother, on the other hand, felt no obligation to put on airs with my aunt.

"*Salaam,*" she called as she entered. My mother jumped to her feet, startling Sitara, who had nearly fallen asleep. She adjusted the top of her dress and walked to the door to greet her mother-in-law.

Khala Shaima took her time but pushed herself up to greet her sister's mother-in-law.

"*Salaam,* Khala-*jan.* How is your health? Well, I hope." She almost sounded sincere. My sisters and I kissed her hands. She sat down across from my mother and Shahla brought a cup of tea from the kitchen.

"Oh, you're here, Shaima-*jan*! How nice of

120

you to drop by again so soon."

I could hear it in my grandmother's voice: *You come too often.* Khala Shaima said nothing.

"You've heard nothing from Arif-*jan*? Any word on when they'll return?"

Madar-*jan* shook her head. "No, Khala-*jan*. Nothing at all. I pray they will return soon."

"In the meantime, I've spoken with Mursal-*jan* and her family has agreed to give their daughter's hand in marriage for Obaid." Obaid was my father's brother. This was surprising news.

"Obaid-*jan*? Oh, I didn't realize . . ."

"Yes. So we'll be preparing for her arrival. We will have their *nikkah* in two months' time, *inshallah.* This will be a blessing for our family. A second wife will bring him more children and grow our family."

"They have five children, *nam-e-khoda,*" Madar-*jan* said softly.

"Yes, but only two boys. Boys are blessings and Obaid wants more sons. Better to have more children than to try to change the ones you have. Anyway, I've made you aware. Fatima may call on you for help preparing a place for his new wife. This is happy news and we'll all take part in it."

"Of course, Khala-*jan*. It's wonderful news." Madar-*jan*'s voice was soft. Khala Shaima watched the interaction with narrowed eyes.

121

"Hopefully, there will be more of it in the future," she said, nodding her head.

My grandmother got back up and walked to the door.

"Anyway, that's all for now. Shaima-*jan*, send my regards to the family, will you please? I guess you'll be leaving soon, as it is getting late."

"You're too kind, Khala-*jan*. You make me feel so welcomed here, it's difficult to leave."

I saw my grandmother's shoulders stiffen before she left and the way Madar-*jan* and Khala Shaima looked at each other. Khala Shaima shook her head. This meant bad news for our household.

"Come, girls, let me tell you more about Bibi Shekiba. I'll tell you how easily women pass from one place to another, from one home to another. What happens once, happens twice and then a third time . . ."

CHAPTER 11
SHEKIBA

Azizullah sat in the living room with his brother, Hafizullah. There were two other men with them as well but Shekiba did not know their names and had never seen them before. They had white turbans on their heads and pale blue tunics and pantaloons. Hafizullah wore a brown vest over his tunic, his prayer beads hanging from the pocket.

"Shekiba, Padar-*jan* wants the food to be ready in twenty minutes," announced Haris. "He says they're going to leave soon so it better not take too long."

Shekiba nodded nervously, knowing the rice would have to be a touch undercooked. She added more oil to the pot, hoping that the extra grease would soften the grains.

Haris leaned over her shoulder and tried to snatch a piece of meat from the bowl next to Shekiba. Her right arm went up instinctively and snagged him by the wrist.

"You know better, Haris. Not until after they've eaten." Her tone was gentle but firm.

Haris was by far her favorite of the children. He would sometimes sit with her when he had tired of his siblings. She didn't mind his company. On the contrary, she enjoyed his chatter and the stories he would tell about his teacher.

"Just one piece!" he pleaded.

"If you have a piece, then your brothers will want some too when they see you licking the sauce off your fingers."

"No, I promise! I won't tell them I had some! I'll lick my fingers clean here before I go back out!" Haris was already an expert negotiator.

"Fine then. But just one —"

He had snatched the largest chunk before Shekiba could finish her sentence.

"Haris!"

He grinned, his cheeks lumpy with lamb. How lucky she was to live in a house that could afford to eat lamb! Shekiba sighed and pretended to be annoyed.

"What are they talking about in there, anyway?" she asked.

"Don't you know? The king is coming!"

"The king?" Shekiba asked. "Which king?"

"Which king? King Habibullah, of course!"

"Oh." Shekiba had no idea who King Habibullah was. It had been years since her father had shown an interest in anything beyond their walls. "Is he coming here?"

"Here? Are you crazy, Shekiba? He is going

124

to Kaka Hafizullah's house."

Azizullah's brother had managed to secure himself a position as a friend of the monarchy. He served as a regional overseer and reported to the authorities in Kabul, the capital. For years, he had served as a loyal delegate and traveled frequently to the palace to meet with the king's advisers. He was vying for royal attention in the hopes of becoming *hakim* to their province. With such a title came an attractive amount of power, and so Hafizullah often shared hearty meals and lavished compliments on anyone with any influence.

Azizullah had no patience for such high-brow relations but he did enjoy the secondary benefits that came with having a strategically placed brother. People in the village showed Azizullah deference, hoping they could curry favor with Hafizullah. This was how influence trickled down from the monarchy into the most insignificant of homes in the countryside.

And while Shekiba had no knowledge of such diplomatic matters, she too became enchanted by the prospect of the king paying a local visit. She imagined horses and regal clothing, guards at his side.

She adjusted her head scarf and poured fresh cups of tea, hoping to distract their appetites for a few more minutes. She carried a tray into the living room and kept her head bowed, wanting to be as discreet as possible.

"It is a huge honor. This is the opportunity I have been waiting for. Thanks be to Allah, I have called in many favors and secured the makings of a fine feast for the night. We will make *qurbani;* a goat will be slaughtered in the king's good name. I am sparing no expense."

"How are you to pay for this? How many people will be with him? Surely, there will be at least a dozen pretentious mouths to feed!"

"There is a price to pay for everything but it is a chance I could not let escape. Sharifullah has been *hakim* of this province for long enough. It is pure good fortune that he has traveled across the country now to attend the funeral of his cousin."

"Good fortune for you!" Azizullah laughed. "But not for his cousin!"

"Forget about his cousin, dear brother. The point is that this is a chance for our family to reach the next level. That is what our father would have wanted to see, may Allah forgive him and keep him in peace. If I am made *hakim,* we will control the entire province! Imagine the life we would have."

"You would be an excellent *hakim,* certainly. And from what I have heard, many of the villages are displeased with Sharifullah's rulings."

"The man is spineless. The kingdom would all but forget our province were it not for the crops our land produces every season. Sharifullah has done nothing for us! When Agha Sobrani and Agha Hamidi disputed that land by the river, it was his idiotic idea that they should each take half."

Shekiba listened as she gathered the empty teacups and brought the dish of nuts closer to the men.

"Now, neither Sobrani nor Hamidi has any respect for him. They are equally dissatisfied with him. He should have given the land to Hamidi. His claim was reasonable and his family carries more clout than Sobrani's. Better to have Hamidi's full support and anger only Sobrani!"

Irrefutable logic. Shekiba quietly crept out of the room. She had grown accustomed to Hafizullah's animated speeches and found him entertaining in some way. At the same time, she was thankful that Allah hadn't placed her in his custody, as she was certain he was a brute in his home.

As soon as she left the room, she heard Hafizullah's tone change. She stopped and tilted her ear toward the living room.

"And how are things going with your new help? Shekiba-*e-shola* is fulfilling her duties around the house?"

"Well enough," Azizullah answered. "Marjan has not had many grievances about her."

"Hmmph. That family must be so relieved to have unloaded her. From what I have heard, Bobo Shahgul was heartbroken at her son's passing. Could not bear to have his child in her home because she was a constant reminder of her dead son."

"You would have heard more than me. The girl does not speak of her family. Actually, she hardly speaks at all. She has that much sense."

"At least your wife doesn't have to worry about your taking her as a second wife!" Hafizullah joked, slapping his hand on his thigh loudly.

"No, she is not for marriage. She is able-bodied and does the work of a man. Sometimes it escapes us that she is, in fact, a girl. Her strength makes me marvel. I saw her just a few days ago carrying three pails of water and walking straight, as if it were no effort whatsoever. Her uncles told me she had been keeping up her father's farm along with him."

"More useful than a mule. Good," Hafizullah said. "Whatever happened to her father? I remember running into him just after his children were taken in the cholera wave. He looked terrible. Too sensitive, that man was."

"His brother told me that he had not been feeling well in the last few months. Agha Freidun told me they had a conversation and he knew his time was coming. He made arrangements for his daughter to live with Bobo Shahgul and distributed his land, his tools and his animals among his brothers."

Shekiba's eyes widened.

A lie! My father had no such conversation!
He had not seen his brothers after her mother died. She wondered if this story was Kaka Freidun's idea or Bobo Shahgul's. Her family was swooping in to pick up any scraps her father had left behind.

That land should be mine. My grandfather gave it to my father. My father wanted nothing to do with his family. I should be the owner of that land.

Shekiba wondered where the deed was. The deed was a simple document signed by her grandfather, her father, a few distant relatives and a village elder to confirm the transaction. Surely her uncles must have been looking for it when they dumped the contents of the house outside.

"Shekiba? What are you doing here?"

Teacups rattled in Shekiba's startled hands. Marjan had come up behind a very distracted Shekiba. She looked puzzled to see her frozen a few feet away from the living room.

"I just . . . chai . . . ," she mumbled, and headed directly for the kitchen, her head bowed to conceal her hurt eyes.

The scent of cumin and garlic filled the room. Azizullah and his brother shared their meal, tearing off chunks of flatbread and picking up morsels of rice and meat. Shekiba wondered if any would be left for the rest of the family. Meat was hard to come by, even in this household, and it seemed that the men

129

were going to finish the week's stock in one sitting.

Her mind began to wander as she dried the pots. What would happen if she were to try to claim that land? The thought almost made her laugh. Imagine that. A young woman trying to claim her father's land, snatching it from her uncles' greedy claws. She tried to imagine taking the deed to the local judge. What would he say? Most likely he would kick her out. Call her insane. Maybe even send her back to her family.

But what if he didn't? What if he listened to her? Agreed with her? Maybe he would think it was her right to have her father's land.

Marjan was in the kitchen with her. She was sifting through the rice for any small stones.

"Khanum Marjan?" Shekiba said meekly.

"Yes?" Marjan paused and looked up. Shekiba spoke so rarely, one had to take notice.

"What happens to a daughter when her father . . . if her father has some land . . . if he is not . . ."

Marjan pursed her lips and cocked her head. She could sense the question buried in Shekiba's ramblings.

"Shekiba-*jan,* you are asking a ridiculous question. Your father's land will go to his family, since your brothers are dead, may Allah grant them peace." Marjan's response was blunt but it was reality — regardless of what the laws might say. Her candor gave Shekiba confidence to speak openly.

"But what about me? Am I not rightfully an heir to the land? I am his child too!"

"You are his daughter. You are not his son. Yes, the law says that daughters may inherit a portion of what the son would inherit but the truth is that women do not claim land. Your uncles, your father's brothers, have no doubt taken the property."

Shekiba let out a frustrated sigh.

"My dear girl, you are being quite ridiculous. What do you think you would do with a piece of land? First of all, you are living here now. This is your place. Secondly, you are unmarried and no woman could possibly live on a piece of land alone! That is simply absurd."

I lived alone on that land for months. It didn't feel absurd. It felt like home.

But Marjan could not know about her time alone. Shekiba did not dare share the details, knowing it was unspeakable for her to have done so. No reason to give the village more fodder for gossip.

"But if I were a son?" she asked, unwilling to let the matter go completely.

"If you were a son, you would inherit the land. But you are not a son and you cannot be a son and your life is now here as part of this home. You are asking questions that will invite nothing but anger. Enough!" Marjan needed to put a stop to the discussion. If her husband heard them, he would surely be displeased. If these were the kinds of thoughts that ran through her head, Marjan was thankful Shekiba did not speak more often.

But I have always been my father's daughter-son. My father hardly knew I was a girl. I have always done the work a son would do. I am not to be considered for a wife, so what is the difference? What of me is a girl?

Shekiba gritted her teeth.

I have lived alone. I have no need for anyone.

Azizullah's family had been relatively kind to her but Shekiba was restless. She felt freshly resentful of her family.

I cannot go on like this forever. I must find a way to make a life for myself.

CHAPTER 12
RAHIMA

Too often, I missed the opportunity to learn from Bibi Shekiba's story. She was determined to make a life for herself and I seemed determined to unravel the one I had.

I wonder how long I would have gone on as a boy had Madar-*jan* not seen us on that day. Most children who were made *bacha posh* were changed back into girls when their monthly bleeding started but Madar-*jan* had let me go on, bleeding but looking like a boy. My grandmother warned her it was wrong. *Next month,* my mother would promise. But I was too useful to her, to my sisters, to the whole family. She couldn't bear to give up having someone who could do for her what my father wouldn't. And I was happy to continue playing soccer and practicing tae kwon do with Abdullah and the boys.

We didn't have any hot pepper at home and Padar-*jan* liked his food spicy. Those peppers changed everything for me.

Abdullah, Ashraf, Muneer and I were com-

133

ing down our small street. The boys walked with us and then continued on to go to their own homes, smaller than ours but in as poor condition. People in our neighborhood weren't starving but we all thought twice before throwing a scrap to a stray dog. This was how it had been for years. Some days we walked lazily. Other days we were boisterous and raced each other to the tin can, to the old lady, to the house with the blue door.

Abdullah and I stayed close together. In our circle of friends, we had something different. Something a little more. His arm across my shoulder, he would lean past me and tease Ashraf. I was a *bacha posh* but it had gone on too long, like a guest who had grown too comfortable to leave.

It was Ashraf who had started it. He had kicked his leg up into the air, though not as high as he thought it went. We tried to tell him he could barely reach our waists but he was certain he saw his foot swoop past our faces. Muneer shook his head. He was tired of Ashraf practicing on him.

We were fans of martial arts. We'd seen some magazines with fighters in different poses, their feet higher than their heads, their arms fired forward. We wanted to be like them and flipped through the pages copying their stances.

We had fought this way before. All of us. Playfully and without giving it much thought.

I had started wrapping a tight cloth around my breast buds. I didn't want the boys to notice them or comment on them. It was awkward enough that my voice had not begun to change as theirs had. Sometimes I came away with bruises. Once, my ankle twisted in under me as I ducked a kick from Ashraf. For one week, I limped from home to school and back. I told Madar-*jan* I'd tripped on a rock, knowing I couldn't tell her how it had really happened.

But it was worth it. Worth it for that moment when, inevitably, Abdullah would have me cornered, or would twist my arm behind me and I could feel his breath on my neck. Somewhere inside I tingled to be that close to him. I didn't want him to let go, even if I could feel my arm pulling from its socket. I reached out and grabbed at his other arm, feeling his adolescent muscles flex under my fingers. When I was close enough to smell him, to smell the sweat on his neck, I felt dangerous and alive. That's why it was often me who started the sparring. I loved where it put me.

That was what we were doing when Madar-*jan* came out of the neighbor's house, a fistful of red peppers in her right hand and the corner of her *chador* in her left hand. It couldn't have been worse. She spotted us just as he'd tripped my foot. I lost my balance and fell to the ground. I looked up and saw

135

Abdullah's handsome grin as he, victorious yet again, straddled me and laughed.

"Rahim!"

I heard my mother's voice, sharp and horrified. I saw her faded burgundy dress out of the corner of my eye. I felt my stomach drop.

Abdullah must have seen the look on my face. He jumped to his feet and looked over at my mother. Her face confirmed that something had gone wrong. He reached his hand out to me so I could get up.

"That's all right," I mumbled, and got to my feet, dusting off my pants and trying to avoid my mother's accusing eyes.

"*Salaam,* Khala-*jan,*" Abdullah called out. Ashraf and Muneer were reminded of their manners and echoed the same. She turned abruptly and went through our front gate.

"What happened? Your mother seems upset."

"Ah, it's nothing. She's always telling me that I come home with my clothes filthy. More to wash, you know."

Abdullah looked skeptical. He knew a mother's angry face and could tell there was something more behind this.

I didn't want to go home. I knew Madar-*jan* was upset but if I delayed facing her, things would be worse.

I couldn't look at Abdullah, already feeling my face flush. My mother had seen something different than everyone else. She had seen her daughter pinned under a boy in the middle of the street. Few sights could have been more shameful.

I felt a crunch and saw red peppers, crushed by my sandal, at our front gate. Where Madar-*jan* had dropped them. I collected what I could from the ground and went inside.

"Madar-*jan*, I'm going to wash up for dinner," I called out. I could see her in the kitchen and wanted to test the waters, without actually meeting her eyes.

She didn't answer me, which I could only take as a bad sign.

I felt my hands start to shake. Sure, I knew better. Even dressed as a boy, I shouldn't have let things go so far. My aunts or uncles could have seen me. And it was possible they had. I would hardly have noticed with Abdullah up against me.

I wondered if she would tell Padar-*jan*. That would be the end of me. Every possibility sent my brain spinning and drove me into a wild panic. I left the broken peppers on the family room table and went to wash up as I'd said I would. I tried to come up with a plan to talk my way out of this mess. I went to the kitchen, my face still wet.

"Madar-*jan*?"

"Hmm."

"Madar-*jan*, what are you doing?" My voice was meek and unsteady.

"Dinner. Go and finish your work now that

137

you're done embarrassing yourself in the streets."

There it was. I felt a tiny bit relieved to hear her say it. Now I could start to defend myself.

"Madar-*jan,* we were just playing."

Madar-*jan* looked up from the pot she was stirring. Her eyes were narrow and her lips tight.

"Rahim, you know better. Or at least I thought you did. This has gone on too long."

"Madar-*jan,* I —"

"I don't want to hear another word out of you. I will talk to you later. Right now, I've got to get your father's dinner ready or I'll have a second disaster on my hands."

I retreated to the other room and worked on my homework assignments for a while before I decided to see if Agha Barakzai needed any help for the afternoon. I didn't want to be around while Madar-*jan*'s anger festered. He kept me busy until the evening and I came home to find that Madar-*jan* had not saved me any food.

She saw me looking into the empty pots.

"There's a little soup left. You can have it with some bread."

"But, Madar-*jan,* there's nothing but onions and water in this soup. Wasn't there any meat left?"

"We finished it all. Maybe next time there will be some for you."

My stomach growling painfully, I suddenly

became very angry.

"You could have left me something! That's how you treat me? You want me to just go hungry?"

"I'm not sure what it is you're hungry for!" she whispered pointedly.

Padar-*jan* walked in just then. He rubbed his eyes.

"What's all the yelling about?" he asked. "What's going on, *bachem*?

I shot my mother a look and spoke without thinking.

"She didn't save me a single piece of meat. She wants me to have onion broth and bread! I was working at Agha Barakzai's shop and there's no dinner for me when I come home!"

I threw my wages on the table for good measure. The bills fluttered in the air and spread out dramatically.

"Raisa! Is this true? Is there nothing for my son to eat?"

"Your son . . . your son . . ." Madar-*jan* fumbled, trying to find a reasonable explanation for why she was punishing me. But Madar-*jan* wasn't quick enough or sly enough to come up with an alternative story on the spot. And as angry as she was, my mother couldn't bring herself to throw me into the fire.

I saw it coming and instantly wished I could take back what I'd said. I saw his face redden with anger. I saw his head tilt and his shoulders rise. His arms began to wave with anger.

"My son is hungry! Look at the money he's brought home! And even with this you can't find a morsel of food for him? What kind of mother are you?"

A clap as the back of his hand swung across her face. She reeled from the blow. My stomach dropped.

"Padar!"

"Find him something to eat or you'll be going hungry for a month!" he barked. He struck again. A drop of blood trickled from my mother's lip. She covered her face with her hands and turned away from him. I trembled when he looked at me. From the corner of my eye, I saw Shahla and Rohila peeking from across the hall.

"Go, *bachem.* Go to your grandmother and ask her to fix you something to eat. Make sure you tell her what your mother has done. Not that she'll be surprised to hear it."

I nodded and stole a glance at my mother, thankful she didn't meet my gaze.

That night I thought of Bibi Shekiba. I liked to compare myself to her, to feel like I was as bold and strong and honorable as her, but in my most honest moments I knew I wasn't.

CHAPTER 13
SHEKIBA

The idea brewed for some time before Shekiba considered actually going ahead with it. The conversation with Marjan should have discouraged her but it hadn't. All she had gleaned from it was that, officially, she had a right to claim at least a portion of her father's land.

She lay awake every night thinking of the deed. A mere piece of paper with a handful of signatures, and yet it carried so much weight. Where would her father have kept it? Shekiba closed her eyes and imagined herself at home. She heard the clapping of the gate against the latch, the metal rusted over. She pictured her father's corner, his blankets laid out and ready for those chilly nights. She saw her mother's kitchen stool and her brother's sweaters, folded and stacked on a shelf.

It must be in his books, Shekiba thought. Since she'd been the only one to tend to it, she knew every inch of the house. She thought of the shelf and how she'd given up on dusting it after her mother died. Padar had collected three or four books over the years and that was where he kept them.

When Shekiba made the realization, she nearly hit herself for how obvious it was.

But how do we know, Padar-jan?

All the answers are in the Qur'an, bachem.

Her father taught them all to read, first with the Qur'an and next with the books he kept. She would follow along as his callused finger traced the words. Her brothers occasionally brought home a newspaper from their adventures into the village and the children would take turns poring over the pages and practicing making sense of the words and phrases. It was difficult but Padar-*jan* patiently let them make mistakes, peering over their shoulders when they faltered and filling in the pieces.

It's in the Qur'an, she realized. What were the chances her uncles had not yet found it? Unlikely — but maybe there was a possibility those bullheaded men had not bothered looking for it. Surely they had no inkling that Shekiba would even think to assert any claim over the land.

Which meant Shekiba was thinking of returning to her home — not a small undertaking.

And if she were to find the deed, what would she do with it? She couldn't expect to show it to her uncles and have a rational discussion with them. No, she needed to bring the deed to an official, the local judge, so that she could argue her case.

It was just like Azizullah and his brother had discussed. A disagreement like this needed to be settled by an official, which meant Shekiba's plan became even more complex. How would she find this person?

And how would she get to all these places? She needed to be out of the house for a day. Shekiba wondered if Marjan would let her venture out on her own. After their conversation, it was hard to imagine Marjan would be supportive of her idea. Shekiba would have to come up with something.

Two days later, Shekiba approached Marjan as she was knitting a sweater for Haris. She rehearsed her question in her mind before clearing her throat.

"*Salaam,* Khanum Marjan," she said, trying to keep her voice steady.

"*Salaam,* Shekiba," Marjan said, barely lifting her eyes from the needles as they crossed, uncrossed and crossed again in her hands.

"Khanum Marjan, I wanted to ask you something."

"What is it, Shekiba?"

"I was wondering if I could take a day to visit my family. I have not seen my family in several months and I was hoping to visit them. Next week is Eid and I know it will be a busy time here, so perhaps this week?" She folded her hands behind her to stop from wringing them.

Marjan stopped her knitting and set the needles on her lap. She looked puzzled.

"Your family? Dear girl, since coming here you have never once mentioned your family. I was beginning to think you were so cold as to not have any affection for them! How is it that you now want to pay them a visit?"

"Oh, I've missed them dearly," she said, trying her best to make her voice sound genuine. "But in my first days here, I did not think it was proper to make such a request."

"And now?"

"Well, now I have been here for some months and with the holiday coming . . . I wanted to pay a visit to my grandmother, out of respect." Shekiba wondered if she was giving omniscient Allah a good laugh or if she'd be damned for her lies.

"Your grandmother." Marjan sighed heavily and pressed her fingers to her temples.

Shekiba braced herself.

"We have much to do to prepare for the holiday. We need to bake some cookies, there will be many meals to prepare, the house needs to be spotless . . . ," she said, listing the tasks ahead. "But I suppose it is only proper that you should pay a visit to Bobo Shahgul. She is your grandmother, after all. I will speak to Azizullah and present your request."

Shekiba tried not to smile. She bowed her head in gratitude.

"Thank you, Khanum Marjan," she said. "I would really appreciate that."

Every once in a while, Shekiba became aware of how painfully naïve she was. The following day was one such occasion.

Marjan walked into the kitchen area as Shekiba sat on the floor, with a heap of potatoes before her. She stopped peeling when she heard her name being called.

"Shekiba, Azizullah agrees . . . hey, girl! What is wrong with you?" Marjan took one look at Shekiba and froze. Her hands flew to her hips and her eyes narrowed.

"Huh? What is it, Khanum Marjan?" Shekiba looked down at the pile before her, wondering what had offended the mistress of the house so.

"Is that how a girl sits?" she said, waving an arm at Shekiba's sprawled legs.

Shekiba turned to look at herself. She was leaning against the wall and had her knees bent, the pile of potatoes in the valley her skirt formed between her legs.

"In the name of God, have some decency! Fix yourself before the children see you! Were you never taught how to sit?"

Shekiba got up and fixed her skirt, tucking her legs under her, and looked up at Khanum Marjan for approval.

"That's better. I heard you had become

your father's son but I did not think it had gone this far."

"Yes, Khanum Marjan." Shekiba felt half her face flush.

"Now, what was I saying? Oh, yes. Azizullah agrees that you should be allowed to pay respects to your grandmother for the holidays. You are to accompany him this Friday when he goes into the village for Jumaa prayers."

Azizullah would take her there?

"Khanum Marjan, a world of thanks, but I do not wish to trouble your husband. I can find my own way and I will not bring him out of his way."

Marjan looked at her incredulously. Shekiba never ceased to amaze her. The girl was quite handy and efficient in the house but when it came to common sense, she was seriously lacking.

"You expect to go wandering around the village by yourself? Have you lost your mind?"

Shekiba remained silent. Her mind raced.

"He will take you, as you requested, and join you to pay a visit to your family, although your uncles usually come by on the holidays. Azizullah will accompany you back home. You cannot expect to be wandering around the village like a street dog!"

Shekiba had done too much on her own while she lived with her father and before her uncles had claimed her. It had not occurred to her that she would have to be accompanied by someone. Her chest tightened with panic. She had not anticipated this stipulation.

"I . . . I had not meant to trouble . . ."

"Well, if you do not want to trouble him then you should not have raised the question." Marjan walked out in exasperation. Shekiba's bizarre questions were getting on her nerves.

Shekiba was left to wonder. She could tell Marjan she no longer wanted to go. It would seem strange but it could work. Or maybe once she was there she could ask permission to collect some belongings from her father's home. But what about taking the deed to a *hakim,* the local official?

Maybe on another day. But even if she were granted another day, she would still need to be accompanied. And she had no idea where to find the *hakim.*

Shekiba would have to ponder that one. *One bridge at a time,* she thought.

Jumaa came and Shekiba steeled herself. It would take all her resolve to face her family again, especially her grandmother. But this was her only hope at getting her hands on the deed.

Marjan had instructed her to be ready in the morning, as Azizullah would not wait on her. He nodded in acknowledgment when he saw her waiting by the outside door, her *burqa* donned and her head bowed.

"Salaam," she said quietly.

"Let's go," he said, then opened the door and led the way.

They did not speak on the way to the *masjid.* Shekiba walked a few steps behind but paid close attention to the road. She tried to memorize everything on the way there. The road was wide and dusty but lined with tall trees. There were a handful of homes scattered on either side, about two acres apart. The homes were uniformly surrounded by six-foot-high clay privacy walls. Shekiba could see rows of plantings in their yards and could spot the potatoes, carrots and onion plants even from this distance. The weather was dry and crops were suffering, which meant the families were probably suffering too.

A *masjid,* three shops and a bread baker constituted the village center. The storefronts were modest, with dull glass windows and handwritten signs. The bread baker didn't really have a store. He sat against a wall of another shop and pulled hot, golden round breads from his *tandoor,* buried in the ground. The smell of fresh bread coming from the open circle in the ground made Shekiba's mouth water. Two women stood waiting for their *naan* to bake. Shekiba recalled walking through the area when her uncle had taken her to Azizullah's as a means of repaying his debt.

Shekiba, the gift, she thought miserably.

Azizullah took her past the *masjid* to a small home about a quarter of a kilometer away. He knocked at the front door.

"Salaam, Faizullah-*jan,"* he said with his hand on his chest.

"Agha Azizullah, how nice to see you! Are you on your way to Jumaa prayers?"

"Most certainly. But I had a favor to ask of you. This is my servant. I am taking her to visit her family after prayers have finished but I hoped I could trouble your wife to watch over her until then. I cannot leave her out in the street."

"Oh, of course! I heard you had taken in Bobo Shahgul's grandchild, the one with the half face. Have her stay in the courtyard. Not a good idea to leave an idle girl in the market-place."

Shekiba was directed to a stool with a view of the outhouse. She rested her head against the wall. The smell from the outhouse was overwhelming but she dared not move her seat, afraid to anger her unseen hostess.

She never met the man's wife or children but she could hear them inside. Crying. Laughing. Running.

The sounds of a family.

I could leave now, Shekiba thought. *What if I just opened the door and left? I can find my home from here. I could look for the deed and maybe even make it back for the end of prayers.*

But Azizullah would probably come back and find her gone. Or the lady of the house would notice that the *burqa* had disappeared from the courtyard and tell him. And then what? Shekiba feared angering Azizullah mostly because she feared being sent back to Bobo Shahgul's house. Nothing would be worse. At least, nothing she could think of.

Azizullah returned and thanked his friend for allowing Shekiba to stay. He gave her a nod and again they were on the dirt road, this time headed toward Bobo Shahgul's house. When they arrived, Hameed answered the gate.

"*Salaam!*" Hameed called out.

"*Salaam, bachem.* Where is your father? Your uncles? I did not see them at Jumaa prayers. Did they not go?"

"No, *sahib.* No, and if you only knew what Bobo-*jan* told them for being so lazy." Hameed never could keep anything to himself.

Azizullah chuckled. "Well, may God forgive their sins even if your *bobo-jan* will not. Tell them your *kaka* Azizullah and your cousin are paying a visit."

Hameed led them into the courtyard and ran inside announcing their arrival at a volume that rivaled the mullah's *azaan,* call to prayer.

"Bobo-*jaaaaaaaan*! Bobaaaaaaaaaa! Kaka

150

Azizullah brought Shekiba baaaack!"

Shekiba panicked even more and turned to look at Azizullah's face. Had he really brought her for a visit or was he returning her to this house? Maybe Marjan had complained about her? About the way she sat? About her odd questions? Her palms grew sweaty. The *burqa* was suffocating.

Azizullah's attention had turned to a flowering bush. He was examining the petals and did not seem to notice Hameed's announcement.

Kaka Freidun appeared in the doorway. He looked unsettled.

"Agha Azizullah! Welcome! How wonderful to see you." Kaka Freidun extended his arms in greeting. The men hugged and exchanged customary pecks on the cheek. "How are you? How is your family?"

"Everyone is well, thank you. And you? Bobo Shahgul is in good health, I pray?"

"Ah, the usual aches and pains of age and unruly children," he joked, shooting me a glaring look. *He thinks I have done something wrong. Already, he would love to punish me.*

"Your family is blessed to have her at this age. I still grieve my mother, God rest her soul, and it has already been two years since she passed."

"May Allah forgive her and may heaven be her place of rest," Freidun said. "Please come in. Join us for a cup of tea."

151

They walked toward the house and Shekiba stood a few meters back. She felt out of place and shifted on her feet. She was within her family's courtyard but she kept her *burqa* on. She preferred its cover for the time being.

"Azizullah-*jan,* we have not seen each other in some time. I hope that things are well at home." Freidun's statement was more of a question. He was trying to gauge the reason behind the visit.

"Yes, yes, things are well. And you? How is the family doing? How is the farm? Are your crops doing well this year?"

"As well as can be expected, with the lack of rain. The dry skies do not help but we are hoping to make at least enough to get by."

"I have heard similar complaints from others around town. And where is Bobo Shahgul? Is she resting?"

"She went to lie down after she finished her prayers," Freidun said. "Did you want to speak to her?" Again, he looked anxious.

Kaka Zalmai and Kaka Sheeragha entered the courtyard, their expressions mirroring their brother's. Azizullah stood and the men hugged and exchanged brief pleasantries.

Her uncles pretended not to notice her in the background. Shekiba knew she should go through the back door and find the women but she had little interest in doing so.

"Shekiba wanted to pay a visit to the family, since Eid is coming next week. She missed everyone a great deal and wanted to say hello, especially to Bobo Shahgul."

Her uncles could not conceal their surprise. After a moment, Kaka Freidun nodded smugly.

"Ah, I see. I am not surprised. Bobo Shahgul is much loved by all her grandchildren."

He thinks I regret how I left. He's even dumber than his wife.

"Her grandmother is probably about to wake up from her rest and will surely be surprised to see her," Freidun said.

Shekiba's lips tightened with frustration.

"Well, you have come all this way. Let us go inside and share a cup of tea with you, dear friend. Surely Bobo Shahgul will be happy for the time with her dear grand-daughter!" Freidun said glibly.

Zalmai and Sheeragha shared a smirk.

Shekiba felt like a puppet; her arms and legs were being directed by her uncle. What else could she do? Her every move was propelled by her desire to stay out of this house. If Azizullah saw her as an insolent girl, she risked being returned to her family.

Her legs obeyed and she walked slowly through the back door of the house. She passed by Khala Samina's son, Ashraf, who was carrying a tray of steaming teacups and bowls of raisins and nuts. The cups rattled with his unbalanced nerves.

Shekiba walked into the hallway and

paused. Should she really go to her grand-mother? Would they check on her? She lifted her *burqa* and let it drape from her head.

Khala Samina appeared in the hallway. She was thin framed, more petite than her sisters-in-law.

"*Salaam,* Shekiba," she said quietly. "She knows you're here. She's waiting for you."

"*Salaam,*" Shekiba answered.

"Shekiba . . ."

She turned around to look at her aunt, who was scratching her forehead. She took a few steps toward Shekiba and lowered her voice.

"She is an ornery old lady. Don't give her any reasons. She knows no other means of entertaining herself."

Shekiba nodded, suddenly feeling her throat tighten. Samina's voice was gentle, a tone rarely used toward Shekiba. She suddenly felt a gaping hole where her mother should have been.

"Thank you, Khala Samina."

Samina closed her eyes briefly and nodded her head in acknowledgment before she resumed her work in the kitchen.

Shekiba walked a few more meters to Bobo Shahgul's room. She could see through the gauzy curtain that her grandmother sat in a chair with her walking stick in her hand. Her bony fingers were wrapped tightly around the stick.

She knows I am here. I have no choice now.

Shekiba pulled the curtain aside and met her grandmother's icy stare.

"Well, well. Look who has decided to disrupt our peace yet again."

"*Salaam.*" Shekiba decided she would take Samina's advice and try not to antagonize the old woman.

"*Salaaaaam,*" Bobo Shahgul said mockingly. "You stupid girl. How dare you come here? How dare you step foot in this house?"

Shekiba steeled herself. She had taken worse. All she had to do was resist the temptation to fire back.

You need to get to your house and get the deed. Do not forget why you came here. Do not let the old lady distract you.

"Eid *mubarak,* Bobo-*jan.*"

"As if I needed to see that face," she replied, turning away in repulsion. "There is no Eid for a disrespectful creature like you — you dare to disrespect the grandmother who took you in even after you robbed her of her son." She rose on her hobbled feet, fueled by rage.

"My father was a wise man who decided for himself."

Shekiba saw it coming but hardly flinched.

Bobo Shahgul's walking stick came crashing down on her shoulder.

She is weaker than a few months ago, Shekiba realized.

"Bobo-*jan,* how is your health? You're look-

155

ing a bit frail, God forbid."

A second blow. She was trying harder.

"You beast! Get out of my house!"

"As you please," Shekiba said, turned and walked out with her chin held high. She had said nothing. And nothing could have made Bobo Shahgul more irate.

Shekiba stopped by the kitchen. She wondered if Khala Samina had heard the conversation.

"Dear girl, there is something about you that makes that old lady crazy."

She had heard.

"Khala Samina, I want to get a few things from my father's house. I will not take long." Shekiba looked in the direction of the living room. She could hear the men laughing.

Samina shook her head. "Do as you must — you are not a child. But understand that there are many people willing to make your life more difficult. It is up to you to find a way to make things easier for yourself."

Shekiba nodded, wondering which one of them was more naïve.

"I won't be long," she said, lowered her *burqa* and headed out the back door.

She crossed the fields quickly, peering over her shoulder every thirty seconds or so to see if anyone was coming after her. After about twenty meters, she broke into a jog, hoping she didn't attract attention. Her father's home looked smaller than she remembered it. She felt her heart quicken as she neared the rusted gate.

For a second, she saw her father standing outside, his face to the sky as he wiped the sweat from his brow with the back of his hand. She heard her mother call out her brothers' names. She saw Aqela's songbird face in the front window, watching their father toil in the fields.

There should have been a word for what she felt, the way her stomach jumped with anticipation to be somewhere she missed so much, to be around people who missed her as much as she missed them. It was a feeling that started sweet and finished bitter, when she realized that she stood in the ashes of those perfect times, as short as they'd been.

No one had claimed the home yet but it looked as if someone were trying to fix it up. Cracks in the walls had been filled with clay. The splintered table outside had a new plank nailed to it. Inside, the two solid chairs were gone, as were the few blankets she'd left strewn about to make believe her parents and siblings still slept in the house with her.

Shekiba wondered which vulture had his eyes on the house but pushed the thought aside for now.

She needed to find the Qur'an. Her father's books had not been touched. They still sat on the crooked shelf above where Padar-*jan* once slept. She looked out the window, half expecting to hear her uncles' angry voices.

She blinked back tears and used a step stool to reach the top shelf. Her fingers reached over the ledge and sought blindly.

That's it.

She pulled at a corner of fabric and the book slid toward her. She grabbed it with both hands and came down from the stool. The Qur'an was wrapped in a thin, emerald-green cloth embroidered with silver thread. This had been her mother's *dismol,* or wedding cloth. Shekiba brushed the dust away and kissed the holy book, then touched it to her left and right eyes as her parents had taught her.

Why do we keep the Qur'an all the way up there, Madar-jan? It is so hard to reach it there!

Because nothing is above the Qur'an. This is how we show our respect for the word of Allah.

Shekiba unfolded the cloth and opened the first page.

Tariq. Munis. Shekiba. Aqela.

Beside each name, Padar-*jan* had penciled in the month and year of their birth.

Shekiba flipped through the pages, the corners frayed. The book opened to the second *sura.* She recognized the line that her father often quoted. She traced the calligraphy with her finger and heard his voice.

It means that we treasure many things in this world, but there is even more awaiting us in

158

paradise.

The paper fell into her hands. Yellowed parchment with two columns of ornate signatures. She recognized her grandfather's name. This was the deed!

Shekiba's senses heightened now that she had what she'd come looking for. She took a quick look around and tucked the deed back into the pages of the Qur'an. It was time to get back to the house before her escapade incited too much anger. She covered the Qur'an again with her mother's *dismol* and tucked it irreverently under her shirt.

God, forgive me, she thought.

As she exited her rusted front door, she could see Kaka Sheeragha across the field.

Lazy, she thought, looking at her uncle. *The others would have come after me.*

Sheeragha met her at the door.

"What were you doing in that house?" he demanded.

"Praying." Shekiba slipped past him and returned to the living room, hoping Azizullah was ready to leave.

"Where have you been? Bobo Shahgul said she had a pleasant but short visit with you." Azizullah took one last sip from his teacup. "We should be going. We have taken up enough of your time."

"Time with you is time well spent," Zalmai said graciously while he eyed Shekiba with suspicion. Sheeragha nodded in tacit agreement. He was not blessed with the social graces of his brothers.

"You are very kind. Please pass my regards along to the rest of the family. I am sure I will see you in the *masjid* for Eid prayers next week."

"Yes, of course you will."

"Absolutely."

Shekiba followed Azizullah through the courtyard and into the street. Her uncles watched them leave, mumbling to each other.

They put on a good show, she thought, knowing they were wondering what spurred her return to the family home.

CHAPTER 14
RAHIMA

"Of course he hit her again! Why did you have to say something like that to him? You know how he is!" Shahla was folding the laundry in the courtyard, her eyes moving back and forth between the clothes and Sitara, who was drawing circles in the dirt with a rock.

"I didn't mean for that to happen. I was just . . . I only meant to . . ."

"Well, you should think before you say something. She couldn't even lift her arm this morning. God knows what he did to her."

I bit my lip. I had gone to my grandmother's as my father instructed. I was hoping he would have left Madar-*jan* alone, but he hadn't. His toxic anger never went away, not without his medicine. I wanted Shahla to stop telling me how awful he had been to our mother. But I needed to hear. I needed to know what had happened.

"You've ruined everything for all of us. You don't think. You're so busy being a boy that

161

you've forgotten what can happen to a girl. Now we all have to pay for your selfish mistakes."

"It has nothing to do with you. He was angry at Madar-*jan* so stop worrying about yourself."

Shahla was fighting back tears. "You think it was all about Madar-*jan*? You think everything stops there? Well, it doesn't. What you do affects all of us."

"What are you talking about?"

"You know what we all are? We're all *dokhtar-ha-jawan*. We're all young women. Me, Parwin. Even you, *Rahim*. Even you."

She was angry. I'd never seen Shahla so upset. Sitara looked up, sensing the tension.

"He hit her again. Parwin and I, we were scared to look but we could hear it. He went on yelling and screaming about how it wasn't bad enough that she had failed him as a wife. Now she was failing as a mother."

I remembered how she'd looked, cowering under him. His face had been red with anger, his eyes bulging.

"She must have fallen to the floor. Her shoulder's hurt badly. I don't know. She tried to get him to calm down but he was . . . well, you know how he can get. And then she said something to him that made him stop."

"What did she say?" I asked quietly.

"She said she was taking care of all of us. She said it was a house full of *dokhtar-ha-*

jawan and it wasn't easy. All of a sudden, he got quiet. Then he started pacing the floor, saying his house was full of young women and that it wasn't right."

"What's not right?"

"Don't you know what people say? They say it's not right to keep a *dokhtar-e-jawan* in your home."

"What are you supposed to do with them?" I sensed the ugly turn this was taking.

"What do you think you're supposed to do? You're supposed to marry them off. That's what's in his head now. And it's all because you don't know what to do with yourself. You think just because you're wearing pants and you strap your breasts down every morning that no one will care what you do. But you're not a kid anymore. People won't pretend anymore. You're no different than me and Parwin."

"You think he wants us to get married?"

"I don't know what he's thinking. He left the house after that and he hasn't come home yet. God knows where he is."

Parwin came out of the house with the second load and started hanging sheets on the clothesline. She reached the twine with difficulty. Most of the sheets she tossed over and then pulled the corners from below. Shahla looked as if she were about to help her, then paused, deciding against it. When Parwin finished, she looked up at the sky,

163

blocking the sun with her hand, and mumbled something under her breath.

I thought of a conversation I'd once overheard. Khala Shaima and my mother thought no one was awake but I was having a hard time sleeping.

"That's why it's important for these girls to go to school, Raisa. They'll have nothing otherwise. Be wise about it. Look at me and think of what might happen to Parwin."

"I know, I know. I worry about her more than the others."

"As you should. I was passed over despite everything Madar-*jan* did. All the friends she talked to, all the special prayers. And look at me, wrinkled and alone. No children of my own. Sometimes I think it's worked out best for me that your husband is away so much, that ass. At least it gives me more chances to come and spend time with your daughters."

"They love having you around, Shaima. They hunger for your stories. You're the best family they have."

"They're good girls. But be realistic. Before you know it, you'll have to seriously consider the suitors. Except for Parwin. You'll be lucky if anyone comes for her."

"She's a beautiful girl."

"Bah. The porcupine feels velvet when she rubs her baby's back. You're her mother. Parwin-*e-lang*. That's what she is. Allah as my witness, I love her as much as you do, but that's what people call her and you have to be honest with yourself and realize it. Just like I'm Shaima-*e-koop*. I've always been Shaima the hunchback. As long as she goes to school, that at least gives her something. At least she'll be able to pick up a book and read it. At least she'll have a chance to know something other than these four walls and the smell of her father's opium."

"She would make a good wife. And mother. She's a special girl. The way she draws, it's as if God guides her hands. Sometimes I think she still talks to angels, the way she used to when she was a baby."

"Men have little need for *special* girls. You should know that."

I couldn't imagine Parwin married any more than I could imagine the rest of us married. I drifted off to sleep after that. I dreamed of girls in green veils, hundreds of them, climbing up the mountain to the north of our town. A stream of emerald on the trail to the summit, where, one by one, they fell off the other side, their arms outstretched like wings that should have known how to fly.

In a three-room house, I couldn't expect to avoid my mother for long. I saw her puffy lip, her long face, and hoped she saw the remorse in mine.

"Madar-*jan* . . . I . . . I'm sorry, Madar-*jan*."

"It's all right, *bachem*. It's as much my

165

fault as it is yours. Look at what I've done to you. I should have put a stop to this long ago."

"But I don't want you to —"

"Things will be changing soon, I'm sure. I'm afraid everything is out of my hands now. We will see what *naseeb*, what destiny, God has in store for us. Your father acts rashly and it doesn't help to have your grandmother whispering things into his ear."

"What do you think he'll do?" I asked nervously. I was relieved my mother wasn't angry with me. She lay on her side, my baby sister next to her. I resisted the urge to curl up with them.

"Men are unpredictable creatures," she said, her voice tired and defeated. "God knows what he'll do."

CHAPTER 15
SHEKIBA

Shekiba faced a new dilemma. She wanted to take the deed to the local *hakim* but she didn't know if Azizullah would allow such an act. Maybe he would. Men were, after all, unpredictable creatures.

She decided against asking Azizullah for permission but that meant she needed to get herself to the town's *hakim.* She had overheard his name in conversations between Azizullah and his brother, Hafizullah, but she had no inkling where she would find this man. Then there was the issue of getting to him. What possible excuse could she make this time?

"How was your visit with your family?" Marjan asked.

"It was pleasant," Shekiba answered. She was elbow-deep in hot, sudsy water, washing the children's clothes.

"And how was Bobo Shahgul? Is she in good health?"

"Yes," said Shekiba. *Unfortunately,* she

thought.

"And the rest of the family? Did you see everyone? All your uncles?"

"I saw Kaka Zalmai, Sheeragha and Freidun. My other two uncles are still away in the army."

Marjan stood over her, a finger on her lip as she pondered something. Shekiba purposely avoided her gaze.

"You know, I ran into Zarmina-*jan,* your uncle's wife, at the *hammam* last week. She told me that she was surprised that you wanted to visit your family for Eid."

Shekiba's neck muscles tightened.

"She said that you did not adjust well to Bobo Shahgul's house after your father's death."

Khala Zarmina. What are you up to?

"Were you angry to be sent here?"

Shekiba shook her head.

"Well, I hope not. This was an arrangement that everybody agreed to so I hope that you are not intending to carry out the same kind of behaviors here in this home."

Shekiba felt a fire burn in her belly. "This is a different place," she said in a bitter voice.

"Good. Just be warned that we do not tolerate disrespectful behavior. I will not have my children learning . . . such things!"

Shekiba nodded.

But Marjan was uncomfortable with her.

Maybe Khala Zarmina had said something more.

She prepared the family's dinner and ate quietly in the kitchen. She liked to listen to the children bickering with each other. Amid the din, she heard Marjan tell Azizullah that she had something she needed to discuss with him later.

Shekiba knew it would be about her.

In the night she heard Marjan's soft yelps and knew that Azizullah was taking his wife. This was something Shekiba had learned in her grandmother's house. From where she slept in the kitchen, she could hear the same grunts and pants through the wall and would see Kaka Zalmai emerge from their room refreshed while Samina avoided Shekiba's gaze and busied herself with her children. The women often joked about it when the children were out of earshot but they did not mind Shekiba hearing them.

"You've been working on that sweater for over a week, Zarmina! When are you going to finish?"

"Sounds like what I hear you saying to your husband in the middle of the night, Nargis!"

Laughter and a hand clapped against someone's back. Shekiba listened closely, intrigued by the rare moments of camaraderie amongst the women.

Nargis giggled and shot back without hesitation.

"Mahtub-*gul* can hardly see beyond her huge breasts to know what is happening below."

Laughter again. Samina looked in Shekiba's direction and seemed uncomfortable to have her in the room. Zarmina noticed and raised her teacup.

"I wouldn't worry about her, Samina dear. Remember, she was her father's son so it's in her best interests to learn the way things are from women. Imagine if you had no idea what your wedding night had in store for you! Let her be aware."

Samina clucked her tongue. "Knowing would only make it worse."

Shekiba had thought of her statement often. What was worse about it? Whatever it was, her aunts made it sound awful but tolerable. They were laughing about it, after all.

Hearing Marjan's soft sighs and gasps came as no surprise. It was the thing that transpired between a husband and wife and it was how women became heavy with child. This much Shekiba had pieced together.

After a few moments, the grunts ceased and Shekiba could hear the sounds of a conversation. She pressed her ear to the wall.

"And Zarmina told you she did that?"

"Yes, that's what she said. And now I know why Bobo Shahgul was so eager to make this arrangement. She didn't want to have this girl in her house."

"I've never trusted those boys. Especially Freidun. They think the world of themselves but not one of those sons is a quarter of the man their father was. Their mother is right to keep a close eye on them."

"But what are we to do with Shekiba-*e-shola*? True, she does her work around the house well enough but I am afraid that she will turn on us as she did with her own grandmother. What if she threatens to put a curse on our family as well?"

Put a curse on the family?

"Hmm. Interesting."

"And Zarmina said that even though she had been doing the chores as a son, that the girl has the spirit of a wild woman. The last thing this home needs to invite is scandal and rumor."

"And what is it that you think we should do?"

"I think you should send her back."

"Send her back?"

"Yes! For the sake of everyone in this house. Take her back and tell her uncles that they will have to settle their debt in another way. We cannot have her."

"I see." Marjan was wise to bring up the matter now, with Azizullah feeling spent and relaxed.

"But we mustn't tell them why we want to send her back. Zarmina specifically asked me to keep all this to myself."

"I bet she did."

There was silence. Shekiba felt betrayed and then wondered why she was surprised by her aunt's accusations.

What does she want? Does Zarmina want me back in the house? Why?

"It's going to be a shame to lose her help but I have a bad feeling about this girl. I cannot shake Zarmina's words from my mind." Shekiba thought of Marjan's nervous behavior the last couple days and almost laughed.

For a while, she relished the idea that she could be so formidable a threat.

"If I take her back, it will create a rift between our families and that is not in our best interests. By the looks of their land, I anticipate that the family will be again knocking on our door to borrow money. Not a single one of them knows how to grow a crop. But I have another idea," Azizullah said.

"What is it?"

"You worry about the children and look after the house. Did I not say I would take care of it?" Marjan's window of opportunity was quickly closing. Azizullah's impatience was returning. "Let me talk to Hafizullah about it but there may be a way to get rid of this girl if she is so bothersome to you. And at the same time, we may be able to secure our position in this community. There are changes coming and Hafizullah has high aspirations."

172

■ ■ ■ ■

Shekiba kept her eyes and ears open in the next few days, looking for any sign of what Azizullah's plan might be. He was out of the house most of the time, undoubtedly meeting with Hafizullah about his mystery plan. Shekiba grew more and more frightened.

Women who brought scandal or trouble to a home were not tolerated. Even a naïve girl like Shekiba knew as much. Shekiba began to fear for her life.

She tried to gauge her situation through Marjan.

"Khanum Marjan," Shekiba said quietly. Marjan was darning socks. She jumped at Shekiba's voice.

"I . . . excuse me! I did not mean to startle you! I was going to prepare dinner."

"Oh, Shekiba!" Her hand covered her chest. Marjan shook her head. "Why do you sneak around like that? Go ahead and begin dinner. Azizullah will be hungry when he returns from outside."

Shekiba fidgeted for a moment before daring to ask.

"Khanum Marjan? May I ask a question?"
Marjan looked up expectantly.

"When you . . . when you spoke to Khala Zarmina . . . what did she tell you? I mean, about me."

Marjan turned back to her socks and looked up at Shekiba from the corner of her eye.

"What does it matter?"

"I would like to know."

"She said that you argue."

"Argue? With who?"

"You don't know?"

"I did not argue with anyone there. I did everything they asked of me."

"Well, seems like you're arguing right now, aren't you?"

"No," she replied adamantly. She was desperate to defend herself. "I am not arguing! But whatever she said about me is not true!"

"Shekiba! Lower your voice! Forget what they said. Just busy yourself with the chores."

Shekiba felt helpless. She retreated into the kitchen to begin dinner, angry and frustrated and forced to hide it.

Two days later Azizullah came home with his brother. They sat in the living room and shared a lunch of rice and eggplant. Shekiba frantically searched for excuses to loiter around the living room door, eager to hear their conversation.

"They will be traveling with around thirty people. I have asked that the house be readied. We are sparing no expense."

"Your home will suit them fine, my brother. Better than our simple home would. Have you enough food for the night?"

"Yes, I've called in all my favors in town and we're going to have a meal that even the king himself will talk about! It is costing me more than I had anticipated but I think this will be a great opportunity. For the both of us, do not forget." Hafizullah was slick with confidence.

"I will be there for sure and if there's anything we can do, we will do it," Azizullah said. "But there is something I would like to offer to the king."

"Oh? And what is that?" Hafizullah said, a half-chewed morsel still in his mouth.

"I would like to offer King Habibullah a gift of a servant."

Shekiba's heart began to pound.

"A servant? Which servant?"

"I do not have that many from which to choose," Azizullah said, chuckling.

"You mean Shekiba-*e-shola*?"

"Yes, that's the one."

"Oh, I don't know about this. Brother, do you really think it is wise to make such a halfhearted offering to the king? You may anger him, you know."

"She is a good worker and will serve the palace well. Is there not a way to make an honorable gesture of her?"

Shekiba, the gesture. Shekiba, the gift.

She felt insignificant and disposable to hear herself described that way. Again.

"Well, let me think on it. It is possible, I suppose. I mean, it's not as if he needs to see her face . . . but you know there may be a good use for this girl in the palace after all. Now that I think of it — I just had a conversation with a general. You know General Homayoon, don't you?"

"Yes, that no-good money-hungry fool. What were you doing with him?"

"He is a money-hungry fool but he's likely going to be promoted, so watch what you say about him. Better to have this fool as your friend than your enemy. He told me that he has been placed in charge of recruiting soldiers to help guard King Habibullah's harem. The king doesn't trust men to watch over his women and he has collected a group of women who are kept as men. This way he need not worry that his guards will take advantage of his ladies."

"Ah, what a brilliant solution! I am telling you, my brother, this girl is well suited for such a role. She walks and breathes like a man, my wife tells me."

"Then we will arrange it," Hafizullah declared. "I will speak to the general so that we can make the entourage aware of the gift before you present her to King Habibullah. This is a historic visit to our town and you will be making a mark. You can expect this to bring you many returns, I believe."

Shekiba had heard enough. She walked

back to the kitchen, her legs wobbly beneath her. Her head was spinning.

The king? The palace?

Words that were foreign to her.

Shekiba, the half face. The girl-boy who walks like a man.

Shekiba was not a whole anything, she realized.

CHAPTER 16
RAHIMA

Khala Shaima liked to keep us hanging. I wondered what would happen to Bibi Shekiba almost as much as I wondered what would happen to us. It seemed that we were both about to leave our homes.

Padar-*jan* spent more time away from home in the following weeks. When he did return, he scowled and barked orders more. Even Parwin's soft singing, which he usually secretly enjoyed, provoked him. Madar-*jan* tried to keep him placated with ready meals and a quiet home but he inevitably found another reason to explode.

I spent more time at Agha Barakzai's shop. It was my way of avoiding the guys without explaining what was happening. I worried that my mother was going to change me back into a girl and I wondered how Abdullah and Ashraf would react. I hated to be away from them, mostly Abdullah, but I was scared to be with them, too.

I lay awake at night, thinking about Abdullah and remembering the day Madar-*jan* had caught us play-fighting. Until the moment she called my name, it had been thrilling. I tingled to think of Abdullah's face over mine, his long legs trapping my hips under him, his hands pinning my wrists. And his grin. I blushed in the dark.

I tried to make up to Madar-*jan* for what I had done. I tried to keep Padar-*jan* distracted from her, even if it meant him yelling at me. Even though I'd been relieved of housework when I became a *bacha posh,* I tried to help when I saw her washing clothes or beating the dust from the carpets.

Shahla didn't say more than a few words to me every day. She was still upset and could sense from Madar-*jan*'s mood that trouble was brewing. She was quiet around Padar-*jan,* bringing him tea or food and leaving the room before he could realize she was one of those young women he had kept home for too long.

My grandmother stopped by more often. She was intrigued by the new wave of unrest in our home and wanted to see it for herself. Madar-*jan* tried to be as polite as she could.

"Tell my son that I want to talk to him. When he gets home, make sure he comes to see me."

"Of course. What is it that you want to talk to him about?"

"Is it any business of yours? Just tell him

what I've asked."

Madar-*jan* knew what the topic was. Maybe this time her husband would be more interested in bringing another wife home.

I listened in when Padar-*jan* went to see his mother. I pretended to be playing with a ball in the courtyard and slowly kicked it further and further until I was right outside my grandmother's living room. I heard her shrill voice loud and clear. My father, mumbling at times, was more difficult to make out.

"*Bachem,* it's high time. You've given her plenty of opportunity to give you a son and she's failed. Now, let's bring a second wife for you so that you can finally expand this family."

"And where am I going to put her? We have one room for all the girls as it is. There's no money to build another space behind our home or to buy something else in town. I can always find a new wife. It's the space and money that are harder to come by."

"What about Abdul Khaliq? Hasn't he promised to help you when you need?"

Padar-*jan* shook his head.

"The men are short on weapons, on supplies. There isn't money to spare."

"Psht. The hell there isn't money. I've heard what he does. I've heard from the people in town about his horses, his wives, all his children. He's got plenty!"

"Madar! Be careful what you say! He's a

powerful man and don't be part of any loose talk about him. Do you understand me?"

"I'm not the one starting this talk. There are lots of tongues flapping about him. That's all I'm trying to tell you," she said, annoyed to be silenced by her son.

"Anyway, I'll be making some changes at home soon and things will be easier on my pockets. It's time I relieved myself of some of these girls."

"And how do you expect to do that?"

"Just watch what Raisa does while I'm gone and I'll find a way to take care of the rest."

Shahla and Madar-*jan* were right. Padar-*jan* was about to shake up our home.

Eleven days later, Abdul Khaliq showed up at our home with seven other men. They pulled up in two black SUVs, their tires leaving clouds of dust in the street. Abdullah saw the car and knew immediately who they belonged to. Most people in our town traveled on foot.

It was my cousin Muneer who opened the front gate and pointed out our home. Not even my father was expecting him. Muneer watched openmouthed as Abdul Khaliq and his entourage walked by. Two men had black guns slung over their shoulders. Abdul Khaliq was a burly man in his late forties, judging by the lines around his eyes and the gray in his beard. He wore a white turban and a beige tunic over loose pants. An antenna stuck out from the pocket of his gray vest, another sign that this man was something other than common folk. He was the first person in our town to own a mobile phone. Few had access to any phone at all.

We usually sent one of the men to the front gate to greet a visitor. People didn't just barge in, since the women of the home could be wandering about the courtyard without their head coverings. But it was either Muneer's stupidity or Abdul Khaliq's presence that changed things from the usual routine. He and his men were in our courtyard, their eyes assessing the situation. I caught sight of them and recognized Abdul Khaliq from the bazaar. I darted inside to warn my mother and send my father out to meet his friend.

"Padar-*jan*, Abdul Khaliq is here — with a lot of people."

My father sat up straight and pushed his newspaper aside. "What are you talking about? Where?"

"Out there. In the courtyard. He's got seven men with him. And guns."

My father's brow furrowed. He got to his feet faster than usual.

"Tell your mother to prepare something for our guests," he said, and went outside to meet the warlord.

Madar-*jan* heard us and stood in the kitchen looking disturbed. She shot a look at the doorway to our bedroom, where Shahla and Rohila were putting Sitara to sleep. Parwin was peeling onions at Madar-*jan*'s feet. She was the only one whose eyes didn't sting and tear when the layers came off.

"He's going to want more than tea," Parwin predicted without looking up.

Madar-*jan* looked at Parwin almost as if she heard some prophesy in her daughter's words. She bit her lip and took out some cups.

"Bring these to them, Rahim-*jan*," she said nervously.

I took the tray and willed my hands not to shake. I could feel their eyes boring into me when I entered the room, their conversation suddenly pausing. The men had spread out, Abdul Khaliq sitting on the cushion across from my father, his fingers nimbly working a string of prayer beads as he leaned back. On either side of him sat older men, more gray in their beards than black. The armed men were closest to the door. I didn't look at their faces and tried to keep my gaze off their weapons as well. Kneeling, I put a cup in front of each person and backed out of the room as quickly as I could to listen from the hallway. Madar-*jan* was doing the same.

"Arif-*jan*, I've come here today to discuss an important and honorable matter with you. For that reason, I have brought my elders with me, as well as a few members of my family whom you have met before. I'm sure you recognize my uncle's sons, my father and my uncle. You have fought with me for years and I respect you for that. From one man to another, we both know that there are traditions in our culture."

"You honor me with your visit, *sahib,* and I have been proud to fight under your leadership. We've done great things for our people thanks to you." I'd never heard Padar-*jan* speak in such a way with anyone. Abdul Khaliq unnerved him. "And I am honored to have your family in my humble home. Dearest uncles, I appreciate you traveling this far to be our guests."

The men nodded, acknowledging my father's platitudes. Abdul Khaliq's father cleared his throat and began to speak. His voice was raspy and he had a light lisp.

"My son speaks highly of you, and of course, your family is well respected in this town. I've known your father for many years, Arif-*jan.* He is a good man. That is why I'm sure we will see eye to eye on this matter as well. As you know, my son is a man who takes pride in meeting his duties as a Muslim. And one of the duties that Allah has outlined for us is to build families and to provide for women and children."

I could feel my heart pounding. Madar-*jan* stood behind me, one hand on my shoulder and the other covering her mouth, as if she thought she might let out a scream otherwise.

"Of course, dear uncle . . ." Padar's voice trailed off; he was unsure what to say. Abdul Khaliq began to speak.

"And you came to me recently talking of your concerns. That you have young women at home and not enough money with which to provide for them. I have been thinking about your situation and am here to offer a solution."

Abdul Khaliq's father gave him a look. *Let me do the talking,* his eyes said.

"We must often think of what is in everyone's best interests. In this case, you have a young woman whom my son would like to honor as his wife. Our family is large and well respected, as you know. Your daughter would do well to join our family and a union between us would be cause for celebration. Of course, as a result, you would be better able to provide for your family as well."

"My daughter?"

"Yes. If you give it some thought, I'm sure you'll see it's the wisest choice."

"But my eldest is —"

"We are not here for your eldest daughter, Arif-*jan.* I'm speaking of your middle daughter. The *bacha posh.* My son has expressed an interest in her."

"The *bacha posh* . . ."

"Yes. And do not be surprised. You have kept her as *bacha posh* beyond what anyone should accept. You are breaking tradition."

185

I turned around and looked at my mother, my face drained of color. Padar was silent. I knew he was wondering how Abdul Khaliq knew about me but word had way of traveling. I remembered the day in the bazaar, the way Abdul Khaliq had looked at me and the way he had smirked and nodded when the man next to him leaned in and whispered something in his ear.

My mother's fingers tightened as she wrapped her arms around me. She was shaking her head, willing her husband to refuse this man and praying he could do so in a way that wouldn't offend him or his guns.

"With all due respect, sir . . . it's just that . . . well, she is a *bacha posh* . . . but I have two other daughters older than her. And as you said, we are people of tradition and usually the younger daughters are not given until the eldest . . . I just don't think . . ."

There was a long pause before Abdul Khaliq's father began to speak again, slowly and deliberately.

"You are right. It would be improper to give your middle daughter's hand without the other two being wed as well."

For a second I could breathe. But it was only a second.

"But this can be easily arranged. My cousins are here, Abdul Sharif and his brother Abdul Haidar. They are looking for wives as well. We can arrange for each of them to take

186

one of your daughters. They are strong men, able-bodied, and will provide well for your girls, who are now young women and should not be kept idle at home. Let these men bring honor to your home and ease your troubles."

"Abdul Khaliq, dear uncles, you know I hold you in the highest regard, but . . . but this is a matter . . . well, tradition dictates that I should consult my family, as you have done. I cannot make such decisions without the presence of my father and our gray-haired family members."

Abdul Khaliq's father nodded in understanding.

"Reasonable. This is not a problem. We shall return in one week's time. Kindly arrange to have your father and your elders here so that we may meet with them."

It may have sounded like a request but Padar-*jan* knew it was more of a command. They would not take no for an answer.

As soon as the last man was out the door, Madar-*jan* ran up to my father.

"Arif, what are you going to do? The girls are so young!"

"It's none of your business what I'm going to do! They're my daughters and I'll do what's right for them. It's not as if you're capable of doing anything."

"Arif, please, Rahim's only thirteen!"

"And he's right! She shouldn't be a *bacha posh* any longer! She's a young woman and

187

it's shameful to have her out on the streets and working with Agha Barakzai at this age. You've given no thought to her decency, have you? Do you know how this looks for my family's name?"

Madar-*jan* bit her tongue. If only my father knew . . .

"You think you can come up with a better plan for this family? There is no money, Raisa! You're thinking of nothing but yourself. And you've seen what happens to girls who stay in their fathers' homes for too long. There is talk about them. There is scandal. Or worse! What will you do if some bandits come and take your daughters by force? This man, this family, they can provide for your daughters! They can give your daughters a respectable life!"

Madar-*jan* searched for a way to argue back. But a lot of what her husband said was true. She was barely able to feed us with what he provided. Padar-*jan*'s brothers were in no better a situation, not to mention the two widows and their children.

"Maybe I can ask my sister, Shaima, to be here when they return. She could reason with them."

"*Khanum,* if your insolent sister dares step foot in this house on that day, I swear to you I'll cut her tongue out and send her hunched back rolling down the street!"

Madar-*jan* shuddered to hear him talk

188

about Khala Shaima in that way.

"Abdul Khaliq is a powerful man and he's in a position to improve our family's lot. This is a matter I'll discuss with my father. You should concern yourself only with fixing what you've done. It's time to undo Rahim."

There was nothing more my mother could say to him. He'd been intimidated by Abdul Khaliq, and from what we'd overheard, it sounded like my father had planted the idea in Abdul Khaliq's mind. I thought back to what Shahla had told me about their fight.

He wants this, I realized. *My father wants to marry us off.*

The thought sent a chill down my spine. I realized what my mother knew as well. Men could do what they wanted with women. There would be no stopping what Padar had set in motion.

Chapter 17
Shekiba

King Habibullah had taken the throne in 1901, just as Shekiba turned eleven years old. This was two years before the cholera epidemic that claimed her family and half her village. That was all she knew about the man. She was a girl from a small village and knew nothing of the palace or life in the capital of Kabul.

Having overheard Hafizullah's brilliant plan for her, Shekiba became terrified. She had no reason to believe that life in the palace would be any better for her. The more powerful people were, the more harm they could do her. Shekiba sat in the night and chewed her lip, her fingers confirming the presence of the deed under her blanket.

I have to get to the hakim. *That's my only chance.*

Shekiba did not know when the king would visit, but it would be soon. She had nothing to lose. She had a plan.

Shekiba tucked the deed into her dress and

crept out of her room at first light. The *azaan* sounded, calling the town to prayer. She remembered the way from Azizullah's house to the village center. There were a few shops there and surely someone would be able to direct her to the house of the *hakim.*

She heard Azizullah's snores and crept past his and Marjan's room. Fortunately, he rarely woke for morning prayers, claiming he would make them up later in the afternoon. The children were still asleep.

She slipped her *burqa* over her head and slowly pushed open the heavy gate. She was outside the courtyard. She paused for a moment, waiting to hear the sound of footsteps behind her. When she heard nothing, she took a deep breath, said a quick prayer and headed down the small dirt road. Shekiba walked quickly, trying not to look back at the house since that might draw more suspicion. But no one was out yet and the two donkeys outside didn't even bray at the sight of her.

Agha Sharifullah, the *hakim.* Shekiba hoped someone in town would be able, and willing, to direct her to him. She rehearsed her appeal in her mind for the thousandth time. She wondered what her mother would have thought of her plan.

The sky was bright by the time she entered the village center and she passed by a family of five, the mother and children following behind their father, probably on their way to visit relatives. They looked at her oddly from across the road but said nothing. Shekiba exhaled when they were finally out of view.

A few moments later, two men exited a house and began walking ahead of her. They looked back at her and commented to one another. Shekiba bowed her head and slowed her gait, wanting to put more distance between them. The younger man pointed at her and shook his head. The older man nodded and fingered the beads on his *tasbeh*.

"*Khanum,* who are you?" he called out.

Shekiba kept her gaze lowered and slowed her step even more.

"*Khanum,* where are you going by yourself? Who are you?"

Shekiba debated asking these men if they knew Hakim-*sahib*. She stopped, afraid to get any closer to them.

"*Khanum,* this is very wrong! Whoever you are, you should not be wandering around alone," he scolded. "What family are you from?"

Shekiba felt her tongue loosen.

"I am from Agha Azizullah's home," she said shakily.

"Agha Azizullah? But you are not Khanum Marjan. Who are you?" called out the older man.

"Khanum Marjan is not well," she lied. "I have been sent to bring her medicine."

"Sent out for medicine? Well, this is just

absurd." The younger man turned to his counterpart. "He is a dear friend of mine but I can't imagine what Agha Azizullah was thinking."

"This is truly bizarre," he said, shaking his head. And then he made a decision. "Follow us into town. I'll speak with Azizullah later."

Shekiba nodded and walked about five meters behind them, now doubly panicked. Surely, by now, Marjan had discovered her absence and she had probably shared the news with Azizullah. Would they come looking for her? Although it seemed this man believed her story, he would surely report back to Azizullah. Although Azizullah already had plans to get rid of her, he could do much worse if he were angered and shamed by Shekiba.

They led her to the village's dry-goods store owner, who doubled as the local apothecary. She entered behind the older man.

"Salaam, Faizullah-*jan."*

"Wa-alaikum as-salaam, Muneer-*jan.* How are you?"

So it is Muneer who will report back to Azizullah.

They exchanged pleasantries before Azizullah addressed Shekiba's presence.

"Azizullah has sent this girl to bring medicine for his wife. I found her walking about in the streets alone. Can you imagine? I think the man has lost his mind."

193

Faizullah shook his head.

"No doubt he is distracted by King Habibullah's visit. It is just two days from now and I'm sure his brother has him running in circles."

Two days from now?

"What illness does she have?"

Shekiba nodded yes or no arbitrarily as he rattled off a few symptoms. She left with a small bottle of blended herbs and Faizullah made a note of the purchase in his records.

Azizullah is going to kill me, Shekiba suddenly realized. She had gone too far.

"Excuse me, *sahib,*" she said outside. There was no reason to stop now. "I must take a paper to Hakim-*sahib.*"

"What? What sort of paper?"

"I was instructed to discuss this only with Hakim-*sahib.*"

The younger man looked indignant.

"Padar, this is ridiculous!" he said.

"It is indeed!" said his father. Shekiba waited nervously.

But they pointed her toward Hakim-*sahib*'s house, which, as Shekiba had prayed, was within the village's central area. They were fed up with her and decided to let her find her own way. Azizullah could clean up his own mess.

A young boy answered the gate and Shekiba asked to speak to Hakim-*sahib.* The boy gave her a curious look before running back into

194

the courtyard. A moment later, a puzzled man with a grayed beard appeared at the door. He peered out from behind the half-open door.

"Please, esteemed Hakim-*sahib,* I have come to you with a most serious request."

"You? Who are you and what are you doing here? Is there no one with you?"

"No, *sahib.* But I have a paper that I need to show you."

"Who are you? Who is your husband?"

"I have no husband."

"Who is your father?" He still had not fully opened the door, uninterested in inviting this strange lone girl into his courtyard.

"*Sahib,* this paper is from my father. His name was Ismail Bardari."

"Ismail? Ismail Bardari?"

"Yes, sir."

"You are his daughter? You are the one who . . ."

"Yes, I am. Please, *sahib,* I have the deed to my father's land."

It all came in one breath. And then she heard her name.

"Shekiba!"

Shekiba almost did not recognize Azizullah. She whipped around to see him walking quickly toward Hakim-*sahib*'s house. Hakim-*sahib* pushed the door wide open. Shekiba turned to him and spoke quickly. Azizullah was a hundred meters away. Her words came fast and furious.

"Please, *sahib,* I have the deed to my father's land and I am his only surviving child. I want to claim my inheritance. That land should belong to me and my uncles are taking it without right."

Hakim's eyes widened. "You want what? Azizullah-*jan,* may Allah grant you a long life," he called out.

Shekiba could not take much hope from his exasperated tone. She pulled the paper from under her *burqa.*

"It is my land and it is my right. Please, *sahib,* just look at the deed and you will see —"

Hakim-*sahib* took the paper from her hand and glanced at it. His eyes returned to fast-approaching Azizullah.

"Please, Hakim-*sahib,* I have nothing else. I have no one else. This land is my only —"

A blow to the side of her head. Shekiba reeled.

"Goddamn you, girl!" A second blow knocked Shekiba off her feet.

She lay on her side, curled. Her hands instinctively rose to cover her head beneath the *burqa.* She looked at Hakim-*sahib.* He was shaking his head.

"Azizullah-*jan,* what is going on with this girl?"

"Hakim-*sahib,* those damned Bardari brothers gave *this* as repayment for their debt and never have I been so swindled in my life!" he screamed, pointing at Shekiba. "We have fed her and housed her and look at how she treats us!" A kick to her flank. Shekiba yelped. "What are you doing? What kind of girl sneaks out of a house? Have you no shame?"

"What is this talk of a deed?" the *hakim* said.

"What deed?"

"This girl is here to claim her father's land," Hakim explained.

"To claim what? Is there no end to this girl's stupidity?" He turned to Shekiba and landed another kick into her side.

The pain threw her into a rage.

"I am only here to claim what is rightfully mine! I am my father's daughter and that land should belong to me! My father would never have chosen his brothers over me! He never did!"

"A family of fools!" Azizullah shouted. He threw his arms into the air in exasperation.

The *hakim* sighed heavily and clucked his tongue.

"Girl, you know nothing of tradition," he said, and tore the deed into pieces.

CHAPTER 18
RAHIMA

Tradition hadn't lost importance between Bibi Shekiba's time and now.

Our home was tense all week. Madar-*jan*'s hands trembled. She dropped forks and food while her mind wandered and worried. I caught her watching me and my sisters. Shahla shook her head and Parwin made comments that made Madar-*jan* burst into tears.

"The pigeons look sad today. As if their friends all flew away and now they have no one to talk to." Parwin looked up from her paper. She'd sketched five birds, each flying off in a different direction.

My mother took one look at the drawing, covered her mouth with her hand and went to talk to Padar-*jan*. We heard yelling and the sound of glass breaking. She returned to us, her lip quivering and a dustpan full of glass shards in her hands.

My father spoke with our grandfather and summoned my uncles to join us at the house.

Kaka Haseeb, Jamaal and Fareed showed up along with Boba-*jan.* They looked solemn. I wondered what Padar-*jan* had told them.

As promised, Abdul Khaliq's family returned in the afternoon. My sisters and I had Sitara look out the window and tell us what she saw.

"Lots of people," she said.

Madar-*jan* came back into the room with us, leaving the discussion to the patriarchs of our compound. She had tried several times to talk to my father but to no avail. He was not interested in hearing her. She stood in our doorway and craned her neck to hear down the hall. In our small home, we could hear every word of the conversation.

"Thank you, *agha-sahib,* for coming today and joining your sons for this important discussion. Our family takes these matters very seriously and we come to you with the best of intentions. This is an issue of honor and family. We have known each other for many years. Our fathers were born and buried in the same soil. We are nearly kin," Abdul Khaliq's father said.

"I have a great deal of respect for your family and always have," Boba-*jan* said simply. It was up to the suitors to do the talking.

"And it is for this reason that we have come to this home. We believe that your granddaughter would make an excellent match for my son Abdul Khaliq, whom this village has

199

come to respect and appreciate for defending our people and our homes for years."

"Our people owe him a debt of gratitude. He has shown great bravery."

"Then you will agree that he would be an honorable husband for your granddaughter."

"Well," Boba-*jan* said slowly. I could picture my father's eyes on my grandfather, hoping he would stick to what they had rehearsed. "With the highest respect, Agha Khaliq . . . we have concerns, which I believe my son Arif expressed to you last week. I understand you are speaking of Rahim. We agree that he . . . she has been kept as a *bacha posh* for too long and should be returned to what Allah created. But, still, there are two sisters before her, and as you know tradition dictates that —"

"This is understood and we have already discussed your other two granddaughters. We have here again my nephews Abdul Sharif and Abdul Haidar. Each of them will be honored to take a daughter as a wife. Even better to further strengthen the ties between our families."

"Hmm," Boba-*jan* said, considering the proposal. My father cleared his throat.

"My second daughter — you probably do not know this, but she was born with a lame leg. She limps . . ."

"No matter. She will not be a first wife anyway. I've seen lame-legged women bear children. You should be happy then, anyway. Unlikely you would otherwise marry her off."

"Yes, unlikely . . ."

Three daughters married off at once would be a huge burden lifted from my father's inept shoulders. While his mind toyed with the idea, my uncle Fareed spoke.

"Abdul Khaliq Khan, *sahib,* you honor us with your proposals but . . . but my family also has traditions. I don't mean to insult you but there is something that has been passed down through generations . . ."

"I can respect tradition. What is it?" I could hear annoyance in his voice. He was losing patience with our family, having had to make a second trip. He'd acquired his last wife with much less fuss.

"Well, my family traditionally asks for a large bride price for our daughters and I am embarrassed to bring up matters of money with a man such as yourself, but it is something that I cannot brush under the carpet. This goes back generations and to break from what our ancestors . . ."

My father must have been nervous. The bride price was the critical part he and his brothers had discussed.

I could tell by my mother's face that my uncle was lying. She was trying to read through the wall if Abdul Khaliq was buying his story.

"What is it?"

"Excuse me?"

"How much is the bride price?"

"It's — as I've said, I'm embarrassed to be discussing this but it's quite hefty. It's . . . it's one million afghanis," he said finally. My mother and I nearly choked at the amount. We'd never heard of such a large figure!

"One million afghanis? I see," he said, and turned to one of the men with a gun slung over his shoulder. "Bahram," he said simply. We heard the door open and close. The room was silent until Bahram returned. Abdul Khaliq was tired of cajoling.

We heard a soft thump. Abdul Khaliq began speaking again. "That should cover it," he said simply. "You'll have plenty there to cover the bride price of each of your three daughters. Of course, as family, we will share with you some of the products of the land to the north. Perhaps that would be of interest to you." I knew my father's eyes were bulging at the promise of opium. My mother shook her head.

"Now we need only arrange the *nikkah* date for these three unions. Wouldn't you agree?"

"I . . . I suppose . . . Abdul Khaliq, *sahib,* what about a wedding? A celebration?" Usually there was something. Guests, food, music.

"I don't think that's really necessary. My cousins and I, we've all had weddings. The most important thing is to have the marriage

202

done properly with a *mullah.* For that, I'll bring my friend Haji-*sahib.*" He waved his hand in the direction of the bag. "Now that this matter has been settled, I'm sure you agree that the *nikkah* is the most important part."

My father, my grandfather and my uncles were silent. My mother and I felt our stomachs drop, knowing they could not resist what Abdul Khaliq was offering — more money than our family had ever seen and the promise of a steady opium supply. I covered my face with my hands and pressed my head against the wall.

I slipped out of Madar-*jan*'s clutching fingers and left her standing there, stunned. Three daughters. Turning me into a boy hadn't protected me at all. In fact, it had put me right in front of this warlord who now demanded my hand in marriage. Barely a teenager, I was to be wed to this gray-haired fighter with bags of money and armed men to do his bidding.

My sisters looked at me, already crying. Shahla was trembling.

"It's terrible, Shahla!" I sobbed. "I'm so sorry, I'm so very sorry! It's so awful!"

"They're really agreeing to it?"

"It's . . . it's just like you said . . . there's too many . . . they're giving Padar so much money . . ."

I couldn't bring myself to form the words.

Shahla understood though. I saw her eyes well up and her lip stiffen before she turned her back to me. She was angry.

"God help us," she said.

I wanted to be outside with Abdullah. I wished I could be chasing stray dogs with him or kicking a ball down the street. I wondered what he would say if he knew I was to be married.

That night, I dreamed of Abdul Khaliq. He had come for me. He towered over me with a stick in his hand, laughing. He was pulling me by the arm. He was strong and I couldn't get away. The streets were empty but as I walked past the houses, gates opened one by one. My mother. Khala Shaima. Shahla. Bibi Shekiba. Abdullah. Each one stood in a doorway and watched me walk by; they all shook their heads.

I looked at their faces. They were sad.

"Why aren't you helping me?" I cried. "Don't you see what's happening? Please, can't you do something? Madar-*jan*! Khala Shaima! Bibi-*jan*! I'm sorry! Shahla, I'm sorry!"

"Allah has chosen this as your *naseeb*," they each called out in turn. "This is your *naseeb*, Rahima."

CHAPTER 19
RAHIMA

Abdul Khaliq Khan was a clever man. A clever man with many guns. He knew all the right buttons to push. My father had never seen so much money and would choose opium over food even if he hadn't eaten for days. What good were his daughters anyway?

We were young but not that young. Shahla was fifteen years old, Parwin was fourteen and I was thirteen. We were flower buds that had just started to open. It was time for us to be taken to our new homes, just like Bibi Shekiba.

My father had come into our room and ordered my mother to make a *shirnee,* something sweet he could put before the guests to show our family agreed to the arrangement. We didn't have much so Madar-*jan* gave him a small bowl of sugar, wet with tears, which he took and laid before Abdul Khaliq's father. The men embraced each other in congratulations. We girls huddled around my mother, looking to each other for comfort.

The arrangements moved quickly. Abdul Sharif was a rugged-looking man in his thirties and his brother Abdul Haidar was probably a few years older. Abdul Sharif had one other wife at home but was content to take on a second, especially since the bride price had been covered by his cousin. Abdul Haidar already had two wives at home. Parwin would be his third.

Come back in two weeks for the nikkah, Padar-*jan* had said, his eyes darting back and forth from the guests to the black bag on the floor.

Shahla was so angry that she did not speak to me for four days.

I tried to talk to her but she wouldn't look at me.

"Why did you have to make Padar so angry? I don't want to go with that man! Parwin doesn't want this either! We were fine! Leave me alone. Go and be with Abdullah now!"

I was stunned. My sister was right, though. I had pushed the situation without thinking about anyone else. I wanted to be allowed to wrestle with Abdullah, to walk to school with him and feel his arm around my shoulder. This was my doing.

"I'm sorry, Shahla. I'm really sorry! I didn't mean for any of this to happen! Please believe me!"

Shahla wiped her cheeks and blew her nose. Parwin watched us, her mouth in a tight pout.

"One by one, the birds flew off . . . ," she said quietly. I looked at her, her left leg tucked under her and her right stretched before her. I wondered how her husband would treat a wife with a lame leg. I could see in Shahla's eyes, she was thinking the same thing.

Shahla blamed me. If I hadn't pushed Padar-*jan* that day, then he and Madar-*jan* would not have had that argument. And we would not have been betrothed to Abdul Khaliq's family.

I wondered if it would have made a difference. I wondered if one small difference in the sequence of events would have altered the paths we ended up on. If I hadn't let Abdullah, sweet, strong Abdullah, pin me down in the street for my mother to see, we wouldn't have argued. I would have eaten dinner with the family. My father would have gone on smoking his own paltry opium supply and he would not have thought to complain to Abdul Khaliq that he needed to marry his daughters off.

Maybe I could have stayed a boy, running alongside Abdullah, making faces behind *Moallim-sahib*'s back and having my father ruffle my hair when I walked by. As if he wanted me around.

207

But that wasn't my *naseeb.*

"It's all in Allah's hands, my girls. God has a plan for you. Whatever is in your *naseeb* will happen," my mother had sobbed.

I wondered if Allah hadn't meant for us to choose our *naseeb.*

With my father standing over her shoulder, my mother reluctantly made three baskets of *shirnee.* She covered a cone-shaped block of sugar and loose candies from Agha Barakzai's shop with a layer of tulle she'd purchased with some of the bride price. She cut swatches from her nicest dress and edged the sides with some lace she'd been given as a gift. Three large squares, one for each basket. These were our *dismols,* as important as the sweets. My father nodded in approval. My mother avoided his eyes. I looked at them and wondered if that was how it would be for each of us with our husbands. Or if they would be more like Kaka Jameel, who never seemed to raise his voice and whose wife smiled more than any woman in our family.

I wondered why they were different.

Padar hardly noticed what was happening at home. He didn't even notice that Madar-*jan* slept in our room with us, instead of at his side. He was busy counting bills and smoking opium at least twice a day. Abdul Khaliq had made good on his promise and my father was enjoying his end of the bargain.

"I've brought home a chicken, Raisa! Make

sure you send some to my mother, and not just the bones, mind you! And if the meat is dry and tough like last time, you'll have no more tomorrows."

My mother hadn't eaten more than a couple of bites since the suitors had left and her eyes looked heavy. She was civil with my father, afraid to rile his anger and risk losing her youngest daughters too.

In the meantime, Madar-*jan* had to undo what she had done to me. She gave me one of Parwin's dresses and a *chador* to hide my boyish hair. She gave my pants and tunics to my uncle's wife for her boys.

"You are Rahima. You are a girl and you need to remember to carry yourself like one. Watch how you walk and how you sit. Don't look people, men, in the eye and keep your voice low." She looked like she wanted to say more but stopped short, her voice breaking.

My father looked at me as if he saw a new person. No longer his son, I was someone he preferred to ignore. After all, I wouldn't be his for much longer.

I lingered around Shahla, brought her food and helped with her share of the chores. I regretted the way things had happened and wanted her to know how sorry I was that I'd pushed her into Abdul Sharif's home. These things I told her while she stared off. But Shahla was too kind to stay angry long. And we didn't have long.

"Maybe we'll be able to see each other. I mean, they're all part of the same family. Maybe it will be like here and we can see each other every day — you, me and Parwin."

"I hope so, Shahla."

My sister's round eyes looked pensive. I suddenly realized how much she resembled our mother and felt the urge to sidle up next to her. I felt better with her shoulder touching mine.

"Shahla?"

"Hm?"

"Do you think . . . do you think it will be terrible?" I asked, my voice hushed so Madar-*jan* and Parwin wouldn't hear.

Shahla looked at me, then at the ground. She didn't answer.

Khala Shaima came over. She'd heard rumblings through the town that Abdul Khaliq and his clan had paid our family two visits. She figured my father was up to something. Her knuckles whitened when Madar-*jan* told her, sobbing, that her three eldest daughters were to be wed next week.

"He's really done it. The ass made himself quite a deal, I'm sure."

"What was I to do, Shaima, with a room full of gray-haired men? And he is their father. How could I have stopped anything?"

"Every man is king of his own beard," she

210

said, shaking her head. "Did you try to talk to him?"

Madar-*jan* just looked at her sister. Khala Shaima nodded in understanding.

"A council of asses. That's what you had gathered here. Just look at these girls!"

"Shaima! What am I supposed to do? Clearly, this is what Allah has chosen as their *naseeb* —"

"Oh, the hell with *naseeb*! *Naseeb* is what people blame for everything they can't fix."

I wondered if Khala Shaima was right.

"Since you know so much, tell me what you would have done!" Madar-*jan* cried in exasperation.

"I would have insisted that I be present. And I would have told Abdul Khaliq's family that the girls were not yet of age for marriage!"

"A lot of good that would have done. You know who we're dealing with. It's not some peasant from the streets. It's Abdul Khaliq Khan, the warlord. His bodyguards sat in our living room with machine guns. And Arif agrees with the plan. Do you honestly think they would have listened to anything I had to say?"

"You are their mother."

"And that's all I am," Madar-*jan* said sadly. Her voice grew quiet. I'm sure she didn't think any of us could hear them. "There is only one thing I could think of doing."

"What is that?"

Madar-*jan* looked down, her voice lowered.

"A death in the family would mean there could be no wedding for at least a year."

"A death? Raisa, what in the hell are you talking about?"

"It happens all the time, Shaima. You and I have both heard stories. Remember Manizha from the other side of the village?"

"Raisa, you've lost your mind! Just think about what you're saying! You think setting yourself on fire is going to solve any problems? You think orphaned girls are better off than married ones? And what about the little ones? What do you think they'll do without their mother? For God's sake, look at your in-laws! You've got two widows in this compound and your brothers-in-law are eyeing them already."

My heart pounded so loudly I was certain they could hear it.

"I just don't know what else to do, Shaima!"

"You have to find a way to turn them down. To make Arif turn them down."

"Easier said than done, Shaima! Why don't you come for the *nikkah*? Bring your big mouth and I'll see what you do then."

"I will be here, Raisa. Don't think I won't."

Madar-*jan* looked exhausted. She leaned her head against the wall and closed her eyes; the shadows under them had darkened since yesterday.

We gathered around Khala Shaima.

"My girls, let me tell you a little more about Bibi Shekiba. As much as I hate to think it, her story is your story." She sighed and shook her head. "I suppose we all carry the story of our ancestors in us. Where did we leave off?"

CHAPTER 20
SHEKIBA

Two days passed before Shekib a could stand. Her lip was swollen and scabbed, her legs and back bore multiple bruises and each breath yanked her ribs in different directions.

It wasn't her *naseeb* to claim her father's land. Instead, Azizullah had dragged her back to the house and beaten her for an hour. Every time his strikes slowed, he would yell and huff about the humiliation she had caused him. His momentum would pick up again and he'd toss her left and right with each blow.

Marjan had watched from the doorway, shaking her head. She had one hand over her eyes and when she could watch no more turned her back and left. Shekiba did not notice. She had let her mind drift long ago.

Marjan came to her three times a day and brought her tea and bread. She would prop Shekiba up and dribble tea into her mouth with small lumps of wet bread. She rubbed an ointment on Shekiba's back and on her cut lip.

"Stupid girl. I warned you not to bring up such matters. Now look what you've done to yourself," she muttered over and over again.

Shekiba wished Azizullah would have killed her. She wondered why he hadn't.

She did not see him, but she could hear his voice. His mood was sour and the children avoided him. Marjan could not.

"Make sure she's up and ready today. No excuses."

"She is weak but I will see what she can —"

"Weak? If she's so weak, what was she doing walking through town, following Muneer and his son around? Why did I find her at Hakim's front door? She's a liar and the sooner we rid ourselves of her, the better. No excuses. She will be up and ready today!"

Shekiba heard the words and the situation began to register. Today was the day King Habibullah would pay a visit to Hafizullah. Today was the day she would be gifted again.

Azizullah left early in the morning and Marjan huffed for an hour before coming to Shekiba.

"Come on. Time to get washed up." Shekiba was lifted to her feet by a woman half her height but twice her width. Marjan guided her to the washroom and let her slide onto the floor. "You stupid girl. You've made

215

more work for me! God knows you won't last at the palace if you pull tricks like this."

"I only wanted what should be mine. You would have done the same," Shekiba said flatly.

"No, I would not have! You think you're the only girl who should have inherited land? My brothers divided our land and not one square inch of it was deemed mine. That's how things are! You accept it or you die. It's that simple."

"Then I should die."

"Maybe so, but not today. Now get undressed so you can take a decent bath."

Azizullah returned in the evening, his mood much improved.

"What a day it's been! Hafizullah outdid himself! Never have I seen so much food. I even met with some of the king's advisers. Good people with a great deal of influence. I think this visit will bring good fortune to our family and our town. We have put ourselves under King Habibullah's nose and he will surely remember how hospitably he has been treated here."

"Did you speak to the king too?"

"Of course I did! What kind of question is that? He's a wise man — this I could see right away. But they'll be leaving at first light and I think the girl should be presented tonight, over dinner, so that everyone can see what a

216

gift we have made to the king! We will make our mark while Hafizullah makes his. Bring the girl! I do not want to sit here and chatter with you now. I want to get back before dinner."

"The girl is ready," Marjan said, and went to bring her. She found Shekiba sitting against the cold wall, her legs tucked under her. "Get up, Shekiba. It's time."

She looked at Marjan blankly. After a moment, she rose, ignoring the pain shooting through her ribs. Marjan led her by the elbow to the living room. She stopped short in the hallway.

"Shekiba, listen to me. You are a girl without mother or father, without brothers or uncles to look after you. Obey the word of God and let Him look after you. Bring your head out of the sky and understand your place in *this* world."

"I have no place in *this* world, Khanum Marjan."

Marjan felt a chill run through her spine. Shekiba's words were cold, resolute. She wondered if this half-crazed girl had finally gone completely mad. Zarmina's warnings echoed in her mind and she decided to keep her mouth shut. If Shekiba was going into a frenzy, she didn't want to invite her wrath.

Azizullah was standing at the door to the courtyard, putting a green and blue vest on over his tunic. His face and voice were stern.

217

"If this girl has any sense in her at all, she will give me no trouble tonight. And if she dares to walk with even the slightest limp, I'll take both her legs off."

The warning was issued. Marjan bit her lip and handed Shekiba her *burqa.* Shekiba slipped it over her head and followed behind her master with a resigned step.

Every footstep jolted her bruises and welts. Shekiba kept pace, though, too hurt to risk more punishment. Within twenty minutes, they approached a home with horses and armed soldiers outside. The horses were tall and muscular; their tails flicked side to side casually. But what caught Shekiba's eye was what stood behind them. For the first time in her life, Shekiba saw a carriage. Four large wheels, a cushioned seat and handsome carvings on the sides.

The king, she realized.

They entered the front gate and walked into a courtyard nearly twice the size of Azizullah's. Shekiba could not help but look around. There were benches and several bushes with striking purple flowers. From the living room came the sound of men laughing loudly.

She walked around to the back of the house to enter into the kitchen area.

"Stay outside, in the back. Behave yourself or I'll let the soldiers straighten you out."

218

Azizullah went in through the living room door and rejoined the gathering. Shekiba closed her eyes and tried to eavesdrop on their conversation. The sky grew dim before she heard something that actually pertained to her.

"We will be leaving in the morning to head back to Kabul. The road ahead of us is long but we hope to reach home by nightfall."

"Amir-*sahib,* you and your esteemed generals have honored us with your visit to our humble village. We wish for many more visits in the future."

"With the roads project, travel will become easier. We anticipate that your village will be more involved in the agriculture projects that have begun. Amir-*sahib* has a new team of engineers that are looking at our current situation."

"Anything that we can do here to assist you, we are at your service. I was born and raised in this village, as was my dear brother, Azizullah. Our roots here are respected by the village and we can serve as your delegates for anything you may need."

"You have made that clear, Hafizullah-*sahib.* Your sentiments are appreciated." The voice was gruff and Shekiba detected a slight exasperation in it.

"I hope so, General-*sahib.* And I hope that you will accept my brother's gift to the *amir-sahib.* It is a small token."

"Yes, he mentioned this earlier. The servant will ride with our entourage in the morning to be taken to the palace."

"Wonderful. Please, General-*sahib,* your journey tomorrow is long and you will need your strength. Have some more sweets . . ."

Hafizullah's wife came to the courtyard and found Shekiba slumped across a bench. She was a petite woman, her face lined with worry and fatigue. By the looks of her, she had done most of the preparation for the king's visit. She clucked her tongue in dismay.

"Merciful Allah. Follow me, girl. I will show you where you can sleep until you leave in the morning."

Shekiba slid to the floor in the corner of a dark room. She could see two small figures curled up and breathing softly. These were Hafizullah's daughters, but Shekiba never did meet them. In the early hours of morning, the mistress of the house came to wake her. Shekiba bolted upright when she felt a hand on her shoulder.

"Wake up. The men are leaving."

Shekiba focused. She heard the sounds of horses, men chattering outside the house.

She rose, made sure her Qur'an was tucked into her dress and walked outside to be taken to her new home.

CHAPTER 21
RAHIMA

There was barely enough room in our small home for Abdul Khaliq's family. They wanted to hold all three *nikkahs* at the same time and brought with them Abdul Khaliq's mother, a gray-haired woman with down-turned lips and narrowed eyes. She needed a walking stick but refused to use one, preferring to lean on her daughter-in-law's forearm instead. They also brought Haji-*sahib*, a *mullah*. Khala Shaima scoffed at the mention of his name.

"Haji-*sahib*? If he's Haji, then I'm a *pari*!" said Khala Shaima, whom no one would describe as an angel from heaven. The title *haji* was given to anyone who had made the religious pilgrimage to Mecca, God's house. Haji-*sahib*, Khala Shaima reported, had dubbed himself with the title after paying a visit to a shrine north of our town. But as a dear friend of Abdul Khaliq, no one contested his credentials. The two men chatted amicably outside.

Shahla kept her head down and pleaded with my crying mother not to give her away. Madar-*jan*'s body shook, her voice trapped in her clenched throat. Shahla was more than a daughter to her. She was Madar-*jan*'s best friend. They shared the housework, the child care and their every thought.

Parwin was her special girl. Part of Madar-*jan* had held on to Khala Shaima's prediction that no one would want Parwin as a wife. Sometimes it comforted her that she would have her singing, drawing daughter with her always.

And me. I was Madar-*jan*'s helper. Her spunky, troublemaking *bacha posh*. I know she wondered if she had made the right decision. If I were a little wiser, I would have told her it had been the best thing for me. I would have told her that I wished I could have stayed a *bacha posh* forever.

The family was here to claim their three sister brides. We listened to hear what Khala Shaima would say.

Haji-*sahib* started with a prayer. Even Madar-*jan* cupped her hands and bowed her head to join in. I was pretty sure everyone was praying for different things. I wondered how Allah would sort it all out.

"Let us begin with a *dua,* a prayer. *Bismillah al-rahman al-raheem . . .*"

The room echoed behind him. Haji-*sahib*,

the *mullah,* went on to recite a *sura* from the Qur'an.

"Yaa Musabbibal Asaabi."

After a moment, we heard Khala Shaima interrupt.

"Yaa Musabbibal Asbaabi."

There was a pause. The room had gone silent.

"Khanum, did you have reason to interrupt Haji-*sahib?"*

"Yes, I did. Mullah-*sahib* is reading the *sura* incorrectly. *Oh causer of the causes,* the verse is meant to read. Not *causer of the fingers.* I'm sure he would want to know he was making such an egregious error, wouldn't you, Haji-*sahib?"*

The *mullah* cleared his throat and tried to pick up where he had left off. He thought hard but recited the verse the exact same way, error and all.

"Yaa Musabbibal Asaabi."

Khala Shaima corrected him again.

"Asbaabi, Mullah-*sahib."* Her tone was that of an annoyed schoolteacher. It didn't go unnoticed.

I feared Padar-*jan* would make good on his threat to cut out Khala Shaima's tongue. I was nervous for her.

"Shaima-*jan,* please have a little respect for our esteemed *mullah* here," Boba-*jan* said.

"I have the utmost respect for him," she said facetiously. "And I have the utmost

223

respect for our Qur'an, as I'm sure you all do. What a disservice it would be for us to recite the verse incorrectly."

Once more, the *mullah* sighed and cleared his throat.

"Yaa Musabbibal Asbaabi Yaa Mufattihal Abwaabi."

"That's better," Khala Shaima interrupted loudly. I could hear the satisfaction in her voice.

We could hear the men beginning the *nikkah* in the next room. Padar-*jan* was giving his full name, his father's name and his grandfather's name to be written on the marriage contract.

Parwin tried to put on a strong front, seeing Madar-*jan*'s condition. Khala Shaima, our only advocate in the *nikkah,* had strategically positioned herself between my grandfather and Abdul Khaliq's mother. No one knew what to make of her presence. Padar-*jan* huffed in frustration but thought it best not to make a scene in front of his guests.

Madar-*jan* spoke softly. We had formed a tight circle in the next room.

"My daughters, I prayed this day would not come so soon for you but it is here and I'm afraid there's nothing I or Khala Shaima can do to stop this. I suppose this is God's will for you. Now, I haven't had much time to prepare you, but you are young women," she said, hardly believing her own words. "Your husbands will expect things of you. As a wife, you have an obligation to your husband. It won't be easy at first but . . . but with time you'll learn how to . . . how to tolerate these things that Allah has created for us."

When Madar-*jan* began to cry, we cried as well. I didn't want to know what it was Madar-*jan* was talking about. It sounded like it was something terrible.

"Please don't cry, my girls. These things are a part of life — girls are married and then become part of another family. This is the way of the world. Just as I came to your father's home."

"Can I come back sometimes, Madar-*jan*?" Parwin asked.

Madar-*jan* exhaled slowly, her throat thick and tight.

"Your husband will want you at home but I hope that he is a man of heart and will bring you here from time to time to see your mother and your sisters."

This was as much as she could promise. Parwin and I sat on either side of our mother, her hands stroking our hair. I had my hands on her knee. Shahla kneeled in front of us, her head resting on Madar-*jan*'s lap. Rohila and Sitara watched on nervously, Rohila understanding that something was about to happen.

"Now, my girls, there's one more thing. There will be other wives to deal with. Treat them well and I pray they will show kindness to you. Older women are spiteful toward younger girls, so be careful how much you trust them. Make sure you take care of yourselves. Eat, bathe, say your prayers and cooperate with your husbands. And your mothers-in-law. These are the people whom you will need to keep satisfied."

A voice bellowed from the next room.

"Bring the eldest girl! Her husband, Abdul Sharif, is waiting. May their steps together as husband and wife be blessed. Congratulations to both your families."

"Shahla!" my father called out unceremoniously.

Shahla wiped the tears from her face and bravely pulled her *chador* over her head. She kissed my mother's face and hands before she turned to us, her sisters. I squeezed my sister and felt her breath in my ear.

"Shahla . . . ," was all I could get out.

It was Parwin's turn next. They started over again, a new contract. For the sake of tradition, they repeated all the same questions, wrote down all the same names.

"*Agha-sahib,*" Khala Shaima interrupted again. "Allah has given my niece a lame leg and I can tell you better than anyone else that it is not easy to manage with such a disability. It would be in this girl's best interests for her to have some time to go to school, to learn to manage physically, before she is

226

made into a wife."

Abdul Khaliq's father was taken aback by the sudden objection, as were the others in the room.

"This has been discussed and I think my nephew has been more than generous in agreeing to give this girl a chance to be the wife of a respected man. School will not fix her lame leg, as it has not fixed your hunched back. Let's continue."

The *nikkah* resumed.

"Bring the girl! May Allah bless this *nikkah* and Abdul Khaliq, who has made this possible. May God give you many years, Abdul Haidar, for agreeing to take on a wife in the tradition of our beloved Prophet, peace be upon him. And a disabled wife at that; truly you are a great man, Abdul Haidar. What a relief this must be for your family, Arif-*jan*."

Madar-*jan* kissed Parwin's forehead and stood up slowly, as if the ground was pulling her back. Parwin stood up and straightened her left leg as best she could. Madar-*jan* whispered to Parwin things she hated to say.

"Parwin-*jan*, my sweet girl, remember to do your chores in your new home. There may not be time for drawing, and sing softly and only to yourself. They'll say things to you, just as the others always have, about your leg, but pay no attention, my daughter."

"*Agha-sahib*, you are keeping this man waiting. Please bring him his new bride," the

227

mullah ordered.

"Bring her out!" My father's voice was cold and loud as he tried to assert control. *Madar-jan*'s delaying made him look small in front of the *mullah* and Abdul Khaliq's family, as if Khala Shaima's behavior hadn't been enough.

"Please, my sweet daughter. Remember these things that I've told you. May Allah watch over you now," she whimpered, brushing away Parwin's tears and then her own. She fixed Parwin's *chador* and had her hold it close under her chin before she turned her around and led her down the hallway and into the living room, where she became the wife of a man as old as my father.

I sat in the room with Rohila and Sitara. I listened to Parwin try to mask her limp, lifting her left leg so it wouldn't drag along the floor as it usually did. Our cousins always teased her, as did the children in the neighborhood. Even for those few months when she attended school, her classmates had mocked her gait and the teacher had doubted she would learn anything, as if walking and reading were related. They wouldn't treat her well, we knew. Our hearts broke for her.

"Rahim, where is Parwin going?" Sitara asked.

I looked at my youngest sister. She still called me by my *bacha posh* name.

"It's Rahima," Rohila reminded her. Her

228

vacant eyes stayed glued to the door, willing Parwin to come back.

"Rahima, where did Parwin go?" Sitara asked again.

"She's . . . she's gone to live with a new family." I couldn't say words like "marriage" or "husband" in the same sentence with my sister's name. It sounded awkward. Like a little girl wearing her mother's shoes.

I knew my mother was watching Parwin from behind the doorway. Their voices faded as they walked out the door. I went to the window to see my sister one last time. Because of her limp, she was shorter than any other fourteen-year-old girl and looked to be half the size of her new husband. I shuddered to think how she would feel to be alone with him.

"When will she come back?"

I looked at my sisters blankly. Madar-*jan* returned, drained. I was next. Khala Shaima had not succeeded in saving my sisters from Abdul Khaliq's family. I knew I shouldn't hope for any better, but I did.

I wish I could say that I put on as strong a front as Shahla or even Parwin, at least for my mother's sake. I wish I could have done something. After all, I'd been a boy for years. Boys were supposed to defend themselves and their families. I was more than just a girl, I thought. I was a *bacha posh*! I had been practicing martial arts with my friends in the

229

streets. I didn't have to crumple as my sisters had.

My father had to drag me from my mother's arms while I cried, the *chador* falling from my head and revealing my absurdly short hair. Abdul Khaliq's family watched in consternation. This didn't bode well. My father dug his fingers into my arm. I only know because I saw the bruises later.

I tried to pull my arms away, kick my legs, twist my body away. It wasn't the same as play-fighting with the boys. My father was stronger than Abdullah.

All we managed to do was embarrass my father. My mother sobbed, her hands in powerless fists. Khala Shaima shook her head and shouted that this, *all* of this, was wrong, a sin. She didn't stop until my father slapped her across the face. She reeled backward. Our guests looked on, feeling it was well deserved. My father had redeemed himself in their eyes.

My struggle changed nothing. I just made it harder on my mother. And Khala Shaima.

My father handed me over to my new husband. My mother-in-law stared with a critical eye. She would have a lot of work to do to set me straight.

And Abdul Khaliq, my new husband, smirked to see me squirm under my father's grip. As if he liked what he saw.

That was my wedding.

CHAPTER 22
SHEKIBA

"First things first. You need a proper bath."

Shekiba stood before a heavyset woman with cropped dark hair. She looked to be in her twenties. She wore ballooned pants and boots with a button-down shirt. If it weren't for her voice, Shekiba would have believed her to be a man. As it was, Shekiba was baffled and had been since Kabul came into view.

Never could she have imagined such a place. All the homes and shops of her village could have fit in Kabul's belly. There were streets lined with stores, striped awnings and men walking through the maze of roads. There were houses with colorful doors at the front gate. People turned and raised their hands, a respectful acknowledgment of the king's entourage passing through. Kabul was a spectacle!

When the royal compound came into view, Shekiba's mouth gaped. The gated entrance was flanked by stone pillars, layer after layer before the palace itself came into view. Through the main entrance, a wide path encircled an imposing tower. Shekiba craned her neck to get a good view.

That tower just about reaches the heavens!

The palace's façade was embellished with carvings and arches, polished and bright. Bushes and greenery lined the path, including the portico that cut through the tower. The palace was an impressive structure with more windows than she had ever seen and incomparable in size to any home Shekiba had ever beheld.

Soldiers guarded every corner. It was only when they came to the entrance of the palace that Shekiba actually saw King Habibullah. On the ride to Kabul, he had been at the head of the caravan, riding in the magnificent carriage that had been stationed outside Hafizullah's house. When they disembarked, Shekiba was sent in a different direction but she caught sight of him entering a main door.

That's the king, Shekiba thought.

He was a stocky man with a thick beard. He wore a military uniform with a row of medals pinned across his left chest and tassels at his shoulders. A broad yellow sash crossed from his right shoulder to his left hip and covered some of the stars on his jacket. A striped belt and medallion clasp sat snugly across the middle of his belly and a tall hat of sheep's wool added five inches to his stature.

The soldiers stood at attention for King Habibullah's return.

Shekiba wondered if she would ever cross paths with him in this enormous place.

"Follow me."

A soldier took her around the corner, behind the palace, where the path opened into a verdant and majestic courtyard. Shekiba's eyes widened. The courtyard had small ponds, flowering bushes and fruit trees. They followed a footpath that led to a smaller stone house, still much larger than even Agha Azizullah's home. The soldier knocked on the door and a guard answered.

"Take her. She is to be a guard with you. Fix her up." The guard nodded and waited for the soldier to turn before the door opened wide.

"Come in."

A woman! Shekiba stood motionless.

"I said come in! What are you doing standing there?"

Shekiba's feet unfroze and she followed the woman-man into the room. There were three women sitting on cushions around the floor, each older than Shekiba but younger than any of her uncle's wives. They had stopped their conversation when she entered. Shekiba noticed four other guards in the room. Were they women too?

"Well, let's take a look at you." She lifted Shekiba's *burqa* and took a step back. "Well,

233

well. That's quite a face. I suppose that's why you were sent here. Ladies, this is our newest guard."

Shekiba's surprise grew when she learned all of the guards in this house were actually women dressed in men's clothing. Ghafoor seemed to be in charge of the five guards. It was evening and she could see the exhaustion in Shekiba's face. Ghafoor had her rest for the night and told her work would begin in the morning. For the first time in a long time, Shekiba slept soundly, surrounded by women pretending to be men.

Her transformation started at daybreak. Ghafoor led Shekiba to the wash area and cut her thick, knotted hair. She was instructed to bathe and given a set of clothing identical to what Ghafoor wore. Shekiba stared in wonder at the pants and could scarcely believe she should walk about in them. She slipped one leg in and then the other, fastening the buttons at the waist. She was given a corseted undergarment that pushed her modest bosom flat against her chest. She slipped her arms into the shirt and buttoned it closed. The boots felt heavy. Shekiba stood and stared down. Then she reached up and ran her fingers through her short hair.

She took two steps and turned. Her legs felt loose and she blushed when she looked down and saw the crotch of her pants. Her hands ran over her backside and she shuddered to think the shape of her limbs would be so visible in these ballooned pants. She had only ever seen women in skirts, draped enough to disguise the curves and crevices that hid underneath.

And yet there was something liberating about her new clothes. She lifted her right leg and then her left. She thought of her brothers and how they would run about the fields in their flowing pants.

Ghafoor understood.

"It is awkward at first, but you'll adjust quickly. The uniform is comfortable enough with time."

"What are we guarding?"

Ghafoor laughed. "They've told you nothing? We are guards for King Habibullah's women."

"His wives?"

"Not exactly. His women. These are women he spends time with, women he takes when he is struck by the mood." Shekiba must have looked confused. "Men can take more than just their wives, dear girl. Sometimes wives are not enough."

Shekiba was certain she did not understand but kept her mouth shut for the time being.

Ghafoor looked at her thoughtfully.

"What happened to your face?" she asked.

Shekiba looked down instinctively. "I was burned as a child."

"Hmm. And where is your family?"

"My village is one day's travel from here. My mother and father are dead. My brothers and sister are dead."

Ghafoor's brow furrowed. "You have no other family?"

"They gave me away to repay a debt. And that man gave me away to the king."

"And now you are one of us. Welcome, Shekiba. But here you will be Shekib, understand? Now let me introduce you to the others."

Four women-men guarded the king's harem. Shekiba found herself staring at their faces as so many others had stared at hers. But with good reason. Ghafoor was actually Guljaan. She was the leader of the group, not only because she was tallest and loudest but also because she had been in the palace longer than the others. She was the most content with her role and seemed to take pride in doing a good job. Her face was smooth, but a fine, downy rim on her upper lip and untamed brows gave her the appearance of a young man, fresh with enthusiasm for his important post.

Ghafoor came from a modest family in a nearby village and had been given to the palace in exchange for a cow. It was mid-afternoon and her mother had been busy with her younger siblings. Ghafoor's father had interrupted her needlework. *We are going to visit your grandmother,* he had said. Ghafoor wondered why the others were not coming but shrugged her shoulders and followed her father two kilometers down the road, where she was delivered to a man dressed in a gray tunic and pants. Her father warned her sternly to follow the man's directions and turned to walk the two kilometers back to their family. She cried and screamed when she realized she would not see her mother or siblings again.

Ghafoor was brought to the palace and watched as a guard brought out a cow for the man in gray. It was a decent cow, not too sickly looking and plenty to satisfy her family's needs. She realized immediately what her father had done and wondered if her mother had been privy to the plan. She cursed him for his deceit and feared what would become of her, an adolescent girl, in the hands of strangers.

It did not take long, however, for Ghafoor to appreciate her father's barter. She missed her mother and siblings terribly but life behind the palace walls, even for a servant, was easier than life at home. The beatings were fewer, the food more plentiful, and she had taken on some authority.

The king needed guards to watch over his harem, but he believed no man to be above temptation. For months he paced and de-

237

bated, the dilemma as perplexing as the tribal disputes in Kurram Valley. When an adviser came up with a plan to dress women as male guards, the king rewarded him for his stroke of genius and had him fill the positions as quickly as possible.

Ghafoor enjoyed the comfort of palace life. All she had to do was give up being a woman, an easy trade. Two other girls were recruited along with her, but they lasted only two or three months. One had argued with a woman of the harem and Benafsha, the other, had been so beautiful that the king took an immediate liking to her and decided she should be guarded as well. She was made to grow her hair long again and reassigned to her new position as a concubine.

Then came two sisters, Karima, who would become Karim, and Khatol, who would be renamed Qasim. This time the king's representatives chose more wisely, recruiting girls who were tall enough to pass for men but homely enough that they would not tantalize the king. Karim and Qasim came from a family of four girls. Their mother cried violently as she told the girls they could not afford to feed all four and that their father had arranged for them to be taken to the king's palace, where they would have a much better life. The obedient girls had tearfully accepted their parents' decision and left home hand in hand.

Karim was two years older and looked after her sister. She quickly overcame her timidity and became second in command, arguing with Ghafoor so that she would not dominate them completely. Qasim was quieter and missed the family. She was taller than her sister by an inch but hunched her shoulders, prompting Ghafoor to poke her repeatedly in the back until she learned to stand as a guard should.

Tariq, the newest addition, was different from the others. She carried out her duties well enough but fantasized that she would be noticed by the king and recruited to his court of women. She was the shortest of the group and plumper in the face, with chestnut hair that she had been told no man could resist. She would not say where the compliment had come from but she refused to let the defeminizing uniform spoil her chances. She made sure her hips swayed when she walked and batted her eyes when the king neared. Of all the women in the harem, she guarded Benafsha most, feeling kinship with the former guard who had enticed the king.

Ghafoor and Karim rolled their eyes at her often but tolerated her occasional fantasies. Every guard had her own way of coping.

Ghafoor introduced Shekiba to a few of the king's concubines, the women who kept the king satisfied. Benafsha was the youngest of the group. She knew why Tariq favored her over the others but refused to indulge any details of the king. Whenever Tariq asked her about the monarch, she would shake her head and adjust her skirt. She was lightest in complexion and her eyes were light brown with speckled irises. Tariq could see why she had attracted the king's attention. She was the most beautiful, now that Halima's face had begun to show her years.

Halima, the eldest of the group, had borne the king two daughters over the years. The girls were two and four years old and bore a striking resemblance to their mother. Halima stroked their hair and sighed wistfully, realizing the king beckoned to her less often and wondering what that would mean for her and her daughters. Halima was kind and motherly and tempered the bickering of the others.

Benazir, the darkest, had ebony eyes that teared easily these days. She was with child and terrified. Her belly had just started to swell but she had been ill for weeks, unable to keep down more than a few mouthfuls of rice at a time. She would stare at the walls and started when Halima put a hand on her shoulder.

Sakina and Fatima were feistier girls, but less beautiful than the others. Fatima had borne a son, which gave her an edge over the others. They were friendly enough, but unlike good-natured Halima, they were usually the instigators of any turbulence in the harem. Sakina in particular despised Benafsha, knowing that her ranking in the harem had dropped notches with the temptress's arrival. And Benafsha knew how to throw that fact in Sakina's face when she needed. Shekiba knew to keep her distance from these two, her instincts telling her they would be unforgiving in their comments about her face.

There were others, she was told. She would see more tomorrow.

Harem life was relatively simple. Shekiba listened in amazement to hear what the women did. And, more important, what they did not do. They did not cook, nor did they carry buckets of water from a well. They did not tend to animals or spend hours peeling vegetables.

"Who does all the housework then?" Shekiba asked Ghafoor as they watched Sakina and Benazir rouge their cheeks and stain their lips with crushed cherries.

"The people for the housework. Everyone has a purpose here in the palace. The guards, the servants, the women, and us. We all do our part in Arg." Ghafoor sat with her right ankle crossed over her left knee. She was comfortable as a man.

"Arg?"

"Arg-e-Shahi. You do not know what Arg is?" Ghafoor laughed with the self-satisfaction of someone who had once been as ignorant.

"This is Arg-e-Shahi, the palace! Arg is your new home, Shekib-*jan*!"

CHAPTER 23
RAHIMA

"Take off your *chador.*"

I kept my face to the wall and pulled my legs in under me. The room was small enough that I could hear each raspy breath.

Abdul Khaliq stood in the doorway, his hands on his hips. From this angle, he looked larger than life. He took two steps in and shut the door behind him.

"I said, take off your *chador.*"

I lowered my head and told myself to breathe. I prayed he would be frustrated and walk away, as he had yesterday.

"I will not tolerate insolence. Yesterday, I let you be. That was my gift to you, to show you I can be kind. Today, things are different. You are in your husband's home, my home. You will behave as a wife should."

I was sharing a house with Abdul Khaliq's third wife. I was his fourth. The other wives lived in separate homes within the same compound, all interconnected. It had been nearly dark when we got to the compound and I hadn't seen much. Bibi Gulalai, his mother, had insisted on using me as a cane to get to the car. She was old and I was not rude enough to refuse, though I only answered her questions with one-or-two-word responses. She was sizing me up.

Bibi Gulalai led me to a small room at the end of a hallway. This was to be my room, she said. There was a bathroom just outside my door, the likes of which I had never before seen. It was modern, with running water and a toilet.

Wife number three was Shahnaz. I saw her for just a moment before I was ushered into my room. She turned her back to me and walked away, uninterested in introductions.

"That's Shahnaz. You'll meet her in the morning when she shows you around."

My room had a cushion in the corner, a pillow and a small table.

"We'll send you a plate of food for tonight. Tomorrow you become part of your new home," Bibi Gulalai said smugly.

I doubted it.

I had nearly screamed yesterday when Abdul Khaliq entered the room. I was crouched in the corner. He wiped the grease from his mouth with the back of his hand. He had just finished eating. My plate was untouched.

"You haven't eaten? My wife is not hungry, eh?" He chuckled.

I said nothing.

He squatted next to me and lifted my chin with two fingers. His touch was rough. I kept my gaze averted. He pulled my *chador* off my head and felt the back of my head.

"Tomorrow," he promised, and walked back out of the room. I shook with fright.

Night came and went and I didn't sleep. I tossed and turned on the mattress, listening for the sound of footsteps, a hand on the doorknob, a knock. I thought of my mother, my sisters. I wondered if Shahla and Parwin were close by. I prayed we were all in the same compound and I would see them in the morning, every morning. I wondered what Rohila was telling Sitara, who every day had been asking more questions that we couldn't answer. I wished I could be laid out at Khala Shaima's feet, listening to her tell another chapter of Bibi Shekiba's story.

I wished more than anything that I could be back in class, *Moallim-sahib*'s back turned toward us, Abdullah and I shooting each other bored looks, kicking each other under the table and tilting our notebooks so the other could see the right answer.

I wished I could be anywhere but here.

When my bladder could wait no longer, I opened the door a crack. I looked into the hallway, saw that it was empty and crept out slowly to go to the washroom. Shahnaz caught me on the way out.

"Good morning," she said plainly. She looked a few years older than Shahla, with features that matched the dullness in her voice. She was thin and stood a couple inches taller than me. She balanced a baby on her hip, no more than six months old.

"*Salaam,*" I replied cautiously. I knew who she was and I remembered my mother's warnings.

"Your name is Rahima?"

I nodded.

"All right, Rahima. Bibi Gulalai has asked me to show you around. So, let's get started. You've hid in your room long enough."

Shahnaz looked disinterested in me but she'd been given a task, and as Madar-*jan* had advised, she was doing what her mother-in-law — *our* mother-in-law — had asked of her.

"This has been my home for three years. I was told I wouldn't be sharing it with anyone else. This room is for my children and me. Here is the kitchen. That is our living room. That hallway leads to the rest of the houses, the better houses. I expect that you'll do your share of the cooking and cleaning. As you can see, I've already got my hands full."

She paused and looked at me carefully.

"Your hair. Why is it cut so short?"

"I'm a *bacha posh.* I mean, I *was* a *bacha posh.*"

"I've never seen a *bacha posh* before. Why

were you made into a boy?"

"My mother had only daughters and my father wanted a son."

"So they dressed you as a boy? And did you go out of the house like that?"

I could hear more curiosity than dislike in her voice. It gave me confidence to continue the conversation. Something about her reminded me of Shahla and I could already tell I would be desperate for an ally here.

"Sure. I went to school. I ran errands for my mother. I even worked and brought money home. I was learning how to fix electronics," I boasted. That was more than I had done for Agha Barakzai but Shahnaz wouldn't know the difference.

"Well, don't expect to be treated like the special son here."

As soon as she said it, I realized that's what I had secretly been hoping.

"Who else lives here in the compound?" I asked, hoping my face didn't show my disappointment. The baby started to whine, her small hands batting at her mother's face.

Shahnaz led me into the living room, where she began to nurse the baby.

"Our home is one of three. Each wife has her own home. Or at least we did, until you came along. His first wife is Badriya. She has the biggest home, with the bedroom on the second level. His second is Jameela. She lives in the biggest part of the house too but on the lower level. Abdul Khaliq's room is in that main house. I thought you would have seen it last night but I'm sure you'll see it soon enough."

I ignored her last comment, scared to think of what that meant. The memory of his touch made me shiver.

"Where does . . . where does Bibi Gulalai live?"

"In the compound next door but she's here often, keeping an eye on her eldest son's affairs. Especially since he's gone so often. Be careful with her. She rules with a heavy hand."

"And what about the rest?"

"What rest?"

"I mean his cousins, Abdul Sharif and Abdul Haidar?" I was nervous to ask. I prayed she would tell me they were next door as well.

"Oh, I heard what happened. So, it's true then? Sometimes Safiya gets the story all wrong. She told me two other sisters were married at the same time. And one of them has a limp, right? Hard to imagine how they arranged that deal. Well, Abdul Sharif lives on the other side of the hill, about four kilometers away. Abdul Haidar lives on the other side of that wall. He's here often since he's Abdul Khaliq's right-hand man."

Parwin was close by! She was on the other side of the wall. I wondered what she was doing and if she knew that I was meters away from her. Shahla. Shahla had been taken the farthest.

"Does Abdul Sharif come here sometimes?"

"He does, but not as often as his brother. If you think you'll see your sisters, though, don't get your hopes up. Neither one of them brings their wives when they come by. The women of this family don't travel much. Get used to these walls. They're going to be all you see."

Shahnaz tired of me and went to put the baby to sleep. She had two children, a two-year-old son and the five-month-old girl I'd seen her holding.

I found out weeks later that Abdul Khaliq had taken her from a village in the south. He and his men had gone there and successfully pushed back the Taliban forces. The village had been saved so Abdul Khaliq and his men felt they earned the right to take what they wanted. They looted houses, harassed women. The village had no one to defend it. Most of the men had perished in the war. The men took whatever caught their eye. In Abdul Khaliq's case, it was Shahnaz. She hadn't seen her family since the day of her *nikkah*.

It could have been worse, she said. At least he took her as his wife. She had heard of many women who had been raped and left with their families. There was nothing worse than that.

I thought about Shahnaz's village often, knowing my father must have been party to that mission. I wondered if he pillaged as the others had. I wanted to believe he hadn't.

I could start with cleaning, Shahnaz said. She needed to bathe her son. I found the broom and began to sweep the floors as I'd seen my sisters do. The broom felt awkward in my hands and I waited for someone to relieve me from the duty. When Shahnaz didn't come back out, I put the broom away and went back to my room to pout. I missed my old life.

Before long, it was evening again. Bibi Gulalai came to eat with us, around the cloth laid out on the living room floor. Shahnaz had prepared a meal of stew and rice. I reminded myself to fold my legs under me and sit like a lady. I could feel my mother-in-law watching me. I helped Shahnaz clear the dishes and wash up before I went back to my room. Bibi Gulalai sat in the living room with her cup of tea, watching her grandson play with a wooden spoon.

I listened for the sound of her leaving but she didn't. My door opened.

"Your husband has asked for you. You should go and see to him as his bride. Shahnaz will take you there."

When I didn't get up, she came after me, pulling me to stand by my ear.

"Did you not hear what I said? Do you want me to repeat myself?"

My twisted ear stung under her gnarled fingers. I yelped and stumbled to my feet. Shahnaz was in the hallway. She looked mildly entertained.

We went down the hallway and into the main house. Had I been less nervous, I probably would have noticed more of my surroundings. I remember thinking that the hallways were wide, the ceilings tall. We passed by many doors. I'd never imagined a house so large!

Shahnaz pointed to a door and told me to go ahead and knock. Before I could ask a question she turned and headed back down the stairs. I ran after her and grabbed her arm.

"Shahnaz, please, let me go back with you!"

She shook her arm free and looked at me with annoyance.

"Let go of me!" she hissed. "Your husband has asked for his new bride. You'd be making a big mistake to keep him waiting. That's my best advice to you."

"Please, Shahnaz-*jan*! I'm scared!" I panicked. I didn't want to be alone here. I wanted to go back to my dark room and my small mattress. I felt out of place and I hated wearing a dress. It felt unnatural, awkward. I was a *bacha posh*! Just like Bibi Shekiba, the palace guard!

"Are you stupid? Get in there or you'll regret it. You'll be punished worse than you could imagine."

She walked away and left me in the hallway, scrambling for options that didn't exist.

He must have heard me. I gasped and jumped backward when the door opened. My reaction made him smile. He beckoned me in. I hesitated, but fearing that Shahnaz was right, I followed.

In subsequent visits, I would realize that Abdul Khaliq's bedroom looked like what I might have imagined of a palace. His mattress sat on a wooden platform a few feet off the ground. A plush armchair sat in the corner and a beautifully woven burgundy carpet covered the floor. Two windows overlooked the courtyard, where three armed men were on guard.

I walked in, too terrified to see anything but Abdul Khaliq. He had already made himself comfortable on his bed. He was sitting up, propped up against pillows.

"Take your *chador* off," he ordered.

I looked at the ground and stood motionless. I had wanted to rip the *chador* off my head when Madar-*jan* put it on me but now, with Abdul Khaliq eyeing me in this way, I couldn't let it go. I watched him from the corner of my eye and saw his intrigued but exasperated face.

"Listen," he said, leaning forward. With his

turban off, I could see that his hair matched his salt-and-pepper beard. He wore a beige cotton tunic and pants. His legs were outstretched. The room was lit by a lamp on his bedside table. "Maybe you haven't received any instruction on what it is to be a wife. From what I've seen of the women in your family, I wouldn't be surprised. Let me explain to you how things are here. I am your husband and this is your home. When I ask for something, you make it happen. In return, you will be given shelter and have the privilege of being wife to Abdul Khaliq."

Again he beckoned me closer. I fought the wave of nausea and took two steps toward him. I was within his reach. My muscles stiffened.

He turned my face toward him. He was so close I could see the lines on his face. I could make out each hair of his eyebrow. I tried to keep my eyes lowered.

"Do you understand what I'm saying?"

I nodded. My mind flashed back to his bodyguards and their guns. I was terrified.

"Good. Now, do as I say and take off your *chador.*"

He could have done it. I thought about it later and realized he could have done all the things he made me do, but that wouldn't have served his purpose. One by one, he made me take off everything I'd been wearing. First the *chador,* then my socks, my pants, my dress. With every piece, I trembled more. When my pants came down, I began to cry, which didn't faze him in the least. I was humiliated. I stood before him, weak and vulnerable, my arms doing their best to cover as much as they could.

He nodded in approval, his lips wet with excitement.

"You're not a *bacha posh* any longer. Tonight I'll show you that you're a woman, not a boy."

CHAPTER 24
RAHIMA

The thought of him made me queasy. I hated the feeling of it. I hated his breath, his whiskers, his callused feet. But there would be no escape. He called for me when he pleased and made me do what he wanted. Thankfully, it rarely lasted more than a few minutes. I wished Madar-*jan* had told me exactly what to expect, but then I think if she had, I never would have made it to the *nikkah*.

Shahnaz seemed to pity me the following day. She must have known. My face reddened when my eyes met hers.

My insides hurt. Raw and angry. I nearly cried when I urinated into the fancy western toilet.

Shahnaz asked me to prepare lunch for the family. She had the children to tend to. I went into the kitchen and looked through the vegetables on the counter, almost thankful to have a task that would keep my mind off what I had endured. There were canisters of flour and sugar as well. I thought of my mother and sighed. Ever since I'd been converted into a *bacha posh,* I'd been relieved of all cooking duties as well. If my father had seen his "son" working in the kitchen, his temper would have turned our home upside down. I had no idea how to make even a simple meal.

I tried to think of the foods my mother and Shahla cooked. Even Parwin could prepare a decent meal, although she spent more time sculpting shapes out of the potatoes than she did actually cooking them.

I set out to make some potato stew. I put the rice in water, as I'd seen my mother do. I tried to focus but my eyes kept drifting to the kitchen window, with a view into the court-yard. Several boys, two of them looking to be almost my age, were kicking a ball around. They shouted and teased each other. I felt my heart beat faster, wanting to be with them instead of bent over a metal pot with potato peels stuck to my fingers.

I wondered who the boys were. I could see they wouldn't have been much of a challenge on the field. They kicked clumsily, barely making contact with the ball.

"Rahima! Why are you sitting like that? For God's sake, aren't you embarrassed?"

Shahnaz's voice jolted me. I looked down and snapped my legs together, bending my knees. I'd been sitting like a boy basking in the summer sun. A bolt of pain shot between my thighs.

"Oh, sorry, I was just —"

"Have a little decency!"

I hung my head, my face flushed again. I cursed myself. Thank goodness my mother hadn't witnessed this. She had warned me over and over again to carry myself as a proper girl in my new home but I'd been living as a boy for years. There was a lot of unlearning to do.

Our mother-in-law joined us for lunch. She hobbled in, her fingers on the shoulder of a young boy, probably a grandson. I kissed her hands and mumbled a greeting, following Shahnaz's lead. Her visit was a surprise to me, but not to Shahnaz. I looked to her for guidance. She didn't offer much.

"She did the same thing to me," Shahnaz whispered. "She wants to see if you're being a good wife. Go ahead and lay out the food, the plates. Sit with her." She went into the living room and spoke sweetly to Bibi Gulalai. "Khala-*jan,* with your permission, I'm going to feed the baby. I'm sorry I can't sit with you but your new bride has prepared lunch for you."

I took out the food as Shahnaz suggested, thinking to myself that she'd just fed the baby before our mother-in-law walked in. But I quickly forgot about it as I began to put the potatoes into a serving dish. Nothing looked like the food my mother prepared. My hands

shook as I laid it out on the cloth. Bibi Gulalai fingered her prayer beads while she eyed
my every move. Once I had spread out the
potato stew and the rice, she spoke.

"A cup of tea would have been a nice start.
Looks like you're rushing us to lunch."

"I . . . I'm sorry. I can bring a cup of —"

"Yes. Bring a cup of tea first. That's how
you treat a guest."

I got to my feet and went back to the
kitchen to boil some water. I sprinkled tea
leaves into the teapot and searched everywhere until I finally found a teacup.

"Did you add cardamom?"

I sighed.

"No, Khala-*jan.* I'm sorry, I forgot the cardamom . . ."

"Tea without cardamom?" She shook her
head in disappointment and leaned back.
"Maybe that's how your family drank tea,
but the rest of us —"

"No, my mother always puts cardamom."

Her eyes narrowed.

"I was saying" — she was not happy with
my interruption — "that the rest of us prefer
our tea with cardamom. So pay attention next
time."

I nodded silently while she slowly sipped
her unflavored tea, the disappointment showing in her eyes. I watched the steam waft from
the rice.

"All right. Why don't we try this food that

you've made now."

I reached over and spooned some rice onto her plate. Large clumps stuck together. The potatoes looked more reasonable. I prayed her eyes were old enough that they couldn't clearly see what I'd made of the rice. She took two bites and shook her head in frustration.

"This is cold. Food doesn't taste good cold. And we're supposed to eat grains of rice, not balls of it. How long did you cook it for?"

"I don't . . . I don't know . . ."

"Too long. Too long. And the potatoes are still hard!" She sighed heavily. "Shahnaz! Shahnaz, come out here!"

Shahnaz came into the living room, her eyebrows raised in curiosity.

"Yes, Khala-*jan*?"

"This girl cannot cook! Did you try this food? It's terrible!"

"No, Khala-*jan,* I didn't. She insisted on making lunch so I let her. Otherwise, I would have been happy to prepare something for you."

I looked at Shahnaz and began to realize that she was not as benign as I had thought. She avoided looking at me. I had the urge to throw a punch at her but kept my cool.

"That's not true! She told me I should make lunch. And she just fed the baby! You did this on purpose!"

"Rahima, this kind of behavior is exactly

259

what I was worried about. You're a wild child and not a suitable wife for my son but he's taken you and now we have to undo what you are. Listen to me carefully. You are to behave like a proper bride and learn to keep house. That tantrum you threw in your father's home will not be tolerated here. I'm leaving now but know that I'll be keeping an eye on you." She got to her feet and wobbled to the door. She said nothing more and let the door slam behind her.

Shahnaz tossed her hair back and walked to her room, a smug look on her face. She had set me up.

*Madar-*jan, *you were right. And this is probably just the beginning.*

I confronted Shahnaz later that day.

"Why did you do that?"

"Do what?"

"You could have warned me. And you lied to her. You wanted me to look bad."

"What are you talking about? I didn't lie!"

I remembered one of Khala Shaima's favorite sayings: *A liar is forgetful.*

"Don't be upset, Rahima. You'll learn soon enough. God knows I did."

Shahnaz was a ball of contradictions. She was angry to have to share her home with me. It was bad enough that she had gotten the smallest of the houses. The other wives had more children and their marriages had been arranged by Bibi Gulalai. Only Shahnaz and I had been chosen by Abdul Khaliq himself and his mother clearly did not approve. Shahnaz was bitter one day but would sit and chat with me as if we were old girl-friends the next. She was lonely, I could see, and missed her sisters as much as I did mine.

"You know why she doesn't like you?" she asked me one day.

"Because I'm a bad wife?"

"No." Shahnaz chuckled. "Although that's not helping matters any. She hates you because she wanted Abdul Khaliq to take her brother's daughter as his fourth wife. Instead, he took you."

"Why didn't he take his cousin?"

"He was going to. That's what I'd heard from the others, at least. But something changed a few weeks ago and he made some excuse to his uncle's family. Next we heard he'd arranged for a *nikkah* with someone else — you. And Bibi Gulalai's brother was more than a little disappointed, since they'd already courted his daughter."

I knew I couldn't trust Shahnaz or anything she said but I was lonely too. She was the only person around me most of the time. Her son, Maroof, took to me quickly and I passed my time showing him how to kick a ball. Shahnaz would watch me suspiciously, as if waiting for me to do something wrong.

And somehow it seemed I did everything wrong. I sat wrong, I cooked wrong, I cleaned wrong. All I wanted to do was get back to school and back to my family, my friends. I felt clumsy in a skirt, my breasts pointy in the brassiere my mother had purchased for me before my *nikkah.* I wanted to tie my chest down again. A lot of days, that's exactly what I did. I would wrap a long strip of fabric around my chest and pin it tight, trying to prevent full womanhood from setting in.

My mother-in-law came back often. When the house wasn't cleaned to her standards, she would pull me by my ear and make me scrub the floors while she watched. Shahnaz blamed everything on me and Bibi Gulalai was more than happy to believe anything she said.

Abdul Khaliq returned, as determined as his mother to make me into a proper wife. I hated to feel his breath on my face, my neck. His teeth were yellowed and his beard rough on my face. I sometimes tried to pull away, to squirm from him like the fighters in the magazines. But the more I struggled, the more forceful he became. And worse than that was the smirk on his face. As if he enjoyed when I put up a fight. I shouldn't have been surprised. He was a man of war, after all.

Each time, I felt dirty and weak. I hated that I was powerless under him. I was supposed to be this man's wife and that changed everything. I wasn't supposed to fight back.

And the look on his face told me that fighting back would only make matters worse.

So many nights I lay curled on my side, crying quietly and waiting for morning to come so the man snoring beside me would stretch his arms and leave.

CHAPTER 25
RAHIMA

"Now taste this. See? It has no flavor at all. You've got to add some salt. Everything tastes better with a little salt. Mmm."

Shahnaz stirred the pot once more, the tomatoes melting into the simmering oil. She was teaching me a few basic dishes. It wasn't easy but I realized she took well to flattery. It was much better than antagonizing her.

"You see the difference? Now just touch the edge of the potato. It should be soft. See? It's cooked. My God, it really amazes me that you don't even know this much. You must have been so spoiled at home. I hope your sisters aren't such oafs in the kitchen!"

I wasn't worried about that at all. Shahla and Parwin could cook nearly as well as Madar-*jan*. But the mention of them made my heart ache. It had been two weeks since we were taken away from our home. I wondered what my mother was doing. I could picture my father, asleep in our living room with a satisfied smile on his face, clouds of heady smoke around him and his stomach heavy with food.

"Shahnaz, how can I see my sisters? I miss them so much! Parwin is so close by. Can I go to visit her?"

"Not a question to ask me. Ask your husband. Or your mother-in-law," she said. I wasn't sure if that was really a good idea or if she was setting me up again.

I saw my mother-in-law most afternoons. My third day at the compound, I was summoned back to the main house but this time by my husband's first wife, Badriya. There was laundry to be done. Badriya was also Bibi Gulalai's second cousin and, therefore, her favorite bride. Abdul Khaliq treated Badriya well, since she had been a good wife to him and because there was a family relation to respect. But as he added newer, younger wives to his compound, she spent fewer and fewer nights in his bed. This was a point of contention, though I couldn't understand why.

Badriya was nothing near pretty. Her cheeks hung low and she had two moles above her mouth, a constellation that looked to me like the letter *tay.* Her face was as thick as her hips, but she didn't need looks. Now in her thirties, she was heavyset, her girth widened by the five sons and two daughters she had proudly borne her husband. Bibi Gulalai loved the grandchildren Badriya had given

265

her and boasted about them to the other wives. This fed the tensions among Abdul Khaliq's wives and kept life interesting for Bibi Gulalai.

"Make sure she does a good job, Badriya. This girl has a lot to learn. She was a *bacha posh,* don't forget. Can you believe that? A *bacha posh* at this age! No wonder she has no clue how to carry herself as a woman. Look at the way she walks, her hair, her fingernails! Her mother should be ashamed of herself."

Badriya was resentful of Abdul Khaliq taking me on as a fourth wife, but he was a warlord and this was common practice for anyone, so she bit her tongue as any good wife did. Badriya had nothing to complain about anyway. She had the best house in the compound, the one with an actual bed and sofas in the living room. She had a cook and a housekeeper to tend to all the chores in her house. She was the most esteemed wife, the one Abdul Khaliq would discuss matters with, and she made sure the others knew as much.

There was a rhythm and routine to life in the compound. The wives tended to their children while Abdul Khaliq tended to his affairs, whatever that meant. There hadn't been any armed fighting lately, but nearly every day he and his bodyguards sped off in his three black SUVs, clouds of dust in their wake. His entourage circled him as he walked, nodding when he gave out orders and keeping away from any of the women in the compound. The men ate meals together, served by the housekeepers that Abdul Khaliq had brought on. They ate in Abdul Khaliq's entertaining room, a carpeted room with a perimeter of cushions and pillows on which the men reclined, licking their fingers and sipping their tea as they discussed the day's affairs. When they were finished, the women and children ate what was left. The servants were the third round, hoping enough had slipped through the many greedy fingers before them.

The women never left the compound. The children played together and fought together as brothers and sisters but subdivided. Half brothers got along most of the time but a casual game of soccer could quickly disintegrate into a scuffle where the sons of the first wife teamed up against the sons of the second. The same held true for the girls, who could become catty in the blink of an eye.

Badriya had no problem putting me to work. Nor did anyone else. Though they had plenty of help at the compound, the women seemed to derive a special pleasure from making me take on the most menial of tasks, especially since I fumbled with them. I swept the floors, washed the diapers and cleaned the western toilets as best I could. My hands burned at the end of the day and all I wanted to do was lay my head down. Most nights, that wasn't possible. Abdul Khaliq called for me to join him in his bedroom to repeat what he had done the night before. And the night before that.

My insides burned and I walked as if a shard of glass was stuck in my underwear. Sometimes I would wake up in the night remembering. It made it impossible to go back to sleep. I would pull my thighs together tight and curl up, praying he would tire of me. I wished my monthly bleeding would come more often but it had only started six months ago and came infrequently. My only escape was training my mind to wander when I was with him. I would close my eyes or stare at a stain on the wall, like seeing shapes in the clouds.

During the day I watched the compound's walls, hoping for a glimpse of my sister. I prayed Parwin would hobble into our courtyard unannounced and surprise me with a visit, a drawing, a smile. I couldn't bear to think of what her days were like. I hoped she didn't have to do all the things I had to do. Parwin's legs moved slowly, clumsily. People didn't like that. If the people around her were anything like the people around me, she was sure to be punished. I'd been smacked around more than once for a job not done well enough.

I couldn't bear knowing my sister was just over the wall. I wanted to see her. I wanted to look at a face that knew me, that loved me. I couldn't bear it anymore and worked up the nerve to ask Bibi Gulalai when I saw her walking through the courtyard.

"Khala-*jan*! Khala-*jan*!" I panted, running up behind her.

My mother-in-law turned around, already displeased. When I reached her she wasted no time and slapped my face.

"What are you doing yelling and running like that? My God! You have absolutely no idea how to behave yourself! Have you learned nothing here yet?"

My face stung and my mouth gaped as I searched for an apology that wouldn't make her angrier.

"Forgive me, Khala-*jan,* but I wanted to speak with you before you left. Good morning. How are you feeling?" I asked, not really caring but trying to show her that I did have some manners.

"You came running across the yard like a rabid dog to ask me that?"

There was no winning with her.

"Khala-*jan,* I wanted to ask you something. I really miss my sisters. It's been weeks since I've seen either one of them or anyone from my family. Would it be possible that I could see my sister Parwin, at least? She's just next door and I —"

"You were not brought here to go playing with your sister and taking her away from her responsibilities as well. It's bad enough that you can't manage what's asked of you here! This is your family now. Stop thinking about anything else and go finish your chores. Your sister is hardly a help over there with her limp leg. Forget about making things even worse."

"But, please, Khala-*jan*. Just to see her for a few moments. I promise I'll have all my work done. I've already washed the floors and beaten the dust from the carpets this morning. I could even go there and help her with whatever she needs to do —"

Another slap across my face. I took a step back and felt my eyes blur with tears. I was always surprised by the amount of force her wrinkled fingers brought.

"You had better learn to hear what I say the first time I say it."

She turned her back to me and walked out of the courtyard, shaking her head.

I shouldn't have been surprised but I was. My sister was yards away but she might as well have been across the country. Bibi Gulalai made me wonder even more how she was doing, with her "limp leg." I prayed the other wives had some sympathy for her, that there was at least one kind face.

In Abdul Khaliq's compound, there was only one person who was genuinely nice to me, Abdul Khaliq's second wife, Jameela.

While Badriya and Shahnaz appeared friendly enough, it took a half day with each to see their true colors. Badriya, with her larger, second-story home, looked down on everyone but even more so on me, the young latecomer.

"Badriya was the same way with me," Shahnaz said when I came back to the house crying one day. "It's not easy being the oldest wife."

"Why not? She's got everything! The best cook, the best maids, the best rooms!"

"It's not about any of those things. Abdul Khaliq doesn't *want* her. He doesn't call for her, now that he's busy with you. He used to be the same way with me and she hated it. Hated me for it."

"But . . . but I don't want to be called to him. I would be happy if he ignored me. What does she do that he doesn't call for her?"

Shahnaz laughed, her eyes lit up with amusement. "Simple, just get old. You see how Abdul Khaliq doesn't like to eat food cooked yesterday? Men want something fresh, hot off the stove." She cocked her head to the side and gave a sly smile.

That night I prayed for Allah to make me old, as old as Badriya, who looked older than my own mother.

But Shahnaz was just as bitter toward me as Badriya was. She, too, hated being called by Abdul Khaliq, but it wasn't much better when she saw me going toward his quarters. She would bang the pots around, huff if I asked her anything and slam her door. The following day, more chores were piled on me than usual, even if I was also called to clean Badriya's house.

Jameela was the only one who was different. She was Abdul Khaliq's second wife and, being such, had the second-best accommodations of the compound. She lived downstairs and down the hall from Badriya. She had been given to Abdul Khaliq by her family as a token of gratitude. No one was sure exactly what they were grateful for — it was always spoken of in very vague terms — but she seemed content enough with the arrangement. She had borne him three sons and two daughters, making him satisfied enough that she was holding up her end of their arrangement.

At thirty, Jameela was much more beautiful than Badriya and even Shahnaz, who was at least ten years younger than her. Her eyes sparkled with kindness and good humor when she spoke. My mother's warnings had been sage advice when it came to the other wives of the compound, but when I met Jameela, I knew I could trust her.

I had met Jameela last. She'd run into me coming out of Badriya's home.

"You must be Rahima! Ay, you're even younger than Badriya predicted."

"I'm not that young!" I'd shot back. I was tired and sweaty and didn't need anyone else making comments about me. "Who are you anyway?"

"Looks like you're off to a good start." She'd smiled gently. Her reaction had embarrassed me. "I'm Jameela. I live in the part of the house here with my children. My son Kaihan is probably your age. My daughter Laila, too. Have you met them?"

I shook my head. I hadn't seen anyone my age yet. I wondered if Laila was as nice as her mother.

"Laila!" she called out. "Laila-*jan,* what are you doing?"

"Zarlasht dirtied her clothes, Madar-*jan!* I'm changing her!"

"Come here for a second, *janem,* and bring Zarlasht with you. There's someone you should meet."

I heard footsteps. Laila was indeed close to my age, probably a couple years younger than me, but the baby on her hip hid the difference. She looked like her mother — her eyes and hair the color of night, dark and dramatic against her gauzy emerald head scarf. She looked at me with curiosity. Zarlasht was about a year old. Seeing them made me think of Shahla and Sitara. As a baby, Sitara spent just as much time in my sister's arms as she did in my mother's.

"This is Rahima-*jan,*" Jameela said, taking

Zarlasht from her daughter's arms. "Remember the *nikkah* we heard about last week? This is your father's bride."

Laila raised an eyebrow. "You are?"

I stood still, unable to bring myself to admit to a title that seemed too heavy for my shoulders.

"She is, so you'll be seeing her around more."

"Why is your hair so short? Like a boy?"

I felt my face flush and turned away. I wasn't sure how much to share. Maybe it wasn't a good idea to tell everyone I'd been a *bacha posh.*

"That's . . . that's how I wore it when I was going to school!" I blurted, hoping that was explanation enough but mostly wanting Laila to know that I'd been to school.

"School?" she exclaimed. "You were going to school like that? Madar-*jan,* she looks like Kaihan, doesn't she?"

"You were a *bacha posh,* weren't you?" Jameela asked. "That's what I'd heard. Bibi Gulalai mentioned it before the *nikkah.* My children have never seen a *bacha posh* but I remember my neighbor's cousin had been one. Up until she was ten years old, that is. Then she changed back to a girl."

"What's a *bacha posh*?"

"Laila-*jan,* I'll explain more later. I just wanted you to meet Rahima-*jan* for now. And this is Zarlasht, my youngest."

274

More footsteps came down the hallway as I tried not to stare too much at Laila, who reminded me how much I missed my sisters.

"Kaihan! Hashmat! Stop running inside! You boys are shaking the walls!" Jameela turned to me and explained. "Hashmat is about the same age as my son. He's Badriya's boy."

I took one look at Hashmat and a knot formed in my stomach. He looked from Jameela to me and grinned.

"Who are you supposed to be?" he said bluntly, his tongue slipping through his teeth and giving his words a wet lisp. It occurred to me that I'd seen him before, that I'd heard him before. We'd played soccer on more than one occasion in the streets a few blocks from our school. My voice escaped me. I wondered if he'd recognize me as well.

"This is Rahima, your father's bride," Jameela said. I turned my face and looked down, avoiding his gaze. Jameela was surprised by my modesty given how I'd spoken to her just a few moments ago.

"Oh. Yeah, I heard about you. You're . . . hey, aren't you . . . you're Abdullah's friend, aren't you?"

I didn't know how to respond. I fidgeted and looked to Jameela. I knew this looked strange to everyone. No girl my age should have been referred to as "Abdullah's friend." Jameela looked at Laila, who seemed more confused now than before.

"Never mind that, Hashmat," she said intuitively. "She's your father's bride and you'll be respectful of that. No one wants to hear anything else from your mouth."

I stared at the ground, knowing now why he looked familiar. I remembered him pushing and shoving his way to the ball, his mouth open and his dirty fingernails clawing at anyone in his way. He had friends only because boys were afraid not to be friends with Abdul Khaliq's son, a lesson they'd learned from their parents. We had made a point to avoid him and his group entirely. It had been a year since I'd seen him.

"You're a girl?" he exclaimed. "What kind of girl are you? That's you, isn't it? That's why you're not answering!"

"Hashmat! Do you want me to tell your mother —"

"Look at that! You've even got short hair and everything! What kind of bride are you? You've been running through the streets with Abdullah and his gang. No wonder you guys couldn't score a single goal!" Saliva sprayed out when he spoke with excitement. I covered my face with my veil, wanting to hide from his wet assault.

"Hashmat! That's enough I said!"

"Maybe Abdullah's a girl too! Maybe you all are!" he laughed.

I would think of lots of clever things to say

later, when Hashmat was not around.

Instead of saying any of those things now, I ran. I ran with the washrags still in my hand, my eyes blurring with tears. I wanted to get away from Hashmat, from this boy who knew me as I wished I still were — a boy just as free as him. I hated that he lived here. I knew he would always bring it up. He would always look at me and laugh at the girl who used to be a boy.

By the time I got to my room and slammed the door behind me, I wondered if he would see Abdullah again. I imagined what he might say and felt my heart drop. I didn't want Abdullah to see me as a girl, as Abdul Khaliq's wife, as Hashmat's stepmother.

I dropped my head into my hands and cried.

CHAPTER 26
RAHIMA

It drove me mad to think of Parwin. Months had passed and there was no hint that I would be allowed to see her. I knew where the adjacent compound was and tried to eavesdrop at the wall between the two homes to hear her voice or even someone speaking of her. I couldn't spend much time out there or Bibi Gulalai would come chasing after me to tend to something that no one else wanted to do. She had taken to using a walking stick these days, a change driven as much by her intensified desire to discipline me as her unsteady step.

I waited a month before making another move. I needed to work up the nerve to try again and to figure out how I could manage to get out of our compound. I set off in the early morning, when I usually went to tend to the laundry. I took the pail and walked across the courtyard as casually as I could. My throat was dry as I scouted the area. A few servants here and there but no one seemed to be paying any attention to me. My husband had left earlier in the morning and wouldn't be back for hours.

I moved closer and closer to the front gate, my palms sweaty.

Don't hesitate, I told myself, and opened the gate to walk out. I waited but heard nothing. No one had even noticed.

The compound sat on an open dirt road, one that I hadn't seen since the day of my wedding. I looked to the right and saw the adjacent compound where Parwin lived. I pulled a *burqa* from the pail and donned it. I walked quickly and tried their gate but it was locked.

I knocked lightly. This was the time of day that only the servants were in the courtyard and that was what I was counting on. If I could just get one of the servants to open the gate, I could find my way to my sister. I waited a moment but no one answered. I tried again, a little louder this time.

On my third try, beads of sweat trickling down the back of my neck, I heard footsteps and grumbling. I stepped back as I saw the gate open.

"As-salaam-alaikum," answered an older woman cautiously. From her worn clothing, I guessed she was one of the servants. I tried to see past her and into the compound. She squinted and narrowed the opening behind her. "Forgive me, I haven't recognized you.

Are you here to see someone?"

I cleared my throat and willed my voice not to betray me.

"*Wa-alaikum as-salaam.* Yes, I am. I am the sister of Khanum Parwin. I've come to pay her a visit."

"Ah, Khanum Parwin! Her sister? Welcome, welcome, but . . . have you come alone?" she said curiously. She looked behind me, expecting to see a chaperone.

"My mother-in-law, Bibi Gulalai, was supposed to come with me and would be here if it weren't for her aching back. She had to rest. But she told me to go on without her," I said, trying to keep my voice steady. "Is my sister around? I just want to see her for a few minutes."

The woman looked confused. Indeed it was strange for one of Abdul Khaliq's wives to show up at the front gate unaccompanied, but then who would imagine that a young girl would lie about such a thing? She opted not to give me, Abdul Khaliq's wife, a hard time and pulled the gate open to let me through.

"I think she's still in her room. I'll show you the way," she said.

The compound was much smaller than Abdul Khaliq's but set up in a similar way. My eyes looked for Parwin. I couldn't believe I'd made it this far! We walked past a few children, no more than six or seven years old.

They glanced at me, too preoccupied with their own games to bother with the stranger in the *burqa*.

"Who is this with you, Rabia-*jan*?" I stopped, as did my guide, whose name was apparently Rabia.

"Good morning, Khanum Lailuma. This is Khanum Parwin's sister. She's come from next door to pay a visit."

"By herself? You are Abdul Khaliq's bride?" Lailuma said, her brows furrowed together with displeasure.

"Yes," I said. I reminded myself to look confident.

"Does anyone know you're here?"

"Of course!" I said. "As I told Rabia-*jan*, Bibi Gulalai was going to accompany me but she was having backaches. I just wanted to pay my sister a short visit. It's been so long since I've seen her."

"Well, that's . . . I just don't think . . ."

"I'm so glad to meet you! I've heard much about the family next door to our compound but I haven't had the chance to meet anyone. Were those your children I saw just now in the courtyard? So adorable, God bless them!"

Lailuma was disarmed by my flattery, which to me sounded much more like something Shahla would say than anything I would have come up with.

"They are, yes, thank you. It's a shame we haven't met. Well, then go on but don't be long because your sister has responsibilities to tend to."

"Of course! I don't want to keep her," I said as sweetly as I could.

Rabia sighed and hurried me along, not wanting to be pulled away from her other duties any longer. We went down a short hallway and as soon as we turned the corner I saw her.

Parwin's back was to us but I could see her limping, a pail of water in one hand. The water sloshed with her wide gait, a trail of splashed water behind her.

"Parwin!" I called out, running to her. My sister turned around, her face puzzled. She dropped the pail on the floor and I could see the servant shaking her head at Parwin's clumsiness.

"Rahima? Rahima! What are you doing here?" she said, her eyes tearing up as I threw my arms around her thin frame.

"I came to visit you! I missed you so much, Parwin!" I turned around and saw Rabia was already shuffling down the hallway. "Let's go somewhere! I want to talk to you before I have to go back."

Parwin nodded and led me to her room, a small rectangular space without windows. It was even smaller than where I slept. We closed the door behind us and Parwin fell back onto her mattress with a sigh. She looked exhausted.

"Parwin, I've wanted to see you for so long but they wouldn't let me come! All they want me to do over there is work and work and I'm so tired of it! I scrub the floors and do the laundry and . . ." My voice tapered as I realized my sister's life was probably no different from mine. I was being selfish to complain to her.

"I know, Rahima. It's terrible here too," she whispered. "I pray every day that something will happen and I'll be able to go back home. I miss Madar-*jan,* Shahla and the girls! I even miss Padar-*jan*!"

I wanted to disagree with her but oddly, I missed our father too, even though I blamed him for putting us all through this.

"What is it like for you there, Rahima? They let you come here today?"

"I snuck away, Parwin. I've asked so many times but Bibi Gulalai won't allow it. So today, I just walked over here. I told the servant that I'd gotten permission."

"Oh no! Won't they notice that you're not there? What are they going to do to you?"

I had given that some thought and only hoped that my reasoning worked.

"I've gotten in trouble a couple of times. The last time, Bibi Gulalai threatened to send me back to my parents. I'm hoping that if she finds out about this, that's what she'll do. I want to go back home. I hate it over there!"

"Do you really think they'll send you

back?" Parwin seemed doubtful. My sister looked different, I realized. Her face looked thinner and her eyes lacked their sparkle. Her cheeks were marked with dark spots.

"I don't know but I really wanted to see you. And I thought it was worth a try," I added with a smile.

"I wish they would send me back too," she said wistfully.

"Are you . . . are you doing all right here? Are they nice to you?"

"I would rather be home. Remember those birds that used to fly over our yard? Remember how mad Shahla got when their droppings got on the laundry — twice in one day! That was so funny!" She was looking past me. Seeing something that no longer existed.

"Parwin, are you still doing your drawings? Have you sketched anything new? I miss looking at your work."

She shook her head. "There's too much to do and I don't want to disappoint anyone here. I have to keep up with my chores. Anyway, I don't really feel much like sketching."

This was completely unlike Parwin. I held her hands in mine and wondered what to say. There were questions I wanted to ask but the answers would only hurt us both. I stared at her while she smiled awkwardly. She talked about Rohila and Sitara, told me stories about them as if she'd seen them just days ago. I wondered what her husband was like. I wondered if she had to tolerate the same things I did.

"Khala Shaima said that Rohila is probably going to go to school now. Isn't that wonderful? She's going to love it."

"Khala Shaima? Did you see her? Did you talk to her?" It sounded like Parwin had completely lost her mind.

"Yes, she came here. About two weeks ago. I just saw her by the front gate for a few moments and then she left again. She asked about you too but I told her I hadn't seen you."

"She came here? Why didn't she come see me too?"

"She tried."

Of course, they'd kept her away from me. They probably didn't want me telling Khala Shaima how they treated me.

"What else did she say?"

"She said Padar-*jan* is the same, but happier now that he can get a lot more medicine. And Madar-*jan* and the girls are doing all right. We didn't really talk for very long. I wished she could have stayed and told more of her stories. I liked hearing about Bibi Shekiba, didn't you? I think about her a lot now."

I thought about her more than anyone could know. I often wondered what she would have done in my place. Or what I would have done in hers. Or if there was much difference anyway.

"Parwin, maybe we should just run away!" I whispered, interrupting her chatter. "Just like I snuck out this morning. We could just take off!"

If only I'd known then what the future held, I would have done just that. I would have snuck away with her in the night. At least that would have given her a chance.

"Rahima, you're always making trouble. I'm all right here. It's a lot of work but it's okay. Madar-*jan* said we should do what's asked of us and I am. You're going to get yourself into big trouble if you try anything."

I felt my throat tighten to hear her talk this way. She wasn't herself but I realized there was no running away for us, especially her. Parwin wouldn't make it more than a few feet from the compound with her limp.

Voices in the hallway grew louder.

"Where is she? Who let her in here?"

"She came alone? Does Bibi Gulalai know about this?"

I heard the footsteps and knew my time was up, quicker than I thought. I didn't bother turning around to see who had come after me. I kissed my sister's face and squeezed her hands as the door flung open.

"I'm sorry, Parwin. I'm sorry about all of this," I said. "I'm not far from you, Parwin, remember that, okay? I'm not far from you!"

I kept my eyes on her as I was yanked to my feet. Parwin looked oddly peaceful amidst the shouting.

"Birds fly away, one by one . . . ," she said meekly, watching as I was pulled away from her once again.

CHAPTER 27
RAHIMA

Bibi Gulalai seethed with anger.

Someone had seen me leaving the compound. Word got back to Badriya, who, probably happily, reported the news to Bibi Gulalai. It didn't matter much. Just made me hate them more. Badriya was a more spiteful person than I'd first thought. I prayed I'd one day find a way to get even with her. No wonder Hashmat was such a jerk.

But I'd invited this round of punishment. I'd asked for it. With every blow, every curse, I held out hope that my mother-in-law would blurt out that she'd had enough, that she was sending me back to my mother. I covered my head with my arms and waited to hear what she'd said the last time. When she didn't say it, I spoke up.

"If I'm so terrible then why don't you send me back?"

She paused. At that moment, I realized I hadn't done myself any favors. She knew that was exactly what I wanted and refused to give

288

it to me, even if it would shame my family and me before our entire community. No, at that moment she decided she would straighten out this pesky bride herself. My plan had backfired but at least I'd seen Parwin. Or what was left of her. My sister, so different and delicate in her disposition, had been changed by her new life. I knew it was partly my doing. This had all come about because of me, the *bacha posh,* and because of the argument I had with my mother. The rest of the blame sat on my father's addicted shoulders.

I thought of Shahla. I wondered if she still blamed me too. She had forgiven me on the day of our *nikkahs,* but I wondered if things were different now. Maybe things were better for her than Parwin or me. Shahla had a way of pleasing people, making people smile. I found it hard to believe anyone could treat her badly.

Now the relationship between Bibi Gulalai and me was forever soured. She focused her energies on making life miserable for me. My husband took from me what he wanted, did to me what he wanted and left the rest of my existence in his mother's hands. He was too busy to care about the details, now that he had even more lucrative business with some foreigners. His power and influence in our area were growing, and with it, so was his aggression and domination at home. We four wives shared a fear of his ready fist.

There was something else that worried me these days. For two weeks, I had been waking up in the mornings, my stomach reeling with nausea. The feeling frightened me and I finally confided in Jameela, who looked at me and sighed.

"Let me see your face," she said, cupping my cheeks in her hands. She turned my head from side to side, looking at my skin and my eyes. I let out a yelp when she felt my full breasts. "Yes, it looks to be true. You're going to become a mother, Rahima-*jan.*"

Her gentle words stunned me. For some reason, this possibility had not occurred to me.

"What? How can you tell?"

"Rahima-*jan,* how long has it been since your monthly illness?"

Come to think of it, I couldn't remember when I had last bled. It happened so ir-regularly that I never could keep track. I shrugged my shoulders.

"Well, it seems that you're pregnant now. The sickness will pass, you'll see, but other things will change for you."

I felt light-headed. Jameela took me by the arm and sat me down on a stool in the courtyard.

"It's all right, *dokhtar-jan,*" she said. "Every woman goes through the same thing. All of us. This will help you, you'll see. Your husband and mother-in-law will be pleased. Bearing children is a wife's duty."

One that Parwin had not fulfilled. Maybe that was why they had made her life so miserable. I wondered if Bibi Gulalai would treat me any better knowing this.

"I don't want anyone to know!" I whispered. I didn't want anyone to look at me differently. I felt ashamed.

"Do not say anything to anyone. It's not proper, anyway. We don't speak of these things. Keep quiet, do your work and let Allah handle the rest. In a few months you will see your child, if Allah wills it. May God keep you in good health," she whispered at the end.

I had no idea what was ahead of me. Jameela looked worried, even as she tried to comfort me. In her wisdom, she kept from me the troubling things she'd seen before she was married. Her uncle had married two girls around my age. When the first delivered her child, she bled for three days until her veins went dry and she could bleed no more. Her baby, with no one to nurse him, followed her ten days later. His second bride survived childbirth but the baby had ripped through her immature body, leaving a hole in its wake. Her husband, repulsed by the constant trickle of urine down her leg, said she was "unclean" and sent her back to her family to hide from the world in shame. Young mothers did not fare well but Jameela did not want to frighten me.

I took Jameela's advice but before long Shahnaz recognized the way my nose turned at the smell of food.

"You're pregnant!" she laughed haughtily. "Now you'll see how tough life can really be!"

Some days I hated her more than Bibi Gulalai. She shared the news with Badriya, knowing it would make her even more spiteful toward me. If I brought a son into Abdul Khaliq's compound, her husband and mother-in-law might not treat me as the lowly servant in the house. I doubted much would change. Bibi Gulalai looked at me as one would look at a flea-infested dog yapping at one's feet.

But surprises were always around the corner and a month later, I was permitted visitors. I wasn't sure if it was because my mother-in-law had learned I was with child. I was shocked to see Khala Shaima standing in our courtyard, looking around with a suspicious eye. Behind her stood Parwin, clutching her *chador* at her chin and keeping her eyes downcast, a model of modesty. I dropped the heap of laundry I was carrying and ran over to them. It felt so good to see their faces, though I prayed they wouldn't be able to see the change in mine. I didn't want to share the news with them.

I held Parwin's hand tightly. Khala Shaima

balked when I tried to kiss her hand. She grabbed my shoulders and looked me over, assessing the changes of the past few months.

Khala Shaima shook her head and sighed when she saw my full face and rounded belly. My baby was three months away. She didn't look surprised in the least.

"Are you feeling all right?"

I nodded. We didn't speak any more on the matter. I was thankful for that.

Satisfied that I was at least whole and fed, she pulled me aside so we three could talk with some privacy. I had so many questions for her. She was my link to my past life.

Our first meeting was bittersweet. Or sweet-bitter, which better represented the order of things. I was thrilled to have them here but I knew how painful it would be when they left. Parwin and I couldn't get close enough to Khala Shaima.

"How's Madar-*jan*? Why didn't she come with you?"

"Your mother is fine. You know how she is. She manages things inside the house but she's been kept under your father's thumb for so long that sometimes she forgets to stand on her own two feet."

"What about Rohila and Sitara?" Parwin asked. "Do they ask about us?"

"Of course they ask about you! They are your sisters. That hasn't changed just because you're living somewhere else now! Don't listen to the garbage that some people say about girls belonging to other people. Bah! Girls belong to their families and always do. You have a mother and sisters and nothing changes that — I don't care *who* you've married."

We nodded but I looked around quickly to make sure no one was within earshot. I knew enough about Khala Shaima to know that her fiery comments invited trouble.

"But why didn't Madar-*jan* come then? Is she all right? Doesn't she miss us?"

"Of course she misses you! She's . . . well, you might as well know. She's been very upset since you girls left. She's been so upset that she started taking some of your father's medicine."

"She what?"

"That's how things go sometimes. Listen, girls, when things are rough, people look for an escape. A way out. Sometimes it's hard to find the right way. Your father's escape has been that damned medicine and now your mother too. It was just a matter of time. It's in front of her face every day."

I was angry. Madar-*jan* was going to be just like our father. I pictured her glassy eyed and snoring on the couch, Rohila looking after the baby.

"What about all the money? What are they doing with it?" I asked bitterly.

"They divided it up. Of course, your father

took most of it but he gave some to his brothers and your grandfather. They feasted on greasy meals, showed off around the village thinking it's going to change the way people look at them. God knows what else he's spending it on. I know your mother hasn't had a finger on any of it."

"What about Shahla? Have you heard anything about her?"

"No, I asked your father about her since he's more in touch with that family than anyone else but he just says she's doing all right. He hasn't seen her. So far away, that poor thing. At least you girls have each other."

"But, Khala Shaima, I never get to see Parwin! She's so close but it's like she's on the other side of the world."

"Hmph. Still? Well, I'll just have to stop by more often so we can all see each other then. How are they treating you girls otherwise? Parwin?"

"I'm all right, Khala-*jan.* They're treating me just fine," she said so sweetly that no one would have believed it.

Khala Shaima's eyes narrowed. "Your mother-in-law? Does she beat you? Do you get enough to eat?"

"She's kind to me, Khala Shaima. She shows me how to do things and I eat plenty. Most of the time I'm not hungry anyway."

Khala Shaima turned to me, unsure what to make of Parwin's answers.

"I'm all right, Khala-*jan*. My mother-in-law, Bibi Gulalai, she's hit me a few times but I've figured out how to keep her happy. And she can't hit very hard anyway, that old witch." I lowered my voice instinctively. Bibi Gulalai always seemed to pop up when I least wanted her to.

"Witch is right," Khala Shaima hissed. "Damn these people, taking such young girls."

"Khala Shaima, can you promise to come often? I miss seeing you so much!" I blurted. Parwin nodded her head in agreement.

"Of course. I'll come as often as I can with this damned back of mine. Somebody's got to keep an eye on you girls. Abdul Khaliq may be the biggest man in this village but you girls have a family too. I want to make sure these people know that."

Her words, her presence, were such a relief, although it did nothing to change our daily life.

"And maybe you could tell us more about Bibi Shekiba?" I asked.

"Ah! Now, there's something we should pick up again. No one likes an unfinished story . . ."

Periodically, she would pick up Parwin and bring her to Abdul Khaliq's compound, where the three of us could sit and talk. She was persistent and managed to get her way. I thanked God for that. Those were the rare occasions when I was able to see my sister. Each time broke my heart and almost made me wish I hadn't seen her at all. The weak smile she gave me and Khala Shaima looked ridiculous on her fragile frame, her sallow skin. I hated her husband's other wives for what they were doing to her.

Parwin never complained to us. She never told us just how things were.

In some ways, I think she was the bravest of all. She, my meek and timid sister, was the one who acted in the end. She was the one who showed those around her that she'd had enough of their abuse. As Khala Shaima said, everyone needed a way to escape.

CHAPTER 28
SHEKIB

Over the next few weeks, and with Ghafoor's help, Shekib became familiar with her new home. Arg was a majestic building and Ghafoor had explored every niche. The palace had been built by Amir Abdul Rahman, while Shekiba was just a toddler. A trench of water surrounded the heavy walls and a tower stood watch at each of the four corners of the estate. At the top of each tower, Shekib could make out a canon aimed into the distance. There were ramparts all around the fortress and soldiers posted everywhere.

"That building over there, on the eastern side, that's Salaam Khana. That's where the king receives his visitors. There are a few smaller buildings behind it where he spends time with his family or his closest advisers. There is where the soldiers sleep and that building is all for weapons."

They walked onward; the soldiers kept their gaze averted but watched their movements with great interest. They crossed the vibrant gardens and walked to the other, western side of the palace grounds.

"What's that one over there?" Shekib pointed to a larger structure, tall enough that you could see it looking over the palace walls. It was a beautiful piece of architecture, stately appearing and just a short walk from Arg.

"Ah, that one! That's Dilkhosha Palace."

"It looks amazing!"

"It is. The inside of it is so beautiful that it can make your heart melt! There are paintings, carvings and gold vases. You could never imagine anything so beautiful!"

"You've been inside?"

"Well, I haven't exactly been inside . . . but that's what I've heard." Ghafoor's voice was full of conviction.

"Where does the king live?"

"Oh, well, he travels a lot but when he's here, he stays in that building over there with his wife."

"His wife? Do the women ever go in there?"

"For God's sake, no! What kind of crazy idea is that? The women of the harem stay in the harem. That's their place. They can wander into their courtyard and they have their own bathhouse that they can use whenever they please but they are not to be confused with the king's wife!"

"The harem?" Shekib took a deep breath. If she wanted to survive this new place, there was a lot she needed to learn.

"Yes, like *haram*. It means that it's forbidden for other men to enter. Except for the king of course. That's part of the reason why we're guarding it instead of his soldiers. But mostly it's because he knows men would be men and they can't be trusted around women, not even women who belong to the king."

Shekib had left the harem with Ghafoor early in the morning. The women were still sleeping and the other guards were just dressing to begin their duties.

"How many women are in the harem?" Ghafoor had only pointed out five or six women yesterday evening but their quarters were large with many rooms. Shekib thought there could be more.

"How many? Hmm . . . by last count there are twenty-nine."

"Twenty-nine?!"

"Sure. Twenty-nine. That is, if you still consider Benazir one of them right now!" she laughed. "She won't really get his attention now that her belly has begun to swell. He won't bother with her until after it's done."

"Until what's done?"

"Until *it* is done. Until the baby is born," she said.

"Oh. And their children, they will live with their mothers in that house?"

"Of course. Did you not see Halima's children there with her?"

300

"Where did he find all the women? For the harem, I mean."

"Same way he found me. And you. Lots of families can do without their girls. Lots of families need things. Anyway, he is the king. He takes what he wants."

"And what of the children? Does he have anything to do with them?"

"Surely. You know" — Ghafoor brought her voice to a whisper — "the king himself was born to a slave mother. He knows firsthand that any child can rise to greatness, not only those who are born to the first wife."

A steady breeze began to blow and Shekib reminded herself that her backside was not exposed. It would take some time to get used to wearing pants, she decided. Ghafoor, on the other hand, looked entirely comfortable in her garb.

"Does it hurt?" Ghafoor asked casually.

Shekiba knew to what she was referring but feigned ignorance. "What?"

"Your face. Does it hurt?"

"No." Shekib kept her gaze straight ahead. It was no accident that Ghafoor was walking on her right side, her good side. With the head scarf gone, she had no cover for her deformity. She wanted Ghafoor to see her face as it should have been.

"That's good."

Shekib was glad the conversation ended there.

They returned to the harem, now bustling with chatter as the women had woken up. With so many new faces around, Shekiba's hand rose up instinctively to bring her head scarf over her cheek but there was nothing to pull.

Past the foyer, there were women everywhere, sitting in groups of four or five. Two or three were feeding young children; one nursed in the corner. Some were in their thirties and some looked to be around Shekib's age. Some were slender and others were plump. Few bothered to look up. Ghafoor put a hand on her elbow and led her into a large room with stone floors. In the center was a large pool. Three women sat with their bosoms half submerged in the water. Their voices echoed against the walls.

"This is the pool room," Ghafoor announced, watching for the astonished reaction she knew the view would draw. Shekib's mouth opened slightly and Ghafoor chuckled. Shekib ignored her amusement. The stone walls rose tall and grand. A balcony on the second level overlooked the pool.

There were plants in the room, lush green leaves that drank in the room's moisture. The women looked over at Shekib and Ghafoor briefly, but seeing only Shekib's good half, their attention quickly returned to their conversation. The guards walked onward.

"These rooms are for the concubines. Some

have to share, but the ones with children each get their own. In about a half hour, the palace will send over lunch. The palace has female servants who come to these quarters but sometimes we help them gather the plates when the meals are done."

"What else are we supposed to do?" Shekib's eyes were busy looking at the maze of doors.

"Just keep an eye on things. Most important is to control the ins and outs. No one is to come in without our knowledge and approval, just as no one is to go out. Every once in a while, especially for someone who is new here, they may want to wander around. It is our responsibility to guard against things like that. And sometimes the women call on us for help with something. Nothing else, really. Like I said before, everybody has a role in the palace. This is ours."

The voices in the large room grew louder in unsynchronized excitement. Ghafoor's ears perked.

"Let's go see what has the women feisty this morning. That kind of chatter means something's going on."

Ghafoor was not wrong. Amanullah, the king's son, had returned to the palace.

CHAPTER 29
SHEKIB

"Why all this excitement for the king's son?"

"Why? Do you not know about his son Amanullah? You poor thing. You have so much to learn still!"

Shekib decided Ghafoor was a snob but tolerable.

"Tell me then. Why all the fuss for him?"

"He's the one. All bets are that he will succeed the king. He's the governor of Kabul and he's in charge of the army and the treasury."

"What's the treasury?" Shekib had never before heard the word.

"You know! It's the group that works with the army. They give out food and uniforms. And . . . and sometimes they take care of the horses too." Something about the way Ghafoor fidgeted told Shekib her answer could not be trusted. "But the most important thing about him is that he is not yet married. Amanullah is of age and his father is in search of the right bride for him. What a lucky girl she will be!"

"When will he marry?"

"The king has not yet decided. But Amanullah is well loved among the women of the harem. He is kind and handsome, more so than his father. The women servants of the palace are always on their best behavior around him, wishing they could be his concubine instead of his father's."

"Does he have his own harem?"

"No. He hasn't yet married. He probably will once he marries."

Amanullah had been gone for two months. Traveling to the disputed British-Afghan borders had exhausted him and he did not care for the usual palace pomp. Shekib would not get a look at him today but two days later, she did see his father.

Amanullah must have brought good news from the front line.

Shekib stood in the corner of the pool room shifting her weight and wondering how long she would be living in this palace. Life was comfortable enough. The rice and vegetables were plentiful, the cakes sweet. She had a blanket to keep her warm at night and the company of women-men who meant her no harm. But Shekib was still restless. She wondered what her mother and father would think to see her living in the king's palace. She wondered if they could see her from heaven, dressed as a man. Her father would likely not notice any difference. He had never seen her as girl or boy while he walked the earth. She still grew angry when she thought of her father's land. *Her* land. Seeing the torn deed scatter in the *hakim*'s courtyard like fallen leaves had hurt more than Azizullah's beating.

Bring your head out of the sky and understand your place in this *world*, Khanum Marjan had said.

Everyone has a purpose here in the palace, Ghafoor had told her.

Shekib wondered what her place in this world was. Something told her it was not her place to be a house servant. And it was not her place to be the unwanted granddaughter. Surely, being a harem guard could not be her fate either, as comfortable as it had seemed in the last couple of days. Shekib knew in her heart that she would need to act if she were to find her true purpose.

If she hadn't been so preoccupied with finding a way out of her current situation, she might have noticed the king sooner. As it was, she had no idea how long he had been on the balcony. She hadn't even noticed that the women in the pool had quieted their loud laughs and started behaving more demurely.

"Guard!"

Shekib jolted at the sound of a man's voice. She looked up and recognized the man from the carriage. Her heart pounded.

Had he seen her daydreaming? Her defenses went up instinctively.

"Guard! Come here!"

Shekib straightened her back, bowed her head and walked up the narrow stairs that led to the balcony. The king had entered from a back stairway, unnoticed. He had his uniform on but no hat. He was leaning over the railing, eyeing the women in the pool with casual interest.

Shekib said nothing and kept her head lowered.

A lifetime passed before he spoke.

"Bring me Sakina."

"Bring her here?"

The king turned around sharply. He was not accustomed to hearing the guards speak. His squinted eyes bored into her face. She instinctively turned to the side.

"You are new?" he said finally.

"Yes, sir."

"Hmph. Tell Sakina I have called for her. She will show you the way."

Shekib nodded and headed back down the stairs. The women had heard the king's voice and awaited Shekib's return. They were familiar with his perch and his habits. Shekib still had much to learn about the palace. The women looked at each other but dared not look up. They spoke in a hush.

Shekib stood at the poolside and looked at Sakina, her thick, dark hair pulled back in a braid and her pale shoulders beaded with moisture.

"He calls for you," Shekib said softly.

Sakina smiled slyly, her lips pulled to one corner. "Me, again? Dear God, I thought he had had enough of me by now." She spoke loudly enough for the ladies in the pool to hear.

Shekib saw some eyes roll, some mouths tighten. Benafsha's green eyes fixated on Sakina's behind.

"Some days men crave *qaimaq*. Other days they make do with spoiled milk." Benafsha's voice was cool and even. The others tried to hide their giggles. Benafsha dipped her head back, her long dark locks fanning into the water. For now, she was the *qaimaq,* the cream of the harem.

Sakina turned and shot her a hateful look. She stepped out of the water and reached for her towel. She wrapped it around her naked body and patted herself dry before standing at Shekib's side. Some of the women noticed Shekib's face for the first time.

"Allah, have mercy! Look at that! I guess after Benafsha, they have made an extra effort to pick guards who won't tempt the king!"

"Mercy, Allah, please! I can't even imagine . . ."

Sakina looked at her expectantly, ignoring the jabbering behind them.

"He said . . . he said you would show me the way," Shekib said finally.

Sakina raised an eyebrow. "Yes, I know the way."

Shekib heard the conversation continue as she turned around.

"It looks like *haleem,* doesn't it?"

Shekib sighed. This was not the first time her face had been compared to the dish of slow-cooked meat with grains, mushy enough that it could be spoon-fed to infants.

"Her face?"

"Oh, you're right! How awful!"

"Damn you, you know how much I love *haleem*! You've just gone and ruined my breakfast for me!"

There were quiet chuckles as Shekiba's new nickname was passed around and adopted by the group.

Sakina took the lead and Shekib followed her into a back corridor and up a separate flight of steps. At the top of the steps was a heavy wooden door. Sakina stopped and turned back to face Shekib. "Now, knock on that door and when you hear an answer, you'll open the door, then turn around and return to the others. This is as far as you go."

Shekib nodded and did as Sakina instructed. From within, she heard the king's voice bellow something incomprehensible. She opened the door just enough for Sakina to enter, holding her towel around her and her head lowered. Shekib closed the door and waited for a moment. She could hear their voices talking quietly. A laugh. A squeal. Shekib felt her face blush remembering that Sakina had nothing but a towel to cover her. She turned back down the stairs, suddenly afraid that she would be discovered lingering outside the room.

Her introduction to the harem was complete. She understood now that the king visited who he wanted, when he wanted. He came often but usually didn't stay long. There were some consorts he favored more than others, some he ignored for the most part but kept in the harem. The nine women who had borne him sons were treated better than the others. These nine women were given dresses with the finest embroidery and the choicest fruits, and they walked taller than the rest. Their places were more secure than the others', thanks to their gifted wombs. Neelab, whose three boys had not lived more than a month, was the exception. She had disappointed the king more than those women who had borne him daughters and she would receive no special treatment until she could give him a son who would live long enough to at least take a few steps.

Shekib watched and learned over the next few months. She paid attention to the way the palace functioned, the way the women interacted with each other and the habits of the king. She was stronger than the other guards and began to take on duties that the others struggled with. It was easy for her to lug the heavy pails of water into the harem. She had no trouble carrying the children when they fell asleep in the courtyard. She was not a threat to anyone, thanks to her disfigurement.

But Shekib did not stop thinking about her own plight. She watched the women of the harem. At least they belonged to someone. At least they had someone to care for them, to look after them. Daughters looked at their mothers' faces, nestled against their bosoms. How that must feel!

But what would become of the guards?

Shekib needed a plan. In the meantime, she made sure to fulfill her obligations and keep Ghafoor and the palace satisfied. She did not want to invite any punishment, thinking back to her grandmother and Azizullah. In more powerful households, the food might have been better but the penalties were that much harsher.

She was in the courtyard of the harem when she saw him. He walked casually with another man, a man with a wool hat and a short beard. Shekib had seen the man in the wool hat before. He was Amanullah's friend, she had been told. His name was Agha Baraan. Shekib wondered what they were talking about. This was the fifth time she had seen

311

the prince and she now understood why his arrival had created such a stir.

Amanullah, the king's son, was striking. He was solidly built, a few inches taller than Shekib. When he walked, his broad shoulders spoke of confidence, even though he seemed to be close to Shekib's age. He exuded a natural boldness, tempered with kind, rational eyes.

Shekib melted into Shekiba.

She had instinctively tried to cover her left face and lower her gaze the first time she saw him. After the third sighting, however, she changed her approach as she realized she could take advantage of her "manhood." She stared at the prince, who did not see her gawking anyway.

He gave her something to think about instead of her father's land. Or her dead family.

They were headed into the palace gardens. Shekib's hand touched her face and hair, wondering what she looked like to him. She knew half her face was actually beautiful. She could tell by the reaction of those who only saw as much.

She had worried that if she were ever to have children, they would turn away from her, repulsed by the demi-mask she wore. But the children of the harem reached out to her, trusted her, laughed when she tickled them. Maybe her own children would do the same. Maybe her own children would see her as her mother had, as unflawed and worthy of love.

And then Shekib realized how she could change her fate. How she could stop being gifted from one stranger to another. But to do so she needed to belong to someone, to a man. And if she had sons, she would seal her fate. A mother of sons would not be passed from hand to hand like livestock.

Amanullah had paused. His companion was pointing to some bushes that had flowered in the last week. He bent over and touched the leaves with an attentiveness Shekib would not have expected from the commander of the army. And the treasury, whatever that really was.

She stood tall, the right side of her face turned in his direction. She willed him to turn and look at her, to see her. She walked a few steps forward, hoping movement would attract his attention. He stood up and, almost as if pulled by her thoughts, turned in her direction.

Shekib's heart leapt into her throat. She froze, watching him from the corner of her eye and wondering what she should do. She gave a half smile and bowed her head just slightly, without diverting her view.

He began to speak and turned back to the friend, without changing his expression. Was he saying something about her? What could it be? Could he tell her apart from the other guards at this distance? Maybe the king had told him about her, the newest of the women-men.

Shekib realized she was smiling and turned back to face the house. She did not want anyone to see her staring at Amanullah and his friend as they walked thoughtfully through the maze of bushes and flowers. She bit her lower lip and pulled her shoulders back. An idea was beginning to take shape in her mind but it would require some work.

CHAPTER 30
RAHIMA

Seasons changed, two years passed and I feared I was forgetting what my mother looked like. I doubted I would recognize my younger sisters if I were ever to run into them. I got updates from Khala Shaima but it usually wasn't good news. She tempered what she told us but she felt we had a right to know. Madar-*jan* had become as much of an addict as my father. Rohila and Sitara were mostly left to fend for themselves, though my grandmother sometimes stepped in to pick up the slack. In return, Madar-*jan* was doing more work around the compound and the already strained relationship between her and her in-laws had deteriorated. Padar-*jan,* when clear-headed, made her life miserable. After all, as his mother pointed out, she wasn't being much of a wife or mother these days.

Part of me was thankful that I wasn't around to see what had become of my mother. Part of me wondered if things would have been different had I been sent back.

Once I started that line of thinking, I could go on for days with what-if scenarios. I always ended up in the same place — wondering how things would have worked out had I never been made a *bacha posh*. I think that's where my family started to crumble. Inevitably, I would wonder if Shahla and Parwin had the same thoughts. And if they still resented me.

I also wondered what Bibi Shekiba was planning. The walls around me were so stifling I couldn't imagine what had given her a spark of hope.

In the meantime, I learned the rhythm of the compound and found my niche within it. The crescent moon rounded and thinned many times over as I found ways to make my life easier, though nothing changed who I was to Bibi Gulalai.

My son, Jahangir, was ten months old at the time, a miracle in his own right. Carrying him for nine months and pushing him out of my body had nearly ripped me apart. I had never seen so much blood. Jameela delivered him, as she had Shahnaz's children. Abdul Khaliq did not like for his wives to go to hospitals and there were no midwives in our area. My husband's wife cut the umbilical cord while I lay exhausted and stunned. I'd never felt so weak. Jameela rubbed my belly and brought thick broths of flour, oil, sugar and walnuts to my lips, urging me to drink. I faintly remember her praying over me, mumbling something about my not having the same fate as her uncle's wives. I wonder if it was her prayers that protected me.

Jameela and Shahnaz cared for my little boy for the first week while I recovered. Even Bibi Gulalai left me alone for a while. At least I had borne a son, she said. Finally, I had done something right.

Jahangir was named after a character Abdullah, Ashraf and I had created, a figure born of our collective imaginations. Jahangir was a strong and mighty man who feared no one. He was the ultimate athlete, the strongest fighter and the cleverest person in the whole country. He was the conqueror of the world, as his name implied. We all wanted to be Jahangir. He could do anything.

It became a running joke between us. When Abdullah huffed that he couldn't learn the newest karate move we'd seen, we told him Jahangir wouldn't have given up so easily. When I couldn't get the soccer ball anywhere near the goalpost, I focused my thoughts on Jahangir and how he would kick the ball. Ashraf channeled Jahangir's persona when he tried to haggle his way through the market, gloating when he felt he'd gotten a real bargain out of a vendor.

While I was pregnant, I hadn't given much thought to a name, as if I believed babies were born with names, just as they were born with two arms or two legs. I was so frightened by the prospect of having a baby that I didn't care much about its name. But Jameela got me thinking.

"You must have a name and it has to *mean* something," she said.

By the time she had finished washing the blood from my thighs, my son was named.

It took me a couple of weeks to adjust to him. I would always be grateful to Jameela for her help. Even Shahnaz, at nineteen, was an experienced mother and couldn't resist teaching me how to feed, bathe and hold this tiny person.

I fell in love with him. Jahangir was my salvation — his face became my escape. He gave me reason to rise in the morning and to hope for tomorrow.

Khala Shaima hadn't been by for months, which was unlike her. I worried that she might be ill but I had no way of getting in touch with her or finding out. I could only wait for her to show up again. I hadn't even seen Parwin in about a month. I wanted them both to see Jahangir. He was starting to clap his hands and would grab on to tables to stand up. I wanted his aunt to see the things he could do now.

I had made up my mind to arrange a visit with Parwin. I had been given a little more freedom these days, now that I'd borne the family a son. Abdul Khaliq was bringing a foreigner to the house to talk business and there would be a lot of preparations to attend to. I knew I would be summoned to help the cook and servants. I decided to put off my visit until the following day.

Just after midday prayers, I began kneading the dough for dumplings when Bibi Gulalai came into the kitchen. I waited for her to point out what I was doing wrong. She looked perplexed, as if there was something she wanted to say.

"What are you doing now?"

"I'm going to roll out the dough for the aushak, Khala-jan. I finished cleaning the living room. It's ready for tonight."

"Yes, well, maybe . . . I guess that's fine. Keep on doing what you're doing."

I was puzzled by her behavior. "Is everything all right?"

"Yes, everything's fine. Why? Why do you ask that?"

"No reason, just that I . . . well, I was just asking," I said, and turned my attention back to the dough. It was getting tough. It was time to cut it into ovals and stuff it with leeks and scallions.

"Fine then," Bibi Gulalai said, and went back out the door.

That was my first clue that something was wrong. I think my mother-in-law, as cold as she was, was working up the nerve to tell me the news. She returned two hours later. This time Jameela was with her. Jahangir was crawling around the kitchen. I had blockaded off the stove, remembering how Bibi Shekiba had been burned as a child. I didn't want my son to carry such a scar. Life was difficult for the disfigured, I'd learned.

Jahangir was pulling on my skirt hem, whining. He was hungry but I wanted to finish the *aushak* before the guests arrived. I kept an eye on him but the expression on Jameela's face put my nerves on edge.

"Rahima, my grandchild is looking for food. I'll have Shahnaz feed him something," Bibi Gulalai said. She looked almost as uneasy as I felt.

"I'm done now, Khala-*jan*. I'll make something for him," I said nervously. "Jameela, what's going on? What is it?"

"Oh, Rahima-*jan,* something terrible has happened! I don't know how to share this sad news with you . . ."

Madar-*jan*. My mind flashed to her.

"What's happened, Jameela? Tell me!"

"Your sister! Your sister Parwin has been taken to the hospital! She's been very badly injured!"

Parwin?

"What hospital? How was she hurt?" I was on my feet, my son in my arms.

"I only know what I've heard from Bibi Gulalai." Jameela turned to our mother-in-law, who scowled and looked away.

320

"Go on, tell her already!"

"They say she set herself on fire this morning . . ."

Nothing Jameela said registered after that. I put Jahangir on the ground as my head closed in on itself. Parwin had tried to kill herself. All I could picture was her unconvincing smile, her feeble reassurance that she was doing all right, that people were treating her well enough. Why hadn't I gone to visit her this morning?

I pieced things together much later. Jameela took me to her house to lie down. She brought Jahangir along and one of the older girls in the house watched him while she sat with me. I asked her over and over again what happened and she explained it as best she could. Parwin had doused herself with cooking oil in the morning, while most of the women and children were eating breakfast. Her husband, Abdul Haidar, had already left the house.

Abdul Haidar's second wife, Tuba, came to help tell me what had happened. Some things she made clear. Others she twisted in vagueness but I understood that my sister had been seen that morning with a fresh bruise on her face.

Tuba claimed they had no idea Parwin would do such a thing to herself. There were no warning signs, no red flags. She hadn't said anything, and as a matter of fact, Tuba

321

said Parwin had smiled at her last night. I wanted to call her a liar. I knew the empty smile Tuba was talking about. I wanted to call them blind and stupid but my tongue was tied with guilt. If I, her own sister, had ignored her behavior, what could I expect of her co-wives? What could I expect of her husband?

They had heard the screams. She'd lit the match in the courtyard and that's where they found her, tried to cover her with a blanket to put out the flames. She'd fallen to the ground. There was a lot of confusion, screaming, trying to help. She'd passed out. They had taken her back to the house and tried to undress her, clean her burns. But it had been too much. They talked about it and talked about it and finally someone had decided that Parwin needed to go to the hospital.

The nearest hospital was not near at all. Her husband was not happy about being called back to the house to deal with the situation.

Somehow, they'd sent word to my parents.

Madar-*jan* must have been crazed with worry. Even Padar-*jan*, who had given us away for a bag of money, had been partial to his artistic daughter. The news must have shaken him. Khala Shaima had been at the house when they sent the message. She was on her way over to see me. I wanted to be with her but feared her reaction.

Please don't make this worse, Khala Shaima.

But Khala Shaima was our voice. She said what others dared not say. I needed her. She arrived in the evening, out of breath and teary eyed.

"Oh, my dear girl. I heard what happened! This is just awful. I can't believe it. That poor thing!"

She hugged me tight. I could feel her clavicles press into my face. I'd never realized just how little flesh she had on her frame.

"Why did she do this, Khala Shaima! I was going to go see her today but I didn't. How could she do such a thing?"

I shuddered thinking of how painful it must have been, how horrifyingly painful.

"Sometimes women are pushed too far, kicked too hard, and there's no escape for them. Maybe she thought this was her only way. Oh, my poor niece!"

We all need an escape. Khala Shaima was right.

"What did my niece say?" Khala Shaima demanded. "Tell me, was she talking when she was taken to the hospital?"

Tuba shook her head. It had been an ugly scene. The smell of burning flesh, agonizing moans, hysteria. She couldn't bring herself to describe the horror to us.

"She wasn't talking at all? Was she conscious?"

"She was . . . she was just lying very still

but she was awake. I was talking to her," Tuba explained. "She was listening to me but she just wasn't saying anything."

"She must have been in so much pain! Allah save her, that poor thing!"

"I'm sure they will give her medicines in the hospital, Shaima-*jan*. Allah is great and I'm sure he's watching over her."

I resisted the urge to spit at her. Pretending. She was pretending that things hadn't been that bad. Parwin hadn't been in that much pain. The hospital, which was a day's journey away and itself in woeful condition, would patch her up in no time. Allah, who had let this happen in the first place, would fix everything. It was all a game of pretend, just as Parwin had pretended every time we'd seen her. There was no honesty in our lives.

Khala Shaima began to lament. I wished she would stop. The sound of her wails made my head spin.

"You people destroyed her," she cried. "If she dies, her blood is on the hands of this family. Do you understand? This young girl's blood will be on your hands!"

The women were silent. Tuba bit her lip and fought back tears. I wondered if she could be honest with me.

I asked Tuba, with one mournful whisper, if my sister would live.

Through tears, she told me that God was great and that the whole family was praying

324

for Parwin and that she was on her way to the hospital, so they really were very hopeful.

I wanted to believe her. I wanted to believe that my sister would be okay.

Tuba's eyes told me it wasn't in her *naseeb*.

CHAPTER 31
RAHIMA

Parwin had stopped pretending.

After ten agonizing days, her peace finally came.

Her body was brought back and buried in the local cemetery. My father attended the burial, as did a few of my uncles and my grandfather.

At the *fateha,* I saw my mother again. The first time since my wedding day. Had I had a life more ordinary, I would not have been able to believe what she'd become.

"Rahima! Rahima, my daughter, oh God! Can you believe this? Allah has taken my daughter, my precious Parwin! So young! Oh, Rahima-*jan,* thank God she at least had you nearby!"

My mother's hair was thin and stringy. Her words came out wet and lisped. She was missing a few teeth. Her skin sagged and she looked much older.

"Madar-*jan*!" I hugged her tightly, surprised at how much like Khala Shaima she felt.

"Madar-*jan,* I've missed you so much!"

"I've missed you too, my daughter! I've missed all of you! This is your son? God bless my grandchild!"

"His name is Jahangir, Madar-*jan.* I wish . . . I wish you could have come to see him. He's a sweet child."

My son smiled, showing off his two bottom teeth. I waited for my mother to reach out to hold him. She didn't. She touched his cheek with her trembling hand and then looked away. Jahangir looked as disappointed as I felt in her lack of interest.

"Oh, I've wanted to come and see you, Rahima-*jan.* Especially when I heard about my grandchild, but it's not easy for me to get away from home, you know that. And your husband's home is not very close. With two kids at home, it just hasn't been possible."

I bit my tongue, wondering why the distance wasn't too much for Khala Shaima and knowing that she could have brought my sisters or left them with one of my uncles' wives if she'd wanted to. My mother was weaker than I'd ever realized.

We women in mourning sat in a row, a wall of misery and tears. Women from our village came to pay their respects, whispering the same words of condolence to each of us one by one. Some even cried. I wondered why. So many of them had laughed to see my sister try to keep up with the other children, had

called her Parwin-*e-lang* and had thanked
God out loud that their own children weren't
similarly deformed. They had made her feel
small and wrong. Today they pretended to
share our pain. I despised the insincerity.

We prayed. The women sat in rows before
us, rocking to the rhythm of the prayer, the
gray haired in the group blowing their noses
into handkerchiefs and shaking their heads.
They cried for us, their hearts softened with
age and they themselves one step closer to
the grave than most others. In the last ten
days, my eyes had dried up. I sat still, blankly
watching the faces in front of me. Madar-*jan*
reached over and held my hand.

Rohila and Sitara sat on my right. I shook
my head. How wrong I was to think I
wouldn't have recognized my sisters! They
had grown taller, more mature, but their faces
were unchanged. They spoke sweetly and I
hurt to think what home was like for them.
Rohila grabbed me and wouldn't let go.

"Rahima, is it true? Is Parwin really dead?
That's what Madar-*jan* told us but I can't
believe it!"

"I wish it weren't true." Nothing good came
of pretending, I'd decided. "How are you,
Rohila? How are things at home?"

"Can't you come back home sometimes?
It's been so lonely since you all left!"

I believed her. I'd felt the same loneliness. I
bet we all had, each in her corner of the

world, separated by so many walls.

"Are you taking care of Sitara?"

"Yes." Rohila nodded. It occurred to me that she was now the same age I'd been when I was married off. I looked at her and wondered if I'd looked just as young. I could see that her breasts were just starting to bud. Her shoulders were hunched forward, her chest pulled in. I recognized her posture. She was uncomfortable with her changing body. I wondered if Madar-*jan* had given her a bra yet.

Sitara was now almost nine years old and clung to Rohila more than she did to Madar-*jan*. She looked unsure around me, as if she didn't trust anyone but Rohila.

"How's Madar-*jan* been, Rohila?" I whispered. I knew I would draw looks for talking, even in a hushed voice, during the *fateha* but this was my only opportunity to see my sisters. What I saw worried me.

Rohila shrugged her shoulders and glanced over at Madar-*jan*. "She just lies around most of the time, just like Padar-*jan*. She cries a lot, especially when Khala Shaima comes over. That just makes Khala Shaima angrier."

At the mention of her name, Khala Shaima looked in our direction. I expected her to give us a chastising look but she didn't. She didn't give a damn about decorum.

"Are you going to school?"

"Sometimes. Depends on what Padar-*jan*

329

says. Sometimes, when she's taken Padar-*jan*'s medicine, I have to stay home to clean up and get Madar-*jan* up and dressed. If Bibi-*jan* sees her the way she is, there's always a big fight."

Sitara stared at the ground but I could tell she was listening to our hushed conversation. She looked so timid, so different from the inquisitive little girl I'd left behind. I looked back to see Madar-*jan* wiping tears away, muttering angrily and fidgeting in her chair. I stared at her cheekbones, the lost look in her eyes. She was every emotion and blank at once. She was as badly addicted as my father.

*Madar-*jan, *what's become of you?*

My stomach sank when I thought of what might happen to my sisters. I prayed for God to keep Khala Shaima alive and present in their lives. I pushed away the thought that they would be addicts soon too.

Things were worse than I'd let myself believe, even with Khala Shaima's dismal updates.

"Rahima, why isn't Shahla here?"

Shahla hadn't been allowed to come. She had just delivered her second child and it wasn't proper for her to be out of the home in her condition. I wondered how she had taken the news, alone and so far from the rest of us.

Respects had been paid. The prayers were complete. The women repeated the procession, again wishing for Allah to ease our suffering, praying for Parwin's place among the angels in heaven and to themselves thinking it was in her best interests that she put herself out of her handicapped and childless misery. I wanted them all to disappear so I could spend this precious time with my mother and sisters.

The *fateha* passed quickly. I was back at the compound, but even more miserable. Madar-*jan* was in bad shape. Rohila had taken over as matriarch. How had this happened to us? I was the only one of my sisters who'd had a chance to live any kind of childhood at all, and that was only because I'd been a *bacha posh.* I looked at my son and thanked God for making him a boy. His lips turned up in a cheerful smile, his eyelashes so long they looked like they could get tangled. At least he had a chance.

I wanted to be alone but there was little possibility of that at the compound. With the *fateha* over, so was my period of mourning. I was expected to resume my duties. Bibi Gulalai treated me just as she always had, if not worse. I think she had convinced herself that Parwin's suicide had been a purposeful attack on her family. With Parwin gone, I took the fall for the tragedy she'd brought to her extended family.

I ignored everything and everyone. I carried out my duties, often with Jahangir a few feet away, playing or napping. I watched him wistfully, vowing to be better to him than my mother was being to my sisters. Thankfully, Abdul Khaliq had no trouble clothing and feeding his family. Jahangir was his son, as much as the other boys in the house. He would go to school and enjoy the privileges that came with being a warlord's son.

And his father loved him in a way that surprised and relieved me. Abdul Khaliq kept his daughters at arm's length but his sons stayed at his side. The older boys even joined their father in some of his meetings. The younger ones nervously scattered when Abdul Khaliq came home, afraid of getting yelled at for spending too much time playing. He didn't have much patience for crying babies but he would watch them while they slept. Except for my son. Often, I caught him gently stroking Jahangir's cheek or whispering something into his ear. He held him with the same adoration I did. He chuckled when Jahangir spilled things and his chest swelled with pride to hear him say *"baba,"* as if he were hearing the word for the first time. The rhythmic breathing of his sleeping son calmed even his foulest of moods. I was happy Jahangir was a favorite, knowing I never would be. At least my son was safe.

The older boys, my son's brothers, both feared and adored their father. They vied for his attention and looked for ways to make him happy — or at least not angry. The older boys stood tall when they recited *suras* from the Qur'an and the younger ones would bring him his sandals when he asked. He was proud to have boys. He smiled for them, and for little else.

My husband was spending more and more time with foreigners and the men he kept around as close advisers. Plans were brewing. The wives were on edge, though only Badriya knew why. If things were not going well for Abdul Khaliq, then things would not be going well for us. When we asked Badriya, she brushed us off dismissively.

"Don't bother yourselves worrying about it. He's worked up because he's renegotiating the arrangement he has with some of these people. It's too complicated to explain to you," she would say, not wanting to divulge the knowledge that set her apart from the rest of us. As his first wife, he discussed these matters with her. It was really the only interaction he had with her since he rarely called her to his bed. Everyone had a role in the house. That was hers.

But walls were thin and I spent most of my time at the main part of the house. I started to hear things when Abdul Khaliq and his men sat in the living room.

"They've got five more open seats for the province. The seat from our region needs to be filled. There are a few other powerful men who will be looking to step in and challenge you, Abdul Khaliq, but a woman candidate would be a sure thing. She would take the seat without question because of these stupid rules they've created."

"I don't like this idea. Why should we put a woman in a man's place? And even worse, you're asking me to put *my wife* in my place? Since when do we have a woman do a man's job?"

"I understand that, *sahib,* truly. And, believe me, I don't like it any more than you do, but these are the rules. I'm simply suggesting we find a way to work around the system so that we don't lose all control over this area. The elections are coming up soon. We must plan for this."

"Damn whoever decided on these shameful rules! Telling us we have to have women representatives? They have no business there! Who do they think is going to look after the children then?"

His advisers were silent. I could hear my husband pacing, grunting. I was surprised at what I was hearing. It sounded like they were suggesting that one of Abdul Khaliq's wives run in the upcoming parliamentary election! Would he really even consider such a move? We wives rarely left the compound. How could he possibly send us out to interact with strangers?

I looked at the clock on the wall. Jahangir

had been sleeping for forty minutes. He would be waking up soon. And Khala Shaima had promised to come over today. Tomorrow would mark forty days since Parwin's death.

"I'm simply presenting an option, *sahib*. I know it's not an attractive one but it may be our only one. I just don't want you to lose the opportunity to have some influence in the government. You're already in good position with the contracts you've secured."

Smoke wafted from under the doorway, the acrid, thick smell of opium. My mind drifted home, to my father asleep in the living room and my mother sewing our clothes.

"It's true," another voice chimed in. "There's no one else who can guarantee the same security — especially over the bridge. Those foreigners, they certainly don't want to send their own soldiers to guard it. They depend on us. This pipeline is not a small project. They've been talking about it for years and this time it looks like it's actually going to happen."

"It's true. There's a lot of money in that pipe. And this area belongs to you, *sahib*. It would be a shame to lose even part of that control." The voice was measured and cautious.

"I know that!" Abdul Khaliq thundered. "Don't you think I know that? I don't need you to tell me things I already know!"

I didn't want to be around for what I knew

was coming next. I picked up my son and walked back toward my own quarters to wait for Khala Shaima. I wanted her to take my mind off things. To tell me about Bibi Shekiba's mysterious plan.

CHAPTER 32
SHEKIB

Shekib waited for the right time. Mahbuba was rarely alone but she was the right person, Shekib had decided. She had borne the king four sons.

The first stage of Shekib's plan was to find out what Mahbuba had done right. How was it that she came to have four sons while other women continued to bring girls? There must have been something she had done differently to not have a single girl in her brood.

Her boys ranged in age from one to seven years old. When Shekib came upon them, Mahbuba was bathing her youngest son. Her eyes searched for a towel, while the older boys ran off to play.

"Thank you! I thought I had something here with me," she said as Shekib handed her a cloth from a nearby shelf. Mahbuba held Saboor's hand as she dried him off.

"Certainly," Shekib mumbled. She had made a point of being quietly helpful with the king's consorts. It was unlike her to start a conversation but she forced herself to speak the lines she had rehearsed.

"You have lovely sons."

"Thank Allah, they are blessings," she said, sighing. The boy was wiggling to escape his mother's grip. His eyes chased after his brothers.

"The others have daughters. Mostly. You are lucky."

"Yes, well, some of us are blessed with sons and others have to bear daughters."

"You have made the king very happy."

It dawned on Mahbuba that this conversation was peculiar. She turned around to see who she was talking to.

"Oh, you! What is your name?"

"Shekib." She looked at Mahbuba straight on. The women of the harem had made her quite comfortable in the last few weeks. They were too busy picking each other apart to pay attention to the woman-man guard with the melted face. Shekib no longer missed being able to pull her head scarf over her cheek. She found it liberating to walk about, her hands in her pockets and the sun on her face.

"Right. Shekib. Let me ask you something. What's your real name, my dear? Your girl name?"

Shekib fidgeted. Mahbuba had surprised her.

"My name is Shekiba."

"Clever. Bet that was Ghafoor's idea. Do

you and the others get along well enough with her? She can be such a nuisance."

"Sure," Shekib said vaguely.

"It's so ridiculous that they have you wearing those uniforms. As if anyone would forget that you are not men. As if we need guards anyway. What we need are more servants to help us with the children. But that would offend the king's sense of security."

"Some people forget."

"Forget that you're women? Do you really think so?" Mahbuba was struggling to dress her son. He scratched at his mother's face in angry protest. She turned him around and locked him between her knees. He looked at Shekib with a defeated pout.

"How did you make it so . . . how did you manage to have boys?"

"What?"

"I want to know how you managed to have all boys. What did you do?"

Mahbuba laughed naughtily. "Do you want me to start with the basics? You are dressed as a man but know nothing about their parts, eh?"

Shekib blushed. "I mean . . . no, that's not what I meant. I was asking how . . . the other women have girls. How did you manage to have boys instead of girls?" she stammered.

"Do you think you are the first to ask me such a question? Most of the women in this house have come to me looking for that very

339

answer. I have borne the king more sons than any other woman!" Mahbuba needed a minute to sing her own praises. Shekib waited. "I have given him son after son and *nothing* but sons! That is why he looks at me with fire in his eyes, with respect in his heart. You are a wise girl-boy. You are looking for the key to a satisfied man."

The humidity of the bathhouse made Shekib's breaths heavy. She wondered if Mahbuba would ever reveal her secret. Maybe this had been a mistake.

"But tell me. Why are you asking such a question? You are a man now, are you not? Are you to be turned back into a woman? Are you to be married?"

Shekib shook her head.

"I did not think so. Then why bother to ask for answers you have no business using? Did someone send you to ask me this? Who was it? Was it Shokria? I've seen the way she looks at my boys. Five girls, she has. Can you imagine? That witch. I'll fix her if she casts a jealous eye on my sons!"

"No, no one sent me!" Shekib panicked. She did not want to cause any fuss among the women. If it led back to her, it would not help her situation.

"Farida? She's another one with her devil eyes . . . can't be trusted. You shouldn't go about the harem doing their dirty work for them!" Her son had managed to finally twist

340

himself free. Mahbuba sighed. He was missing one sock.

"Forgive me, I have not been sent by
anyone. I was . . . I was just asking out of my
own curiosity."

"Are you wanted by a man?"

"Am I . . . no, I just —" Shekib decided
she should close this conversation.

"I am teasing you. I will tell you a few tricks
if you promise —" Mahbuba paused and
looked from left to right dramatically. Her
voice turned into a hush. "If you promise that
you will not share these secrets with anyone
else. You can use them if you find yourself
under a man one day and in the mood to give
him a son."

Shekib squatted next to Mahbuba, her ears
hot.

Some of what she was told, she never would
have anticipated. And would never have been
able to repeat.

But she committed the tips to memory,
hoping that they might prove useful. The
shape of the moon, the seeds of the yellow
flowered plant, the juice of an apple with no
brown spots. These were simpler. But the
other things, the things with the man, these
made Shekib wonder if Mahbuba was not
looking to make a fool out of her. But there
had been no glimmer of trickery in her eye.
She spoke casually, as if the things she talked
about were commonplace and ordinary. To

Mahbuba they were. To Shekib, they were not.

Did the women really allow the king to do such things? She thought of Halima and could not imagine it. Then she thought of Sakina, the way she had walked, half-naked, to the king's chamber and knocked on the door with feigned timidity. It could be true.

She could not stop her mind from drifting to Amanullah, the governor of Kabul. She thought of the way he walked, the confidence of his step, his fingers grazing the petals with delicate respect. She wondered what it would be like to be near him, to feel his breath on her face, moist and warm like the air of the harem's bath room. She thought of her fingers tracing the borders of his neatly trimmed beard and the medals of his uniform pressing against her unfettered bosom.

Shekib shook her head and hoped her face did not betray her thoughts.

At night, the guards slept in a room just outside the concubines' quarters. They took turns standing guard. Tonight was Shekib's turn. Kabul's air was brisk but she did not mind it. She wrapped her coat tighter around her and rubbed her hands together. She thought back to her first night on duty, a night she spent standing at attention, terrified that someone would find her asleep or sneak up on her. By morning she had drawn her weapon, a heavy baton, a half dozen times, only to frighten the frog who had wandered too far from the pond. She nearly collapsed when Ghafoor came to ask her how her night had gone.

"Why are there so many noises at night? There are frogs and lizards and soldiers coughing and pacing! You said I should just stand in the quiet night until morning. It wasn't a quiet night at all!"

Ghafoor had laughed uncontrollably. Two soldiers had turned, their brows furrowed in disapproval to hear a woman laugh so loudly, even if it was a woman-man.

"Did the frogs shake you up? Well, little girl from the village, I didn't think a few little night critters would make you so nervous!"

Shekib had felt a little embarrassed. "It wasn't the frogs, it was mostly the soldiers . . . they are loud but I couldn't see them. I just thought . . ."

"Don't worry about it. The next night will be easier on you. You'll grow accustomed to the sounds of the palace at night. You might even enjoy it more than the days."

Ghafoor was right, although Shekib kept that revelation to herself. Over the next few months, she grew content to sit in the dark, the dim light from the king's main residence and a few oil lanterns casting enough of a glow to make a game of shadows. Shekib smiled when some resembled animals, laughed when one took the shape of her grandmother.

Tariq joined her on those nights when she could not sleep. She had been in the king's presence more than a few times and he hardly glanced at her. She was losing hope for being that rose that is plucked from the garden, as she had put it. She fretted, bit her nails and creased her forehead but Shekib did not mind her company.

"Ghafoor is snoring again."

Shekib nodded.

"It's like sleeping next to a congested horse. I can't take it. I don't know how the others ignore it."

"She'll deny it in the morning."

Tariq smiled. "Anything happening in the palace?"

"No, not so far." It was quiet in the gardens, but the palace was unpredictable. People came and went at odd hours sometimes. And from time to time, King Habibullah hungered for a concubine in the darkest hour.

The guards were silent. Tariq sighed. Something was on her mind.

"Are you happy here?" she asked.

"Happy? What do you mean?"

"I mean, are you happy? Are you satisfied with this?"

"I've seen worse."

"You don't miss your family?"

"I miss them as much as they miss me."

Tariq did not know how to interpret Shekib's response. She understood from her tone that she would not elaborate. She pulled at her bangs, tried to make them reach her eyebrows.

"But how much longer do you think we will be here?"

"I don't know."

"I wonder sometimes."

"About what?"

"I wonder what the palace will do with us. How long will they keep us here? I want to be married. I want to have children and a home. I want to live somewhere else, don't you?"

Tariq, dressed as a man, was a woman after all. Her voice was nearly cracking. Shekib understood better than she let on. She had to protect her own plan.

"I don't know. We have a comfortable life here."

Tariq sighed heavily. "It's comfortable, but this can't be it. I'm not like Ghafoor. Or even Karim. I don't want to wear pants for the rest of my life. I was happy as a girl."

Tariq's laments were interrupted by the sound of a door slamming shut. The guards froze and looked for the source of the noise. They focused their eyes in the dark, trying to locate the footsteps.

"Where was —"

"Shhh!" Shekib hissed.

A shadow scurried away from the harem's

345

side door. The figure was running back into the palace.

"Do you think it's the king?"

Shekib did not. King Habibullah never left from the side door. And he had no need to sneak past the guards either.

"Who goes there?" she called out. She wrapped her fingers around her baton.

The figure scurried faster, passing under the yellow glow of a lantern. From the breadth of the shoulders and the shape of the pants, they could see it was a man. A man in the harem?

"This is bizarre. Stay here. I'm going to check on things inside," Shekib said.

But the harem was peaceful. Shekib could hear the light snores. The man had come from somewhere though. She waited, cocked her ear for any movements. She tiptoed through the hallway slowly. Carefully.

When she had crossed through the bath and checked the hallway on the opposite side, she retraced her steps. Something stirred by the foyer. She focused her eyes in the dark as the figure turned toward her.

"Did you find anything?"

It was Tariq.

Shekib sighed and shook her head. They stepped back into the night air and looked into the courtyard, across the gardens, to the palace. Nothing moved. Shekib wondered who it could have been. Someone had paid a visit to one of the king's concubines. Who could be so bold as to trespass here? And which woman had allowed him into her chambers?

Shekib and Tariq sat in silence, chewing over the same thought. If the palace were to find out, the guards would be held responsible.

CHAPTER 33
SHEKIB

Shekib and Tariq entered their sleeping quarters when daylight broke. They had neither seen nor heard anything else throughout the night. The soldiers were walking about now and the servants looked hurried. The king was likely expecting a visitor.

Ghafoor was awake, her arms stretched over her head as she yawned. The others rubbed their eyes.

"Tariq? You're up already? Did you not sleep last night?" Ghafoor asked, puzzled.

"Something happened last night," Shekib said softly. "Something you all need to know about."

Her words, rare as they were, got everyone's attention.

"We saw someone leaving the harem through the side door, which should have been locked. It looked like a man. He ran off toward the palace but in the dark we couldn't make out his face."

"It must have been the king. You know his

urges come at odd hours."

Tariq shook her head. "It wasn't the king, trust me. I know his shape. This man was leaner, taller. And the king doesn't sneak in and out of the side door. He comes and goes as he pleases, even when the hour is late. This was someone else."

Ghafoor and Karim leaned forward; they were just now making the realization that Shekib and Tariq had made last night. Qasim looked at her sister's concerned face.

"Did you hear anything inside? Was anyone awake?" Karim asked.

"Nothing. I walked through the hallways and heard nothing at all, saw no one. Whoever it was that let him in was not making a sound," Shekib said, her tone flat and serious.

"Of course not," Ghafoor said. "But if this has happened once, then it has probably happened twice and three times and more. We have a serious problem on our hands, guards. If the king learns that someone has been sneaking past us and paying secret visits to his private harem, we can start saying our final prayers."

"Should we tell someone in the palace?" Qasim asked nervously.

"No, absolutely not!" Ghafoor cried. "We have to find out what we can on our own and stop this from exploding on us."

Karim and Tariq nodded in agreement.

Shekib stood in silence. Ghafoor was taking charge now.

"First of all, we need to speak with the concubines, privately, one at a time, and see if anyone can give us any information."

"You think whoever brought him in is going to tell us?" Qasim asked.

"No, she won't tell us anything, I'm sure. But if this has been happening, someone must have heard something and I'm sure that someone *else* will be willing to talk about it. You know how these women are with each other. They can't wait for a chance to rip the others to shreds."

"I can't believe we haven't already heard about this," Tariq said.

"This was bound to happen. It was just a matter of time. There are just too many women in one house. One of them was going to invite trouble." Ghafoor spoke confidently, as if she had predicted this months ago.

Shekib and Tariq lay down to get some rest. The others assumed their posts, rotating to cover Tariq's position as well so that she could close her reddened eyes for a few hours. The situation had given Ghafoor new energy. Her face was serious and her tone urgent. She gave orders as if she were a palace general commanding her soldiers.

Karim and Qasim shot each other looks but let her be.

Shekib could not sleep. From the moment

she had seen that shadowy figure, a feeling had taken root in her stomach. Something would come from this. She lay on her side, looking at the cracks and crevices of the stone wall. She was not in her village now. She was not even in Azizullah's house. She was in the king's palace. Bigger people meant bigger problems.

Sleep claimed her finally but briefly. In the afternoon, she rose and dressed. She found Karim in the bathhouse. Five women soaked in the pool. Shekib looked up and saw the balcony was empty.

"Have you heard anything?"

Karim shook her head. "Ghafoor says she has her suspicions but no one is talking yet. I've asked two of the women, Parisa and Benazir, if they heard anything odd last night but they said they hadn't. We have only asked those women who have children since it's unlikely young ones would sleep through a visitor in the dark."

Shekib nodded. The reasoning made sense.

"But it is best not to create too much of a stir since one of the women might actually tell King Habibullah what we've been asking." Karim sighed heavily. "There are just so many ways for this to turn on us."

"That's how things are. There always has to be someone to blame," Shekib said. She could still see Bobo Shahgul's crooked finger

351

pointing at her, her beady eyes filled with hatred.

The next week brought no revelations, no clues as to who had come to visit the harem. The only proof that Shekib and Tariq had not imagined the whole thing was that the visitor had returned. Just five days after the first sighting, he was seen again leaving the house. This time it had been Qasim's turn for night duty.

Qasim's description seconded what Shekib and Tariq had described.

"Did you go after him? Did you see his face?" Ghafoor had demanded.

"No . . . I only saw —"

"You just stood there? We're trying to find out who this is and you just stand there? Great job *guarding* the harem!" She threw her arms up in exasperation.

"He was walking so fast. I didn't think I should . . ."

"Forget it. It's fine. There's no point chasing this man down. He probably already knows that we've seen him and obviously he doesn't care. He's only concerned about getting caught by the palace. He knows we cannot do anything," Karim said with annoyance.

"What are you talking about? If Qasim would have had half a nerve, she could have —"

"Then you can take her night duty and you

can chase him down yourself!" Karim shouted. She was tired of hearing Ghafoor's complaints. Ghafoor pursed her lips but was silenced.

The bickering had seeped through the harem and into the guards' quarters. Their small troupe now felt the pressure and it was straining the thin friendships that had formed among them. Shekib watched as the cracks grew, week by week.

The man visited the harem about once a week and though we posted a guard at the side door, we were somehow unable to confront or identify him. By Ghafoor's account, he never appeared on her overnight shifts but the others doubted this. More likely, she was turning a blind eye since she too did not want to be the one to chase him down in the middle of the night. Better to find out from the woman and put a stop to it there.

In the meantime, Shekib decided to continue laying the groundwork for her own plans. She approached a few women with two purposes in mind. She asked if they had heard anything, any strange noises in the night. And she found ways to make mention of her own family. She awkwardly and clumsily told a story about them, about the string of boys her mother had borne, her aunts had borne, her grandmother had borne.

Women in our family have many sons. I was

the only daughter.

Curious looks. The women were not sure why the disfigured guard was sharing such information but they nodded politely and moved on. Or they shooed her off and crossed their brows. But Shekib persisted.

Something told her she did not have much time.

CHAPTER 34
RAHIMA

"She looked terrible, Khala-*jan*," I said. "I just never thought I would see my mother looking like that. Shahla would have been in tears to see her!"

It occurred to me, though, that Shahla too had likely changed. None of us were what we had been three years ago. Shahla now had two children. I thought of her when I looked at Shahnaz. I wondered how her new family was treating her. I prayed she was faring better than Parwin had.

"Rohila is a smart girl. I just wish they would send them to school." She sighed. "That's all I wanted for each of you. A bit of education that you could carry with you through life."

"What good did it do me?" I asked in frustration. "I went to school for a few years and it did absolutely nothing to change where I am now."

"You'll see later in life. Every bit does some good. Look at me. I'm lucky I know how to read. It's a candle in a dark room. What I don't know, I can find out for myself. It's easier to fool someone who can't figure things out on his own."

I bit my tongue. I still didn't see what use it was. Khala Shaima had been the only one of her sisters to make it to the eighth grade, since no suitors had come for her. Other than her being able to read a newspaper or a book here and there, I didn't see how her life was any better. She hadn't been able to stop anything from happening to my sisters or me.

"Your mother will be all right," Khala Shaima said, misreading the doubtful expression on my face. "The human spirit, you know what they say about the human spirit? It is harder than a rock and more delicate than a flower petal."

"Sure."

"Your mother is protecting herself. She's protecting her spirit, making the delicate petal as hard as rock with the medicine your father brings home because it's the only way she knows to survive. You should do the same, in a different way, of course. Don't forget that you are part flower petal and part rock too."

She sighed.

"That damn medicine. Now that Abdul Khaliq is your father's *damaat,* he can get as much as he wants. There was just too much of it for your mother to resist."

"They made out well in this whole arrangement," I said with more cynicism than I'd intended. Sometimes I saw my mother as a victim. Other times I thought of her as my father's coconspirator. Either way, my sisters were the ones who suffered. I looked at Jahangir and swore never to do the same to him.

"You can blame your mother but it won't do any good. You don't know what it was like to be in her position. In an ant colony, dew is a flood."

"But you said it too! You were the one telling her that she shouldn't give us away. I remember you arguing with her!"

Khala Shaima sighed and looked away, frustrated. "Of course I told her all those things! And she tried. She tried to talk to your father but he's —"

"I know what he is."

Khala Shaima quieted. She bit her lip. It was time to change the subject. "How has Abdul Khaliq been with you lately?"

"He's so busy with his own affairs that he's hardly around the house at all."

"Good. Busy with what?"

I shrugged my shoulders. "I'm not sure exactly but I heard him talking with his advisers and guards the other day. Something about his soldiers doing what the foreign soldiers can't do."

"Or don't want to do. He's got a good racket. These other countries come in here and throw a few bombs around. Friends today with yesterday's enemies. They just change their hats and all of a sudden, they're allies to these western countries. No one cares what Abdul Khaliq was doing for the past few years."

"What was he doing?"

Khala Shaima's lips pursed together. "He's your husband, Rahima, so I would have thought you'd have a better idea by now. How do you think he got to be so rich and power-ful? Off the blood of our own people, that's how. By ransoming, stealing, killing and then washing up and looking pretty for the west-erners who either don't know any better or pretend not to. Your husband is not the only one and he's probably not even one of the worst. You were too young to really know how things worked and no one in your house would talk about it since your father was fighting under him." Khala Shaima's voice was a cautious whisper.

I remembered how Shahnaz had come to be Abdul Khaliq's wife — pillaged from her home as if she were a piece of jewelry or silver serving tray.

"You should know these things, Rahima, since you're living here in this house. As his wife, no less. But don't speak of them, ever. Not even with his other wives. Understand me?"

I nodded. Her warning was unnecessary. I

already knew how loose the lips in this house were.

"His advisers were telling him he should have one of his wives run for parliament," I said, thinking of the conversation I'd overheard. "It sounds like such a crazy idea."

"Run for parliament? Those conniving bastards!"

"They really want him to. That would be a big change for him, Khala Shaima, wouldn't it? Imagine, one of his wives in the parliament."

"To hell it's a big change! It's a charade. There's a rule that a certain number of seats have to be filled by women. They made this rule part of the constitution because otherwise no one would give any woman the time of day. But he'll put one of his wives in and tell her exactly what to say, how to vote, who to talk to. It's no different than Abdul Khaliq taking the seat himself!" Her words were bitter, underscored by the way she spat some letters out.

I hadn't thought of the situation that way but Khala Shaima's reasoning made sense. And it explained why Abdul Khaliq was even considering the option. It was as his adviser had said — this might be the only way to keep control over the region.

"Did he say which wife he wanted to have run?"

"No, they didn't." I had wondered the same

359

thing myself.

"Probably Badriya."

"Why Badriya?"

"Because Jameela is too pretty. He won't want men's eyes on her. And you and Shahnaz are too young."

She was right.

Over the next few weeks Badriya was groomed for the election. Abdul Khaliq spent more time with her behind closed doors. We didn't know what they were talking about and Badriya was tight-lipped, or at least put on the appearance of being so.

"It's going to be a difficult election," she said, tapping her finger against her lips. It was obvious she was feeling very special to have been chosen for the task. "We've been discussing getting the word out, getting my name out."

"What kinds of things will you have to do if you're part of the parliament?" Shahnaz asked. It was a warm afternoon and the children were all in the courtyard. Abdul Khaliq had gone on an overnight trip and Bibi Gulalai was in bed, recovering from a cold that she said had nearly killed her three times over. The compound could breathe now that Bibi Gulalai swore she couldn't.

"Silly thing! Don't you know what the parliament does? Good thing it's me and not you that's running!"

I saw Jameela swallow a smile. We both

knew Badriya was trying to come up with an answer.

"It's a lot of work once you hold a *jirga* seat. There are things to vote on, decisions to make . . ." She waved her hand about as if it was just too much trouble to bother explaining.

Shahnaz raised her eyebrows. "But you're going to be covered, right?"

"Of course! I'll be wearing my *burqa.*"

"And if you make it into the parliament, then what? It's mostly men, isn't it? You'll have to go and meet with them?"

"Yes, that'll be my responsibility as an elected official. We'll have to talk about the voting, the issues."

"When are the elections?"

"In two months. There's a lot to be done." Badriya sighed as if she had just realized how much work awaited her.

Badriya, the first wife, had been accustomed to a status within the compound but she had started to resent all the attention the other wives were getting. This development was just the boost she needed to reclaim her distinction. But not all attention was good attention.

About a week after our conversation, I woke up in the morning, tied my hair behind my head and slipped on my work dress. I was to clean out the chicken coop. The smell always turned my stomach so I brought a square of

361

cloth to tie around my nose and mouth.

I walked outside and went to the far edge of the compound. The chickens were up early and clucked with excitement at my arrival. Feathers flew into the air, making me cough. I adjusted my mask and took a deep breath.

Before I could pick up my broom, the clucking heightened, and the chickens started to pace the area as if they'd been upset by something. I turned back toward the compound and saw Badriya walking behind the house. She had her left arm tucked in under her side and walked with a slight limp that made me think of Parwin.

I watched her and realized she hadn't seen me. She stopped at the clothesline and reached up to pull off a *chador* and a dress. It took her three tries before she was able to get the dress down; each time she reached upward, she would stop short and withdraw her arm sharply, shaking her head. I wondered what had happened and was happy for an excuse to delay my task anyway.

"Badriya-*jan! Sobh bakhair!*"

Badriya whipped around, her surprised expression interrupted by a wince. "Oh, Rahima! Yes, *sobh bakhair.* Good morning to you too. What are you doing back here?"

Her arm was still tucked in.

"I have to clean out the henhouse," I explained. "It looks like you're having a hard time with your arm. What happened?"

362

Badriya frowned. "It's nothing," she said unconvincingly. As she went to turn back to the clothesline, I caught a glimpse of her neckline and saw bruising around her collarbone. I started to say something about it but caught myself. She tried to move around as usual but her face betrayed her.

"Just get on with whatever you were doing, Rahima. I'm too busy to chat," she said dismissively. I walked back toward the chickens, looking over my shoulder to confirm that she was still limping. Hashmat met her at the door of the house and helped her in. He noticed me watching and shook his head. I kept my distance from him these days. By now I'd figured out that I shouldn't be around boys my own age or older, no matter what their relation to me. And I didn't want to invite any talk about Abdullah, who now seemed like a character I'd created in my imagination.

In the afternoon, I returned to Jameela's house. Most of the time, my son joined me while I did my chores, but cleaning the henhouse was impossible with him around. Jahangir had taken to spending time with Jameela while I was attending to some of the more taxing work. She enjoyed having him around now that her own children were grown and I trusted her more than anyone else. Even though I lived with Shahnaz, it was Jameela I turned to with every question about feeding and bathing Jahangir. She even knitted a sweater and cap for him to keep him warm through the winter.

"He hasn't been too much trouble, has he?" I asked, knowing what her answer would be.

"Oh, he's getting sweeter every day, Rahima. Tomorrow we should *espand* him, to keep the evil eye away. Before you know it, he's going to be talking his mouth off. You should see him trying."

"Have you seen Badriya today?" I asked, wanting to talk to someone about what I'd observed.

"No, are you looking for her?" She was feeding morsels of tea-soaked bread into Jahangir's open mouth.

"I saw her this morning, outside behind the house. She looks like her arm's pretty badly hurt. And she's not walking right."

"Hm. Did you ask her about it?" Jameela said, shaking her head.

"Yes, but she brushed me off."

"She expected too much." Jameela sighed. "A man has to feel that he's in charge of his home, at the end of the day. Especially a man like Abdul Khaliq Khan."

"What are you talking about?"

"You know it's not easy for him to agree to have her run for election. Her name has to be publicized in the area for people to vote for her; she will be talked about. And it will be big news that the powerful Abdul Khaliq's wife is out of the house, running for parliament. It's not what he wants."

I felt stupid for not figuring this out on my own.

"Last night, I heard him."

"What happened?"

"He warned her not to turn into one of those women, the kind who make a lot of noise, talk with lots of people. He wanted her to know that it was his decision to put her into the election and that it had nothing to do with her. I think he's heard her talking about it. That's not what he wants of his wives. I don't know what exactly she said but he was rough on her last night." Jameela shook her head and clucked her tongue. "It sounded like he was at his worst."

As much as her smugness had irritated me, I pitied Badriya. We all knew Abdul Khaliq's heavy hand. I wondered if Badriya regretted being chosen to run for the *jirga* seat.

"Is he still going to go through with it? I mean, to have her run for the parliament?"

"I think so. He wants the power. Through her, he would have his finger in a lot of different projects. He's not going to give that up, as much as he might hate to have his wife's name written on ballots and know that she's going to have to be away from the house sometimes to fulfill her duties. I'm sure he's trying to think of a way around all that anyway."

Abdul Khaliq had indeed taught Badriya a lesson. She didn't talk about the upcoming election after that. He met with her from time to time as well as his advisers. I caught bits and pieces of conversations. Things weren't going well. His advisers weren't sure Badriya would win the seat in the *jirga* but Abdul Khaliq had a way of convincing them.

My husband was used to getting his way. If he wanted Badriya elected, she would be.

CHAPTER 35
RAHIMA

Abdul Khaliq and Badriya traveled to Kabul frequently. He hated it. She claimed to enjoy it but we could see that she didn't. Abdul Khaliq was always tense before they left and even worse by the time they returned.

Badriya had won the election, mostly thanks to the women's votes, according to local news. To me and my husband's two other wives, it seemed unreal that something as important sounding as the parliament would let women vote. Khala Shaima had come by again. I asked her about my family and Bibi Shekiba. She asked me about Badriya and Abdul Khaliq. By this time, my naïveté had been washed away. I knew just what kind of man I was married to and I knew he had done terrible things to people. Jahangir, my son, was starting to look like his father, which frightened me. Sometimes I worried I might grow to dislike him if he did. I cringed when he became angry or frustrated, his shrieks taking on a familiar hostility. But his moods were nothing in comparison to his father's and he was otherwise very loving and affectionate, pulling my face to his and patting my head as if I were the child and he the parent.

Khala Shaima's breathing was more labored today. It could have been the dust in the air, her waning health or my own paranoia. She was the only family that I had left and I often worried about what I would do without her visits. I prayed for her health selfishly.

"He's telling her exactly how to vote. She's got no choice but to follow his orders."

I nodded. "You should see how exhausted she looks every time they return from Kabul. She looks completely drained."

"But there must be some way, some way for her to vote on her own. He doesn't go into the parliament, you know. Once she's in a session, he's not there to sway her."

"I'm sure he's got ways of knowing or watching every little thing that happens behind those doors." I pried Jahangir's small hand open and took away the stone he had found. He had watched his older half brothers playing and now wanted to imitate them. His round eyes lit up when he saw them, his mouth broke into a wide grin and he would pull my face and point for me to look at what he was seeing.

"Yes, *bachem,* I see them. You're going to grow up to be just as big and strong. Just wait." Sometimes I tried to imagine what he would look like in ten years but my mind couldn't envision him as anything but the sweet toddler he was. When I tried to picture myself in ten years it was frightening. My hands were already rough and knobby. My back ached at night, partly from carrying Jahangir for nine months and partly from being bent over to wash clothes and scrub floors most days. This home, this life, had aged me. Maybe that was what Parwin had seen, life in ten years. Maybe it was a sight too ugly to bear.

Everyone needs an escape.

"Maybe you can go to Kabul with her," Khala Shaima suggested. She started to cough, a rough cough that rattled her whole body. I put my hand over hers and pushed a glass of water closer to her. "Thank you, *dokhtar-jan.* Bah! The dust is irritating me more than usual today."

I hoped that was all it was.

"Anyway, what was I saying? Yes, why don't you see if you can go to Kabul with her?"

"What am I going to do in Kabul, Khala-*jan?*"

"Who knows," she said vaguely. "But in Kabul you'll see different things. It's an education of sorts. See how people live there, see the buildings and see what the parliament is doing. It's an opportunity for you."

The idea was tempting. I wouldn't have

369

minded seeing what the big city of Kabul looked like. I'd only heard about it through the story of Bibi Shekiba, which I hoped Khala Shaima would continue today. It was as if she read my mind.

"I know you enjoy hearing about your *bibi* Shekiba. She lived in Kabul, you know. It's a different life there."

"But you've never seen it, have you?"

"Look at me, Rahima! I'm thankful my ragged bones bring me this far. When I was younger, though . . ." Her voice softened. "I did dream of going to Kabul. I wished a carriage would come down the road, pick me up and take me to see the presidential palace and the shops and the streets and the airport. I wanted to see all the places I had read about."

That was her escape, I realized. Where her body couldn't take her, her mind went.

"Maybe you could go now?" I suggested. The yearning in her voice made me wish she could go.

"My time has passed. But think about it. Badriya is going back and forth between here and the city. It shouldn't be a big deal for her to take you along. Offer to help her."

"Help? The only help she needs of me is right here, washing, scrubbing, ironing, rubbing her back even . . ." The list went on and on.

"I know Badriya's type. I doubt she can

read. I wonder how she's managing that with her role in the parliament. Let her know you can read and write. That would be a much better way for you to be useful to her."

That was true. Badriya had never learned how to read. I'd once seen Hashmat reading her a letter from her family. She listened eagerly as he deciphered the scribble. She wasn't alone. Most women in our village didn't know how to read. My sisters and I had only learned thanks to Khala Shaima's insistence. Rohila and Sitara may not have been getting the same opportunity, I thought, now that Madar-*jan* had retreated into herself and Khala Shaima's health was not what it used to be.

"She can't read. Neither can Shahnaz. Jameela can read a little bit, I think."

"Well, there you go," she said. She leaned forward and exhaled slowly, her lips pursed. "Talk to her, nicely. I think it would be good for you to see the places your *bibi* Shekiba saw."

The idea excited me even more once she brought up Bibi Shekiba. I had already experienced her double life, living as a boy. I wanted to see the places she'd seen. But I wanted more than she had too. I didn't want to be a pawn the way she had been, passed from one set of hands to another. I wanted to be bolder. I wanted to make my *naseeb,* not have it handed to me. But from what my mother had always said, I didn't know if that was possible.

"Khala Shaima, do you think you can change your *naseeb*?"

She raised an eyebrow. "Tell me this, how do you know what your *naseeb* is?"

I didn't have an answer for her. "I don't know. Madar-*jan* said it was my *naseeb* to be married to Abdul Khaliq. And for Shahla to be married to Abdul Sharif and Parwin to be married to Abdul Haidar."

"And what about this morning? What did you eat for breakfast?"

"I ate a piece of bread with tea."

"Did someone bring you the bread?"

"No." I nearly laughed at the thought of someone bringing something to me. "Of course not! I got it myself."

"So maybe this morning it seemed it was your *naseeb* that you shouldn't have any breakfast at all. And then what happened?"

"I changed it?"

"Maybe. Or maybe it was your *naseeb* all along that you should have the bread and tea. Maybe your *naseeb* is there but waiting for you to make it happen."

"But wouldn't people say that is blasphemous? To change the *naseeb* that Allah has for us?"

"Rahima, you know how deeply I love Allah. You know I bow before God five times a day with all my heart. But you tell me which of those people who say such a thing have spoken with Allah to know what the true *naseeb* is."

That night I lay awake thinking of what Khala Shaima had said. Jahangir breathed softly, tucked in next to me, his small hand on my neck.

Was it Parwin's *naseeb* to die that way, her skin a mess of melted flesh? Or had she missed an opportunity to change things? To realize her actual *naseeb*? Was it Madar-*jan*'s *naseeb* to lie dazed with opium while Rohila and Sitara fended for themselves? Dodged my father's angry rages on their own?

It baffled me. I sighed and pulled the blanket over my son's shoulders. I traced his pink lips with my finger. His face twitched in his sleep and the corners of his mouth turned up in a dreamy grin. I smiled.

I didn't know what my *naseeb* was, much less that of my son. But I decided that night I would do whatever I could to make it the best *naseeb* possible. For both of us. I was not going to miss any opportunities.

From what Khala Shaima had told me about Bibi Shekiba, she looked for chances to make her own *naseeb*. I, her great-great-granddaughter, could do the same.

CHAPTER 36
SHEKIB

Shekib's heart pounded; her mouth was dry. Amanullah was again walking through the gardens. Shekib was standing at her post, just a border of shoulder-high shrubs between them. He was walking with the older man again, his friend. Shekib recognized him by his wool hat. They took a seat on a bench and made Shekib's palms sweat.

It was naseeb *that they should walk through here now, while I am on guard.*

"There are many forces at play here. Your father will have to tread carefully. We are mice in a field of elephants but if we are smart about our moves, we can save ourselves from their heavy feet."

"The problem is that we have unrest within our borders and unrest at the borders. Our attention cannot lag or we will be weakened." Shekib could hear the respect in Amanullah's voice. He trusted this man.

"This is true. But the two are linked. A country secure in itself will stand strong against those who eye it hungrily. And those who eye us know that troubles at home make for easy prey."

"Our army is weak compared to theirs."

"But our will is strong," he said firmly.

Amanullah sighed thoughtfully.

Shekib stiffened at the sound of his breath. She took a step to the right and then two to the left, stirring to make her presence known.

"Our people know so little of what goes on outside these borders. They are barely aware what happens one province, one village away from their own."

Shekib held her breath. She wondered if Amanullah realized it was her. Her back was facing the two men but she kept her head turned just slightly, her right profile to them — if they had bothered to look. They stood and walked back toward the palace. Shekib could not resist the opportunity to look at Amanullah when she was close enough to see the color of his eyes. She twisted at the waist and looked from the corner of her eye.

He looked back. A nod.

He looked! He nodded! He saw me!

Shekib felt her breath quicken. Nearly an hour passed before she realized that Agha Baraan, too, had nodded in her direction, a subtle acknowledgment. She rubbed her moist palms on her uniform pants. She had made contact with Amanullah. He had noticed her and nodded. She had not detected any repulsion in his expression, not an ounce of disgust. Was it possible? Could Amanullah have looked past her disfigurement?

The afternoon reenergized her. She needed more contact with the palace, with anyone outside the harem. But the guards were insulated, were they not? Shekib considered the situation. She had more freedom than the concubines. She could travel the palace grounds without restriction. She could interact with the servants who came to deliver meals to the harem.

Karim came to relieve her of her post.

"You can get some dinner. I think they were going to bring the carts over soon."

"I am not that hungry yet, actually. I may just go for a stroll."

"Whatever you want. Just keep your eyes open. It's been weeks and we know nothing."

The women were tightlipped. Each guard had her own suspicions but the questions they asked had gotten a spectrum of useless and curious answers.

Shekib traversed the gardens, passed the statues, the pond, two soldiers talking quietly to each other, eyeing her from afar. She looked out at Dilkhosha Palace, impressive and forbidden. She wanted to see inside but she had no business there. She let her imagination tell her what might be within.

Maybe there were doves inside, graceful white winged birds that fed on warm palace bread and chirped blessings for the monarch. Or perhaps there were mountains of food, delicacies baked by cooks to tickle the king and queen's palates.

Things were so different here in Kabul, in the palace. So many things Shekib had never before heard of, things she had never heard her parents speak of. She wondered if the palace thought of the villages as much as they thought of these other things. Why were they so preoccupied by these Russians, whoever they were, when villages were struggling without water?

She was so lost in thought that she hadn't noticed Agha Baraan sitting on a bench, sheets of paper in his hand.

"As-salaam-alaikum," he said gently.

Shekib turned sharply. When she realized who it was that had startled her, she turned her shoulders and head so her right faced him.

"Wa . . . wa-alaikum as-salaam," she whispered.

He turned back to his papers, reading thoughtfully.

Shekib took a step to leave but realized she had walked into a rare opportunity. Here was a link to the palace, a man very close to Amanullah. There were no walls between them, no interferences. She could speak to him, if she could make her voice follow her command.

"I . . . I guard the harem," she said simply.

Baraan looked up, his brown eyes surprised. "Yes, I remember. We saw you earlier today by the courtyard. You have an important position here in the palace."

Everybody has a role in the palace.

"Yes. And it seems you do as well."

He chuckled. "That will depend on who you speak with."

"What is it that you do?"

"What do I do? Well, I am an adviser, you could say. I work with one of the viziers. An assistant to the assistant, so to speak."

Do palace people always speak in riddles? Shekib wondered, thinking of his earlier conversation with Amanullah. "Are you in the army?" she asked. Her voice no longer trembled. His demeanor, his voice, his words told her he was not a threat.

"I am not. I work with them but I am not a soldier myself."

"I don't know anything about Kabul."

"You are from a village. That is not surprising."

There was condescension in his voice but Shekib chose to ignore it.

"What is your name?"

She paused before she answered. "Shekib."

"Shekib, I see. And the name your parents gave you?"

"Shekiba."

"Shekiba-*jan.* My name is Agha Baraan. I

378

am pleased to make your acquaintance. Is your family nearby?"

"I have no family." The words rolled off her tongue before she could reconsider. But it was the truth. Bobo Shahgul and her uncles had made that abundantly clear.

"I am sorry to hear that."

Shekib suddenly remembered her plan. If she wanted to change her *naseeb,* she could not waste an opportunity like this. She tried to recover from her misstep.

"I mean, I had a family but now I live here. I no longer see my family. But I had many brothers. I am the only daughter in a long line of sons. My aunts all had boys. My grandmother too."

Agha Baraan's lips tightened slightly. He looked away for a moment before returning to Shekib. "Their husbands must be happy."

"They were." She fidgeted; her tongue felt thick with lies. He watched her. She wondered if he had sensed the dishonesty in her voice.

"Are you content here in the palace?"

"Yes . . . mostly." Shekib hesitated. She was not sure how much to say. "The palace is beautiful."

"It is. You are in Kabul, in the king's palace, the heart of Afghanistan. It is here within these walls that history is made."

Such grandiose talk, she thought, but she let her expression reveal nothing. "The king's son." She could not bring herself to utter his name. "He is an important man?"

"He is and he is not."

"That's not possible."

Baraan raised an eyebrow. "Why is that?"

"Because he either is or he isn't. He cannot be both," she said bluntly.

He chuckled again. "You disapprove of contradictions. Well, you are ill prepared for life in the palace then. These walls are home to all that is and is not."

Two soldiers walked by and looked at them curiously. Shekib saw one whisper something to the other. She turned away from Agha Baraan abruptly and straightened her back.

"I need to get back to the harem."

She was clumsy and unrefined, Baraan thought, but interesting in an odd way. He wondered how she had gotten her scar and how much of what she had said was true.

CHAPTER 37
RAHIMA

Badriya looked surprised.

"It's just that you look like it's bothering you. You've been holding your back all day long. I think you'd feel better if you let me rub it."

"That's just what I need. You're right. I have some oil here. Let me lie down." She wasted no time leading the way back to her bed, where she stretched out on her side, her back to me. She wiggled her dress up to her neck, looking over to make sure the door was closed.

I dipped my fingers into the tin of animal fat and started to knead into her back. Rolls of skin hung loosely around her waist.

"Wooeee wooooeee," she moaned. I rolled my eyes. She tended to complain about her back only when there was something to be done around the house. Other times, she loved to point out that she was more active than Jameela and even Shahnaz, who were both much younger than her. Just another

381

one of her contradictions.

She was putting on a good show now, although it wasn't necessary.

"*Akkkh,* you're young. You have no idea what aches and pains are. Have a couple more children and you'll see. My back, my knees, even my neck! Every part of me hurts from morning to night. And the road from here to Kabul is long and bumpy. My muscles get so stiff that by the time we get to the city, I can barely straighten my legs."

I kneaded harder, knowing she loved the attention. She had brought up Kabul, though, and I searched for a way to broach Khala Shaima's idea.

"Are you going back to Kabul soon?"

"In about three weeks. The parliament is meeting again. We have to vote on a couple of laws and there are some subjects up for discussion. Things you wouldn't understand."

My massage must have relaxed her. She was falling into her old habits and boasting about her position. This was what had gotten her black and blue under Abdul Khaliq's fist before she'd even taken the seat in the *jirga.*

"It must be a lot of work for you to do while you're there."

"Oh, it is. It's a huge responsibility. And going back and forth from here to Kabul is exhausting. It's not easy."

"You must be so tired." My tongue felt heavy and awkward saying things I didn't mean. Badriya hardly lifted a finger around the house and her children were mostly grown. They helped her with what little she had to do. And if she was so happy to have been elected to the seat in the *jirga,* then she should have been happy to travel to Kabul.

"I am — I am so tired. Push harder here," she said, pointing somewhere in her lower back.

I told myself not to huff. My fingers started to cramp but I dug my palms in where she had pointed. I needed her cooperation for the plan that was starting to take shape in my mind. Khala Shaima had planted a seed.

"You know, I was thinking, maybe I could help you in Kabul."

"You? Help *me*?" Badriya balked. I gritted my teeth. "You're young, just a girl! You know nothing about the *jirga* or what goes on there. It's government business, not child's play."

It had been a long time since I'd had time for any kind of child's play. And, as Khala Shaima had explained, Badriya had no experience or knowledge to qualify her to participate in the parliament. She was there only because Abdul Khaliq wanted her to be.

"I just thought I could help you with some of the smaller things, like filling out any paperwork or reading through the Kabul newspapers . . ."

Badriya's breathing paused. I could feel her hips tense under my hands. "You . . . you wouldn't mind that kind of thing? You can read?"

"Sure."

"And you can write too?"

"Yes."

"And you can do it well? Not just a couple letters here and there?"

"Yes. I got high marks in school on writing and reading. Better than my classmates," I said before reminding myself not to reminisce too long on that time of my life.

"Hm. I'll think about it. It's a demanding job and I could use some help with it . . . but I wonder what Abdul Khaliq would say. You know he doesn't like for us to be away from home. He made an exception for me," she said with an arrogance that could not be contained.

"He is different with you. I think it would be best if you would explain to him that I would be there for you, to make things easier on you. Because obviously he likes you best."

She looked satisfied with my reasoning. For a moment she forgot how often Abdul Khaliq called me to spend the night with him. As if the night was not bad enough, I always had Badriya's bitterness to look forward to the following morning. Once she beat me with her sandal for breaking a plate when she had seen her son knock it from my hand. Everything was reported back to our mother-in-law, who took exceptional pride in reinforcing my punishments.

"What about your son? Jahangir is still young. You would leave him behind? Bibi Gulalai is not going to like that idea."

She was seriously considering my proposition. I hadn't thought my idea through so I spoke slowly, making it up as I went along.

"I think I could bring him along. He's not a difficult child so I don't think he would disturb you much. I could look after him in Kabul and still help you out." I stopped myself before I said anything about Bibi Gulalai. She hated everything I did anyway.

"I don't know if Abdul Khaliq wants his son traveling to Kabul." She seemed skeptical but I felt an opening. I pushed it.

"Just bring it up with him. Please. I think I could be useful to you."

"But why? Why do you want to do this?" She turned around to see my face. Her eyes narrowed to slits. I shifted and moved my hands to her shoulders, trying to divert her attention.

"Because . . . because you have so much to do and I thought . . . well, I've always wanted to see Kabul. I thought this would be a good chance. As you said, Abdul Khaliq makes exceptions for you, so maybe if you discussed it with him, and told him that I could help you . . . maybe he would agree?"

She closed her eyes and let out a sigh as I worked my way over to her shoulders. She liked the idea. Now we just had to work on our husband.

I hoped she would be as convincing as I was.

Every time I asked her about it, she shrugged me off. She either hadn't had a chance to ask him or she had forgotten, or he wasn't in the right mood to bring it up. Her next trip to Kabul was coming up soon. Two weeks away. One week away. I became discouraged. She didn't have the nerve, even though I knew she liked the idea. A few days after I approached her, she'd asked me to read a few things around the house. I think she was testing me. Not that she could tell the difference but she seemed reassured that I actually could make sense of letters.

When just two days remained Badriya finally approached Abdul Khaliq. The way Badriya told it, he wasn't excited by the idea, but after much cajoling, she managed to get him to agree. I asked her again when I brought her the dresses she'd asked me to press.

"Make no mistake, he wasn't for the idea at all. And for all the reasons I had predicted. I really didn't think that even I could get him to agree, but he did. So there you go. You got your wish. We'll leave Sunday to be there in time for Monday's session. You'd better make yourself very useful to me there or I'll regret going to such trouble for you."

"You won't regret it — you'll see! Thank you so much! I'd better pack some things for me and Jahangir!"

"Just you," she said, and turned her back toward me. She put the clothes directly into a duffel bag. "You won't need to pack anything for Jahangir."

"Why not?" I asked, confused.

"He's not going. Abdul Khaliq says he's too young to travel. He said Jameela can take care of him while we're away."

I became tense. I'd never been apart from Jahangir. The mention of leaving him made my heart fall. Should I insist? Should I stay behind?

"Oh, I didn't think . . . he said that? For sure?"

"For sure? Do you think there's any mistaking what Abdul Khaliq says? It's always for sure, Rahima. Just pack a few clothes together. Jahangir will be fine with Jameela. She's got a soft spot for little children."

I squirmed still. "How long would we be gone for?"

"Rahima, enough with these idiotic questions. Parliament is in session for four months. I've been going back and forth to get things prepared and we get breaks."

"Breaks for what?"

"Breaks are for us to come back to the areas we represent. To meet with people and get an idea of the issues at home."

"But you've never met with anyone."

"Do you think Abdul Khaliq would have me running around town talking with this and that one? Honestly, it doesn't matter. No one is checking up on us and I don't think any of the others actually go back to talk to constituents. Who needs to? I'm sure everyone in this region has the same issues we do."

"And what issues are those?"

Badriya looked frustrated. "Maybe you don't have enough to do around the house! Have you been sitting and thinking of nonsense to ask me? You won't be talking with people in Kabul but you might be seen, so bring your nicer clothes. Not that ratty blue housedress you always wear."

The ratty blue housedress. I'd worn it so much I could almost see through the material, as Shahnaz had snickered and pointed out one day. I'd been embarrassed but it was hard retiring it. The navy blue reminded me of a pair of blue jeans I'd happily worn for a few months. Denim. In denim, I had been free to run down the block, to walk with my best friend's arm around my shoulder, to kick a soccer ball between the goalkeeper's legs. That ratty blue housedress was my freedom flag, but no one else knew it.

"How long would we be gone?" I was calculating. I knew Badriya had made several trips back and forth in the last session but

I'd never paid attention to how often she came back for a break.

"Two weeks, I think. Then we come back for a short break before heading back to Kabul . . . that's the way it goes."

"Two weeks? Oh, wow. Two weeks . . . I suppose I could . . ."

"You *suppose*? You brought this all up, so don't be such a child about it."

She wants me to go with her, I realized, and nearly smiled. *She needs me.* It almost felt like I had a card to play.

I learned later how things really worked. Badriya, like all the other parliamentarians, was given a stipend to hire one assistant, one driver and two personal security guards. So far, Abdul Khaliq had been garnering her stipend and salary since he'd already sent her with his own driver and guards. Unable to do any of her own paperwork, Badriya had been going to the director general's office more often than any other member. They were tired of seeing her and had insisted that she find an assistant as soon as possible or they would take part of the stipend away.

It was an empty threat but an assistant would make things easier for everyone.

But I didn't know how things worked at the time. I surely didn't know that Abdul Khaliq and Badriya were doing what so many other parliamentarians were doing too. It seemed that no one in Kabul followed up on money. Or promises.

All I could think was that I could do this. I trusted Jameela would take good care of my son. Maybe this would be good for Jahangir and me in the end. Anything had to be better than waiting on every person in this house.

"All right," I said in agreement, thinking this might be my crossroads, my *naseeb*.

CHAPTER 38
SHEKIB

When Shekib had first arrived at the palace, she could barely make eye contact with anyone she came across, even the women. She had been veiled for so long and had worked in homes where people wanted neither to hear nor see her. The first time she'd crossed paths with a soldier, her heart had nearly pounded out of her chest because he'd muttered some unintelligible greeting to her. The second time, it was a gardener. It took an hour for her hands to stop trembling and for her to get over the awkward eye contact they had made.

It was hard for Shekib to believe that she could look directly at a stranger and speak. Instinctively, she wanted to run away. But as days passed and her legs grew more confident in their pants, she slowly became more accustomed to small interactions. She forced herself to speak with the other guards and listened when they spoke with each other.

Some days, Shekib came across people who

worked in the palace, not just outside it. Each time, it became the slightest bit easier for her to strike up a conversation. And inevitably, she would find a way to interject something about the long lineage of sons in her family. She wasn't very deft about it, but that was of no concern to her.

It had been a year since she had first arrived at the king's palace. She walked the grounds with confidence. She knew more about each concubine than she had thought possible. She had watched their children, the king's children, take their first steps, write their first words. Habibullah seemed to be a good king, according to the palace workers. He had expanded the network of roads across the country. He had founded a military academy and other schools.

King Habibullah was gone for weeks at a time and occasionally returned with a new concubine, girls, doe-eyed and nervous. Shekib watched as the new consorts floundered until they settled into the harem.

Everybody has a role in the palace.

New concubines made older concubines purse their lips and reconsider their position. Sakina grew feistier, gave the newcomers facetious advice and stayed silent for days when King Habibullah passed her over for a fresh face. Benazir had given birth to a little girl. She had named her Mezhgan and lined her eyes with kohl, as Halima advised.

Fatima had grown pale in the last few weeks. Her son had just turned a year old but spent a good deal of time with Halima, since she rarely had enough energy to keep up with him. Her illness unnamed, she was visited often by the harem's physician, a British woman named Mrs. Brown. Kabul had only male doctors, which would not suit the king's insecurities. Mrs. Brown had been brought in from abroad, a kind but firm woman who satisfied the monarch in both her competence as well as her demeanor. She stayed at the palace and traveled back to England infrequently. Mrs. Brown ("Khanum Behrowen," as the women called her) placed her stethoscope on Fatima's chest and back, her hands pressed into her belly. She would sigh and tap her forefinger against her lips, thoughtful.

Despite its tensions, the harem was a family. The older women were mothers to the younger concubines, while the younger consorts had rivalries with each other like siblings with only one toy. King Habibullah visited when he chose, appearing sometimes in daylight and other times well into the night. He came with minimal fanfare but he made no secret of his visits. Unlike the other man.

The other visitor, whoever he was, came rarely. The guards would almost believe he had tired of his mistress when he would make another appearance, always under the cloak of darkness. He must have known the guards had seen him and probably surmised that they felt powerless to stop him. Whoever he was, he boldly betrayed the king with the most sinful trespass and then returned to slumber in his palace.

Shekib wondered who could be so brazen. And why.

Amanullah stayed closer to the palace while his father ventured out into the country to check on the roads he had commissioned. He came to the harem's courtyard from time to time, leaning over to pat his younger half siblings on the back, ruffle their hair and kick a stray ball back in their direction. Shekib watched him, her heart beating in odd tempos, wistful and hopeful. He would acknowledge her and give her a light smile, a formal nod. Like a secret handshake between them, Shekib thought.

I probably look a bit older than him but I haven't outgrown the possibility of marriage. I am young yet, able-bodied and strong. I hope the others have told him about me, how I help the gardeners replant shrubs, how I carry the children when they grow sleepy, how I bring trays of food into the ladies' quarters. My back is as strong as that of any soldier in the palace, my arms solid and my mind rational. Think of me, Amanullah-jan, and I am certain I would not disappoint a man like you.

Shekib was not the only one thinking of Amanullah's *naseeb*.

King Habibullah also believed it was time for his son to be given a bride. In his mind, there were a handful of contenders — daughters of the viziers or his closest advisers. In his own words, words Shekib overheard one day as she stood outside his suite in the harem, "I cannot force his hand. He will choose for himself, my boy. Amanullah is different than his brothers. He is more like me than the others. And so unlike me in other ways. I sometimes wonder how I would feel about him were he not my own son."

Shekib felt a clock ticking. Amanullah would choose a bride soon. She charged ahead with her humble efforts. She found a reason to speak to nearly anyone who crossed her path and made certain to mention that women in her family rarely bore anything but boys.

She saw him again with Agha Baraan. They crossed the palace's grounds, returning from a meeting at Dilkhosha Palace. Shekib dug her hands into her pockets and looked around. She floated in and out of genders easily now, aware of her flattened bosom and hidden curves only in Amanullah's presence. She tingled for him. She hoped he knew.

The men stopped at the bench. Agha Baraan plucked a red rose, breathed in its perfume and stuck it in his blazer pocket.

Shekib was a good distance away but slowly and casually made her way toward them, pretending to inspect the shrubbery as she wandered over. Once seated, their view was blocked by the greens and they were unaware of the woman-man guard at their side, eavesdropping and flirting.

"So you have decided?"

"I am ready, Agha Baraan. I think it is time for me to take a wife. I want to have a legacy of my own and I must start a family to do so. I want to have at my side a woman who is thoughtful and who will be as dedicated to Kabul as I am. I am confident in my decision. She is strong-willed and has undergone hardship; people have turned against her and yet she walks with her head held high. When I see her face, I see that she brings with her a gentle understanding because of what she has experienced."

Shekib froze. *Her face? Could he be talking about my face? Yes, people have turned against me! Nearly everyone has turned against me! But I would work so hard for Kabul! I would do anything he needs!* She did not move, terrified that she would give her presence away.

Maybe Agha Baraan had told him about her? Maybe he had shared those morsels she had laid out for him and maybe they knew she was listening at this very moment.

"And what will your father say? I mean,

given where she comes from . . ."

"I know that, but it was my father and this palace that introduced me to her."

Shekib's eyes widened. Indeed, it was King Habibullah who had brought her to the palace and into his son's life. She straightened her shoulders, wanting to comport herself as a palace woman would.

"I will speak with him again tonight. I have brought this up before but he did not believe I was serious."

Baraan took a deep breath.

Shekib said nothing to the other guards but for two days they shot each other looks, noticing a change in her. Ghafoor had to repeat herself three times before Shekib would notice she was talking. Karim and Qasim watched her meals go barely touched and shared her leftovers when she walked away. Tariq tried to approach her, to talk about her dreams of motherhood. Shekib blankly nodded and shook her head in a way that told Tariq she might as well have been talking to the pigeons.

Two days passed as such. In the nights, Shekib stared at the wall, pictured Amanullah's face and imagined how someone from the palace might approach her with his proposal. Where would she live? She would grow her hair. She would wear makeup, as some of the women in the harem did from time to time. A British woman visiting the palace had brought rouge and powder, showing the women how to lighten their complexions and bring an alluring tint of color to their cheeks. Shekib wondered if the powder could conceal her disfigurement, her half mask.

On the third night, Shekib was on duty. She stood outside the harem, watching the palace and wishing her mother was alive. She took longer than she should have to react to the footsteps and talking inside the harem. Halima was at the front entrance just when Shekib was starting to realize something was going on.

"It's Fatima! She's not well. We need to send for the doctor!"

Fatima had taken a dramatic turn for the worse and with it, Shekib's *naseeb* changed course.

CHAPTER 39
RAHIMA

The road was bumpy. My sides ached with every jolt. Badriya watched me from the corner of her eye. The experienced first wife wasn't surprised. Last night Abdul Khaliq had asked me to visit him. I entered his room quietly. Although I was no longer a new bride, the nights with my husband still repulsed me. I had to take my mind elsewhere, think of the chores I still needed to do or school days when the *moallim* would teach us to sing our multiplication tables to memory.

Whenever my wifely obligations were fulfilled, I would wait to hear my husband's snores, a signal that I could put myself back together and retreat to my room. Last night was different.

Badriya and I were set to leave in the morning for my first trip to Kabul. I was excited but anxious about leaving Jahangir behind. Abdul Khaliq's even breaths told me he was relaxed but not yet asleep. I took a chance.

"I wanted to ask something . . . ," I said hesitantly. I looked for the combination of words that wouldn't anger him right away. He looked surprised to hear me speak. With a raised eyebrow, he told me to explain.

"Tomorrow . . . because I will be helping Badriya-*jan* . . . I was hoping I could take Jahangir with me so that —"

"Jameela will watch him."

"But I didn't want to trouble her. She's already got her own to look after."

"He'll be fine."

"And I want to be sure that Jahangir eats well. Sometimes he can be so picky . . ."

I had said too much.

"Then don't go!" he thundered. "It was an idiotic idea to start with! Now I have to listen to you nag! You appreciate nothing!"

He was up now, the sheets pulled behind him, leaving my legs uncovered.

"I'm sorry —" I started to say, hoping to stymie the reaction I could see coming.

It was too late. Abdul Khaliq spent the next thirty minutes making me regret I'd spoken.

I realized then my husband understood people. He knew just how to get to people to do what he wanted, to make them angry or sad or fearful. I realized that was probably how he had been successful at whatever it was that he did.

Morning came and I kissed my sleeping son before laying him on a cushion in Jameela's

400

bedroom. I touched his cheek and watched as his lips turned slightly in a dreamy smile.

Jameela bit her lip when she saw my face. My cheek was starting to turn a deeper red, a bruise in the outline of a hand taking shape.

"He'll be fine, Rahima-*jan*," she said warmly. "I'll have Jahangir sleep right next to me with your blanket. We'll talk about you until you come back. This will be good for you, you'll see."

I was grateful and knew Jahangir loved being with her and her children. Still, I hated to leave my son.

Two weeks, I thought. *We'll be back in two weeks for our first break. It's not that long, right?*

I ran my fingers through his dark locks once more and leaned over to kiss his head. He turned onto his side, his perfect lips parting just wide enough for me to see his petite teeth.

"It's okay, Rahima-*jan*. He'll be fine, you'll be fine. You'll see," Jameela said. She hugged me delicately, knowing one bruise heralded the presence of others.

I carried my duffel bag out to the car. Bibi Gulalai and Badriya were outside, as was Hashmat. He looked over and smiled snidely.

"Good morning!" he called out.

"Good morning," I mumbled, my mind still on Jahangir's soft face. I was in no mood for Hashmat's facetiousness today. "*Salaam,* Khala-*jan*."

She ignored my greeting. "You're ready for your trip to Kabul I see. I don't know how you could leave a young boy to go off doing things you've no business doing. My son is being kind in allowing this, so you better make yourself very useful to Badriya."

"That's right," Badriya echoed.

"I doubt she'll be worth the trouble she'll cause," Bibi Gulalai muttered.

Hashmat laughed. "Isn't that nice that you'll be joining Madar-*jan* in Kabul! I bet all your classmates would be jealous if they knew you were going to see the city," he said.

I shot him a sharp look that went unnoticed by Bibi Gulalai and Badriya. Hashmat made a point of talking about my *bacha posh* days and my male classmates as often as he could. He used to do it in front of his father but it sometimes resulted in such an explosion of anger that he would be caught in the overflow. Something about me as a *bacha posh* had piqued Abdul Khaliq's interest, but now he could not tolerate hearing about me even sitting next to boys in school.

Abdul Khaliq's guards put our bags in the back of the car. We donned our *burqas* and climbed into the backseat.

Don't speak to the guards. They'll watch out for you but if you do anything . . . let me assure you . . . you'll regret it. And in Kabul, I have people. I will hear about everything you do. If you do anything to embarrass me, I promise

402

you that you'll wish you never stepped foot in that city.

He was clear. I was thankful Jahangir was too young to cause much trouble. Abdul Khaliq's temper came hard and fast and often without warning. I had asked Jameela to make sure Jahangir did not get in his father's way. I wouldn't be there to shield him.

These thoughts played over and over until the rough road finally lulled me to sleep in the backseat. Badriya was in no mood to talk. She leaned her head on the window and started to snore lightly.

I don't know how many hours passed before structures came into view again. There were buildings, houses, horses and cars. I sat up straight. We were in a jeep with tinted windows so I dared to look out and see what the people of Kabul looked like. My mind jumped to Bibi Shekiba and her first impressions of the capital, as Khala Shaima told it.

I was the same, wide-eyed and amazed, but in a different way. I had never seen so many cars and people in one place! It looked as if everyone who lived in Kabul owned a car. And store after store, the streets were lined with exotic wares and different foods. Bakeries, tailors, even a beauty salon! This was so different from home. I wished Shahla could be here to see it all with me. Or the boys. There were so many places we could have explored if we'd grown up here!

"Kabul is . . . Kabul is amazing!" I exclaimed.

Badriya seemed entertained by my reaction. "Of course it is! There's a lot going on here. We won't have time for me to point everything out to you." I saw Maroof and Hassan in the front seat look at each other. It was unlikely Badriya had actually seen any of Kabul. She had complained to Jameela that the guards took her from her hotel to the parliament building and back. "We're almost there. We're going to be staying at a guesthouse run by some Europeans."

Down a tree-lined street, a building came into view.

It had a gated entrance flanked by porticos with stone pillars, Through the main entrance, a wide path led to and encircled an imposing tower with a flag flapping from its summit. I craned my neck to get a good view.

That tower reaches the sky! I thought.

The palace's façade was embellished with carvings and arches, dull and chipped, but it surely once looked very majestic. A woman walked past the front gate, her green-yellow head scarf pulled across her face, hiding everything below her nose and cascading down her shoulders. As we drove past, she turned slightly and looked directly at my tinted window, her eyes meeting mine as if she could see through it. This first glimpse of a Kabuli woman was exciting for me, a girl from a village.

"What's that building?" I asked, already knowing the answer.

"That's Arg-e-Shahi, the presidential palace."

"Bibi Shekiba . . . ," I whispered. I got a chill thinking of how my great-great-grandmother must have felt when she first saw those gates. And to think of what she had seen on the other side. As usual, Khala Shaima had left her story unfinished. The turn of events in her life was unpredictable. I wanted to know what became of her almost as much as I wanted to know what would become of me.

"God have mercy, what the hell are you mumbling about?"

Badriya's question went unanswered. I stared at the palace, where my legacy began. *What happened to you here?* I wondered.

Maroof turned left, then right and left again, weaving through the crowded streets and cursing every car in his path. There were tanks and soldiers in fatigues and helmets. They didn't look Afghan. These were the foreign soldiers Badriya had told us about. Just like my husband's guards, they had large guns hanging at their sides. Little boys stood in front of them, looking curious. The soldiers laughed and chatted casually.

"Are they American?" I asked Badriya.

"They're from everywhere. Some are

American, some European or whatever they are." She pointed to a building coming up on our left. "We're here," she announced.

"Is this where you always stay?"

"Yes, it's a nice place. You'll see."

Badriya was right. We pulled up to a metal gate on a small street, tucked away from the busy market.

Our driver rolled down his window when we pulled up to the blue-uniformed guard at the gate. He mentioned Abdul Khaliq's name. I thought the men were shaking hands but I realized Hassan's fingers held a folded stack of bills that the man slipped into his pocket.

I looked over at Badriya but she either hadn't noticed the exchange or didn't care.

Hassan opened the gate and our driver, Maroof, pulled into a circular drive that looped in front of the largest building I'd ever seen. It was three stories tall with rows of windows lined up like a hundred eyes. Two columns framed the glass, double-door entrance.

"And this is where the meetings are?"

"No, you fool. The *parliament* meets in the *parliament* building." I was too excited to be annoyed with her condescending tone.

We were led into an elegant lobby with a reception desk. A man wearing a crisp dress shirt and slim pants was talking on the phone, but he nodded when he saw our driver and the other guard. He cradled the receiver and looked up at our guards. I stood behind Badriya, not wanting to make an inappropriate move. Three women walked in from outside dressed in fitted tunic tops and denim pants. Their head scarves were demurely tied under their chins but wisps of hair framed their faces and their delicately arched brows. Their shoes got my attention most. Black leather pumps broke the silence in the room.

Looking at their clothes, I was thankful the *burqas* hid our faded, baggy dresses. I felt suddenly unsophisticated and awkward. I tried to hide my feet behind Badriya. The women were busy talking and hardly noticed us.

The conversation between Abdul Khaliq's bodyguards and the man at the reception desk went back and forth until finally there was another handshake. Another wad of bills slipped into the receptionist's palm and from there was quickly tucked into his jacket pocket, while he made a quick glance around the room to make sure no one else was watching, not that anyone would have cared.

We were led to a room on the third floor with two single beds and a bathroom with a western toilet. The window looked out on the courtyard behind the hotel, a small stone area surrounded by flowering plants and shrubs. I saw a pigeon waddling in the shade of a tree.

Like the palace gardens where Bibi Shekiba used to stand guard, I thought.

"I can't believe this is where you stay in Kabul! No wonder you like coming here so much!"

"Don't get used to this," she said, opening her duffel bag and pulling out a sweater.

"Why not?"

"Because we'll be in an apartment soon. Abdul Khaliq is only using this place temporarily. He's been looking to find a place in Kabul where we can stay with more privacy, only his guards outside."

"Has he found a place yet?" I asked.

"How the hell should I know?" she replied. She sat on the bed and took her sandals off. Her heels were cracked and yellow. She rubbed one of her soles and sighed. "Look, Rahima, I know why you're doing this. Don't think I'm stupid."

I looked at her but said nothing. I thought it best I let her explain.

"But as long as you help me with what I need to read and write for these meetings, then I don't care much. Just don't expect to see much of Kabul."

Badriya was right. Our personal guards kept to themselves but were never more than twenty feet away. Most of the time they stayed in the small seating area on the third floor, just two doors away from our room. I hated knowing that Abdul Khaliq was keeping tabs on us at all times, but Jameela had told me about the threats against parliament members, especially the women, so there was something comforting about knowing Abdul Khaliq's trusted bodyguards were watching over us in this new, busy town. I felt safer because of them.

Work started the following day. Our guards drove us to the parliament building in the morning. We wore our *burqas* until we got there. Badriya slipped hers off and instructed me to do the same. I looked over at the guards to see their reaction. They had turned away but watched peripherally while we entered a long and stately building with a row of columns before it.

People walked in and out, men and women who looked to be from all different regions. Some of the men were dressed in the flowing caftans and pants common to our village, their heads wrapped in turbans, one end cascading over a shoulder. But it was the women who made my jaw drop. Some were dressed as we were, in simple flowing calf-length dresses with loose pants underneath. But others wore button-down shirts and long flowing skirts. Some even wore jackets and slacks. They wore their colorful head scarves smartly. As we got nearer, I could see that a few women wore lipstick or rouge, while others had outlined their eyes with kohl. I wondered what their husbands thought of them walking uncovered, with painted faces.

We came to a security station. Four uniformed guards stood at the entrance, two men and two women. The mass of people slowly melded into three lines. Badriya took me by the elbow and led me past the others. She paused briefly when she came to the security guard, dressed in the same khaki color as her male counterparts but in a long skirt.

A woman guard. Just like Bibi Shekiba, I thought. I couldn't help but stare at her face, wondering if she looked anything like the woman I'd heard so much about.

Badriya muttered a quick greeting and waved at her. The guard nodded and turned her attention back to the woman in front of her. She pulled her behind a partition.

"What are they doing?"

"They're here for security. They're checking people for weapons. That room back there is where the female guards check the women. We're not supposed to bring anything into this building. And we're not supposed to take anything out of it either."

"We don't have to go through the checkpoint?"

"Well, we're supposed to but I don't. The guards know me. And no one else from the parliament goes through either. We are the parliamentarians, after all! How ridiculous if we were to be patted down every time we walked in! I wouldn't stand for it!"

I bit my tongue, knowing she would stand

for it if she were ordered to.

Badriya smiled politely to a few people she knew. Two women, wearing dresses and longer head scarves, approached with bright and cheerful faces.

"Badriya-*jan*! Good to see you again! How are you? How's the family doing?" They were of similar height and build and even face structures. But their ages differed by about ten years, the older woman's face with more lines, her hair with more wisps of gray.

Cheeks pressed to one another, kisses in the air, an arm around a shoulder. The women greeted each other.

"Sufia-*jan, qandem, salaam*!" My eyes widened to hear Badriya greet her with such syrupy sweetness. "Thanks be to God, everyone is well. How are you and your family doing? And you, Hamida-*jan*? How are you?"

"Fine, thank you. Ready for another busy session?" Hamida replied. Her face was plain, unpainted and serious.

"Yes, I am. When do you think it will start?"

"They said we should be starting in half an hour," Sufia said, scanning the entryway. She was the older of the two. There was gentleness in her eyes that put me at ease. "But my guess is that we don't have enough people here. We'll probably begin in about an hour. Maybe two. You know how it is."

Badriya nodded politely and was silent.

She doesn't know what else to say to them, I

411

thought.

"And who do you have here with you? Is this your daughter?"

Hamida and Sufia were looking at me expectantly and smiling. I looked at Badriya and felt the urge to step away. I didn't like the idea of her being mistaken for my mother. She didn't like it either, but for different reasons.

"Her? Oh, no, she's not my daughter. She's my husband's wife."

"Your husband's wife? Oh!" Hamida's smile tightened. She disapproved.

"Have you brought her to see how the parliament runs?" Sufia asked, trying to distract us from Hamida's reaction.

"Yes, er . . . she wanted to see for herself what it is that I do. That we do. So I've decided to hire her as my assistant."

"Oh, she's going to be your assistant! What's your name?"

"Rahima," I said. "I am pleased to meet you."

"And we're pleased to meet you as well," Sufia said, looking impressed with my manners. "I think it's a great idea for you to come see what the parliament does. Maybe you would want to join your . . . er . . . Badriya-jan and take a seat in the *jirga*. We need women to get involved in our government."

Badriya nodded but looked uncomfortable.

"Why don't you both come to the resource

412

center tonight? After the session is over."

Badriya shook her head. "No, we can't make it. Some other time."

"Why not, Badriya-*jan*? They have some instructors there who have helped us very much. Tonight we're going to work on the computers. It's not easy. You really have to spend some time to figure those machines out. It would be good to get familiar with it."

"I know that. I've seen computers. It's not that hard," she said, her eyes shifting nervously.

The look on my face confirmed for Hamida and Sufia that Badriya was not in the least familiar with computers. Hamida decided to ignore the obvious lie.

"What else do they teach there?" I asked. I had been away from school for so long. The idea of instructors and lessons excited a part of me that Abdul Khaliq's compound had buried.

"They teach lots of things," Sufia said, happy to hear my curiosity. "How to speak English, how to do research, how the parliament is supposed to function . . ."

"It's a school? Can anyone go?"

Hamida nodded. "You could come, as her assistant. It's only for women parliamentarians. It's run by a foreign organization and it's open after the sessions end for the day. Maybe you can convince Badriya-*jan* to come along. There are too many people doing nothing in this building. We all need to do something more."

"Excuse us, ladies. I want to show Rahima-*jan* around the building and then we're going to get to our seats," Badriya said, her fingers wrapped around my elbow firmly. She wanted out of this conversation.

I followed her lead but my heart lightened at the talk of classes. I was starting to taste the possibility of change here.

CHAPTER 40
SHEKIB

Shekib stood frozen.

"Don't just stand there! She needs the doctor. Go and get Khanum Behrowen!" Halima threw her hands up in frustration. Shekib nodded and turned around but stopped short, realizing she had no way of summoning the doctor without walking right into the palace in the middle of the night. She turned back to the guards' quarters.

"Ghafoor! Ghafoor, wake up. We need to get the doctor for Fatima. She's ill and needs help."

Ghafoor, the consummate guard, bolted upright and answered the call to take charge.

"She's ill? Worse than before?"

"I suppose so. I haven't seen her."

"What? You haven't even gone in to check on her? What were you . . . never mind! Karim, get up. Go and see how Fatima is doing. Take Qasim with you. I'll go to the palace and ask for the doctor."

"What should I do?" Shekib asked.

415

"Nothing. You can do that much, can't you?" Ghafoor said with annoyance. She brushed past her and went to pull on her uniform quickly. She fastened her belt brusquely before shooting Shekib one last glare.

People from the palace will be awakened. I should resume my duties, she thought, and returned to her post outside the harem. Karim and Qasim soon walked past her and entered the harem. Tariq, hating to be alone, followed after them, her arms folded against her chest in the cool night air. She half smiled through tight lips as she passed Shekib.

Shekib tapped her foot. She could see the way they looked at her, the distance. The same look Khanum Marjan had given her — some pity, but no friendship.

I am on my own, Shekib thought. *Nothing has changed.* She began to pace in front of the harem, walking around to the side entrance and making sure she looked like she was actively guarding the building.

Ghafoor and Dr. Behrowen emerged from the darkness. Ghafoor carried a lantern and Khanum Behrowen a black bag, their pace hurried. Two men followed behind them, sent to observe and bring word back to the palace. Shekib turned to walk back to the front entrance when she heard a door open. Before she could turn, she had been pushed aside, just roughly enough to make her stumble.

She braced her fall with her hands and knees and looked up to see the man's back as he darted off.

She started to call out after him and then caught herself. She looked over at Ghafoor and the approaching team from the palace. They hadn't seen the man knock her down, nor did they see him disappear behind the shrubs. She kept her mouth shut and scrambled to get back to her feet. She wanted to meet them by the front entrance.

"The others are inside with Khanum Fatima," Shekib announced as they approached. "I am standing guard here." She made sure to be loud enough for the men to hear. They stood back, rubbing their hands together and speaking quietly as they watched the women enter the harem. "Should I come in with you?"

Ghafoor did not pause. "Do whatever you wish," she called out from the foyer.

Shekib followed them in. The hallways were lit with multiple lanterns. They followed the sounds to Fatima's chamber. It was a small room toward the back of the house. Nabila and a few others stood in the narrow hallway, shaking their heads and muttering to each other. Inside the crowded room, Shekib could see a circle of women. Sakina sat behind Fatima, holding her head up on her lap. Fatima's face looked wan, even in the amber glow of the lanterns.

Dr. Behrowen knelt at Fatima's side and opened her bag. She laid a hand on her forehead and called out for some wet cloths in rudimentary Dari. Halima rushed past Ghafoor to bring them. The doctor picked up Fatima's wrist and placed two fingers on it, her forehead tightened and her lips pursed. She took out her stethoscope and bent over Fatima with her head turned to the side, listening carefully. The chatter in the room had grown louder with the doctor's arrival. She finally lifted her head up and pointed an angry finger toward the door.

"Hush! Step outside if you wish to chat!" Though they did not understand English, the room was immediately silent.

Beads of sweat lined Fatima's brow, like soldiers preparing for battle. She moaned softly and turned her head to the side. Her son began to whimper and pulled at her sleeve. Benazir picked him up and whispered something into his ear that quieted him, his bottom lip still curled out.

"She is feverish. I want to bring her to a cool bath. Ladies! Help her to the bath area!"

The women looked at Dr. Behrowen, puzzled by her instruction. Dr. Behrowen had learned a few words of Dari over time but most of her communication with the harem was through gesture. Sighing with frustration, she motioned for Sakina and Nabila to lift Fatima and then pointed at the doorway.

They nodded and Karim and Qasim jumped in to help. Grabbing limp arms and legs, they carried Fatima into the hallway. Dr. Behrowen pointed toward the bath area.

"Aab, aab!" she called out.

"She wants us to go to the baths!" Qasim called out. They hurried down the hallway. Khanum Behrowen pointed at a shallow bath and instructed the women to place Fatima in the water.

"We have got to bring her temperature down," the doctor muttered to herself. "She is burning up."

Fatima reacted to the water, but Qasim held on, her hands under Fatima's armpits to keep her head above water. She looked more awake, more alert, turning her face to Khanum Behrowen.

"I feel so weak, doctor," she said.

Dr. Brown nodded. That much was already clear to her.

"What's going on in there?" It was a man's voice echoing from the front entrance. The women jolted at the sound. Ghafoor looked up at Shekib.

"Go and tell them she has a fever and that Dr. Behrowen is bringing it down. Go!"

Shekib nodded and hurried to the front door. The two men were pacing just outside the entrance. They were growing impatient.

"She has a fever. She is in the bath now to bring it down. She is weak."

"Is she going to be all right?"

"I don't know much more than this. Dr. Behrowen will have to tell you."

They huffed, dissatisfied with the answer but helpless to find out more for themselves.

Shekib returned to the baths. They had pulled Fatima out of the water.

"Let's have her lie down!" Dr. Behrowen pointed at the nearest door, just a few feet down the hallway. It was Benafsha's room. The door was closed.

"Khanum Benafsha, open the door please!" Ghafoor called out. She knocked a second time, louder, when there was no answer. "Khanum Benafsha!"

"Please, I am sleeping!" she called back. The women looked at one another in surprise.

"Khanum Benafsha, please, this is an emergency. Khanum Fatima is —"

"Oh, may God have mercy. Just open the door!" Sakina said angrily, and pushed the door open into Benafsha's chambers. Benafsha's mouth opened in surprise to see them lay a pale-faced Fatima on her floor. Benafsha's face was flushed and she had pulled a robe around her nightgown. Someone had thought enough to bring dry cloths and a dry gown for Fatima. They began to strip her wet clothes when Sakina looked over at Benafsha.

"What is the matter with you? You can hear us, can't you? She's not well!"

Benafsha bit her bottom lip and rubbed her eye. "I was sleeping. I didn't hear anything."

"You must sleep well if you —" Sakina paused. "What is that?"

A dozen eyes followed her finger.

On the floor of the room, behind the door, was a gray lamb's-wool hat. A man's hat.

Benafsha's mouth gaped. Her face grew as pale as Fatima's.

"This is a man's hat!"

She was speechless. The women looked at each other, slowly realizing the implications. Benafsha tried to recover.

"It is his, it belongs to our dear Habibullah . . . come on, Sakina, what are you trying to . . ."

"It's you, isn't it? The guards have all been asking about strange noises, any odd events! It's you they've been asking about! Where's Ghafoor? Where's Karim? Here!" Sakina stormed to the door, picked up the hat and waved it wildly in the air. "Is this what you've been looking for? Benafsha dares to have a lover!"

"Sakina, you tramp! Watch what you say or you'll regret it! I don't have to answer to you! You of all people with your . . . your . . ." Her eyes searched the room for an ally. Unfortunately, in her time in the harem, Benafsha's haughty attitude had made her no real friends. She looked at Tariq, her eyes pleading. Tariq looked away, her face conflicted.

Benafsha's attempts to retaliate failed. Her eyes welled with tears and her tongue floundered as she looked at a room of hostile stares. Only Dr. Behrowen's attentions stayed on Fatima, who had been stirred both by the cool bath and now by the fresh scandal. She had propped herself up on her elbows, her bleary eyes looking around with the others.

Sakina could hear the panic in Benafsha's voice. She pounced.

"Well, if it is Habibullah's hat, then we can just take it to him and ask him to confirm it. That's easy enough," she said sweetly. She pushed the hat into Benafsha's face and then tossed it to Ghafoor. Ghafoor looked at the gray hat with almost as much trepidation as Benafsha. Her mind scrambled, knowing nothing good came from bringing bad news to the palace.

Benafsha was crazed.

"Sakina, sisters," she cried, looking around the room. "You can't possibly think . . . please, don't say such things about me to Habibullah! He will think things . . . he will . . . please! I have never been unkind to any of you! Please just stop and think before you act on such wild ideas!"

"Wild? Look who talks of wild!"

"*Khanum-ha,* please! Hush!" Dr. Behrowen grew frustrated with the storm of tears and screaming. Her patient still needed attention. "I don't know what you women are arguing about but surely it can wait," she muttered.

"Sakina, let's consider this a moment," Halima said, her voice feigning calm. "Let's just stop for now and focus on Fatima-*jan*. We will address this later. Let's see what Khanum Behrowen needs for the moment."

Shekib watched but her ears tuned out the talking. She saw nervous glances, hot whispers, tongues clucking. There was pacing, head shaking and hot tea. Children walked in and were sent back out. Benafsha's green eyes blurred behind tears. She pitied herself. She hated Sakina.

Shekib noticed something the others had not. A single red rose petal on the floor, trampled under the many slippers of the king's concubines.

Shekib knew exactly whom Benafsha had welcomed into her bed.

CHAPTER 41
SHEKIB

Fatima's condition improved. Benafsha's worsened.

The harem was tense. Periodic updates were sent to the men outside. Nothing had been said yet about Benafsha, but it was just a matter of time. A matter of hours. Some of the more sensitive women had regressed into their own chambers, knowing the palace, the king, would not take Benafsha's transgressions lightly. She had made a fatal mistake and they could do nothing for her.

No one wanted to break the news to the palace, fearing they would strike broadly at anyone remotely involved.

"Have mercy, please. Have mercy," Benafsha whimpered in the corner. She was on her knees, her head touching the ground in supplication.

The guards and a few of the concubines had gathered outside her room. Fatima had been returned to her own chambers, Dr. Behrowen still at her side.

"It should be one of the guards," Sakina decided. "You are the ones responsible for the happenings of the harem. It is your duty to report back to the palace what happens here."

"What if we say nothing?" Nabila suggested meekly. "I am sure she will put an end to this sinful behavior after tonight. She looks as if she's suffered enough now."

"You would dare hide this from the king? And what if he comes to find out some other way? We will all be blamed!" Sakina said. "I can't take that chance with my life."

A few others nodded, agreeing with Sakina's reasoning. What if the men outside had actually heard everything? What if they were going to report everything to the king? The harem had to be forthcoming if they were to save their own hides.

"Khanum Sakina, maybe it would go easier on the king's ears if he were to hear it from someone he fancies. And since you were the one who made the discovery, I am sure he will reward you for sharing this with him and putting an end to such a shame," Ghafoor said.

She is impressive, thought Shekib. *She could have Bobo Shahgul's blood in her veins.*

"You are talking as if it is your first day in the palace. You know very well that you are the ones who report to the king's people. We, women of the harem, are not to be involved

425

in this discussion. I will not hide anything from my dear Habibullah but it is not my place to march up to his chambers and make such an announcement."

Ghafoor chewed her lip and looked at Karim. She shook her head, having nothing to add to the argument. Ghafoor grew more nervous, knowing that, as leader of the guards, she was responsible for direct communications with the palace. The onus sat heavily on her shoulders. She could be rewarded for her service or she could be struck down for bearing such devastating news. She motioned with a subtle tilt of her head for the other guards to follow her into the foyer. A quick peek outside confirmed that the two men were idling by the far end of the courtyard, their backs to the harem.

"Karim, why don't you and Qasim go and ask those men for a chance to speak with the king directly. It may be worse for this message to go through too many ears before reaching his."

"With all due respect, Ghafoor-*jan*," Karim said facetiously, "since you have always been in charge of our troupe, this does not seem to be something you can delegate out like a night shift. Neither one of us would dare infringe on your responsibilities."

"Nor us," Tariq said, glancing at Shekib. She, too, felt the need to pair up with someone.

Ghafoor huffed. "Fine. Fine! Cowards. I'll go and speak to them myself." Her eyes betrayed her confidence. She paced the foyer for ten minutes before putting her hand on the doorknob.

Karim had her ear to the door, trying to listen in, but the voices in the courtyard were hushed. The guards looked at each other, paced and sighed frequently. Eyes were bloodshot with fatigue and conflict. When Karim cracked the door open ten minutes later, the courtyard was empty. They had taken Ghafoor to the palace.

An hour passed, painfully, before Ghafoor reappeared. Qasim and Karim had fallen asleep leaning against the foyer wall. Tariq sat near the door as if ready to make a quick escape. She tapped her foot nervously. Her eyelids were heavy and dark. Shekib sat against the wall opposite the sisters, her stomach uneasy. A house under stress had never boded well for her. She had no reason to believe she would emerge from this unscathed.

Ghafoor looked about nervously and took stock of the situation.

"How is Fatima?" she asked quietly, her eyes shifting around the room, hesitant to land on anyone in particular.

"She's a little better. She's had some tea with sugar and was talking for a bit. Now she's fallen asleep. Dr. Behrowen left a few

427

minutes ago. You probably passed her on the way here," Tariq said, her voice as exhausted as her eyes.

"Good."

"Aren't you going to tell us what happened?" Karim asked impatiently.

"I spoke with the men outside and they took me back to Agha Ferooz, our king's most trusted adviser. They did not want to disturb the king himself. I explained the situation and they are, of course, very upset. They notified the king."

"And? What will happen now?" Qasim asked.

"He is angry. He wishes to speak with Shekib."

Shekib was not in the least surprised.

"What is that they want to speak to me about?" Her tone was measured, even. It made Ghafoor nervous. She looked at the others while Shekib saw through her act.

She's done something.

"How should I know?" she said defiantly. "They asked me who was on night duty tonight and I gave them an answer. I had better check on Khanum Fatima. There's a soldier waiting outside, Shekib. He'll escort you to the palace. I'm sure it's not a big deal."

Shekib was sure that it was.

But she said nothing, staring at the back of Ghafoor's bobbing head as she scampered down the hall, putting distance between them as quickly as she could.

The others watched her leave and then turned to Shekib. She said nothing but rose and walked to the door. As Ghafoor had promised, outside stood a soldier. A baby's face in a man's uniform. He looked nervous in the brisk dawn air. He motioned for her to follow, turning back once to steal a glance at her face.

He walked her to the palace's heavy front doors, intricately carved and oddly inviting even at this moment. He opened the door and led her in, down one long hallway with ornate patterns on the walls, gilded pedestal tables and richly embroidered chairs. Shekib noticed her surroundings with vague interest.

"In this room," he announced, and cracked the door open enough for her to enter. He stayed back and looked thankful that his duties ended there.

Shekib entered, remembering to keep her back straight and her eyes focused. Weariness was blurring her judgment as well as her vision.

In the room, King Habibullah paced behind a handsome wood-carved desk, his fingers pulling at the fringes of his beard. Two men sat anxiously in armchairs to his left, opposites of each other. One was heavyset and short, the other tall and lanky. Had Shekib been less nervous, she might have noticed how ridiculous they looked as a pair. They

429

looked up at Shekib, their lips tightening.

"You!" King Habibullah called out. He had stopped pacing abruptly, his blue *chappan* flapping as he whirled to a stop.

"*As-salaam-alaikum,* Your Highness," she said in a hush, keeping her head bowed and her eyes downcast.

"*As-salaam-alaikum,* eh? As if nothing has happened? Do you know the meaning of the words, you idiot?"

"I apologize, esteemed sir. I meant no disrespect —"

"Don't patronize me, guard! You are here to answer questions, to speak up for your actions — or inaction, as it appears! It was you who was on guard tonight, when a man somehow managed to evade your attention and enter *my* harem!"

A conversation began to take shape in Shekib's mind. She could imagine Ghafoor standing in this very room, not too long ago, painting a picture of an idle guard, passively allowing a man to violate the king's sanctuary, to indulge in his private stock of women.

"Dear king, I was on guard tonight but I saw no one enter."

"You saw no one enter? But someone did enter, didn't he!" His face was the color of the carpets on the floor. A blue vein pulsed across his forehead like a lightning bolt. He fell into his chair and looked at his two counselors expectantly.

"Guard, did you see someone leave the harem tonight?" The thinner man rose to his feet and spoke up.

Shekib did not have much time to consider her answer. "No, sir."

"And you saw no one enter?"

"No, sir."

"Are these the kinds of guards we have for my harem!" The king exploded, his fist rattling the table with a thunderous clap. "We might as well have brought donkeys!"

"Guard, explain to our dear king what happened tonight. Was there a man in the harem?" the lanky man demanded.

Shekib searched for the right answer, her hands trembling at her sides. She was afraid to move. They took turns shouting questions at her.

"Answer!"

"I . . . I did not see —"

"Don't tell us what you did not see! Tell us what happened!"

"Tonight we found a hat in one of the chambers." Shekib was not sure how to phrase such a finding. It was a sensitive matter and the wrong words could be dangerous. They were waiting for her to continue. "There was no one there but the hat . . . the hat suggested that someone . . . a person had been there. We asked but —"

"Whose chambers were you in?" the king asked, his eyes slits. He spoke slowly and precisely.

"We were in Khanum . . . Khanum Benafsha's chambers," she answered, her eyes cemented to the marble floor. Benafsha had shamed the palace with her iniquity but Shekib still felt reluctant to expose her. She pictured Benafsha back at the harem, prostrated, her face wet with misery.

Why did you do this? Why did you bring this upon us?

"Benafsha." Habibullah turned his back and faced the window. Heavy burgundy drapes framed his silhouette. "That vixen."

"Have you seen anyone before? Coming in and out of the harem?"

What did you tell them, Ghafoor?

"I . . . I have not."

"This was the first time you learned of this?"

"Yes, sir."

Three men brooded. Shekib could hear their measured breaths.

"You. You believe this happened once?"

"I . . . I . . . believe so."

"And who was it guarding the harem tonight?"

"I was, sir."

"You are a liar. We have heard differently. Ghafoor has already told us that you saw this man before! And you kept it from everyone until tonight!" the short man shouted.

432

"With respect, *agha-sahib,* I had not seen
—"

"Liar!"

Ghafoor, you scoundrel! You fed me to the lions!

It was clear now. Her word against Ghafoor's, and they were taking Ghafoor's. Shekib was not a bystander. She was a guilty party.

"Did you know of Benafsha's activities? Did she ask you to cover up for her?"

"No, sir! I had no —"

"What about the man? Who is he? Did he bribe you?"

"Please, dearest king, I had nothing to do —"

He barely heard anything she said. He was more interested in how this made him look.

"Know this, guard! An offense this grave does not go unpunished. My name has been besmirched. One look at your face and it is obvious you are damned! Have her locked up! And Benafsha too! We'll make swift examples of them both."

CHAPTER 42
SHEKIB

"Why did you have to do such a thing?"

"You wouldn't understand."

The room was dark and smelled of rotted meat. The stench reminded Shekib of cholera, of mourning and loneliness.

Benafsha's face had changed. Shekib was struck by the difference. Just eight hours ago, she had been the most striking woman in the harem. How quickly her face had grayed! Her hair was stringy and her green eyes looked defeated and bloodshot.

One of the king's most prized concubines. A life of luxury by any standards. The choicest foods, clothes. What had driven her to take all these for granted?

An hour passed in silence. Shekib wanted to ask her about Agha Baraan. She was sure it was him. The hat. The rose petal. But why? He was Amanullah's friend. Why would a man like him commit such an act against his friend's family, especially when his father was the most powerful man in Afghanistan?

"I am sorry you are here."

Shekib looked up. "So am I."

She thought of Amanullah. What would he think when he heard of the night's events? How disappointed he would be in her! She wasn't much of a guard, according to the palace. What made her think she could be much of a wife? Benafsha had ruined everything. She looked at the girl with disgust and pity. Then there was Ghafoor, that split-tongued viper. She had set Shekib up, saving herself. No wonder she had run off. Coward.

The dank room was unfamiliar but the rest of the experience was not. Angry fingers had often pointed at Shekiba.

On the king's orders, Shekib had been led away — through the hallways, through the kitchen and into the small room where the cooks once kept cured meats and vegetables. The room smelled of flesh and earth. Shekib closed her eyes and imagined her father's house. Her mind floated to those bare walls, her brother's shirt thrown across a chair as if he would run through the door looking for it. Her sister's amulet on the table. Her father, sitting in the corner clicking the beads of his *tasbeh* while he stared through the window onto fallow fields, a fallow home.

Shekib stood up and began to pace. The walls were tight but light crept in, framing the door with a yellow glow. The palace had electricity courtesy of a foreign company commissioned by the king. All of Afghanistan twinkled by lanterns but the palace shone, a beacon for the rest of the country.

The king must have his way. How much it must burn him that another man has had his way with his precious Benafsha. She's pretty, I suppose. If she doesn't show her teeth when she smiles. All pushed together, her teeth look like chickens climbing over one another in a crowded coop.

Benafsha had her head between her knees. Shekib couldn't tell if she was awake or asleep.

"What do you think they're going to do with us?" Shekib asked quietly.

Benafsha shoulders lifted and fell with a deep breath.

"How long do you think we'll have to be in here?"

Benafsha looked up. Her eyes were flat with resignation. "You really don't know?"

Shekib shook her head.

"When the crime is adultery, the punishment is *sangsaar*. I will be stoned."

CHAPTER 43
RAHIMA

The large auditorium, a room larger than any I'd ever seen, held hundreds of parliamentarians. Their chairs were arranged in rows that went from one side of the room to the other, leather chairs behind a row of desks. Each member had a microphone and a bottle of water.

Badriya's and mine sat in the center of the room, sharing our row with Hamida and Sufia. In the front of the room sat a man with a neatly trimmed mustache and salt-and-pepper hair. He listened, nodding his head from time to time.

The men intimidated me. Some of them were my husband's age, gray haired with beards that nearly touched their chests. Others were younger, their faces shaved and their clothes different from what the men in my village wore. Pants, button-down shirts, jackets.

As we broke for lunch during the first week, Hamida had asked me what I thought so far.

I was nervous to tell her, afraid I would sound stupid. And I worried that if they saw me reading and writing, they would realize how basic my knowledge was.

"They come from where?" I asked, astounded by the accents I was hearing.

"What do you mean?" She looked to see where I was pointing.

"I mean, I've never seen men dressed like . . . dressed like that." I pointed with my head to a man wearing brown pants and a military-style vest over a white shirt.

"That's what you'll see in Kabul, Rahima-*jan*," Hamida said, proudly. "This parliament is where every corner of Afghanistan comes together."

"Comes together?" Sufia scoffed. "More like this is where Afghanistan comes apart!"

Hamida laughed. A man one row away turned around and shot her a look. He shook his head and leaned over to mutter something to the man seated next to him, sharing his disapproval.

The session was called to order. Rahima tried to look around without anyone noticing. Badriya picked up a pen and held it to the blank paper before her as she watched the speaker. She was playing the part.

"Ladies and gentlemen, the matter of the president's cabinet members will now be introduced. Seven people have been nominated by the president. It is up to this parlia-

438

ment to approve or reject the nominations."

"Badriya, are we going to see the president?" I whispered. It was hard to believe I might come face-to-face with our nation's most powerful man.

"No, you fool! This is the parliament. He does his work and we do ours! Why should he come here?"

"We'll talk about the candidates one by one. I'll call on you to ask whatever questions you may have. We need to decide if these individuals are suited for the job. And if they'll help take our country in the right direction. First up is Ashrafullah Fawzali, nominated for position of minister of justice."

The speaker went on to talk about Fawzali's background, his home province and his role in training the police force.

A woman parliamentarian sat in the seat beside me. I heard her huff, frustrated. I watched her from the corner of my eye, slouched back in her chair and shaking her head. As the candidates' virtues and experience were extolled by a man who had taken the floor, she became more and more displeased, fidgeting in her seat and tapping her pen.

The next candidate was introduced, someone equally distressing to her. She raised her hand to speak but the director looked past her. She waved her hand more dramatically.

"Excuse me, but I would like to say some-

439

thing about this candidate," she said, leaning forward and speaking into her microphone. "Excuse me!"

"*Khanum,* the time for the discussion of this candidate is up. We're getting close to ending today's session. Thank you all, please return for tomorrow's voting. The parliament is dismissed."

"Of course it is! God forbid we actually talk about these candidates!" the woman hissed.

"Who is she?" I asked Badriya.

"The one next to you? Oh, that's Zamarud Barakati. She's trouble. Make sure you stay away from her," Badriya leaned forward to tell me. "She's one of those you don't want to get mixed up with."

"Why? What's wrong with her?"

"She's a troublemaker. You see what she did today? Always interrupting things. That woman's lucky they haven't condemned her to *sangsaar.*"

Stoning. I shuddered and thought of Bibi Shekiba.

As far as I had seen, Zamarud hadn't done anything that several other parliamentarians hadn't done. Just like the men, she had raised her hand and asked to speak. But I could see many people didn't appreciate hearing from her. Several men had rolled their eyes or waved their hand in annoyance to hear her ask for the floor's attention.

"She pushes her ideas too much. People

440

don't want to listen to her all the time." We were walking out the security checkpoint by this time. Our driver saw us coming and went to turn the car on. Our guard was already with him. Zamarud walked angrily past us, her own security guards struggling to keep up.

She reminded me of Khala Shaima, the only woman I'd known who would speak up to men outside her own family. I wondered what Khala Shaima would have thought of Zamarud. Picturing the two of them in the same room made me smile. They could have the entire parliament up in arms.

But what I saw in that first day was just the beginning. The parliament was a fiery mix of personalities and politics. There were so many women there, but only a few of them spoke during the sessions. And there was only one Zamarud.

As the discussion of the cabinet nominations went on, Zamarud became more and more agitated. She was given opportunity to speak and took the floor like a storm, questioning the intentions and honesty of the candidates. She implied that the candidates had been chosen for reasons other than their qualifications, since one was the president's brother-in-law while another was the president's childhood friend. And there was no diversity, she said critically. They were all from one sect of the Afghan population.

441

Afghanistan needed to represent all of its many colors, Zamarud insisted, or it would fall apart. Again.

On the fifth day of sessions, we took our seats. I missed my son more today and saw his round cheeks and almond eyes when I closed my eyes. I wondered if he was walking at this moment, one hand tightly gripping Jameela's. I wanted to hear his voice, the tiny sound of *"maada";* he was still unable to roll his tongue to produce the proper *"madar".*

Zamarud's voice brought me back.

"It's imperative that we think of the future of this country. We Afghans have become complacent, letting almost anyone take on these positions of power and influence. Let's think about it carefully and then decide."

"*Khanum,* I believe it would be wise for you to consider before you speak. There are many people here and you're not thinking —"

"I'm not thinking? I'm thinking about it a great deal! It's you and the rest of you that need to start thinking. I'm going to speak my mind right now."

Badriya looked over at me. Waves of anger were rippling through the room. The men were leaning over and complaining to their neighbors. Hamida and Sufia looked over at Zamarud nervously.

"From what I have seen, the nominations that have been presented thus far have been of men who worked alongside the most

442

sinister characters in our country's recent history. The money in their pockets comes from drugs, from alliances with warlords and mercenaries. They have the blood of their fellow Afghans on their hands.

"And there are candidates who are family members, getting special treatment from those in the highest position."

It was obvious she was talking about the president's brother-in-law, who traveled between Kabul and other cities like Dubai, Paris, London and Islamabad, importing and exporting goods. He had built a successful trade business and a life of luxury for his family. But everyone knew his business didn't account for all of his income.

"We must watch who we place in these official positions. They should be there for the right reasons, for the development and protection of our beloved Afghanistan. We have suffered enough in the hands of others in the last decades. Our people deserve to have right-minded individuals in power. I wonder, as do so many others, how it is that some of our nominees have been able to amass a fortune when our people go hungry. How is it that they are able to live lavishly when they are engaged in simple businesses? We all know the answer. We know that there are sources of money that are not talked of, that are not openly discussed. Bribes. Nepotism.

Drugs. These practices will bring our country down."

The room began to talk. Zamarud continued, louder.

"I will not stand for this. I will not approve the election of such people, brothers and cousins taking under the table what rightfully belongs to our country. Are we to sit here quietly and let them suck the blood of the Afghan people? Getting fat off of government money?"

"That's enough!" one man called out. Others echoed after him.

"Shut her up."

Zamarud went on, unfazed by their comments. She raised her voice over the protests.

"Every person in this room, every man and every woman, who would dare to approve these nominations will share the responsibility for keeping those lips greasy with the money that should go to the Afghan people, to the Afghan country. And for what? For a chance of fattening your own pockets! You know who you are. You come here and pretend to represent your provinces when really you represent nothing but your own pockets!"

"Who does this woman think she is?"

"I will not listen to this harlot babble on!"

The yelling became angrier. Hamida and Sufia, not far from Zamarud, had gone over and pulled her back to her seat. Sufia was talking to her, saying something in her ear, while Hamida put a hand over the microphone. We were close enough that we could still hear her.

"I will not be silenced! I have had enough of their nonsense! Which of you will speak up if I do not? Call me what you like but you know I speak the truth and it is you all that are damned for what you're doing! It's a sin! It's a sin!"

Two men went to confront her directly. Fingers were pointed, just inches from her face. I felt my body tense with their aggression. I wanted to pull Zamarud back but I sat frozen, my eyes wide. I prayed for her to stop talking.

The room was on its feet. Arms were waving. A group of men had gathered in a corner of the auditorium, pointing in Zamarud's direction and shaking their heads. Two other women had joined Hamida and Sufia in trying to restrain a belligerent Zamarud. Others were on their feet, watching the fray with interest or enjoyment.

I was nervous for her, as was every other woman in the room. I'd never seen a woman speak so boldly, so directly, and in a room full of men! Everything I'd ever seen in my life told me Zamarud wouldn't make it out the door.

"This is bad," Badriya muttered, keeping her head low. We had not stirred from our seats. "We can have no part in this, under-

445

stand me? Just stay where you are. We're going to leave just as soon as things calm down."

I nodded. The last thing we wanted was for Abdul Khaliq to get word we'd been involved in a shouting match between the parliament's most outspoken woman member and the group gathered by the door. They were men like my husband, older and with fearful constituencies back home. They were warlords.

Hamida walked over to us when things calmed.

"Unbelievable," she said. "These people are wild!"

Badriya nodded politely, not wanting to weigh in with an opinion.

"I mean, she's a bit bold, I'll give them that. Actually, she's a bulldozer. But she's right. Especially about Qayoumi. He has friends in the Ministry of Defense and they fed him every contract that came through their office. As if he needs any more money. Have you seen his car? His house?"

"No, I haven't," I said, intrigued. Badriya was so silent around these women that I almost forgot she was there. It was completely unlike her but she tensed, fearful that Abdul Khaliq would hear about any idle chatter.

"Let me tell you, his house is one of the nicest houses in Kabul. He tore down an old, run-down home in Shahr-e-Naw and then built himself a two-story mansion! And you know how expensive that area is! No Afghan can buy anything there. All those properties go for at least half a million U.S. dollars. At least!"

Half a million U.S. dollars? My mind reeled at the staggering amount.

"Half a million . . . ?"

"Yes, that's right! He'll do anything to get what he wants. Anything. He was a Taliban ally not too long ago and they pillaged one town, robbed the people of everything they had. Setting fires, lining up the men and killing them. By the time they finished with that town, whoever they left alive had only the clothes on their back. Sinful!"

"And they want to vote him in?" If this was common knowledge, why weren't people more upset about him?

"Yes, they do. That's how it is. For God's sake, warlords make up at least a third of the parliament right now. Those people who led the rocket attacks, the bloodshed — they're all sitting in this assembly room. Now they want to fix what they broke. It's almost comical," she said, shaking her head. "If I thought of it too much, I'd go crazy. Like Zamarud!"

Had I been anyone else, I might have been more surprised. But I was a wife of Abdul Khaliq, a man who inspired fear in every corner of our province. And I was sure I didn't know a quarter of what he had done in the years of war. Actually, I still didn't know what he did when he set out with his guards and his automatic weapons. Someone could nominate him for a post as well.

"What can you do? Our politics are full of people like that. But I can tell you, I won't be approving the nomination of that corrupt butcher. Sufia's talked to the other women. They're going to be rejecting him as well."

"If so many people are going to vote against his nomination, he won't stand a chance, right?" I watched Badriya, her lips pulled down in a frown. I was asking too many questions.

"He stands a very good chance, actually. Warlords make agreements, alliances, to serve their own purposes."

I wondered if Hamida knew who Abdul Khaliq was. I wasn't sure how far his name had reached. Where we came from, he held a lot of power and he was trying to grow that. Badriya's involvement in the parliament was a step in that direction.

"Hamida-*jan,* we're going to get a cup of tea from the cafeteria, if you don't mind," Badriya said. The conversation had touched a nerve. Her voice was stiff. "Can I bring you anything?"

"No, I'm fine, thank you. Let me go see what Sufia is up to. The session will probably resume in another thirty minutes."

In our hotel room that night, I asked Badriya about Zamarud's allegations.

"Is it true? Are there that many people in politics who are that corrupt?"

"Don't bother yourself with things like that. It's none of your business."

That angered me. I was fairly sure Sufia would not have agreed with her. "But it's yours, isn't it? You're going to be voting on those nominations tomorrow. Are you going to approve them?"

"Of course I am."

"Why?"

"Why? Because that's who I will vote for! Have you finished filling out that form yet? The director's office has been asking about it all week."

"It's almost done." I sighed. I wondered how Badriya had coped in her last stay in Kabul. She could barely scratch out her own signature. "But how do you decide how you will vote?"

"I decide, all right? I know what the issues are and then I choose."

I thought back to today's heated session, Zamarud's determined look. "Does she have a husband?"

"Who? Zamarud?" she snickered. "They say she does but I can only imagine what a mouse of a man he must be! Can you believe the way she behaves?"

"She's not afraid of them."

"She should be. Zamarud's gotten more threats than any other woman in that assembly. Not surprising, the way she carries on. Shameless," she said, clucking her tongue.

"You haven't gotten any threats, have you? Hamida said most of the women have. Her family begged her not to run for parliament again but she wanted to."

"She's another mule of a woman. I haven't gotten any threats because I know what I'm doing. I mind my own business and do only what needs to be done. I'm not here to embarrass myself or my husband."

I shuddered to think how Abdul Khaliq would put Zamarud in her place. But I didn't think Badriya had any special business in the parliament. My instincts told me it had something to do with our husband.

"This form asks if you want to join the group traveling other countries with parliaments. As a learning experience, it says. Europe. It says, 'the director highly recommends that all parliamentarians go to learn how other assemblies function.' "

Now that I was in Kabul, I was hearing of places even grander and more unimaginable, like Europe. I wondered what a place like that could look like. We'd come all the way to Kabul. Maybe we could go to Europe too? Badriya lifted her head, as intrigued as I was by the exotic name.

"Go to Europe? Really?" Once she'd said it, Badriya realized how ridiculous it sounded. "Forget it. Not interested. Put that damn thing away. I'm tired. You can finish it in the morning. I'm going to bed."

Chapter 44
Rahima

"We will now take a vote on the candidate Ashrafullah Fawzali. Please raise your paddles with your vote on his nomination."

The parliamentarians each had two paddles, one red and one green, which they raised to vote aye or nay in the assembly. This was the first vote to be taken and Badriya looked nervous.

"Are you going to vote for him?" I whispered.

"Shhh!" she hissed at me, her eyes scouting the room. Paddles were going up, many at a time. Badriya reached for the green paddle and raised it halfway, still unsure.

I followed her eyes to a man sitting toward the front of the room. From our position, we could see his profile. He was a burly man with a heavy beard and thick features. His gray turban sat coiled on his head like a serpent. He held a green paddle.

I saw him look in our direction, giving Badriya a subtle nod. Her green paddle went up and she kept her eyes fixed on the front of the room. I was puzzled. I didn't recognize this man but it looked like Badriya did.

"Badriya, what are you doing? Who is that?"

"Shut up! Just take notes or whatever it is that you're doing."

"But he's looking over here!"

"Shut up I said!"

I crossed my arms, shut my mouth and watched. That's how things went for the rest of the session. Each time the director asked the parliament to vote on a candidate, Badriya waited until this man raised his paddle. And each time she would pick the paddle that matched his. Green, green, red, green, red, red. And each time he looked over, his face was smug with approval to see her vote his way.

The ladies looked over at Badriya, seemingly confused. Sufia whispered something to Hamida, who shrugged her shoulders.

Qayoumi. It was time to vote on his nomination. I looked over at Hamida and Sufia. They were shaking their heads as the director prepared to take a vote. A small murmur wove through the assembly as the parliamentarians prepared to decide on one of the most controversial figures in Kabul. Tongues clucked with disapproval even before the paddles went up.

"Ladies and gentlemen, please raise your votes. Raise them high so we can see them!"

The man voted green.

I looked at Badriya. I was sure she could feel my eyes on her but she avoided my gaze.

She watched as the ladies both raised their paddles red. The representatives around them raised their red paddles as well. There were pockets of green here and there, almost all men.

The mumbling got louder as green paddles went up.

Badriya kept her head down and picked up her paddle. I opened my mouth to say something.

Green.

"Badriya! What are you doing? Didn't you hear what they said about him? Why are you voting for him?"

"Please, Rahima, shut up!"

Hamida and Sufia looked over, eyebrows raised. They looked away and leaned toward each other. I thought of our conversation with Hamida. I couldn't ignore everything she'd told us.

"But Hamida said —"

"If you can't shut your mouth, leave then! Just get out!" she snarled. "I don't need you."

I stared at her. There was nowhere for me to go. I sat beside her, fuming, even though I had no right to. Maybe I would have done the same if I were her. Maybe I would have aped the votes of the man in the corner.

Abdul Khaliq. He set her up for this. That man

must have something to do with that security contract he wanted to land. Just like Hamida talked about.

I was surprised only that my husband's influence was this far-reaching, into the parliament building of Kabul. And wherever that man was from.

Hamida looked over, her lips pursed.

Maybe I wouldn't have been like Badriya if I were in parliament. Maybe I could have been more like Hamida. Or Sufia. Or even Zamarud. Maybe I would have sat in that assembly seat and made up my own mind.

But I probably would not have. It wouldn't be easy to go home to Abdul Khaliq after going against his instructions. Especially in a matter this big.

The session closed for the day. Badriya rose quickly from her seat and gathered her bag. She made her way down the row and out the main aisle without turning around to see if I was following.

We ran into the ladies near the security check. Not even a polite smile. It was obvious they were disappointed in Badriya's voting. They could tell her reds and greens were decided by outside forces. She was part of the problem.

"I'm glad the day is finally over," Sufia said neutrally.

"Yes, so am I," Badriya said, agreeing demurely.

"Interesting day," Hamida murmured, adjusting her head scarf.

I watched the exchange, wanting to shout out that I wasn't part of this. I wanted to say that I wouldn't have voted for Qayoumi. Even though I was almost certain I would have. I was learning that cosmopolitan Kabul was, at least in that way, no different from my obscure village. Many of our decisions were not decisions at all. We were herded into one choice or another, to put it gently. I wondered if the other women representatives truly felt free to make their own judgments.

I sat in the car and leaned back, wishing I was home with Jahangir. He was probably taking a nap now, his mouth half open and his eyelids fluttering with innocent dreams. Thank God Jameela was there to look after him.

Badriya got in from the other side, slid across the seat, turned and slapped my face so hard I fell against the car door.

"Rahima, you question me again and I swear I will go straight to Abdul Khaliq and tell him you're opening your idiot mouth in the assembly. We'll see if you're so eager to wag your tongue then! Learn to control yourself, you bitch."

Maroof looked into the rearview mirror. An expression of surprise twisted into a smirk. He was entertained. My face stung but I said nothing. I had the rest of our stay to get through and I refused to become a spectacle for our bodyguards.

The following morning, we wove through clusters of foreign soldiers and returned to the parliament building. Late, because of Badriya. But there was no voting today, only discussions. Nothing of importance to her, though she was obligated to make an appearance.

I wasn't speaking to her, just answering her questions and keeping out of the way. I was beginning to reconsider if being in Kabul was worth putting up with her attitude. As bad as she was at the compound, she was worse here. There was only me to take all her attention and the pressure of following our husband's plan was getting to her.

I took notes for her and filled out a survey distributed by some international organization looking to improve the parliament, and then we broke for lunch. I gravitated toward Hamida and Sufia. Badriya reluctantly followed with her tray.

"How are you two doing?" Hamida said. They looked at us differently now. Yesterday had changed things.

"Fine, thanks. You?" Badriya was curt. It wasn't helping the situation.

"Still surprised from yesterday. We were hoping to block more of those nominations. But I guess it was their *naseeb* to get approved."

Naseeb. Did Sufia really believe that? If she did, why bother voting?

"Maybe so," Badriya said in agreement.

I searched for something to say that would tell the ladies I was on their side but without riling Badriya's nerves.

"Sometimes people surprise you, don't they?" I said. "Maybe something good will come of it."

"An optimist — there's something we don't see often."

I had no reason to think Qayoumi was anything but the bastard they said he was. I had almost no reason to believe anyone would do anything good, really. My "optimism" was just words, strung together in hopes of making me look neutral. I wanted to be friendly with these women. They were independent and happy, something I'd tasted only as a young boy.

"Sufia and I are going to the resource center this evening. Maybe you would want to join us?"

"Thank you but I can't," said Badriya. "I'm going to my cousin's home tonight. I haven't seen her in over two years."

I looked at her, surprised. Was she telling the truth? She spoke up, seeing the look on my face. "My mother's cousin lives here in Kabul. I haven't seen them in so long and my aunt is getting older. They've insisted that I come by and visit them. They live on the other side of the river, by the women's hospital."

"Well, if you ladies are going there tonight then maybe another —"

Badriya looked startled. "Us? Oh, no. I'm going alone. Since it's my cousin, you know," she said, fumbling her words as she tried to undo my accompanying her. "And Rahima-*jan* said she didn't want to go anyway."

Eyes on me for confirmation.

"Well, you kept saying they were such nice people. Maybe I should go after all, huh?"

Badriya's eyes widened. "Really? You want to go? Are you sure that's what you want to do?" she said. Her glare told me the answer she expected.

"No," I said. "You know what? I think I've changed my mind. You should go and see your aunt and cousins. Maybe I'll go to the resource center instead. It would be great to see what they offer. I wouldn't mind taking some lessons while we're here."

Hamida's eyes lit up. It was as if she saw me in a new light.

"That's a great idea! That's what we'll do. While Badriya visits her aunt, we'll go to the resource center. We can go meet directly after the session closes today and then head over to their office. You'll be ready to go then, right?"

I agreed, satisfied that I'd gotten my way, even if Badriya had gotten hers as well. We parted ways when the session closed and I followed Hamida and Sufia. Badriya had taken Maroof and the guard. I was left with no one, which made me feel more free than alone. We picked up some dinner from the cafeteria and carried the plastic bags with us.

"Do they have these classes all the time? Is it like a school?" I asked. I was getting more and more excited at the thought of returning to a classroom. Even if nothing came from the lessons.

"They have different instructors. Haven't you heard Sufia speak English? Where do you think she learned to say so nicely, 'Hello, how are you?' " Hamida mimicked cheerfully.

I had no idea what she'd said but I was impressed that they were learning English. Even more than that, I wanted to learn how to use the computers I'd seen in the parliament's library. The library was a small room in the basement level with three bookcases, two of which were empty. The book collection was sparse but the woman in charge was determined to amass a collection with works on politics, law and history. I thumbed through the books and realized how much there was to learn about government. It was not as simple as raising paddles.

The computers caught my eye. There were three of them but more were coming, we were told. The three were all being used by men whom I recognized from the assembly. I tried not to stare over their shoulders but I wanted to know what they were looking at on those screens. I watched from the corner of my eye as they punched slowly and carefully at the keyboard, piecing letters together in a way I'd never before seen.

The women took me to a small, newly constructed building with small windows and a sign out front in both English and Dari.

Women's Training Center, it read.

"This is really just for women?" I asked. "The men can't come here?"

"Absolutely not, just like the *hammam.*" Sufia chuckled. "Thank God, someone finally took our involvement seriously. You know, Rahima-*jan,* international organizations send teachers and computers. All of it is available. We just have to use it."

"Do many of the women from the parliament come here?"

"Hardly!" Hamida said. "So many of those women have no idea what they're doing. I had no idea what I was doing either but now it's my second term and I am just starting to realize how much we still have to learn before this assembly is really functional. We're like babies, just learning to crawl."

An image of Jahangir, his knees rough and dark from crawling about, his palms slapping against the floor with excitement. I missed my son.

Sufia must have read my face.

461

"You have children?"

I nodded. "I have a son."

"How long have you been married?"

"Almost three years."

"Hm. You were how old when you married?"

"Thirteen," I answered quietly, my mind still on my little boy's face. I wondered what he was doing.

"Your husband must be much older, judging by Badriya's age," Hamida said, pausing before she opened the door to the training center.

I nodded. I realized they both were trying not to look as curious as they were.

"Your husband . . . what does he do?"

I drew a blank. I wasn't quite certain what he did and I was even less certain how to avoid explaining it.

"I don't know," I said. I blushed when I saw the way they looked at me.

"You don't know? How can you not know?"

"I never asked him."

"Never asked him? But you live there! You must have some idea what he does."

This outing was not as innocent as it appeared. They were interested — probably after seeing Badriya's bizarre voting trend. But talking too much would come back to haunt me.

"He has some land. And he provides security for some foreigners, some people who are trying to build something in our province. I don't really know the details. I keep out of his business."

"I see," Sufia said in a way that made me feel like I had just given everything away.

I needed to stop talking.

"Did Badriya talk to you about the candidates? The people she voted for?" Hamida tried to sound casual.

"No," I said, reaching for the door. This conversation had to end. "We don't really discuss the parliament issues. I'm just here to help her with paperwork and reading the documents."

"Can she not read?"

From the first day, I'd liked these women. I really had. But they were making me very uncomfortable right now, hitting every nerve. I was certain I was going to pay for this later.

"Let's go in, please. I can't wait to see what they have inside."

They relented. I followed them into the center, where an American woman was sitting at a computer, her fingers flying across the keyboard. She looked up and smiled brightly to see us, the first visitors she'd had all week.

She came over and hugged us, greeted us warmly. Sufia, her confidence growing, practiced her English and asked her how she was doing, how her family was getting along.

"Why isn't anyone else here?" I whispered.

463

"Not interested. They just show up to the sessions and then go home. No one cares to learn anything new. They think they know what they're doing, even though they've never done it before. Born experts!" Hamida laughed.

The ladies introduced me to Ms. Franklin and explained to her that I was an assistant to another parliamentarian. She seemed thrilled to have me there. I stared at her light brown hair, soft bangs peeking out from under her head scarf. She looked to be in her thirties, with a brightness in her eyes that made me think she'd never experienced sadness.

If that's true, lucky her, I thought.

"Salaam-alaikum, Rahima-*jan,"* she said, her accent so thick it made me giggle. *"Chotoor asteen?"*

"I'm fine, thank you," I answered, and looked at Hamida. I'd never before seen an American. I was amazed to hear her speak our language. My reaction looked familiar to Hamida.

"Her Dari is good, isn't it?" she laughed. "Now, dear teacher, what can you show us today?"

We spent almost two hours there, Ms. Franklin patiently guiding us through the basics of using a computer, guiding the mouse across a table to move a pointer on the screen. I was thrilled, feeling an excitement I hadn't felt since my days as a *bacha posh.*

Imagine if I learned to use this machine. Imagine if I could work like this woman, Ms. Franklin. To know so much that I could teach it to others!

I felt privileged. A new feeling! I doubted even Hashmat had ever seen a computer, much less received personalized instruction on how to use it. I would have loved to see the look on his face if he ever learned what I was doing in Kabul.

But it was going to get dark soon and it was time to leave. The women had promised Badriya that one of them would escort me back to the hotel with her guard and driver. I hugged Ms. Franklin before we left, making her laugh out loud, her blue eyes twinkling with kindness.

"I want to come back here, please! I like it very much!"

If only our day had ended with that sentiment.

Sufia had a hand on the door when a large explosion startled us all. We dropped to the ground, out of the way of windows. Nervous stares.

"What was that?"

"Something. Couldn't have been too far. But it didn't sound like a rocket."

We were a people of war; explosions were familiar to our senses. But not for Ms. Franklin. Her face drained of color and she was shaking. Hamida put an arm around her young teacher, trying to reassure her. Sufia squeezed my hand. No other sounds came. Sufia got up cautiously and went to the door. People in the street were yelling, pointing. Her driver and guard jogged over to the door. They looked frustrated. They were panting.

"What is it? What's happened?" she asked.

"Some kind of bomb. Looks like it was right by the parliament building. Stay here. We're going to find out what happened."

We were huddled by the window, trying to read the faces of the pedestrians. Hamida called out into the street.

"What's going on? Was that a bomb?"

The street was chaotic. Either no one heard her or no one bothered to answer.

We inched out the door, our curiosity overwhelming. I was nervous. Although my father and my husband had been in the throes of battle, the war had always been at least one village away from me. I wondered if Badriya was anywhere near here.

Sufia's driver came back, shaking his head and muttering something under his breath. Hamida's guard stopped him, wanting to know what he'd found out.

"It was two blocks from the parliament building. A bomb in a car. Looks like they were trying to get Zamarud."

My stomach lurched. I pictured her storming out of the building, remembered the hateful leers she'd drawn from some of the men. Even some of the women had shaken their heads as she walked by. People thought she was out of line, and the punishment for being out of line was severe in our world. It always had been.

"Zamarud! Not surprised, with the finger-pointing she's been doing. This isn't good. Is she all right?"

"I don't know. Someone said she was killed. They took her away. I didn't see her there, or her guards. We'd better get out of here."

CHAPTER 45
RAHIMA

When Abdul Khaliq got wind of what happened, he told his driver and guard to bring us back to the compound. The bombing had scared me badly. Badriya and I stayed in our hotel room, afraid that other women parliamentarians would be targeted, and heard a hundred versions of yesterday's events from our guard and the hotel staff.

She was dead. She was alive but had lost a leg. She was unscathed but three children walking by had been killed. It was the Taliban. It was a warlord. It was the Americans.

I didn't know what to believe. Badriya believed each and every story wholly until the next one came along. My head spun. I prayed for Zamarud, thinking there was something inspiring about the way she had riled the entire parliament with her irreverent behavior. The guards came back; our driver was smoking a cigarette, his eyes red from the lingering smoke of the bomb. He'd been too curious to walk away. When he nodded that the car was ready, I sighed with relief. I wanted to hold Jahangir.

I imagined how my little boy might squeal and laugh when he saw me, how he might run to my arms. I couldn't wait to hold him, praying he didn't hate me for leaving. Though I regretted thinking it, I hoped I wasn't like my mother. I didn't want to abandon him and leave him to raise himself. I opened my small bag and checked for the ballpoint pen and a few sheets of paper I'd taken from the parliament building. I smiled, thinking how happy it would make Jahangir to scribble.

My son was the bright spot in my return to the compound. I went directly to Jameela's room and called his name. He froze at the sound of my voice and toddled to greet me at the door, an innocent grin on his face and a twinkle in his eye.

"Maa-da! Maa-da!"

My heart melted to hear him call for me.

"Play ball outside! *Maa-da!*"

He wasted no time trying to recruit me to play with him. I smiled, wishing I could join him in the courtyard, where we could kick his brother's soccer ball back and forth. I was close enough to childhood that playing still appealed to me. But they had just killed a chicken for Abdul Khaliq's dinner guests and there was little time to pluck and clean the bird for tonight's dinner.

"Forgive me, *bachem,* but maybe later I can

469

come outside with you. Right now I have to get some work done. Maybe your brother can go outside with you."

I think I secretly hoped that my work in Kabul would change how I was treated at the compound, but that idea was quickly dispelled. Bibi Gulalai stopped by the next day to make sure my time in the city hadn't undone all the work she'd put into me.

"That was Kabul, this is here. In this house, remember who I am. There are no meetings or papers for you to look after here. Now go wash your face. You look filthy. How embarrassing."

I sighed, nodded and walked away before she talked herself into a worse mood on my account.

I kept to my room. My last night here with my husband had been exceptionally unpleasant, exceptionally violent, and I didn't want to put myself in his way again. I wondered if he'd let us go back to Kabul after this. I still didn't know if Zamarud was alive or dead.

And something was happening at home. I didn't know what it was but Jameela looked anxious and distracted. She was polite with Bibi Gulalai but she would quickly excuse herself. Bibi Gulalai seemed to be surveying our home with a discriminating eye. I asked Jameela but she smiled and changed the subject. Shahnaz, bitter because I had been allowed to travel to Kabul, was curt and snide with me. There was no use approaching her.

Through Jameela's younger son, I sent word to Khala Shaima that I'd returned from Kabul. I wished very much to see her. Where before I was a listener, we could now exchange stories. I wanted to tell her about Zamarud and the bombing. And about Hamida and Sufia and the resource center. But a week passed and Khala Shaima had not come. I asked Jameela if she'd heard anything about my aunt but she hadn't. A second week went by and still nothing.

I was worried and frustrated but there was nothing I could do. Already I was feeling the differences between home and Kabul. That taste of independence, even the possibility of it, made me yearn to go back.

Three weeks passed. Badriya and I were waiting on Abdul Khaliq's decision. He was most likely going to allow us to return to Kabul and complete the remaining three months of sessions. He hadn't said anything to Badriya and she was my source of information. Abdul Khaliq did not discuss these matters directly with me. In that respect, he treated me more like a daughter than a wife. It didn't matter to me. The less interaction I had with him, the better.

Badriya finally approached Bibi Gulalai and asked her what was going on. Leaning against the living room wall, her shawl across her lap, Bibi Gulalai began to speak to her in a hush. When I paused by the doorway, the two of them looked up, annoyed.

"Go on, get to the carpets! And do it right this time. I don't want them looking dingy," Bibi Gulalai said.

I moved away from the door but lingered in the hallway.

"When did this come up?" Badriya said when I was out of view.

"Right when you all left. He knows her brother. I wish he never would have taken this stray. I don't know what he wanted with Rahima. Such a worthless family."

"I agree. Why he wanted a *bacha posh* for his wife, I'll never understand. But, Khala-*jan,* why do you think he would want to get rid of her? She is the youngest here and he wanted her for something . . ."

"He will. I think he knows now that she was a mistake. And he wants to make up for it with this one. He's going to marry her."

"But why not just keep her and marry this girl?"

"Because he's living by the *hadith*! He is a respected man in this village, in this province! He leads by example, so he is doing as the Prophet said. And the Prophet, peace be upon him, said that a man should take no more than four wives at a time. This wouldn't have been a problem if he wouldn't have taken that *bacha posh.*"

My throat went dry. What was my husband

planning? A fifth wife?

"Well, God bless him. It's admirable that he wants to be such an upright, devout Muslim."

Bibi Gulalai gave a quick hum, agreeing with Badriya's praise of her son.

"Just don't say anything to Rahima about this. She's wild enough as it is. We don't need her or her insane aunt Shaima making a fuss about this. It's none of their business anyway."

"I won't say a word but she'll find out soon enough . . ."

The kids were coming down the hall. I slinked away from the door and melded into their footsteps.

I needed to talk to Jameela. Would Abdul Khaliq really try to get rid of me? How?

"Why? What did you hear?" Jameela said, her eyes narrowed.

I recounted the conversation for her. She listened intently.

"I don't know anything more than that. Bibi Gulalai will only talk to Badriya, of course, her angel. The rest of us will only hear when something happens. But God help us all. If he really does this, it's going to be a disaster."

"But do you think he'll take a fifth wife? He wants to get rid of me, Jameela-*jan*. Can he do that?"

"He can do —" Jameela started to say, but changed her response after a brief pause. "I

473

don't know, Rahima-*jan*. I really don't know."

We left it unsaid. If he wanted to take another wife without going over the limit, that would mean getting rid of one of us, and Bibi Gulalai had already made it clear that I was the expendable one. I'd once prayed my husband would send me back to my parents. Now that would mean leaving my son behind. Jameela had told me of one girl who had been sent back to her father's house, her husband dissatisfied with her as a wife. The girl's family, unable to tolerate the shame, refused to take her in. No one knew what happened to her.

Four weeks since our return. Jahangir came into our bedroom, where I was mending a tear in my dress, the blue housedress Badriya had warned me against wearing in Kabul. And after seeing how most of the women parliamentarians dressed, I could see why. But it was in fair shape and there was little chance of new fabric coming my way.

Jahangir called out to me. I looked up, surprised to see Khala Shaima hobbling a few steps behind him. She had never come into this part of the house.

"Khala-*jan*! *Salaam,* Khala Shaima-*jan,* you came! I was so worried about you!" I scrambled to greet her.

Khala Shaima put a hand on the door frame, leaning forward and steadying her breathing.

"*Salaam . . . ah . . . salaam, dokhtar-jan.*
Damn Abdul Khaliq for building his compound so far from town," she panted as I kissed her hands. I could hear the air whistle in her lungs. I quickly glanced in the hallway to be sure no one heard her curse my husband.

"I'm so sorry, Khala Shaima-*jan.* I wish I could come to you."

"Eh, forget it. I'll walk as long as my feet allow. Now, let me sit and get myself together. You must have something to tell me from your trip. And what the hell are you doing back here for so long?"

I told her about everything, the hotel, the guards, the buildings and the foreign soldiers. Then I told her about the bombing and the reason we came back.

"I heard about that on the radio. Bastards. Can't handle a woman with a voice."

"Who do you think was responsible?"

"Does it matter? They may not know who brought the bomb there but we all know why. She's a woman. They don't want to hear from her. The last thing this country needed is one more cripple. And that's what we've got now."

"She's not dead? What happened to her?"

"You don't know?"

"We heard so many things before we left. And here no one cares to find out. I'm sure Abdul Khaliq knows, but . . ."

"But you're not going to ask him."

I shook my head.

"It seems the bomb went off just next to her car. Exploded and killed one of her guards. But she survived the attack. I think they said her leg was burned but nothing more."

"Is she going to come back to the parliament?"

"She wants to."

I didn't doubt that. Zamarud was not one to be scared off easily. I wished I could be more like her — so determined and brave.

And I should be, I thought. I'd been so self-assured when I was a *bacha posh.* Walking around with the boys, I feared nothing. If they had dared me to wrestle a grown man to the ground, I would have done it. I thought I could do anything.

And now I trembled before my husband, before my mother-in-law. I had changed. I had lost my confidence. The dress I wore felt like a costume, something that disguised the confident, headstrong boy I was supposed to be. I felt ridiculous, like someone pretending to be something he was not. I despised what I was.

Khala Shaima had read my mind.

"She's taking risks and she just might be a total lunatic, but she's doing what she wants. And I bet she doesn't regret it. I bet she'll keep doing it. That's what people have to do sometimes to get what they want. Or to be what they want."

Khala Shaima was like no one else. Everyone else thought Zamarud was a fool to say the things she did and an even bigger idiot for willingly offending men.

Carefully, quietly, I told Khala Shaima about Abdul Khaliq wanting to take another wife and what Badriya and Bibi Gulalai had said about me.

She said nothing but I could tell the news unsettled her. She looked anxious.

"Did they say how soon?"

I shook my head.

"Dear God, Rahima. This is not good."

Her words made me more nervous.

"We have to figure something out. But keep this to yourself for now. Remember, the walls have mice and the mice have ears."

I nodded, blinking back tears. I had hoped Khala Shaima would say something else. That the rumor was absurd. That I was safe here as Abdul Khaliq's wife.

"Things don't always work out the way you think they will. I bet you've been wondering what became of Bibi Shekiba. Shall I pick up where I left off?"

I half listened to my great-great-grandmother's story. My mind was preoccupied.

I did have to figure something out. And I should be able to, shouldn't I? Why did it matter if I wore a dress now? Why did it matter that I no longer bound my breasts flat? I wanted to be the same person I had been. Zamarud let nothing get in her way. She wore a dress and she had married and she campaigned to get a seat in the *jirga*. A seat she occupied as a real parliamentarian.

The dress didn't hold her back as it did me. I felt restless. I thought how much more comfortable I would be if I could just button my shirt and walk into the street. If I could just slip into my old clothes . . . how much more capable I would be. Zamarud might have disagreed but the clothes meant something different to me because I'd lived in them.

The dress, the husband, the mother-in-law. I wished I could toss them all aside.

CHAPTER 46
SHEKIB

When Shekib had been a girl, she'd heard about a woman in a nearby village condemned to stoning. It was the talk of their town as well as the neighboring towns.

The woman had been buried shoulder-deep in the earth and encircled by a crowd of onlookers. When it was time, her father had thrown the first stone, striking her squarely in her temple. The line continued until she slumped over in atonement.

Shekiba had listened to the story being recounted by her uncle's wife. Her mouth gaped at the horror of such a punishment and the grains of rice she was sifting fell through her drifting fingers and missed the bowl. An anthill of rice collected on the floor.

"What had she done?"

Her uncles' wives turned around and paused their conversation, surprised. They often forgot she was there.

Bobo Shahgul's eyes narrowed seeing the wasted rice on the floor.

"She ruined her father's life and gave her entire family nothing but grief!" she said brusquely. "Watch what you're doing, you absentminded fool!"

Shekiba looked down to see the mess she had made. Her mouth closed sharply and she turned her attention back to the rice. Bobo Shahgul tapped her walking stick in warning.

Sangsaar? A chill coursed through Shekib's veins as she looked at Benafsha and pictured her half-buried. Stones hurled at her head.

She asked no more questions of Benafsha. The room was silent but for the grumbling of two empty stomachs.

Two days passed without food or water. The door did not open once, though Shekib could see people walking behind it, stopping and listening before walking off. From the slit beneath the door, Shekib could make out the soles of army boots and knew soldiers were guarding them.

On the third day, the door opened. An army officer looked down at the two women, curled up on the floor. Shekib pulled herself to stand. Benafsha barely stirred.

"Guard. Khanum Benafsha."

Shekib dusted her pants off and straightened her back.

"Your offenses against our dear king are grave and reprehensible. You are both to be stoned tomorrow afternoon."

Shekib gasped. Her eyes widened in disbelief. "But, sir, I —"

"I did not ask you to speak. You have
shamed yourself enough, have you not?"

He turned around abruptly and slammed
the door shut behind him. Shekib heard him
order a soldier to lock the door. A chain
clanged and a key turned, leaving the two
women with their fate.

Benafsha let out a soft moan once the door
closed. She had known.

"They're going to stone us both!" Shekib
whispered, her voice tight and unbelieving.
"Even me? I did nothing!"

Benafsha had her elbow tucked under her
head. Her eyes gazed at the wall in front of
her. She had known exactly what they would
do to her. Why had she brought this upon
herself?

"This is your fault! They're going to stone
me because of you!" She knelt at Benafsha's
side and grabbed her shoulders roughly.
"Because of you!"

Benafsha rattled limply in her hands. "With
Allah as my witness, I am sorry that you are
here," she said softly, her voice tearful and
resigned.

Shekib pulled back and stared at Benafsha.
"Why? You knew what they would do to you.
Why did you do this? How could you do such
a thing in the king's own palace?"

"You would not understand," she said for

the second time.

"No, I do not understand how you could do something so stupid!"

"It is impossible to understand if you do not know love," Benafsha whispered. Her eyes closed and she started to recite lyrics I'd never heard before. Phrases that I memorized because they echoed in my mind after she'd stopped talking and meant different things to me at different moments.

There is some kiss we want with our whole
   lives,
The touch of Spirit on the body.
Seawater begs the pearl to break its shell.
And the lily, how passionately it needs
   some wild
Darling!
At night, I open the window and ask the
   moon to come
And press its face against mine. Breathe
   into me.

Her melancholy verses pulled at my heart. I knew nothing of that kind of love. I knew nothing about pearls and shells either except that one had to free itself from the other. We were both calmer than we should have been, Benafsha because she had lived her love, and me because I had never known it.

The hours crept by.

Day turned into night and night became

morning. One final morning.

Maybe this is how it is meant to be. Maybe this is how I will finally be returned to my family and saved from this wretched existence. Maybe there is nothing for me in this world.

Shekib swung wildly between anger, panic and submission in those hours. Benafsha whispered words of apology from time to time but mostly prayed. She held her head between her hands and atoned for her sins, said there was no God but Allah.

Allahu akbar, she whispered rhythmically. *Allahu akbar.*

There was talking outside their door. Shekib could not make out what they were saying but heard a few words here and there.

Whores. Stoning. Deserved.

Whores? Shekib realized she was a woman again. As guilty as the woman lying a few feet from her.

I have been both girl and boy. I will be executed as a girl. A girl who failed as a boy.

Stoning. Today. Stopped.

Stopped? What was stopped?

Shekiba listened carefully.

King. Pardon. Gift.

At hearing "gift," Shekiba realized something was happening to her. She strained to hear the voices more clearly but could not make out most of what they were saying.

The door opened. The same ranked soldier

reappeared, his face cross.

"Khanum Benafsha, prepare yourself. You," he said, looking at Shekiba with disgust. "You will attend the stoning and then you will be punished for your crime. After that, you will be given in marriage. You should thank Allah that you have been shown a mercy you do not deserve."

The room went dim again and the chains were locked in place. Shekiba's heart pounded.

They will not stone me! I will be given in marriage? How could this be?

Benafsha looked at her, the corners of her mouth almost turned up in a weak smile.

"Allahu akbar," she whispered; the condemned's prayer had been answered.

Shekiba's hands trembled. Was it Amanullah? He must have intervened! But why would he want her now that she had been accused of such treachery? Now that she had made herself an unworthy wife?

Everyone spoke of Amanullah's noble character. Maybe he had seen through the accusations. Maybe in their brief exchanges he had seen something, something that told him she was more than just a woman-man, more than just a harem guard. Was that not what he had told his friend Agha Baraan?

Tears ran down Shekiba's cheeks. Now all she could do was wait. The hours passed slowly. It became painful to sit in the same room with Benafsha. Shekiba looked at her glazed eyes and broken spirit. She crawled over and crouched at her side.

"Khanum Benafsha," she said, her words a hush. "I am praying for you."

Benafsha's eyes focused on Shekiba. She looked hollow but grateful.

"I cannot understand why you . . . but I want . . ."

"I fulfilled my destiny," Benafsha said calmly. "That is all I did."

When they came for Benafsha, Shekiba was holding her hands. Two soldiers dragged Benafsha to her feet and another two pulled Shekiba up by the shoulders. Shekiba's fingers lost their grip when they bound Benafsha's wrists together and covered her with a blue *burqa*. Benafsha looked at her and began to wail, long slow moans that grew louder as they walked through the hallways.

"Shut your mouth, whore!" a soldier snapped, whipping his hand against the back of Benafsha's head after he had made sure they were not being watched. Though she was about to be executed, she was still the king's concubine.

Benafsha's head bounced forward. She began to pray loudly.

"Allahu akbar. Allahu akbar. Allahu . . ."

They shook her gruffly by the shoulders and warned her again. Her prayers went on.

Through the palace, out a back door and

into the courtyard, where the afternoon sun nearly blinded the women. Shekiba looked at the harem and saw the women lined up outside, head scarves pulled across their faces. Halima in silhouette, her shoulders shaking as she sobbed. Sakina stood among them, her arm linked with Nabila's.

You did this, Shekiba thought bitterly.

Ghafoor, Karim, Qasim and Tariq stood in front of the women, solemnly watching the dead woman walk by. Even from this distance, Shekiba could see Tariq trembling. Ghafoor kept her eyes averted, whispering something to Karim as she looked back at the concubines.

Coward. You can't even look at me.

"Allahu akbar. Allahu akbar . . ."

Soldiers stood everywhere. The palace grounds were quiet, an eerie silence given the number of people in sight. Benafsha's prayers echoed through the gardens, her toes dragging through the ground. The women of the harem shrank into the distance. Shekiba could hear someone crying. Others tried to hush her but the sobs continued. Shekiba thought it sounded like Nabila.

"Do not weep for those who damned themselves!" a voice boomed.

Shekiba turned around to see where the voice came from. Ahead of them stood a general. From this distance she could not tell if it was one of the men who had come to

486

their makeshift prison cell. Three soldiers stood on either side of him, their backs straight as rods.

A hundred times Shekiba had crossed the palace grounds but never had it seemed this far. They inched along.

"Allahu akbar. Allahu akbar. Allahu . . ."

Shekiba began to mouth the words too. Her voice was barely audible, her throat so dry it burned to talk.

As they neared the general, he nodded to the soldiers and they walked past the fountains, toward the far limits of the palace. They marched solemnly to a clearing where a semicircle of soldiers stood at attention. Shekiba's heart dropped. In front of the soldiers lay two separate piles of stones, most the size of a fist. The heaps reached the soldiers' knees.

Shekiba's prayers grew louder, synchronizing with Benafsha's. She tasted tears. They walked to the edge of the palace; high walls shielded the onlookers. King Habibullah emerged from the palace and stood beside the general he had placed in charge of the execution. The men whispered to each other, keeping their eyes on Benafsha.

The general nodded at something the king said and approached the condemned as she was brought to the center of the semicircle. A deep pit had been dug in these outskirts of the palace, behind a row of fruit trees, a place

Shekiba had never before ventured. The soldiers, about fifteen feet away, stared at Benafsha. Shekiba was still within earshot.

"Tell me, Khanum Benafsha, are you ready to divulge the name of the man you welcomed in your chambers?"

Benafsha looked up and met his stare.

"Allahu akbar."

"You could be granted mercy if you would at least tell us who this man is."

"Allahu akbar."

The general threw his arms up and looked back at the king, exasperated. The king nodded, his face a contorted mix of wrath and disappointment.

"Very well! Khanum Benafsha, your crimes have been reviewed by the scholars of our beloved Islam and according to the laws of our land, you are to be stoned for the grave offense you have committed." He looked at the two guards and pointed at the hole. Benafsha let out a wail as they held her by the armpits and lowered her into the pit, her legs kicking, her blue *burqa* flailing like a goldfish pulled from the palace fountain.

Shekiba took a step toward her and felt two hands tighten on her arms. She looked over at King Habibullah. His arms were folded, a finger over his lips as he mouthed something. At the sound of Benafsha's voice, he shook his head, lowered his gaze and walked away. He would not stay for the execution.

The soldiers shoveled the earth back around Benafsha until she was buried to her chest. She continued to twist and turn but she was deep in the ground and her arms stuck to her, useless. As the dirt piled up around her, she moved less but moaned louder. Shekiba closed her eyes and heard the wails: *"Allahu akbar. Allahu akbar. Allahu . . ."*

Suddenly a sharp yelp. Shekiba opened her eyes, startled. A thin line of darkness formed above the eye mesh of Benafsha's *burqa*. Three stones lay near her.

It has started.

The soldiers bent over, picked stones from the arsenal before them and mouthed something before hurling them at Benafsha, the blue half person.

May Allah have mercy on you, Khanum Benafsha!

Her body jerked with each stone that hit her. The soldiers took turns. Picking, hurling, and moving to the back of the half circle. Ten minutes passed, a hundred stones. Benafsha's voice grew weaker; she slumped forward, her *burqa* stained in a dozen places, dark circles bleeding toward one another. The earth around her grew dark as well, blood soaking into the soil. Two stones had ripped through the blue fabric, gashed flesh showed through the holes.

Shekiba turned around, unable to stomach any more. She saw the row of blue *burqas* behind a row of spectator soldiers. Benafsha was to be an example to the dozen or so who had been brought out to bear witness. As horrified as Shekiba, the blue cloaks were half turned away.

Stone after stone, scream after scream, until Benafsha went silent and still. The general raised his hand. The execution had been carried out.

CHAPTER 47
SHEKIBA

Benafsha's limp body flashed over and over in Shekiba's mind as she received her own punishment. She had been sentenced to a hundred lashes, which were delivered precisely by one of the soldiers, a general standing watch over him. Shekiba had been made to kneel while they stood behind her, her wrists bound as Benafsha's had been.

Though her face twisted in pain with each blow, she did not make a sound.

Her back stung, hot and wet. The soldier had a book tucked under his arm, as law instructed, to soften the striking force. They counted out loud and when they reached a hundred, Shekiba's wrists were untied and she fell on her side in exhaustion. The men said nothing and left the room.

Her mind drifted. She felt water on her lips. Hands rubbed ointment on her back. It was nearly a day later before Shekiba realized Dr. Behrowen was tending to her wounds. The British woman clucked her tongue and shook her head, almost as an Afghan would, muttering something that Shekiba did not understand.

Shekiba closed her eyes to block the horror but it was still there, the images seared onto the insides of her eyelids. She opened her eyes again and looked at Dr. Behrowen. She was squeezing water out of a wet rag. She considered Shekiba carefully.

"Dard?" she asked, her British accent blunting the letters so thickly that the word was unrecognizable. She had to repeat herself twice more before Shekiba understood she was asking about pain.

Shekiba shook her head. Dr. Behrowen raised her eyebrows and turned her attention back to the bucket of rags.

Shekiba looked down. She was wearing thin pantaloons that tapered at her ankles. A head scarf lay strewn across a chair in the corner of the room. Shekiba realized she was in Benafsha's room in the harem. Through the walls, she could hear women chatting. She remembered how Benafsha had begged and prostrated herself before them, asking forgiveness and mercy from a crowd focused only on saving their own skins.

The door opened and Halima peered in.

"Can I come in?" she asked quietly, looking at Dr. Behrowen.

Dr. Behrowen must have understood; she nodded and waved Halima into the room.

"How are you feeling?"

"Better." Her throat felt like sandpaper.

"I'm glad." She knelt at Shekiba's side. "Things have been ugly here the last few days. Never have we experienced such things."

Shekiba had nothing to say in reply. Halima sighed heavily and looked quickly at Dr. Behrowen with tears in her eyes.

"Tariq is outside. She wants to see you but she's very nervous. Is it all right if she comes in for a few moments?"

Shekiba nodded. She remembered seeing Tariq when she turned her gaze from Benafsha's stoning. Tariq's mouth and eyes were open wide with horror, a small pool of vomit at her feet.

Halima placed a gentle hand on Shekiba's forehead before she stood and quietly walked out. Shekiba wished she would come back, stroke her hair and hold her hands as a mother would. Instead, Tariq rushed in and fell at Shekiba's side; the trembling in her hands vibrated her voice.

"Oh, Allah have mercy! Are you all right? Are you badly hurt? What did they do to you?"

"I was punished."

"How?"

"One hundred lashes."

Tariq scanned her body, her brows furrowed together in angst. "How awful! How very awful! Oh, Shekib! Did they say why they were punishing you?"

"Because I did not do my job as a guard."

"Oh, Allah forgive us! We were all as guilty as you!" she whispered, as if afraid the palace would hear her.

"But only I had been on duty that night. Ghafoor made sure to tell them that."

"She . . . I never would have imagined she could be so . . . I mean, I know she thinks only of herself but I just never thought she would do something like . . ."

"That's what people do. She's no different than anyone else."

It suddenly occurred to Shekiba that Benafsha had been different. The general had offered leniency in exchange for a name. Although she must have known his offer was a lie, even the possibility of mercy didn't faze her resolve. She never named the man. Why had she done that? Why had she protected Agha Baraan?

"She said that they only wanted to talk to you. She said she did not know they were going to punish you."

Shekiba recalled Ghafoor's shifting gaze on that night and on the day of the stoning.

"What did they tell you? Benafsha . . . she brought such shame to the palace but I never thought . . . I just cannot believe this happened here! I thought things were different here in Kabul, in the king's palace!"

494

"No man could tolerate such an offense. The king would have shamed himself if he had agreed to a lesser penalty."

"And what will become of us guards?"

"I do not know."

"What about you? Will they send you back to your family?"

Shekiba remembered that she had been spared for a reason — she was to be married! She pictured Amanullah's face. Could it really be? Had he rescued her from execution to live on as his wife? Or maybe as a concubine? Even curled up on the floor with her raw back covered in salves, Shekiba yearned to be in a new home, her own home, and with child. She wanted to feel tiny palms pull at her face with unquestioning affection.

"No. I do not know where they will send me." She decided to say nothing about the marriage until she knew more. She did not want word getting back to Ghafoor, lest she find a way to ruin things for her.

"Oh, what an awful mess! I'm so sorry, Shekib. I'm so sorry that you took the fall for this. The whole harem is terrified. They're worried more will be punished, just to set an example, or maybe if they believe others were involved . . ."

Shekiba decided Tariq was exhausting her. She asked her to leave so that she could close her eyes. Tariq looked disappointed but nodded and walked out, her uniform looking bulky and awkward. She was less of a man now than she had ever been.

Shekiba was just drifting off when Tariq burst back into the room.

"Shekib!" she said excitedly.

"Please, Tariq, I just want to sleep for a few —"

"I know and I apologize, but the palace sent over a messenger. They asked me to tell you . . . to tell you to be ready in two days."

Shekiba looked up.

Tariq's face flushed with a nervous smile.

"They said you're going to be married!"

CHAPTER 48
RAHIMA

It was the holiday of Eid. Five weeks since the attack on Zamarud. Badriya had received several letters from the director general. If she didn't return to her duties immediately, she would be stripped of her position. Abdul Khaliq had made up his mind. We would be going back after the holiday.

Jameela told me what it was all about.

"He's got a deal with a foreign company. You know these westerners he's always going out to meet. He wants them to pay him to provide security. But it's up for vote in the parliament whether or not that company should be allowed to build a pipe through our province. If they aren't allowed to build, they won't need his security."

"That's why he put Badriya in the parliament? To get her to vote for the pipe?"

"Yes. And to vote for all the right people for other positions, the people who will give him what he wants."

Badriya's voting made perfect sense now.

497

Abdul Khaliq must have told her to watch for his friend's signals. She wanted us to believe she actually mattered but she was a stooge. She was nothing like Hamida and Sufia. No wonder she seemed so awkward around them.

I was happy we would be returning, although this time I knew it would be even harder to leave Jahangir. This time I knew just how much I would miss him. But I dared not ask again if I could take him with me.

We, the four wives, went to Bibi Gulalai's compound next door to pay our obligatory respects on the first day of Eid. After that, we went home and braced ourselves. For three days, our house received visitor after visitor. I spent three days in the kitchen with the cook and the maid, drying dishes, filling bowls with nuts and raisins and pouring cups of tea. I wasn't invited to sit with any of the guests as Badriya and Jameela were. Even Shahnaz came out from time to time and chatted with the women who came by.

And if my husband were to marry again, I had no reason to expect things would get better for me. I knew my family would not take me back. It was a matter of pride. My uncles would never tolerate having a rejected wife, a dishonored woman, back in their fold.

It was possible that he would keep all his wives. But there was no room in the house for that. We were all uneasy with the possibilities. Bibi Gulalai and Abdul Khaliq were remarkably tight-lipped about the idea.

"Rahima! Rahima-*jan,* come out here! Look who has come to see you!"

I dried my hands on my skirt and hurried into the living room, hoping to see Khala Shaima. My jaw dropped to see that my eldest sister, Shahla, stood before me, a little boy holding her hand and another baby, no more than four months old, in her arm.

Shahla smiled brightly to see me while I simply stared. Her face and hips had rounded, taking her out of adolescence. She looked cheerful.

"Rahima! My dear sister!" She let go of her son's hand and took a step toward me. I couldn't believe I was seeing her after all this time. It felt so good to have her arms squeeze me, to have her hands touch my face.

I felt her tears against my cheek, mixing with mine.

"It's so good to see you, finally!" she whispered. "Forgive me, Rahima. I couldn't come to be with you when . . . when everything happened."

I had missed Shahla so much, and never more than when Parwin had taken her own life. Seeing her reopened the hurt.

"I wanted to be here. I wanted to come but it was so close to the time when this little one . . . ," she said, pointing to the baby girl in her arms.

I touched the little girl's face, her skin soft and smooth like Shahla's.

"I know, Shahla. I wish you could have been here too. It was . . . it was so terrible!"

"Allah forgive her, I'm sure it was. Poor Parwin! I can't imagine what she must have gone through!"

Bibi Gulalai stood in the corner of the room, eyeing us suspiciously and looking displeased. I looked and saw there were other guests I hadn't greeted. I exchanged quick kisses with Shahla's mother-in-law and two of her sisters-in-law. Shahla had taken a seat on one of the cushions, her little boy beside her and her daughter in her lap. I sat next to her, Bibi Gulalai's eyes following me.

"Oh, Shahla, look at your children! They're beautiful! I have a —"

"Rahima!" Bibi Gulalai barked. "Don't you think it would be more polite to bring our guests some tea before you start boring them with your yammering?"

My face flushed with embarrassment and anger. At least five Eid holidays had passed and this was the first time my sister had been able to pay a visit to the compound in that nearly three years' time. I hadn't seen her since the night of our miserable weddings. I could see the surprise on Shahla's face to hear the way Bibi Gulalai spoke. Jameela intervened.

"Let me, Khala-*jan.* Rahima's dear sister is

here and it would be nice if the girls could spend some time together."

I loved Jameela for understanding. And stepping in. She brought cups of tea and passed around a dish of nuts and dried mulberries. The ladies chatted amicably while Shahla held my hands. Her son, Shoib, grinned shyly while her daughter's tiny arms waved this way and that, her eyes glued to her mother's face.

"Shoib, did you say *salaam* to your *khala-jan*?"

"*Salaam,*" he said quickly, then hid behind his mother's shoulder.

"He's very timid," Shahla said, smiling.

"I want you to meet my son, Shahla." I rushed into the hallway and called out for Jahangir. The ladies in the room thought we looked ridiculous. Everyone had children. They didn't understand why we were making such a fuss over them.

I heard footsteps from Jameela's room. My son had become quite comfortable staying with her while I was in Kabul. Whenever he wasn't with me, I knew exactly where I would find him.

"Come, *bachem,* come and meet your *khala-jan,*" I beckoned. My son, looking curious, took my hand and followed me into the living room.

"He's a darling, *nam-e-khoda*!" she said, praising God's name and blowing three times to ward off the evil eye. "He's got your face."

"Do you really think so?" It pleased me to hear that.

"Absolutely! And Madar-*jan*'s hair. Look at the way the curls twist behind his head."

We both winced at the mention of our mother.

"Have you seen her?" I tried to be discreet.

Shahla shook her head. I looked at my feet, dark with dust. This was a sore spot for both of us and I didn't want to tell my sister everything I'd heard about Madar-*jan*'s downward spiral. With all these women present, it felt like a betrayal. But I wanted to pour my heart out to her, to tell her about our younger sisters, left to fend for themselves even with two parents at home. I wanted her to tell me she would talk some sense into Madar-*jan,* even if Khala Shaima couldn't. I kept it bottled.

"And your little girl — she's so sweet! What's her name, Shahla?"

I put my hand in front of her hand. Her long, graceful fingers wrapped around mine and squeezed tight.

Shahla lowered her voice and looked to see if anyone was paying attention to us.

"I named her Parwin," she said quietly.

A second look and I realized Shahla's daughter had our sister's doelike eyes and pink, puckered lips. My throat tightened. Shahla smiled wanly.

"Parwin?"

"Yes. My mother-in-law wanted to name her Rima, actually, but I asked if I could choose the name. She agreed to let me."

I stared at my niece's face. The longer I stared, the more of Parwin I saw. Then I thought of my own mother-in-law. She had only gone along with my son's name because my husband had approved of it. He must have liked it very much or she would have changed it for sure.

"I can't believe she agreed."

"I know. It was difficult because she thought it would be bad luck, you know, to name a child after someone with a lame leg. Thank goodness I named her before . . . I mean if she had been born after, I couldn't have convinced anyone. The name would've carried too much shadow."

Shahla looked at her daughter's face wistfully.

"Then after all that happened, everyone started calling her Rima. I could barely bring myself to say her name either so for a long time it was a relief to call her Rima. But now, when it's just me and her, I call her Parwin. It makes me feel better. Funny, isn't it? We hear the same name and while they see dark, I see light."

I knew just what she meant.

Had the guests been anyone else, I would have returned to the kitchen long ago. But it was my sister and I wanted to spend every second I could with her. Jameela refilled the teacups, passed around a plate of cookies and made small talk. She kept an eye on Bibi Gulalai and when it looked like our mother-in-law was about to say something to me, Jameela would ask a question or say something to distract her. When our eyes met, I thanked Jameela silently. She smiled.

"Shahla, you look so well!" I exclaimed. And I meant it. My sister looked more mature but otherwise unchanged. And she looked content. I even saw her make eye contact with her sister-in-law once or twice and smile. Genuinely. Her mother-in-law was a soft-spoken woman, nothing like Bibi Gulalai and her searing glare. She must have been in her sixties, wisps of gray hair peeking out from under her head scarf. She listened to Jameela talk about our mother's illness with a look of sincere concern.

"Really, Shahla, are things okay?" I whispered when the room was divided in conversation. "Are you happy?"

"I miss you so much, Rahima! I miss everyone. I wish so much that I could see Rohila and Sitara. I want to know how big they've gotten, what they're doing. But I'm happy."

I smiled. I believed her.

"What about you?" Jahangir pulled at Shoib's sleeve, inviting him to play in the hallway. Shoib shrugged his shoulders and followed.

"Me?" I could feel Bibi Gulalai's stare boring into the back of my head. I nodded. My sister knew me too well. Her face grew somber.

"Good, I'm glad to hear that," she said in a way that told me the opposite was true.

"I go to Kabul now. Did you hear about that?"

"I heard something, but . . ."

I told her about Badriya's seat in the *jirga* and how I worked as her assistant. I told her how different Kabul was, just like in the stories Khala Shaima told us. I was proud when I saw how impressed Shahla was.

If only I could have suspended time. I would have sat beside my sister, our children playing together in a picture of innocence, our hearts supporting each other as we mourned our dead sister, the mother we once had, and the sisters we'd left behind.

"You see Khala Shaima still, don't you?"

I nodded. "She comes by when she can. It's getting harder for her but I miss her so much when she doesn't come."

"Does she still tell you stories of Bibi Shekiba?" Shahla asked. She started to rock when she noticed her daughter's eyes begin to close, just as I did with Jahangir. It was amazing how quickly girls took on the instincts of motherhood.

"She does. I love hearing those stories. It

makes me think of . . . it makes me think of other times."

Shahla sighed. She missed it as much as I did.

"I know, Rahima-*jan*. But times change. Everything changes. Birds fly away, one by one."

CHAPTER 49
SHEKIBA

Shekiba was told nothing more. A *nikkah* was to be performed in two days' time. Word spread through the somber harem quickly and several women came together to prepare the new bride.

"Who is this man? How fortunate you are! You were spared by our dear king for marriage! That is quite an honor!"

Those voices were in the minority. Shekiba heard the whispers around her, angry and incredulous. Some said that she had probably conspired with Benafsha and that she should have been stoned alongside her.

You see how comfortable she is in Benafsha's room? As if it's been hers all along!

I bet she helped hide Benafsha's lover. I'm sure of it. I heard her footsteps in the middle of the night from time to time and I knew — I just knew something had to be going on!

They must be giving her to a blind man. Who else could stand to look at such a face!

How quickly they turned on her! How

quickly they forgot how she had carried their children, brought hot water for their baths and even scrubbed their backs when they asked. All the while she had been Shekiba-*e-haleem* to them; they winked to one another when she served the bowls of the hot dish to the women from the breakfast delivery.

Shekiba-e-haleem, *serving up her special dish!*

Maybe she should pour a bowl over the other side of her face — I swear it's just the right color to match her complexion today! The cook must be a genius!

But there were a few, namely Halima and Benazir, who pitied Shekiba and knew that she needed help preparing for her *nikkah.*

"Who is this man?" Halima asked as she combed oil through Shekiba's dull, short hair.

"I don't know, Khanum Halima. No one has said anything to me."

"Maybe it's one of the servants from the main palace. Maybe they will have you work there now?" Benazir suggested. "Would you like that?"

"I suppose," Shekiba said, her voice contained. That was not what she wanted at all, but she could not bring herself to share her secret with anyone. It was Amanullah that she hoped for — not a palace servant!

"Well, it is a bit strange that they have not told you anything." Halima looked hopeful but reserved. Shekiba had misfortune written all over her and it was hard to imagine that even a marriage would bring her peace.

"You know, there are many things that come with marriage. You have seen this harem and you know what happens between a man and a woman. Your husband will expect you to fulfill wifely duties. You will not want to disappoint him," Halima said gently.

Shekiba felt her stomach drop. She had not given much thought to what would happen between her and a husband. She thought of the squeals and grunts that came from the king's chambers. She thought of what Mahbuba had told her and felt something between her legs tighten with anxiety.

"It is painful the first time," Halima said.

"So painful!" Benazir echoed.

"But each time after that will be easier. And maybe Allah will bless you with a child."

Benazir smiled and looked at Mezhgan, who lay sleeping a few feet away.

"You have said that the women in your family all bear sons. If you do so, you will make your husband a happy man. Especially if it is his firstborn."

"Do you really think she'll be a first wife?" Benazir asked.

"Anything is possible," Halima said, looking at Shekiba and thinking of the last few days in the palace.

Later that afternoon, a second wave of news

rippled through the harem. Nabila came running into the bath area. Shekiba could hear her through the door.

"Have you heard the news? He is to be engaged! Our dear prince Amanullah is to be engaged! He has finally chosen a bride!"

No one else connected the two stories. No one but Shekiba, who closed her eyes and prayed with a nervous heart.

As promised, a soldier came to the harem two days after Tariq brought word to Shekiba. Ghafoor was standing outside and called into the house for Shekiba. They had not spoken since that dark night.

"Shekiba!" she called unceremoniously. "The palace has sent for you."

Shekiba had spent her last night in Benafsha's chambers, wondering about tomorrow. Her back still sore, she slept on her side. She stared at the door and imagined Agha Baraan entering to take the king's concubine in secret. Why hadn't Benafsha given her lover's name?

Shekiba stood up slowly and smoothed her skirt, trying not to wake Tariq who had quietly joined her last night. She pictured Amanullah in his military uniform, his pants neatly pressed and his hat perched perfectly on his head. Looking at her own clothing, she felt embarrassed. She picked up her head scarf and crossed the corners under her chin.

Tariq woke up, stretched and jumped to her feet. She threw both arms around Shekiba's neck and squeezed her tightly. The gesture caught Shekiba by surprise.

"Is it time already? I wish you all the best, dear sister! May Allah bless the steps you are about to take and give you a lifetime of happiness." Tariq's eyes were tearful. "And don't forget to pray for me sometimes too. Pray that I'll be so lucky!"

"I'll pray that you'll be even luckier."

With the palace waiting, there was no time to find Halima or Benazir to say good-bye. Shekiba walked past Ghafoor to the front door.

"How are you, Shekiba-*jan*? I hope you're feeling better. I heard your punishment was severe." She looked uncomfortable; her eyes wandered past Shekiba to the soldier waiting outside.

"I was delivered to them, blame already assigned. What else were they to do?"

"They must have assumed —"

"They assumed what they were told." Shekiba spoke coolly.

"I did not . . . regardless, congratulations."

"And to you too."

"To me too?"

"Certainly. It's not every day that one can successfully escape a fire."

"Just wait a minute! I did not —"

Something in Shekiba made her turn

around and look Ghafoor in the eyes. She was tired of holding her tongue.

"There's something you do not know about me, Ghafoor." Shekiba turned to glare at her directly. Her eyes narrowed with hate. "Do you wonder why my family sent me away? My family sent me away because I carry a curse and those around me ended up in a grave years before their time. And now, under these clear skies and with Satan listening, I curse you. May you suffer a hundred times over for each lash I bore. Mark my words, you snake, you will get what you deserve," Shekiba said quietly.

Ghafoor's shoulders stiffened with anger but her face went pale. Satisfied, Shekiba turned and walked toward the soldier.

Shekiba was led into a small room in the east wing of the palace. The two men who had questioned her only a few days ago sat waiting. The short man looked at the lanky man, waiting for him to begin speaking.

Will Amanullah come here? Is it possible I will meet him today? Is it possible that there will really be a nikkah *between us?*

"*Salaam,*" she said quietly with her head bowed. She fidgeted with her clothing, her head scarf, wanting every piece to look perfectly in place. They motioned for her to sit in the chair across from them. One man spoke while the other nodded in agreement and parroted his words.

"You are a fortunate girl."

"Very fortunate."

Shekiba did not look up.

"You have been shown mercy that you did not deserve. You should be very grateful."

"Very grateful."

"Someone has agreed to take you on as wife, a title one would have hardly expected for you. But this is a chance for you to redeem yourself. To attempt to live a respectable life and fulfill your duties as dictated by our holy Qur'an. Do you think you can do this?"

"I was raised with love for our holy book, sir. I want nothing more than to live an honorable life."

He raised an eyebrow. Maybe he had anticipated a more insolent response.

"Very well then. As you can imagine, our dear king Habibullah has no desire to lay eyes on you again after the tragedy that befell this palace. But he has given his blessing that you be given in marriage."

Shekiba's heart pounded. Still they had not mentioned the man's name. She waited on each word he uttered, anxious to hear that name, that sweet name — Amanullah!

"Your future spouse is in the room next door with the *mullah*. He is signing the marriage certificate." The door opened and a third man appeared. He gave the other two a nod and they turned back to Shekiba.

"He has agreed, stating his intentions clearly thrice over. Now it is your turn. We will speak on your behalf. Do you agree to take Agha Baraan as your husband in life?"

Shekiba began nodding before she heard the name. She kept nodding even when she heard the name and even for a few seconds after, before her mind was able to process it.

"Agha Ba. . . . ?"

"It is a simple yes-or-no response. Do you agree to take Agha Baraan as your husband? And might I add that you would be a bigger fool than we already know you to be if you should even consider any response other than yes."

Shekiba sat speechless. They stared at her expectantly while her mind spun.

What is happening? Why would Agha Baraan want me? Agha Baraan? Benafsha's secret lover? This doesn't make any sense at all.

Shekiba felt her face tingle.

"Yes or no?" Louder, impatient.

"Are you stupid? Just say yes so we can send word to the *mullah* to close the *nikkah*! Maybe we should just speak on her behalf. I'm in no mood to wait."

"Fine, then it's agreed. She hasn't said no. I'll tell the *mullah*." The stocky man stood and walked out the door.

What about Amanullah? Then who is he to be married to? How could I have thought . . . ?

Shekiba thought of the conversation she

had overheard in the garden. Her throat knotted with anger. Maybe she was as foolish as everyone said.

A paper was brought to Shekiba and she took the pen that was handed to her, already dipped in ink, and wrote her name on the line. She was dazed but aware enough to know there was nothing else she could do. She'd seen how the palace disposed of people.

They led her into the hallway, where she was instructed to don her *burqa*. She did as she was told and Agha Baraan emerged from a nearby room. He looked in her direction, his face more somber than she remembered; his eyes heavy, dark and mournful.

He nodded at her and walked down the hallway toward the door. She followed, hearing the sighs of relief from the king's lanky and stout advisers behind her. She was leaving the palace with Agha Baraan. Her *nikkah* had been signed, the contract official and binding. Shekiba was married to Agha Baraan.

CHAPTER 50
RAHIMA

Seeing Shahla made me miss her more. And Parwin. As the car bumped down the dirt road to Kabul, I thought about my sisters. Shahla looked like she was being treated well. Her mother-in-law seemed to be kinder, gentler than Bibi Gulalai. Just last night, Bibi Gulalai had taken her walking stick to my shoulder as I swept the hallway. She snapped the stick against my kneecaps when I fell to my side. She didn't like the way I was crouched, she said. It was shameful.

I shifted in the seat, realizing the seat belt was pushing against a sore spot below my collarbone. I sighed heavily. Badriya pretended not to notice and I was grateful for that. I had no intention of crying on her shoulder.

But there was something else that I'd been thinking about since Shahla's visit. Something that had been creeping into my mind since we sisters left our father's house. Shahla had chosen to name her daughter Parwin. I loved

Parwin with all my heart but it was undeniably bold and bad luck to name a child after someone with a lame leg. I wondered if I could have brought myself to name a child Parwin. Or Shaima. I hoped my aunt would never know. I felt a surge of shame to think it but I wouldn't have used either of those names.

Bringing Jahangir into the world had nearly killed me. I prayed I would not become pregnant again and for once Allah had answered my prayers. But by now my body had regained strength and my mind had blurred the memory of his birth; I had started to want another child. I wasn't sure why I hadn't become pregnant again but I thought maybe Allah had a plan for me. Maybe next month. As foolish and illogical as it was, I prayed my next child would be a girl.

What name would I choose? Raisa. My mother. Absolutely not. I was less embarrassed to admit that. I could picture her eyes in a toxic glaze, red with smoke, while Rohila and Sitara watched on helplessly. No, I could never use my mother's name. But I couldn't think of my mother without missing her, missing the way she held me on the day of our *nikkahs,* the day that broke her.

Zamarud? Maybe, but probably not. Too many people disliked her, enough to try to kill her. If they tried once, they would likely try again and maybe succeed. Then it would be the name of a murdered parliamentarian. No, I thought. That wouldn't do.

Hamida? Or Sufia? Very possibly. I liked them both, Hamida a bit more because she had pushed Badriya to let me see more in the parliament, to do more outside.

Shekiba. That was it. That was the name I would have chosen. The name of my *bibi*'s *bibi*. The woman who lived the double life I had, walked in a man's clothes, worked with a man's strength and fended for herself. That's what I would want to name my daughter, if I were to have one. If.

"I'm not going to babysit you just because of what happened with Zamarud. You better look out for yourself," Badriya said sharply. Kabul's busy streets were coming into view. I turned and looked at her, not sure what she was implying.

"Fine with me. I didn't think you were looking out for me before," I said flatly, but I was too late to catch myself. Badriya's eyes widened.

"Why, you insolent little . . ." Unable to find the words, she whipped the back of her hand against my face. My eyes watered and my nose stung. I prayed it wouldn't bleed on my freshly washed dress. "Don't you dare talk to me like that, you worthless girl. Just remember you're here only because of me and I can change my mind about your usefulness anytime."

I bit my tongue and looked out the tinted window.

We checked back into our room at the hotel. The apartment our husband had purchased needed a lot of work before we could stay there. He'd asked his guard and driver to find some local workers to replace the flooring and cover the windows. He didn't want people or neighbors catching a glimpse of his wives.

Badriya set to unpacking right away, hanging her dresses in the closet.

I saw something that made my jaw drop. Our room had a television in it! It hadn't been here on our last trip and Badriya had never mentioned having one before. I turned it on and saw Badriya watching me, very interested.

There was a knock on the door. I looked at Badriya.

"Don't just stand there like an idiot. Find out who it is!"

It was the man we'd seen downstairs when we checked in. Our driver stood behind him, his arms crossed.

"Excuse me, *khanum-ha,* forgive me for intruding but it seems that we've forgotten one thing. May I enter please?" He looked back at Maroof, who nodded.

I stepped away from the door, turned to the side, and kept my head scarf pulled across my face. I didn't need Maroof reporting anything back to my husband about my behavior. The man entered our room, turned the television off and unplugged it. He wrapped his arms around it and lugged it out the door while I watched, brokenhearted. I had seen about thirty seconds of a woman singing in a grass field, the small mirrors on her traditional Afghan dress catching the sun.

The door closed. Abdul Khaliq had a television back at the compound. A large box he kept in his own room, with an antenna that tracked to the roof of the house. We weren't permitted to watch it. Once he'd caught me in there, eyeing it and fingering the buttons, daring myself to turn it on. I didn't expect him to be home. He'd thundered into the room and grabbed me by the neck so hard I couldn't breathe.

"What do you think you're doing? Let me catch you watching television and I'll rip your eyeballs out of their sockets!"

Khala Shaima had explained his reaction to me when I asked her if she had a television at home.

"Your husband is a lot of things but he's not a stupid man. He knows what he's doing. He doesn't want you to see what's going on in the rest of the country, what the other women are doing. These television stations now have so many programs, female singers, female news reporters. Even men advocating on behalf of women. Can you imagine that?

Now can you imagine how you would feel if you were to see women like that every day? He needs to keep you blindfolded."

The hotel manager had forgotten to remove the television before we got there. It angered me to realize how tight our leash was, even this far away from Abdul Khaliq. I felt like I was being buried in a hole, deeper and deeper every day until I could hardly see daylight.

At least returning to the *jirga* sessions was a break for me. And I was thankful to see Hamida and Sufia again. They greeted us with hugs and asked about our children. I couldn't help but notice, happily, that they were warmer with me than they were with Badriya. I liked that they liked me.

The attack on Zamarud had frightened Badriya, as it had many other female parliamentarians. Hamida told me two women had decided not to return, afraid that they would be in danger as well. Zamarud was badly hurt, she said. Her wounds had gotten infected and she'd been hospitalized. She was not expected to survive.

The session opened with a prayer. I sat with Badriya, our heads bowed and our hands cupped. I spent the day filling out her papers and reading documents to her. She snapped at me for reading too slowly but I said nothing. It was easier that way. After the sessions and during our breaks, I would tag along with Hamida and Sufia, who were kind enough not to ask why I didn't accompany Badriya. It was only within the parliament building that my husband's driver and guard did not keep track of my whereabouts. Here, the leash slackened.

After the sessions, Badriya wanted Maroof and our guard to escort her back to the hotel. She had no interest in attending classes at the women's training center but I certainly did. The guards had more stock in looking after Abdul Khaliq's first wife, so they watched nonchalantly as I climbed into Hamida's car, leaving me under the watch of her guard and driver.

We opened the door to the training center, which was, as usual, empty until we got there.

"Hello!" Ms. Franklin called out happily.

I wondered how she could be so cheerful all the time.

We alternated every day. One day she would teach basic English, and the following day we were back on the computer, learning to navigate the Internet or type notes. I thrilled at being a student again and longed for a real classroom, one full of boys my age whom I could learn with, joke with and play soccer with.

Ms. Franklin was proud of our progress. She said she'd told her parents all about us, about how impressed she was with our dedication, with our desire to work in government as women. I liked her praise. It had been a long time since I'd heard any.

So when the door opened, thirty minutes into our session, we were understandably intrigued to see who it was.

A tall, thin woman in her forties entered and looked around, unsure.

"Hello, come in!" Ms. Franklin said.

The woman wore a calf-length black jacket over a deep-plum-colored tunic and pants. Her ponytail was hidden by a plum-colored head scarf.

"Salaam!" she replied. "You are Ms. Franklin?"

Her name was Fakhria and she put Ms. Franklin in a tricky situation. She worked at a women's shelter here in Kabul and wanted to attend the classes at the resource center. Ms. Franklin looked mildly perplexed. The funds that supported the center were specifically allocated to women parliamentarians. The classes were not open to the public because, theoretically, the center couldn't accommodate more than the women *jirga* members. But so few of them came.

Ms. Franklin pursed her lips and waved Fakhria in, as I would have done. Somehow, she was not a woman you could turn away easily.

At the end of the class, Hamida asked Fakhria about the shelter. She and Sufia had heard of a women's shelter but hadn't ever seen it. I was surprised to hear such a place existed.

"My sister was killed by her husband. I decided I needed to do something and then I came upon this shelter. It was founded by an Afghan woman who was living in America. She raised money and emptied her pockets into building this place for girls. She travels back and forth now but we have a few people who look after the shelter."

"And your husband, he doesn't mind you spending time there?" Sufia asked gently.

"No, he is very supportive actually. He's a kind man, my husband. After what happened with my sister, he knew I would go crazy just sitting there in mourning. We've got five children to keep me busy at home but I needed to do this. I wanted my children to see me do something."

Fakhria started to tell us about the shelter, about the girls who came there. She told us about a girl she called Murwarid. Murwarid was only fifteen years old, she said, and had come to the shelter two weeks ago, bruised and desperate. At the age of eight, she'd been married to a man in his sixties, living in the countryside. Her husband had abused her in every way possible. Her nose was crooked after he'd broken it twice. When he'd tired of her, he'd started to take her around to other villages, selling her off to men to have sex with her. She had tried to run away once before but he caught her and sliced off one ear, dragging her home by the other.

Six months later Murwarid decided again that she wouldn't survive if she stayed with this man. And this time, if he killed her, she would be better off. So she ran.

She came to Kabul and found the women's shelter, where she was living now, recovering. She still woke in the night screaming.

Fakhria invited us to visit the shelter. It would be great, she said, if the parliament could help support such a place. Maybe offer some training or jobs to the women living there.

Hamida and Sufia clucked their tongues to hear the stories Fakhria told.

I sat frozen. Too much of what she said sounded familiar.

You see that? Murwarid found her escape, I could hear Khala Shaima say. *Why haven't you found yours?*

CHAPTER 51
RAHIMA

"Read this one to me."

Badriya had unfolded Kabul's weekly news-paper on the table. She pointed from one column to the next. She stopped me one paragraph into a story about drought conditions in a province to the south.

"Forget it. Who needs to know about that? I want to know what's happening here. Try this one," she said, picking out a column on the following page. I sighed and got ready to read about a new bank opening next month when I was interrupted.

A knock on our door.

"There's a phone call from home. Come down to the lobby to take the call." It was Hassan, our bodyguard.

"Now?" she huffed. "As if we haven't had a long enough day!"

Badriya and I had just gotten plates of food sent up from the hotel kitchen. I loved the food there. Maybe it was that I had no part in cooking it or cleaning up after it. Maybe it was the pretty floral pattern of the plates. My mouth watered at the smell of the cumin-infused potato stew. I tore off a piece of bread as she resentfully left the room. I dipped a piece of bread into the stew and brought it to my mouth. The grease felt good on my lips. No reason for us both to eat cold meals, I figured.

Badriya returned a few moments later.

"The *qorma* is really good," I announced as she walked in. I looked up and saw that her face was drained of color.

"Are you . . . are you all right?"

She looked at me, her mouth open slightly. Her eyes searched.

"Badriya-*jan,* what is it? Who was on the phone?"

Her hand covered her mouth. Something wasn't right.

"Badriya-*jan,* are you all right?"

Suddenly, something in her shifted. She straightened her shoulders and pulled her lips together tightly.

"It was Abdul Khaliq on the phone. He called about Jahangir."

My stomach fell at the sound of his name.

"He's not well," she said, choosing her words carefully. "He's not well. Seems he's been very sick since we left."

"Since we left? Why didn't he call sooner?"

"I don't know, Rahima-*jan.* I don't . . . he's going to have Maroof take us back."

"I want to go back now!"

"We are. Maroof is bringing the car around."

I wanted to be there already. I wanted to see my son. The last time he had been ill, he'd spent two days in my arms. Whispering every prayer I could remember, I stroked the moist hairs from his sweaty forehead and watched his cherry lips tremble until the fever released him. I knew he must have cried for me and I hated that I wasn't there.

We packed our belongings in a matter of minutes. Badriya moved surprisingly quickly. Forty minutes later, Abdul Khaliq's SUV was on the main road leaving Kabul, whizzing past tanks and western soldiers, their curious eyes shielded by sunglasses. Maroof grunted something to Hassan in the passenger seat.

There was something peculiar about Badriya's behavior. Jahangir, like all the other children in the compound, had survived fever and illness. I looked over at her. Badriya busied herself folding papers neatly and putting them away in her purse. Papers she couldn't read.

"What did he say, Badriya? Do they want to take him to a doctor? Has he been eating anything?"

"I don't know, dear girl. The connection was lousy and you know Abdul Khaliq. He doesn't explain much."

The hours dragged on. I tried to fall asleep,

hoping I would open my eyes and find myself back at the compound, Jahangir coming to the gate to welcome me. It would be midnight before we got back. I hoped Jameela had made him a cup of the herbal tea she had given him last time. I hoped the other children were not disturbing him.

Just as I was beginning to drift off, it occurred to me that there was something odd about my conversation with Badriya. Something other than Jahangir being ill.

The way she had looked at me. What was that look?

Concern? Annoyance? Fatigue?

Pity.

I don't know, dear girl.

Never before had she addressed me with endearments.

My mouth went dry. I started to pray.

CHAPTER 52
SHEKIBA

Shekiba and Agha Baraan did not speak on the way to his home. Shekiba sat beside her new husband but kept her gaze straight ahead. Agha Baraan guided the horse expertly down Kabul's busy streets, small shops and pedestrians everywhere. He looked in her direction only once but his expression told Shekiba nothing.

He turned down a narrow, house-lined street, homes packed so close together that a child could toss an apple into his neighbor's courtyard. Shekiba thought of her village, the homes divided by kilometers of open fields.

Agha Baraan's home was in the middle of the street; the royal-blue door set it apart from the rest.

Shekiba suddenly felt a panic set in at the thought of being behind those walls with this man. She briefly considered running — disappearing into Kabul's maze of roads. But she remembered Azizullah dragging her back from Hakim-*sahib*'s doorstep and decided against it.

He opened the door and she followed. The courtyard was small, much smaller than houses in her village, but it was neatly kept and had bright flowers and a birdcage with three small canaries. She followed her husband through the house door.

A woman in her twenties looked up from her needlework. She did not seem surprised.

"Gulnaz, this is Shekiba. You can show her to her room please. She has no belongings so you'll have to give her a dress or two for now."

Gulnaz stood up and looked at the blue cloak before her. Agha Baraan walked out, uninterested in how the two would take to each other.

"You can take your *burqa* off. You look ridiculous wearing it inside." Shekiba understood by the tone of her voice that Gulnaz was Agha Baraan's first wife and that she was not happy to see her. Shekiba lifted her *burqa* but kept her right profile toward Gulnaz.

"I hear they call you Shekiba-*e-haleem.* Let me see your face."

Shekiba turned, making a point to look Gulnaz in the eye. Each woman took a moment to consider the other. Gulnaz was a beautiful woman but nowhere near as striking as Benafsha. She had almond-shaped eyes and gracefully arched brows. Her hair looked soft and thick, loose curls tossed over her shoulders.

"I see," she said, wincing. "Well, come this way. I'll show you to your room."

The layout of the house was similar to Bobo Shahgul's. Behind the living room was a small kitchen. Off the main hallway were three other rooms, which Shekiba was not shown. The last room was to be hers, an eight-by-ten-foot space without a window. A thin cushion lay against the wall and a lantern sat on a narrow round table.

"I'll bring you some clothes later. For now you can stay here. We won't be eating dinner for a while. I've prepared the meal for tonight. You can start helping tomorrow."

"Khanum Gulnaz, I —"

"Don't call me that. It doesn't sound right. Just call me by my name. You're his wife now and it would sound strange if someone were to hear you say that."

"I'm sorry."

"Let me warn you. This is my home. I do things the way I like and you better not expect to change things. You're here because he wants you to be here but that does not mean you can do as you please."

"I had no intention —"

"Good. Then it's understood and I'll expect no problems from you. I asked him to have you in a separate house but there just isn't room for that right now. You'll have to be here."

Gulnaz was only slightly older than Shekiba

but she spoke with such condescending authority that Shekiba felt like she was being chastised by one of her uncles' wives. She had no reason to expect Gulnaz to be any kinder to her, but Shekiba thought Gulnaz might be able to shed some light on her situation.

"Excuse me, but can I ask one question, Gulnaz-*jan*? Can you tell me why I am here?"

"What? What do you mean?"

"You said he wants me to be here. Why does he want me here?"

"You have no idea?"

"No."

Gulnaz shook her head and walked out of the room, leaving Shekiba with more questions than answers.

She heard from Gulnaz once more that night, when she walked by the room and announced that there was food left in the kitchen if she wanted some. Shekiba stared blankly at the door but did not respond. She felt terribly out of place. And she was now a woman again. Her dress felt cumbersome and heavy. She had just about forgotten how to keep her head scarf in place. She had left her guard's uniform in Benafsha's room but took with her the corset used to bind her breasts. She could not tolerate their jiggling, even though the corset chafed her raw wounds.

Shekiba wondered how things would be here, with her living as a second wife to

Benafsha's lover, the man who had betrayed the king in the worst way. How had she become involved in such a twisted affair?

She listened, nervous, for the sound of Agha Baraan approaching. She knew, from watching the king's habits, that men came for women at odd hours of the day and night. She felt unprepared to be near him behind closed doors. Shekiba dozed off sometime near morning.

"Look, you've got to get up and eat something. It doesn't really matter to me what you do but I won't have the blame on my shoulders if you get ill from hunger. Looks like you're not in great shape to start with. Here's a dress too. That's all you will be getting from me. He can buy you fabric if you need another."

Shekiba sat up and rubbed her eyes. She watched Gulnaz put a plate with bread and butter on the floor, along with a cup of black tea.

"And if we're to share the house then we'll share the work. You can't expect to just laze around all day long."

"Sorry, I didn't realize the time . . ."

Gulnaz did not wait for an explanation. She was gone before Shekiba could finish her sentence. The butter melted on her tongue. She walked out of her room hesitantly and found the washroom. It was summertime and a bit of cool water felt good, especially on her scabs. Shekiba wondered how badly scarred her back was. She cursed Ghafoor again but Ghafoor wasn't the only one to blame. Agha Baraan and Benafsha had created the mess as well. Shekiba had been caught in an elephant stampede.

I am not welcome here. I am his wife, but only half. Nothing about me is whole. Why did he do this?

Shekiba went out to find Gulnaz and make herself useful. This part was nothing new to her. It felt the same as being in Marjan's home. Or Bobo Shahgul's. She found the kitchen empty, a pile of raw potatoes on a counter. Shekiba looked around. Agha Baraan had a nice home. The walls were smooth and flat and intricate hand-knotted carpets covered the living room floor. There was a tufted sofa with carved wooden arms as well as a chair that Shekiba had not noticed the day before. On the walls were framed pieces of calligraphy, Allah's name written in graceful curves, slants and dots.

Shekiba went back into the kitchen and looked around. There were cups and plates in the cabinets and a pile of pots and pans underneath the counter. Shekiba found a knife and sat down to peel the potatoes. It was a relief to be doing something and when Gulnaz came back in from the courtyard, she pretended not to notice the second wife in her kitchen, walking to her room instead.

They have no children, Shekiba realized. That was what was different in this house. No excited footsteps, high-pitched voices or crying. They lived alone and apart from the rest of Agha Baraan's family.

It would be hard to get lost in such a small household. Gulnaz said nothing more to her than household instructions. She left dirty clothes in a pile and told her Aasif, Agha Baraan's first name, needed his shirts for the morning. They did not eat together. Gulnaz and Agha Baraan shared their meals when he was home but Shekiba kept herself occupied with chores and made no motion to join them. Nor was she invited. She took her meals to her room or ate a few bites in the kitchen.

Aasif said no more than a few words to her each day, mostly small greetings in passing, his eyes averted. Shekiba would mumble something to complete the exchange. Aasif was different with Gulnaz. He chatted about the people he had seen and told her of Kabul's local news. Gulnaz listened and asked questions. Sometimes they even laughed together. Shekiba wondered how things had been for Aasif and Gulnaz when they were first married. Had Aasif been as cool with her as he was now with Shekiba? Would he ever say anything more to her?

The silence was uncomfortable, but Shekiba dreaded a conversation with Aasif.

That day in the palace, when she had spoken with him, he had seemed a gentle person, a noble man. But what she knew now made her question her first impression.

Four nights passed before he came to her room. Shekiba had begun to believe he had brought her only to help with the housework when she heard her door open. It was late and her eyes were just beginning to feel heavy with sleep. In the darkness, she could make out his thin silhouette.

He stood there for a moment, watching her. Shekiba kept her eyes mostly closed, feigning sleep and praying he would turn and walk back out. Her heart beat so loudly she was sure he could hear it. He came in and closed the door behind him. Shekiba nearly stopped breathing.

He sat beside her mattress on the floor, his back turned to her. His head was lowered.

"Things turned out badly," he said quietly. "I regret that it happened this way."

Shekiba stayed silent.

"She was a good woman and did not deserve what they did to her. I did not want . . . I did not think it would go so far. But once they found out, there was no stopping it. I was foolish to ignore what might happen — what *did* happen," he whispered, his voice cracking. "She warned me and I ignored it. I ignored it. Still, she spared me or I would not be sitting here now. I am very aware of that."

Ramblings of a guilty conscience. He knew Shekiba was aware of their affair. Maybe he thought Benafsha had revealed his identity to her or maybe he thought she had recognized him as he stumbled past her on that night. Shekiba did not know why he was making this admission but she listened carefully.

"Gulnaz is not happy. Things will be difficult for a time but it will get better."

And without a word from Shekiba, Aasif, her husband, walked out of her room and closed the door behind him.

CHAPTER 53
RAHIMA

It was pitch-black when we arrived at the compound. Never had I been so relieved to see those gates. Maroof parked the car, looked at Hassan and sighed. Badriya had fidgeted so much in the last hour of the drive back that I'd thought she might just jump right out of the car. I didn't bother with my *burqa*. Our car had barely stopped before I jumped out and opened the gate. There were lights on.

I opened the door to find Jameela rushing toward it. Her face told me everything.

"Jameela!"

"Oh, Rahima-*jan*! Allah, help us — dear, young mother!" Her voice rose and fell, my heart with it.

"Jameela, where's my son? Where's Jahangir? Is he all right?" I grabbed her by the arms and moved her aside, pushing my way toward her room. Shahnaz emerged, holding her *chador* tightly at her chin. She was looking down, avoiding my gaze. I stopped short when I saw her. Her lips were trembling.

"Why are you all out here? Who's watching my son? Where is he?"

Jameela rushed back and grabbed me before I could run into her room. By this time, Badriya had joined her.

Jameela hugged me tightly and held my head to her chest.

"Rahima-*jan,* Rahima-*jan,* God has decided to take your son! He's taken your little boy, dear girl. God give him peace, that darling little boy!"

I froze. That was what I'd read in Badriya's face. I looked at her now but she, like Shahnaz, diverted her tearful eyes.

Someone wailed. Someone moaned *no, no, no, no.* My son's name.

It was my voice.

This couldn't be true. This couldn't be real. I looked around, thinking everyone I lived with had gone mad.

Abdul Khaliq came into the hallway, his eyes red, his lips tight. He looked at me and shook his head. I saw my husband's shoulders heave. Bibi Gulalai stood behind him, sobbing into a handkerchief.

"Why? Why would you leave a sick child? His mother should have been here with him!" she cried out.

I looked into my husband's eyes, our first truly intimate moment. It was as if no one else existed.

It's true . . . It's true, Rahima. What they're saying about Jahangir, our son, is true! Our beloved boy is gone!

Abdul Khaliq covered his eyes with his hands before he looked up, took a deep breath and yelled for someone to find his prayer cap. His voice cracked and my chest caved in as the air was sucked out of the house.

CHAPTER 54
RAHIMA

I'm not altogether sure what happened after that. There was whispering, wailing, cursing and praying. All at once and then one at a time. Voices and faces blurred around me.

Let me see my son, I screamed. *I want to see Jahangir.*

Have a sip of water. You look as if you're about to pass out.

Someone brought a glass to my lips.

The other children were in the living room, the older ones somberly watching over the babies and trying to keep them quiet.

Abdul Khaliq's compound had never experienced such tragedy. Even I, who had lost my father, my mother, my sisters and myself, even I could not believe God would add this to my lot.

They led me to Jameela's room. My little boy. His tiny face looked pale, his lips gray. I fell to my knees and put my head on his small chest. I stroked his chestnut hair, touched his full cheeks. I talked to him as if there was no one else in the room, as if there was no one else in the world. I wanted to comfort him and breathe life back into his little body. I was his mother. I had given him life and when he was ill, I had nursed him back to health. Why should now be any different?

I snapped when I felt a hand pull at my elbow.

"Leave us alone! I need to make my son better. He always wakes when I whisper his name. You'll see him yawn, rub his eyes and look around in confusion. He's going to tell me he missed me and that I shouldn't go away again."

There were traditions, rules that needed to be followed.

One hand became two, or maybe it was four. When there were enough, the hands became stronger than I and the room shrank away from me. I was in the hallway. I was on the floor. I was outside of myself. The arms melted away.

That is enough, they whispered. I hated them.

Bibi Gulalai was there. Wailing louder than anyone else.

Why? Dear Allah, what a sweet little boy he was! Too young, too young to take! His face, I picture his face before me as if he were still here. I can't believe it. I just can't believe it! Oh, my poor son! Why should you have to have such a tragedy happen to you, my God-fearing son! My lion among men! If only I'd known sooner! I could have done more for him! I could have made him better!

I hated her.

I was numb. Days passed. Rituals were performed. All the right prayers were said. All the wrong people came to pay their respects. I noticed little of it, only the absence of my own family. My mother, my father. They never came to their grandson's *fateha*. My father was not there to carry my son or throw fistfuls of dirt onto his grave. It mattered, though it shouldn't have. Jahangir had never known them anyway.

Khala Shaima came, as did Shahla. My aunt and my sister sat by my side as I rocked back and forth, their eyes red and raw. Someone asked Khala Shaima about my parents, if they were coming. Shahla bit her lip and looked at the ground. I heard my husband curse my father. He was insulted, not only as a son-in-law but also as a former commander. Whatever respect he owed his father-in-law, out of tradition, was lost now. And I didn't care.

"Oh God, Rahima-*jan*," Shahla whispered. "I can't believe this! He was so full of light!"

I closed my eyes.

Khala Shaima looked thinner than she had the last time I'd seen her but I couldn't bear to think on it much. She shook her head and whispered to me that the medicine had gotten the best of my parents. It was hard to tell which of them was worse than the other. She clucked her tongue in dismay and squeezed my limp hand.

"They can barely get themselves up and about in the house," she said.

"You're there a lot," I said blankly.

She nodded. She was concerned about Rohila and Sitara. She had mentioned in her last visit that rumors were circulating of suitors for my younger sisters. She wanted to make sure the girls were not given away in a careless stupor.

My aunts and uncles came. Even my grandparents. I kissed their hands. They cried and made sorry excuses to my husband and mother-in-law for the notable absence of my mother and father. They were embarrassed more than anything else.

You never saw him, I wanted to scream. *You didn't know how sweet he was.*

I'd never expected much from my grandparents. They'd had little to do with my sisters and me since we were married off. It was as people said. Once married, girls no longer belonged to the families that raised them. Especially if they only raised them halfway. But Madar-*jan,* she'd been so different once upon a time.

"She's that bad?" I asked Khala Shaima.

"She's that bad, *dokhtar-jan,*" she said,

545

confirming it. "Your sisters, Rohila and Sitara, they really wanted to come see you. But your grandmother didn't think it was proper for them to come without your mother. And, of course, she wouldn't let them come with me. Rohila cried when she heard. She wanted to hide under my *burqa* and sneak over here. Sitara, she's very reserved but she's a strong girl. You girls would be very proud of your sisters."

I was sure she was right. They were surviving in a home without a mother or father, essentially. They'd been abandoned just as much as my own son.

"I should have taken him, Khala Shaima. I should have taken him to Kabul with me. He wouldn't have gotten sick with me. And even if he had, I could have taken him to a hospital. They have the best hospitals there. Lots of doctors. Even foreign ones."

"Your husband never would have allowed it. He keeps his sons at his side, my dear. You know that."

"Then I should have stayed with him. I didn't have to go to Kabul."

Khala Shaima said nothing. We both knew it had been her idea.

My son was buried in the family plot, a half kilometer from the compound. It was sacred earth for Abdul Khaliq's family.

My husband was quiet, different. I knew he was hurt.

"He's with his ancestors now. They're watching over him, as is Allah. His fate is our fate," Abdul Khaliq said to me when the men returned from the burial.

Naseeb. Was it really Jahangir's destiny to be taken so young? Was it my *naseeb* never to see my son grow taller than me, to go to school, to help his father at work?

Abdul Khaliq asked Jameela to look after me. I saw him pull her aside and have a few words. They watched me. Badriya too, although a week after Jahangir was buried, she quietly asked Abdul Khaliq when she could return to Kabul. His hand flew across her face so fast that she'd barely finished her sentence.

I closed my eyes and wished for everyone to disappear, including myself.

Every Friday, Abdul Khaliq's friends and family members gathered at our compound for a *khatm.* Each person read one of the thirty parts of the Qur'an. Prayers were said at the completion, or *khatm,* of the holy book. I could hear them from down the hall and prayed along with them, hoping it did Jahangir some good. It did me none.

Khala Shaima came back more often than before, even though the trip had become very difficult for her. She was worried. I was losing weight; my clothes hung loosely on me. When I looked in the mirror I saw someone I barely recognized. My face had dark spots

547

and my eyes were heavy. I saw Jameela and Khala Shaima exchange worried looks.

Abdul Khaliq let me be for the most part. He wasn't speaking much either. His guards tiptoed around him. His friends kept their voices low and their comments brief. My husband, the warlord, was not one to express or show emotion, but it was clear that he was grieving. He was short even with Bibi Gula-lai.

My head felt like an empty, dark room. My insides were painfully hollow. I missed my son's face, his smile, the way his small fingers held on to mine. He was supposed to be safe. He had survived infancy. He had learned to walk, to talk, to tell me when he was hungry and when he was happy. Jahangir. His name was a dagger. His name was a salve.

Four weeks passed before I was able to ask the questions that remained.

"Jameela-*jan.*"

Jameela stopped short, surprised to hear my voice. "Yes?"

"What happened to him?"

Jameela stood still for a moment, pondering my question. Then she sat on the cushion next to me in the living room, tucking her legs under her and straightening her skirt. She put her hand on mine.

"Rahima-*jan,* he became ill. Everything happened very quickly. So quickly." Her mind traveled back to that day. "Abdul Khaliq called Badriya right away."

"I want to know what *happened* to him," I said insistently.

After me, Jameela probably carried the most guilt. I'd left Jahangir in her care and come back to find my son dead. She felt terrible about it. She wasn't sure how much to explain and how much to leave unsaid. She told me in bits and pieces, filtering as she went along.

First came the fever. His body was hot. *From his head to his toes, so hot,* Jameela said. She had tried to fan him, to cool him down with baths. His bowels were loose. Jameela looked for worms but saw nothing in his stool. When he started to complain about his stomach hurting, she'd talked to Abdul Khaliq. He saw Jahangir's trembling body and immediately called for Bibi Gulalai. Bibi Gulalai set to work making a soup heavy with garlic and herbs to clear the germ from his body. But instead of getting better, things got worse.

On the fourth day, Jahangir's belly was freckled with red spots. Jameela tried again to cool him with moist cloths on his forehead and sips of water. When Jahangir stopped whining and complaining about his belly, she thought he was finally getting better. She thought he needed a few days of rest and that by the time we returned he would be back to his usual self, just as I'd left him.

549

We were both crying. She paused her story two or three times, collecting herself and then looking at me. I nodded for her to continue. I needed to know.

By that afternoon, Jameela realized that Jahangir was delirious. He wasn't answering her questions but he was mumbling and batting away something that wasn't there. She called his name. His eyes were glassy. She called again for Abdul Khaliq, who had just returned from an overnight trip with his guards. Never before had she seen our husband so shaken, Jameela said. He took one look at his son, then flew out the door and summoned his driver and guards. He came back into the room and cradled Jahangir in his arms while he yelled for Jameela to pack some water and bread for the drive to the hospital. Before she knew it, Jameela was standing at the front gate, watching the tires of Abdul Khaliq's black truck spin and screech as they tore off down the road.

She didn't want to go on. I put my hand on hers. She looked tortured. She sighed and continued, trying to get her words out in one short burst.

They came back the next day, heavy, morose faces. Jameela ran out to meet them. Abdul Khaliq looked at her and shook his head.

"Crying," she said. "I've never seen him looking like that. I never thought . . . the doc-

550

tor wasn't able to do anything for him. He was too weak and they think he had developed a terrible infection of his stomach. Horrible. Something that just took over, making his belly stone-hard when the doctor tried to touch it. He was in the hospital until morning and they were giving him serum but it didn't work. I suppose . . . I suppose it was his *naseeb,*" she said, sobbing. "Rahima-*jan,* I'm so sorry. I don't know how he got so sick so quickly! He felt better for a bit. He let me rub his stomach. I thought it was helping . . ."

"Why didn't he take my son to the doctor sooner?" I knew she felt badly. At the moment, I didn't care very much. I wanted to know if something could have been done. I wanted to know who to blame.

"Abdul Khaliq? He . . . he wanted to. Before he left for his meetings."

"Then why didn't he?"

Jameela shook her head in frustration. "Rahima-*jan,* what's done is done now. It won't help anything to ask so many questions. It's best you think of your son, pray for him to be in peace."

"I'm tired of praying, damn it. I want to know. What happened, Jameela?" I said insistently. She was glossing over something.

"Abdul Khaliq was going to take Jahangir to the hospital but . . . but Bibi Gulalai stopped him."

"*What?* Why on earth would she do that?"

"She thought . . . she thought she could heal him with the teas and soups she was making for him."

My heart sank. Bibi Gulalai was going to save him. I nearly laughed. Her concoctions had never saved anyone from anything. She had stood in the way of my son getting to the doctor. My husband had tried, I thought.

"He really did try," Jameela echoed, as if she could read my thoughts.

I had a fresh hatred for Bibi Gulalai. She'd been the one to delay Jahangir's treatment. She'd been yelling and carrying on about the absent mother being to blame. Now I knew why. Bibi Gulalai always boasted about the powers of her remedies. She claimed she could heal any ailment with her potent, homemade brews, and that she had. The family humored her. She wanted to look good, the grandmother who stepped in and cured her grandchild while his shameful mother played in Kabul.

One more question to ask, the question I dreaded because there was no good answer. It haunted me.

"Jameela-*jan* . . . ," I said, my voice breaking.

"Yes, *janem*," she said gently.

I was looking over the edge of a cliff.

"Jameela-*jan* . . . did he . . . did he cry for me?"

Jameela, loving mother of six, had also

given birth to two children who had been claimed by Allah before she could see their smiles. Jameela pulled me into her arms and kissed my forehead. She read my heart.

"My dear *madar-ak*" — *little mother* — she whispered, though I wasn't one anymore. "What child doesn't call out for his mother? What could be more comforting than a mother's embrace? I believe, in his sleep, that's where your little boy was, feeling your arms around him, *janem*."

"But I wasn't there!" I cried. "I wasn't there to hold him, to wipe away his tears, to kiss him good-bye! He was just a baby! How scared he must have been!"

"I know, Rahima-*jan,* but he wasn't alone. No one can replace you but at least his father was there with him. His father held him. And you know, Abdul Khaliq loved his little son very much."

It wasn't until weeks later that this conversation would bring me solace. For now, I stored her words, saving them for when my heart had healed enough to believe that my son had felt my embrace. That his father had held him lovingly in his last moments. That he did not feel as alone as I did now.

CHAPTER 55
SHEKIBA

Shekiba swept the floor of the living room, beating the dust from the rug section by section. She had breathed a huge sigh of relief after Aasif had left her room, thankful that he had not touched her as his wife. At least for now. He felt remorse for what he had done. And Shekiba could hear something in his voice that she hadn't heard in a long time. Aasif sounded as if he *cared* about Benafsha. Maybe her first impression of him hadn't been that far off. There was still a lot to learn about him but it seemed he had a heart.

Shekiba had spent the rest of the night replaying his words in her mind and trying to piece together how she had come to be his wife.

He could not stop her execution. So he stopped mine. How did he propose this deal to King Habibullah? Does Gulnaz know all this?

Shekiba wondered why the king bothered to agree to it. And another question still lingered. How had he come to know Benafsha? As a concubine, her activities were limited to the harem. It wasn't as if she had been roaming around the palace grounds. Benafsha had originally been a guard before she had caught King Habibullah's eye and he must have seen her then.

And Benafsha let him in? Willingly?

You wouldn't understand, was all she had told Shekiba. She was right about that.

The canaries were singing — three yellow songbirds in a white wire cage suspended from a tree branch. They sang in the morning mostly, bright and melodic. Shekiba paused to listen to them, to decipher their chirps.

Two weeks had passed. Her back was healing. Her skin itched more and burned less, which was how she could tell it was better. With better days came better nights. She learned the routines of the house and found a way to fit in without being a nuisance. She knew from experience that she should not consider herself a permanent fixture in any man's house, even if she was his wife.

Aasif now said a few more words to her, but their exchanges were still brief and polite. He looked past her face and made only fleeting eye contact. Gulnaz watched their interactions from the corner of her eye and seemed satisfied that the second wife was not her equal. She began to see Shekiba more as a housekeeper than a second wife.

Through the window she could see one of the canaries pecking at the other's head. The two others tried to retreat. Peck, peck, peck. They tried to fly from one side of the cage to the other but hadn't enough room to flap their wings more than once before they crossed the cage. Contained. Three caged canaries singing.

Aasif came home that night. Shekiba kept her door open to listen in on their conversation.

"There will be a wedding in three months' time. The palace is preparing for a monumental event."

"I wonder how many people they will invite."

"Plenty. And it will be all the most important families of Kabul. His fiancé's family is well respected and they carry a great deal of clout. They could not have chosen better for Amanullah."

"What is her first name? I know her aunt, Aalia Tarzi. I have seen her in the market from time to time and she is a friend of my cousin Sohaila. Aalia-*jan* speaks very highly of her niece. She was educated while they lived in Syria. I wonder what kind of queen she will be."

"It's a powerful match, Amanullah and Soraya Tarzi, although I know Habibullah is not thrilled that his son is taking Agha Tarzi's daughter."

"Why is that?" Gulnaz asked.

"Tarzi writes what he thinks. And what Tarzi thinks is not always what Habibullah thinks. But the problem is Tarzi thinks Habibullah is not doing enough to bring Afghanistan to modern times. He thinks we should look to Europe and learn from them."

"But we are a different people. We are a Muslim country. Why should we learn from them?"

"Because they are making progress and we are not. Habibullah has made some roads but not much else. Tarzi wants science, education — and not just the religious kind. But Amanullah, his ears are open to Tarzi's ideas."

"But, Aasif-*jan,* he is not king."

"He will be. I don't see his brothers taking the position. Amanullah has been groomed for this since a young age. He'll make a much finer king than his father, who spends his days quail hunting and riding around the countryside for attention."

Gulnaz sighed. Her husband detested the king and she feared his dislike would eventually be the subject of gossip. If it did, he could expect no mercy. And he had already done enough to jeopardize them. He didn't talk about it and Gulnaz wasn't sure if her suspicions were true. She'd heard things from others. A stoning. One of the king's concubines. She would not ask him about the girl. She did not want to know more.

Aasif saw his wife's eyes turn away. He knew her burdens were his doing.

"Anyway, I'm busy with my own work. I don't have time to be Amanullah's counselor anymore." His way of saying he would stay away from the palace.

Gulnaz looked at the door, pictured the hallway and the scarred woman hiding in the far room, her husband's other wife. She wondered if her husband's plan would work or if he had only added another barren wife to his home.

Shekiba listened carefully to every word. Amanullah was to marry Agha Tarzi's daughter. She marveled at her own naïveté.

Why should he look at me? I'm no one. I have no father or mother, no family name. I am a half woman with a half face. How stupid I was to believe anything else!

Shekiba waited till Aasif had gone out before she went to the kitchen to fix herself some food. The spinach and rice she had made earlier had cooled but she didn't care. She took a piece of bread and retreated to her room. She moved about so quietly that Gulnaz almost didn't hear her from the living room.

In the night, Shekiba woke with a start. Aasif was in her room again. The door stood open behind him while he considered walking back out. Shekiba's heart galloped. She prayed he was here only to talk some more.

She did not move.

He closed the door and Shekiba pressed her eyes shut, hoping to ward him off. He sat next to her, with his back to her face for a few moments. Shekiba felt his presence. Her body was tense.

What does he want?

Aasif sighed and turned to her.

"Shekiba," he whispered. "You are my wife. You have an obligation to fulfill."

Shekiba did not answer. His voice was raspy and low. He did not sound like himself.

She clutched her blanket tightly with her two hands, knowing she had no right to resist. She was his wife and she had a responsibility to lie with him, even if it terrified her. Her breathing quickened. He turned toward her and pulled the blanket away. Shekiba could keep her eyes closed no longer. She saw him, saw him looking at her nightgown, the thin white cotton that surrendered without a fight. He undid the drawstring of his pants and lifted her hem over her hips. Shekiba pressed her back into the mattress, wishing she could melt into the floor. A wave of panic rolled over her body as Shekiba closed her eyes, clenched her teeth and became Aasif's wife.

CHAPTER 56
SHEKIBA

In a way it was a relief. She knew now what to expect. He came to her infrequently and briefly, leaving when he had finished his grunting and sighing to sit in the living room. Sometimes he retreated back to Gulnaz. Shekiba always avoided Gulnaz the following morning, embarrassed and feeling as if she had committed an offense against her.

Her only reprieve was her bleeding. Only then could she whisper in the dark, her face flush with humiliation, "Forgive me, I have illness."

He understood right away and would leave her chambers, seemingly relieved. Only last night was different. She had started bleeding two days ago.

"I have . . . I have illness," she said softly, pushing her thighs together.

But he didn't leave. Instead he sat again with his back turned toward her. He put his head in his hands.

"Things are not going well. Why are you

still having your illness? Are you lying about it?"

Shekiba was surprised. His voice was gruff. "No, I would not lie about . . . about such a thing."

"What happened to all that talk? All the talk about the women in your family and the lines of sons they birthed? You've been here for five months and you are still having your illness!"

Shekiba once again realized just how simple she was. That was the reason Aasif had taken her from the palace. Gulnaz had given him no children at all. He didn't want Shekiba — he wanted sons.

"I . . . I . . . it was not talk. I had brothers . . . I —"

"This is a joke! How can this be possible? They were going to execute you. Do you understand that? Do you understand what you escaped?"

Shekiba understood better than anyone what she had escaped. She had been close enough to see the blood seep through Benafsha's *burqa* and pool in the earth. She understood exactly what she had been spared.

"I understand."

"Do you? Do you really? What are people to say? Two wives and not a single son! Do you know what that does to me?" He was livid. Gulnaz could hear him through the thin walls. She turned on her side, knowing that

Shekiba was receiving the anger that he intended for them both. "A harem guard! Did you like being a man? Maybe that's what it is! You liked being a man so much that now you refuse to be a woman! What are you? You are not a man! You are not a woman! You are nothing! Do you have anything to say for yourself? Where's all the boasting now?"

"I . . . I . . ." Shekiba did not know what to say.

"I feed you and clothe you and for nothing! This is what you do to me! I should throw you out on the street! I should throw you back to the palace and let them do with you what they planned! You and your cursed face! Damn you!"

Shekiba braced herself for the blow but it never came. She cowered in a corner of her mattress. Aasif stormed out and slammed the door shut behind him. A few seconds later, Shekiba heard glass breaking and the metal gate clanged loudly. Her throat clenched, she could not help but agree with her angry husband.

Not a man, not a woman. I am nothing.

Gulnaz slipped quietly into Shekiba's room a few moments later. Through the open door, a sliver of moonlight lit the floor of the hallway. The two wives stared at it, Aasif's rant still echoing through the house. The first wife finally spoke.

"We have been married for one year and I

have been unable to bear him a child. Your head would spin to know how many herbs I have ground under the pestle at my grandmother's instruction. I have prayed at the local shrine and given alms to the poor. Nothing. My bleeding comes month after month, as does yours. He thought you would be different but I suspect now that Allah may have cursed him and no matter what woman or how many women he beds, a son is not his *naseeb*.

"And now, now that he has heavy sins on his shoulders, he may have poisoned his *naseeb* even more."

This was the first reference Gulnaz had made to Aasif's involvement in the palace scandal. Shekiba was not sure how much she knew.

"You were a guard there for the harem. He told me this much. You were living as a man. Your short hair, the way you walk, the way you hide your breasts. I think you may have been more content that way. To be honest, I would not mind trying it myself. I wonder what it would be like to be able to walk through the streets freely, without a thousand critical eyes. Do you miss it?"

This was something to which Shekiba, the woman-man, had given a great deal of thought.

"It did feel good. But . . . pants or a skirt, it changes nothing in the end. When it mattered, I was as vulnerable as any woman . . ." Shekiba decided against talking about the lashing. "And now I am here."

Gulnaz intuited what Shekiba meant. "It must have been awful, what they did to you."

Shekiba felt her back stiffen. There were still three raised scars she could feel when she bathed. She wondered how many more scars she had that she could not see. Gulnaz sighed.

"He was so angry. He did not say much about it but a wife knows her husband's moods. He was angry from the beginning and I didn't understand why until Aasif's sister told me about *her*. She wanted me to know I wasn't her brother's first choice."

Her. Shekiba looked at Gulnaz from the corner of her eye. Her expression was blank. She was talking about Benafsha.

"He knew her from before. She was nobody. Her family is as poor as they come and with three daughters, her father cursed his luck. She was just some girl who lived near his uncle's home. I don't know how, but he saw her once or twice.

"Aasif wanted her but his father rejected the idea. Not a proper family, not good enough for his son. But he kept at it. Kept trying to convince his father, and he had almost gotten his way when her father sent her to the palace. One less girl to provide for. Aasif was angry, but she was out of reach behind the palace walls so he let his father choose another family. And then we were married."

Shekiba listened intently. Gulnaz was speaking to no one in particular.

"Men don't like being denied something. Even if it is by the king. He won't say exactly what happened there but I know something happened. I know it must have been terrible because he came home with eyes so red he looked like he could cry blood. He didn't eat, sleep or speak for days."

Shekiba looked away. She did not want to explain and hoped Gulnaz wouldn't ask.

"And then he came home one day looking like he'd just met Shaitan himself. His eyes were dark and serious and he sat around staring at the walls, muttering something about atoning for his sins, begging forgiveness of God. He announced that he was going to bring home a second wife since I haven't been able to bear him a child. There was nothing I could say to that, especially when I saw the look on his face. His family had spoken to him about the idea months ago but he hadn't seemed all that eager. But I thought . . . well, when he said he would bring a second wife I wondered if he was crazy enough to think he could bring her here, but then it was . . . you."

Shekiba kept her eyes on the ground. Her head spun. Benafsha had not turned him away. She had loved him, enough to protect him with her own life. How could a woman love any man so much?

Because of Benafsha, Aasif had saved her life. For that, Shekiba was grateful.

CHAPTER 57
RAHIMA

I was a little girl and then I wasn't.

I was a *bacha posh* and then I wasn't.

I was a daughter and then I wasn't.

I was a mother and then I wasn't.

Just as soon as I could adjust, things changed. I changed. This last change was the worst.

"Rahima-*jan,* remember that life has typhoons. They come and turn everything upside down. But you still have to stand up because the next storm may be around the corner." I hadn't changed much since I lost my son. Abdul Khaliq had become withdrawn. Bibi Gulalai was more present than before, making sure that the family was carrying itself properly. We had to mourn appropriately or our neighbors would talk. Her narrowed eyes fell on me, checking the color of my *chador,* the dress I wore and the expression on my face.

When my mind wandered, she caught me and told me to stop staring. She told me to get back to work. I couldn't expect to just lie around forever. There were still floors to clean. There were clothes to wash. It would be good for me to get back to the routine.

A mourning mother should have been given her forty days to grieve, our visitors were surely thinking. Bibi Gulalai, mother to the most powerful man in our province, knew their concern was driven by fear, not respect, and she did not care.

Khala Shaima summoned the strength to visit me still. Each time she left, I wondered if she would make it home. And I worried that she wouldn't make it back. I needed her. In a house full of people, I still felt totally alone. There was something on my mind, something I didn't want to admit to myself or to Jameela. I didn't know how to feel about it.

"Khala-*jan,* do you know what the people of Kabul think of us?"

"What are you talking about, Rahima?"

"Kabul is different from here. Just like Bibi Shekiba thought. It's amazing how many cars, how many people, how many posters. There is so much noise there."

"What does that have to do with anything?" Khala Shaima looked concerned that I was losing my mind.

"I wonder what those people think of us. They've got buildings, banks, taxis, hotels. People from all over the world, construction companies working on new buildings. Beauty parlors and restaurants. Hospitals."

"You've seen a lot of good places in your travels, haven't you? Seems like you haven't shared some stories with me!" She smiled wanly.

"And the parliament . . . sometimes I can hardly believe that so many people could come together in one room. And they talk about things, even some of the women. Sometimes they talk about things people in this village don't think about in a lifetime."

"Rahima-*jan,* what's on your mind? Did something happen in Kabul?"

"Lots of things happen in Kabul. It is so different from here."

Khala Shaima looked thoughtful. "Is that a good thing?"

I looked at her. Anything different from here was a very good thing.

"But there's something else," I said, my heart heavy with worry.

"There is?"

I nodded.

"What is it?"

I looked away, my eyes starting to tear.

"I see."

I knew she did. Khala Shaima knew me better than anyone else.

"Well, that's something to think about then." She sighed heavily and shook her head.

I'd given it much thought. Thoughts I

didn't care to admit.

People close to death have little to lose. They can think things, say things, do things that others wouldn't. Khala Shaima and I were both in that position, she because of her health and me because I felt no desire to open my eyes in the morning. A conversation began to take shape between us. A conversation that happened in unspoken words, in false words, in knowing glances. It was difficult to say what we were both thinking but it was something to be explored.

Because, as Khala Shaima had so often said, everyone needs an escape.

CHAPTER 58
SHEKIBA

Shekiba and Gulnaz kept house together and endured Aasif's outbreaks, episodes where his frustration got the best of him. He ranted, berated and slapped. He threw things, twice breaking windowpanes. The cost of replacing them sent him into a new rage.

The tension drew the two women together. They shared a husband, they shared blame, they shared punishment. They bickered as well. Shekiba hated Gulnaz's lofty attitude and her bland cooking. Gulnaz thought Shekiba dull and plain, a lousy conversationalist. But they made the situation work. Shekiba added spices when Gulnaz turned away and Gulnaz talked enough to make up for her husband's boring second wife.

There were a few months of nervous respite when Gulnaz's belly began to swell. She told Shekiba when she realized that she had not bled for two months. They wondered on the possibilities until Gulnaz began throwing up once every four days. Shekiba confirmed that these were the signs that a child was growing, as she had learned in the harem. Nothing was said to Aasif, since it was improper to discuss such delicate matters with men, but when he noticed her belly protruding, he smiled with satisfaction and entered Shekiba's room after dark with renewed zeal.

Aasif came home and shared meals with his wives. They had taken to eating together, the three of them, from time to time. Shekiba was cautious not to join them too often, knowing now that Gulnaz was carrying Aasif's child he would see Shekiba as an even bigger failure than before.

But Aasif was busy anticipating the birth of his first child. Aasif's family was quieted, their whisperings that he should take a third wife silenced temporarily. Gulnaz and Shekiba knew that he had been debating the idea but simply could not afford a third wedding and another mouth to feed.

Ramadan came and went. Gulnaz, excused from fasting, glowed with satisfaction as her belly grew large, her cheeks fattened and her breathing grew loud. She huffed walking from the living room to the kitchen. Shekiba had seen many women with child but none had looked as uncomfortable as Gulnaz. It was hard not to notice that she only panted and sighed when she knew Shekiba was around to hear it.

When the pains came, Shekiba hurriedly

walked the four blocks to summon the mid-wife. Gulnaz bit her lip and twisted in agony, her triumphant grin gone for now. Aasif came home and, hearing the midwife coaching Gulnaz through her moans, left again. Hours passed.

The baby finally came, just before Aasif nervously returned to a silent house. The midwife smiled politely and congratulated him as she wrapped her shawl around her shoulders and headed out the front gate. Aasif nodded and walked into Gulnaz's bedroom. Shekiba pretended not to hear him enter and kept her head over the stove, pouring flour into the hot oil and stirring as it thickened. *Litti*, the hot flour soup with sugar and walnuts, would help Shahnaz's womb heal and make her milk come in. Shekiba waited.

"After all that? A girl? How can this be?"

Gulnaz mumbled something that Shekiba could not make out.

"Is there no end to my humiliation?" he shouted. The baby began to cry.

Even a newborn can tell she is not wanted, thought Shekiba. Aasif walked into the living room and yelled for Shekiba to fix him something to eat.

"And it better be hot," he shouted. "I've had enough disappointment for today."

He fell asleep in the living room, his snores echoing down the hallway. Shekiba tiptoed into Gulnaz's room. She was lying on her side, trying awkwardly to get her daughter to nurse. Shekiba sat her up and showed her how to tuck the baby under her swollen bosom. Small pink lips slowly opened and pulled together, her mouth closing in on Gulnaz's nipple.

Shekiba noticed the funny look Gulnaz was giving her.

"I guarded a house full of women and children. I've helped with plenty of newborns."

"Well, I haven't. If only my mother were alive. It would be different then."

Shekiba sighed. *If only my mother were alive.*

"What will you name her?"

"Shabnam." *Morning dewdrops.*

"Beautiful. I made you *litti.* You are *zacha* now. Warm foods will heal your body."

Warm and cool foods had nothing to do with temperature but everything to do with a mysterious inherent property of the food. Walnuts and dates were warm. Vinegar and oranges were cold. Joint aches and childbirth made the body cold and were treated with a diet of warm foods.

Gulnaz took the bowl readily. The hours of straining had left her pale, exhausted and ravenous. She spooned the hot soup into her mouth, pausing just once to look up at Shekiba with gratitude.

"I am glad you are here, Shekiba."

Shekiba froze. It was not like Gulnaz to make such a statement and it made Shekiba fidget. She picked up the baby instead of responding.

"I thought it was going to be a boy. We waited for so long. And in the end, God gave me a girl."

"Aasif is upset."

"He says it's my fault. He didn't want to hold her. He was too upset."

"You will have another. You had one baby. The door is open now. God will give you another."

"Maybe. He wanted to name her Benafsha."

Shekiba looked up in surprise. Gulnaz's face was calm.

"Think of that. To name my daughter Benafsha. He's mad."

"What did you say?"

"I told him I've never put up a fight before but there was no way I could call my daughter by that name."

"And?"

Gulnaz's face twisted with pain. Shekiba instinctively put a hand on her shoulder and leaned toward her.

"What is it?"

"She warned me it would be painful."

"What would?"

"It's my womb. The midwife said my womb would be angry and looking for the baby that

575

used to live in it."

"It is angry?"

"It must be. Oh . . ." Gulnaz moaned.

The spasm passed after a moment and Gulnaz remembered their conversation.

"He wasn't happy. He stormed out. He said Benafsha would be a fine name for a girl, but I think he knows it's wrong."

And if word got back to the palace, it could cast suspicion on him, Shekiba thought. She smiled to think of Aasif not getting his way.

"I'm going to wash her up some more. She still has blood in her hair."

Gulnaz gave a weak smile and closed her eyes, thankful for a moment's rest.

Shabnam's first year passed with two mothers. Gulnaz and Shekiba took turns bathing her, feeding her and rocking her to sleep. Shekiba held her head while Gulnaz lined her eyes with kohl and again a month later when she shaved her head to make her hair grow in thicker. Shekiba served tea and nuts when Aasif's family came to visit, days that reminded both wives how fortunate they were not to be living at the Baraan family compound. Aasif's mother made no attempt to hide her repugnance for Shekiba. She had been first to suggest her son take on a second wife, since his first appeared to have been defective, but this deformed creature with another barren womb was not at all what she had in mind.

She held her granddaughter but kept her eyes roaming around the living room, looking for evidence that her son's home was not being kept well by his two wives. She had a talent for masking criticisms with compliments.

"The colors of your carpet finally show! Looks like someone took the time to beat the dust from it, eh? How long had it been? I had to wash my dress last time I went home from here."

Neither Shekiba nor Gulnaz replied to her comment. It would only feed the flames.

"Gulnaz-*jan*, those cookies that you sent over, they were delicious! How lovely that you've finally started baking sweets!"

"I cannot take the credit for Shekiba-*jan*'s hard work. She made the rosewater cookies and sent them over for you," Gulnaz said, pretending to ignore the snide comment.

"Oh, well, I wondered how it was possible that after this much time you would have started to treat your husband's palate to something tasty. Shekiba-*jan*, they were better than the cookies Khanum Ferdowz makes every year for her family and neighbors."

"*Noosh-e-jan, Khala-jan,*" Shekiba said quietly as she refilled her mother-in-law's teacup. "Please help yourself to another."

"Maybe I will. It's not often that my *aroos* makes such goodies." She shook her skirt, a shower of crumbs raining down on the newly cleaned carpet.

"Who knows, Madar-*jan,* maybe it's just not often that *we* get to taste them," Parisa said, laughing. Parisa was Aasif's eldest sister. She often accompanied her mother on visits, leaving her four children at home as she joined her mother's social circuit.

Aasif's mother smiled at Parisa's comment. Her lips curled up at the corners and the dark hairs on her upper lip cast a shadow. Shekiba opened the teapot and, although it was still full, headed back into the kitchen to refill it.

Gulnaz and Shekiba breathed a sigh of relief when Aasif's mother and sister finally left. Shekiba beat the cookie crumbs from the carpet and tossed the larger pieces into the cage for the canaries. They chirped and tweeted with excitement, watching Shekiba as they flitted from one side of the cage to the other.

Two had bald spots where the aggressive one had pecked their feathers away. Still, they looked content. They watched Shekiba cautiously, occasionally hopping a few inches closer to her for a better look. She reached her finger through the wires and wiggled it. All three birds retreated to the opposite side of the cage immediately, horrified that she would dare trespass into their home.

Shekiba withdrew her finger and watched their wings relax, their syncopated chirping less alarmed.

CHAPTER 59
SHEKIBA

Shekiba did not have to guess. Though she recognized the signs, pregnancy was no less of a shock to her. She chewed on a piece of raw ginger and tried to ignore the nauseous rumblings in her stomach.

I will be a mother. I will have my own baby. Is this possible?

It meant a permanent break from her previous life. She could no longer float between genders like a kite carried by the wind. No more binding her bosom to disguise her figure. She would fool no one.

She watched Shabnam pull on her mother's sleeve and try to pull herself up. She had learned to crawl only one month ago and had already tired of it. Shabnam was a beautiful girl. She had dark curly locks and lashes on her pleasantly plump face. Her loveliness softened her father's disappointment. But Aasif only smiled at her when he thought no one was looking. He let her crawl onto his

lap and paw at his face until he heard footsteps.

"Come and get your daughter! She's driv-
ing me mad!" he would call out.

"Shabnam, come and leave your father
alone," Gulnaz would say as she swooped the
smiling baby off her father's lap.

Shekiba had seen him caress her cheek, the
corners of his mouth turning up in a quiet
smile as he watched her slap her palms
together clumsily. He laughed at the way she
rolled around on her back, her feet in her
hands.

"But he'll always resent her," Gulnaz said
with a sigh.

"That's how it is for girls. A daughter
doesn't really belong to her parents. A daughter belongs to others," Shekiba explained.
Gulnaz should have been wiser in such matters, Shekiba thought.

She tried to hide her condition from Gulnaz, thinking her husband's wife might be
envious. Shekiba dallied in the washroom
until the waves of nausea had passed and her
stomach had emptied itself. She knocked
basins over to mask the sound of her retch-
ing. Gulnaz was so preoccupied with Shabnam, Shekiba needn't have worried so much.

Aasif did not notice either. After Shabnam's
birth, disappointment temporarily cooled his
fire. He opened Shekiba's door less often and
she was thankful for the reprieve. There was

nothing about his sweaty grunting that appealed to her and she hated the way he pressed her face to the side, as if her disfigurement might spoil his momentum even in the darkness. But after three months, he had a renewed determination. Shekiba could hope only for her monthly bleeding to save her from her wifely duties.

With her queasy stomach, Aasif's visits were even more repulsing. He suddenly had an odor that made her stomach reel. She would hold her breath for as long as she could, taking deep gasps in between, which her husband mistook for pleasure. He paused and looked at her, surprised.

"So, you're enjoying this, aren't you? Such a performance you put on!" he said with a crooked smirk.

He did not notice her belly growing until she had missed six cycles of her bleeding. He looked at her curiously as she leaned against the wall to rest after dinner. Gulnaz was knitting while Shabnam slept beside her. Shekiba instinctively tried to bunch her dress over her growing abdomen. Aasif's eyes zeroed in on her belly.

"Maybe there is hope for this house after all!"

Shekiba's face reddened. Gulnaz's lips tightened, just enough that Shekiba could see the tension in her face. Gulnaz had confronted Shekiba two months ago, having noticed the way she kept Shabnam's kicking legs away from her belly.

When Shekiba had nodded, Gulnaz smiled, but with hesitation. She knew what it would mean if Shekiba delivered the son Aasif so desired.

Aasif let out a guffaw, an awkward sound in a room with air so thick.

"We'll see what Shekiba can do."

Gulnaz had whispered to Shekiba as she scrubbed the pots clean.

"He's so different from a couple of years ago. Can you imagine that he used to like to take walks in the evenings with me? This same man! The last two years have soured him. I don't know what he'll become if he's handed another daughter. There's nothing you can do now, is there?"

Shekiba lay awake at night pondering that very question. She thought back to all the mechanisms Mahbuba had described but it was too late for any of them. Someone had told her about the powers of chicken livers, she remembered, and headed to the market the very next day to buy as many as she could find. She did not miss a single prayer and whispered to the ceiling, her palms open, with a fresh desperation.

Please, merciful Allah, I am begging you to give Aasif the son he so desires. Satisfy his wish so that we may live in peace with this bitter man.

Whether it was the chicken livers or the prayers or just God's will, Shekiba gave birth to a son.

Aasif walked with his head high, a smug smile on his face as his family came to visit. Shekiba hardly noticed him. She was fascinated with the ten fingers, the perfectly formed pink lips and the tiny chin that nuzzled against her bosom. She had checked him over head to toe but there was nothing wrong — nothing about him was marred or mangled.

"His name will be Shah. My son, a king among men! And a real one! Not like the coward we bow to now!" Aasif had chosen a name. Shekiba could see the spite in his choice. When he mentioned Habibullah his jaw clenched in a way that made Shekiba shudder. She fretted as she stirred the *litti*. Gulnaz had tried to make some but had filled the house with thick smoke instead. Gray soot clung to the once-white ceiling.

Shekiba was not pleased with her son's name. She had secretly hoped to name him Ismail, after her father, but she knew she would not be as successful as Gulnaz in this battle. So his name was Shah and on the sixth day, they celebrated his birth with a prayer and *halwa*.

As the days passed, Shekiba became terrified. There were too many pats on the back, heartfelt embraces of congratulations, baskets of sweets sent to their house. She worried about *nazar,* that their good fortune would be cursed by someone with a jealous eye. Her king sleeping peacefully, she fired the *espand* seeds and wafted their protective powers over him.

Nazar was not the only danger. Shekiba remembered what she had seen Dr. Behrowen doing in the palace and boiled everything that came near the baby. She boiled his clothes, even the evil eye that she had pinned to his tiny blanket. She scrubbed her breasts raw before she let him nurse. Her fears multiplied when Aasif came home shaking his head.

"What is it?" she asked. "Has something happened?"

Aasif was cordial with her these days, engaging in conversations as his first wife listened bitterly from her room down the hall.

"It's that damn illness again, sweeping across the villages. Even in Kabul."

"What illness?" Shekiba asked, suddenly alarmed. Shah was only three weeks old. Instinctively, she pulled her swaddled baby closer to her.

"Cholera. Maybe you've never heard of it. It's a powerful disease. God help whoever it strikes. I've heard that at least twenty families in Kabul are sick with it. The doctors can't do anything about it."

Shekiba knew better than anyone else just

how powerful cholera could be. Her back stiffened.

"We mustn't let the baby get ill," she said, her voice quivering. Panic was setting in.

"Don't you think I know that? Just take good care of him and keep him inside. You're his mother so it's up to you to keep him from getting sick!"

Shekiba's mind flew back to her village, watching her siblings waste away in a corner of their rank home. Thinking of her mother, broken at the sight of her dead children, Shekiba boiled, washed and prayed fiercely.

Please, God, don't let anything happen to my little boy. He's the most perfect thing I've ever had. Please do not take him away!

And when the cholera wave passed, there was time for Shekiba to think of new dangers. She would not let the baby near the kitchen and kept him away from anything made of glass. She surrounded him with pillows and did not take her eyes off him. It was clear she did not trust Gulnaz to watch him. What if he broke his leg and walked with a limp? What if he was hit and lost an eye? Shekiba could hear the names, the teasing, a crestfallen little boy. She wanted better for her son.

"You know, I have managed to care for Shabnam reasonably well this past year. I think I am capable of holding a baby! What is it with you? What do you think I'm going to do? Drop him from a window?"

"I'm just . . . I'm just nervous. Don't be offended, please. It's just that I don't want anything to happen to him." Shekiba turned away so she wouldn't see the angry look on Gulnaz's face.

Shah changed every dynamic in the house, even for his half sister. When Shabnam waddled toward Shekiba, Gulnaz was quick to pull her back, and if she caught Shabnam eating something Shekiba had prepared, she would hold a hand in front of the baby's confused mouth and make her spit it out. But only when Shekiba was watching.

It hurt Shekiba to see Shabnam yanked away from her. She loved the little girl as much as she could love any child that was not her own. And Shabnam, who had grown up with two mothers, did not understand why one was now off-limits. She looked at Shah with suspicion, as if she knew he had disrupted her happy home.

Aasif made the situation worse. Gulnaz no longer joined them for dinner, always making some excuse about Shabnam needing to eat or sleep. Aasif, having just proudly celebrated his son's fortieth day, hardly noticed that his first wife had retreated into her room for over a week. What he did say to Gulnaz only made her more resentful of Shekiba.

"Long overdue, but worth the wait. Look at my son! Look at the healthy color in his cheeks! He's a lion, my son!"

Gulnaz, listening from her room, bit her tongue, thankful that her daughter was not yet aware of her father's partiality.

"*Nam-e-khoda.* May evil eyes stay away," Shekiba murmured nervously as she looked at her fingernails, another superstition she had picked up from one of her uncles' wives, though she couldn't remember which one.

Gulnaz nearly laughed. An evil eye could hardly find its way to Shah, with all the talismans and prayers and *espand* that Shekiba used in the house. It occurred to her then that Shekiba was probably worried about her. She thought on it for a moment and realized it made sense. That was why she wanted to keep Gulnaz away from her precious son!

And so Gulnaz retaliated. She showered Shah with compliments, purposely not invoking the name of God.

How plump his cheeks have gotten! How quickly he's learned to roll over! He'll be walking before you know it, Shekiba-jan.

How well he nurses! He'll grow up to be bigger and stronger than his father! And look at how alert and curious he is!

Shekiba was frenzied. She knocked on wood, burned *espand* and prayed even more. She tried to downplay the compliments as quickly as they came.

Oh, it's just today. Yesterday he barely wanted

to nurse at all. I don't think he's gained any weight in the last couple weeks. He feels so light when I lift him.

You don't see how skinny his legs are? He'll probably end up short and bowlegged, at the rate he's eating.

Animosity simmered as Shekiba slowly realized what Gulnaz was up to. Frustrated, she decided to turn the game around. They sat in the courtyard, giving the children some sunlight while Shekiba hung the laundry on a clothesline. Gulnaz was watering the flowers.

"Just look at Shabnam! She's walking as if she's been doing it for years! I bet she could run right across Kabul with those strong legs!"

Shekiba watched Gulnaz's mouth open slightly and her eyes widen. She mumbled something incomprehensible in return.

"Coo coo! Coo coo!" Shabnam called out, her word for the canaries.

"Yes, my little one, coo coo is there," Gulnaz said without turning around.

"Coo coo! Coo coo!"

The two mothers turned around and saw only two yellow birds flitting about the cage. Gulnaz walked over, her head cocked to the side.

"Where is the other? How could he have gotten . . ." Her voice trailed off as she neared the cage. "Oh no!"

"What is it?" Shekiba said as she walked over. Gulnaz's eyes were wide.

"He's dead."

The feathered creature lay lifeless on the floor of the cage while his roommates huddled close to one another and chirped softly. Both women were silent. The omen did not go unnoticed.

We're just like Aasif's mother, Shekiba thought with a sigh. *Making daggers of words.*

CHAPTER 60
SHEKIBA

The relationship between Shekiba and Gulnaz had cooled now that Aasif had warmed
toward his disfigured second wife. Shekiba
prayed Gulnaz would have a second child, a
boy, to even their score, but months and then
years passed and Gulnaz had no other children. They learned to be civil with one
another and make the house function as it
had when Shekiba had first arrived — two
wives embittered against each other.

Shah and Shabnam made up for the relationship between their mothers. By the time
Shah turned one, he was chasing after his
older half sister, who giggled and watched
him with a toddler's curiosity. Shabnam was
much more beautiful than her mother, her
perfect curls in a ponytail behind her head
and bangs that shadowed her forehead. Her
cheeks were full and rosy, her eyes almond
shaped and chestnut colored. She had inherited the best of her parents' features, and a

cheerful disposition that was foreign to their home.

Shah, as Gulnaz had so facetiously predicted, grew to be strong and taller than most boys his age. He had walnut-colored hair that curled just slightly and a grin that melted hearts. The two made a perfect set of siblings, despite the rancor between their two mothers.

In February of 1919, Shabnam was five and Shah was four. The temperature was barely above freezing. Hundreds of miles from Kabul, someone brought the country to its knees. Gulnaz and Shekiba were tending to the chores when they noticed that the streets were loud and boisterous. There were people shouting and doors slamming. Shekiba sent the kids into the house from the courtyard and opened the gate. Men were walking down the street in a hurry, consternation on their faces and arms waving wildly as they shouted.

"No, it's true! My brother is in the army! They have no idea who it was!"

"What's going to happen?"

"I don't know but it's best to get home and stay there until we find out."

Shekiba closed the door and leaned against it, the metal sending icy shivers down her spine. What could have happened?

Gulnaz met her at the inner door. The two canaries, brought inside during the winter months, tweeted loudly, egged on by the agitation in the streets.

"What is it? What's happening?"

"I'm not sure. I just heard someone saying it's best to stay home. Something is going on."

"Where is Aasif?"

"God knows."

Four hours later, their husband showed up. The women had locked the doors and closed the windows, fearful without knowing what it was they were afraid of. His face was heavy with worry and his forehead sweaty, even in the cold.

"Aasif! What is it? What's happening?" Gulnaz said, meeting him at the door.

"It's the king. Someone's killed Habibullah!" he announced, his voice quiet and his breaths heavy. He took off his hat and scarf.

"Allah!" Her hand covered her mouth.

"The city's in a panic. I was at the Ministry of Foreign Affairs when we got word. He was on some kind of hunting trip, as usual, and he was shot. For a while, they were trying to keep it quiet, but stories began to leak out. You can't keep something like that hidden for long! We thought it might have just been rumors — you know how easy it is to spread stories in Kabul — but it seems to be true. The army is on alert and they sent for Amanullah. Thankfully, he's in Kabul already."

"The shah is . . . ," Shekiba said incredulously. She could not bring herself to use her son's name and "dead" in the same breath.

"Did you not hear everything I just said!? Yes, Habibullah is dead! He's been assassinated, the bastard."

His wives winced. However Aasif might have felt, it was unwise to speak ill of the dead.

"How could this have happened? Was it here? In the palace?"

"No, he was in Jalalabad. It must have happened two days ago at least, if word is getting to us now. I can't believe someone killed him."

"What's going to happen now?" Gulnaz said while Shekiba put a hand on her son's head. Shah had just entered the room and looked at his father with concern. He had no idea what "dead" meant but he could sense that something was not right.

"I don't know. My guess is that Amanullah will take his father's place. And he rightfully should. But it's impossible to say. If his assassination was a coup, then his assassin will have to get through the army. They've sworn allegiance to Amanullah."

"Allah, have mercy on us. This could be a disaster for Kabul!"

"We'll sit tight and see. Just keep the children inside and keep your mouths shut. This is no time to speculate with the neighbors. Be smart."

Shekiba turned away so Aasif would not see her roll her eyes. It was hard to swallow such words of wisdom from a man who had violated the king's harem and condemned Benafsha to a horrible death. Where was his sense of caution then?

But they did as he said and Aasif nervously returned to his post in the Ministry of Agriculture in the morning. The streets were desolate as panic spread through the capital. Aasif stockpiled extra food as a precaution. The assassin was still unidentified and no one had made any moves toward the palace but the army was on high alert, all the same.

Aasif had not seen Amanullah in nearly a year, but now it was critical he reconnect with his friend. He needed to pay his respects and make sure he was aligned with the man who would most likely be taking Habibullah's place as ruler of Afghanistan. He stopped by the palace, his nerves on edge.

Amanullah was heartbroken and enraged, Aasif reported to his wives. His father's brother Nasrullah had accompanied the king on his hunting trip. Word came from Jalalabad that Nasrullah had been proclaimed Habibullah's successor, which angered Amanullah. Amanullah's eldest brother, Inayatullah, seemed to be in support of his uncle, as were many of Habibullah's sons.

Amanullah, born to the king's chief wife, knew his father would have selected him to take the throne. And as leader of the military and treasury, Amanullah was in position to assume the reins of the country and declared himself the new king from his post in Kabul.

Shekiba could picture him, his heart heavy with grief, his noble face drawn and sad. He would be a just and wise king, she knew. She blushed to think of how stupid she had been five years ago, to think that such a man might want her.

I have no reason to complain, though. I am married to a man with a respectable position in the Ministry of Agriculture. He keeps us fed and clothed in an esteemed neighborhood of Kabul. He provides for his children and does not beat me. What more could I have asked of Allah?

Aasif carefully worked to bring himself closer to Amanullah and the new king welcomed his friend's counsel in such a difficult time. He wanted to avenge his father's death and there were a handful of people under the cloud of suspicion, including his own uncle Nasrullah, who, it was rumored, had not shed a single tear at his brother's death. Amanullah made an announcement. He would find the assassins and bring change to Afghanistan. Reform was on the way. He banned slavery. He vowed to increase pay for the army. Afghanistan would maintain its friendly relationship with India.

He is not like his father. He is a better man,

Shekiba thought as she heard the declarations. *God be with you, King Amanullah.*

By April, an investigative committee had looked into Habibullah's murder. Amanullah jailed his uncle Nasrullah and a dozen others in the palace dungeons. Aasif stood by his friend as the palace prepared to spill blood.

Amanullah brought with him many new ministers and Kabul braced itself for the changes that would come with their new leader. Shekiba and Gulnaz felt more secure when it became apparent that there would be no bloody challenge to Amanullah's claim to the throne. Kabul transitioned relatively peacefully, eager to see their bold young king fulfill his promises. Shekiba smiled, ruffling her son's hair, feeling that Amanullah would make Afghanistan better for her Shah.

Their link to the palace revived, the Baraan family became host to some of Amanullah's other advisers. Gulnaz served guests tea and nuts that Shekiba prepared from the safety of the kitchen. They eavesdropped on conversations, feeling privileged to have the first scoop on Kabul's political affairs. Compared to the other wives of the neighborhood, they were much more informed, and Gulnaz, the more social wife, enjoyed flaunting it in conversations with other women. She made sure their audiences knew how well connected their household was. In a city like Kabul, connections counted for everything, so she didn't mind the extra work that came with Aasif's many guests.

Gulnaz and Shekiba wished the men would talk more about Amanullah's wife, Soraya. What they did hear was astonishing. She was educated and beautiful. She was born in Syria and spoke many languages. Amanullah took her everywhere and consulted with her. They wanted to hear more about their mysterious queen but the discussions usually centered on what Amanullah's next move would be, since he had promised big changes when he assumed the role of king.

"How much of Tarzi's reforms do you think he'll take on?"

"He'll take on them all, if you ask me!" Aasif said. "He thinks the world of his father-in-law, probably even more than he thought of his own father, may Allah grant him peace in heaven."

Gulnaz shot Shekiba a look of surprise. It seemed Aasif finally knew how to speak respectfully of Habibullah when he needed to.

"You're as mad as Tarzi himself. This is Afghanistan, not Europe. We are not like those people and shouldn't try to be. Let us concentrate on our own country and stop ogling others."

"What's wrong with learning from others?" someone asked.

"Depends on what you learn from them."

"What's happened with his brother In-ayatullah?"

"He and a few other brothers have sworn allegiance to Amanullah. He's going to release them from the dungeon tomorrow. His uncle will remain in prison. There is too much doubt over his head. He'll stay in chains for the time being."

"People are angry about that. They do not feel it is just."

"They will forget when they see what our king is capable of. Soon, they will not remember Nasrullah's name."

In May, Amanullah did what Aasif had suggested many years earlier while Shekib, the guard, had eavesdropped in the gardens. Amanullah flexed his muscles and sent soldiers into northern India. Amanullah had had enough of British dominance and acted on his father-in-law's teachings.

"Ya marg ya istiqlal!" Demonstrators in the streets shouted for death or freedom. Gulnaz and Shekiba listened nervously, hoping the crowd would not turn on anyone.

Amanullah had embroiled the country in the third Anglo-Afghan war. Kabul was tense. Everyone talked about the fighting. The army was small but fierce. The Baraan household braced itself. If the Afghans lost, there would surely be another regime change and it was impossible to know what that would bring.

"It's over," Aasif announced as he entered

the house three months later.

"It's over?" Shekiba repeated, a habit that drove Aasif mad. She knew it as soon as she said it but it was too late to undo. Shah ran into the living room to greet his father.

"Yes, that's what I said! Let me see my son! Shah, good news! It's over. We've won our independence from England!"

CHAPTER 61
RAHIMA

Forty days after Jahangir's last breath, the house was still. It was the final day of mourning.

"The forty days will be complete today," Bibi Gulalai reminded us. "People may come to say prayers with us or with Abdul Khaliq. Watch how you talk."

Shahnaz bit her lip and went to bathe her children. She kept her distance and, more important, made sure her children stayed clear of me. I made her nervous, as the mother of a dead child. Maybe I was cursed. Or maybe I would be jealous that her little ones were alive and my son was dead.

Forty days. What was so magical about forty? I wondered. Was I to feel differently today than I did yesterday? Was I to forget what happened just six weeks ago?

We Afghans marked both life and death with a forty-day period, as if we needed that much time to confirm either had truly happened. We had celebrated Jahangir's birth forty days after he'd left my womb, unsure if this child was here with us to stay. And now his death. Forty days of praying, alone, with others and everything in between.

"It's been forty days, Rahima," Badriya reminded me.

"And tomorrow will be forty-one," I shot back. Nothing would change.

But something did change. For forty days, Abdul Khaliq had kept to himself, sitting with the many men who came to pay their respects and read with him. He didn't look at me much. If we had been a different husband and wife, I might have approached him. I might have asked him about our son's last breaths, about how he was feeling now. I was thankful that he'd been good to our son in his last moments but nothing more. Now, more than ever, I wanted nothing to do with him.

On the forty-first day, the house breathed a sigh of relief. Badriya and her children no longer spoke in hushed voices. Jahangir had been given his due period of respect.

Abdul Khaliq called for me that night. With a heavy step, I went to him. He was standing by the window, his back to me. I knew I should have closed the door behind me, but I did not. I hoped I wouldn't have to stay.

"Close the door," he said, his back still turned. His voice was firm, a warning buried in his tone.

I obeyed.

"Come closer."

I wanted to scream. I wanted to run far from him, from the scent that lingered behind his beard, from his rough hands, from the disdain in his eye.

Haven't I suffered enough? I wanted to yell.

He turned around and looked at me, reading the reluctance in my face. He took another step, now within reach. I sighed and turned my head away, staring at the floor.

A slap thundered across my cheek. My knees buckled.

"No wife of mine looks at me in that way! How dare you?"

My eyes watered from the stinging blow. He was angry still. His fingers gripped my arm so tight I thought my bones might snap.

"I didn't — I'm sorry, I didn't mean to . . ."

He tossed me to the floor. My right knee hit the ground first.

"Worthless! You've been good for nothing since you came here! A waste. A waste of my money, my time. Look at you! A big mistake for me to take you. I should have listened to what others said but I pitied your father. He suckered me, that rat! Made me believe his girls would make decent wives. Look what's happened! One worse than the other."

He was in a rage. Nothing he hadn't before said or done, but there was a renewed enthusiasm in his vitriol. He swung again as I pulled on the edge of the bed to stand.

"A *bacha posh*. I should have known better. You still don't know what it is to be a woman."

I felt a trickle of blood from my lip and realized I should have anticipated this. I steeled myself for what I knew was coming. The blow that would shatter me. True or untrue, I didn't want to hear him say it.

"Hard to believe you could be even worse as a mother than you are as a wife! My son deserved better! He would be alive if he'd had a mother better than you!"

I closed my eyes, a surge of pain. The worst blow. I crumpled to the floor with my hands over my head. I crouched forward, almost as if praying. He was muttering something. I couldn't hear him over my own sobbing.

"Do you want to be a boy? Maybe that's what you want! Is that what you want?"

My ribs.

"My mother couldn't make a woman out of you. Then maybe you should go back to what you were! That's what you want?"

I never saw where it came from. Maybe under his pillow. Or maybe in his jacket pocket. In a flash, Abdul Khaliq grabbed my hair and pulled my head off the ground. My head slipped forward. He snatched again and jerked my head up. My scalp screamed. When I saw locks of hair on the floor around me, I realized what he was doing. I tried to pull away, begged him to stop, but he was barely there. He was trying to take me apart, to disassemble the pieces that were hardly holding together as it was.

More hair on the ground. I tried to crawl away but his grip was tight. I shrieked as I felt my scalp lift off my skull.

"Please," I begged. "Please stop! You don't know!"

He had taken a knife to my hair, a blade I'd seen him tuck into his waistband before he and his guards went off for his meetings. The blade was dull and he had to chop at my hair again and again, holding it taut by the ends.

"One child! You've brought only one child and you couldn't even take care of him!" My stomach lurched.

One child. One child.

I wanted to let him end my misery, to give me the punishment my heart believed I deserved, those dark, dark thoughts that haunted my days and nights. I wished he could end it for me. Maybe I would have even taunted him, if it weren't for . . .

He was on the edge of his bed, his breaths slowing. My husband lacked the endurance to exact the punishment he intended.

I lay motionless, curled up on my side at the foot of the bed. I waited for the signal.

"Get out," he hissed. "I can't stand the sight of you."

I crawled to the door, then pulled myself to stand by the chair. I heard footsteps scamper in the hallway as I exited. I held one hand over my throbbing belly and one hand on the wall to steady my slow step.

One child.

In my room, I waited. It didn't hurt as much as it should have, maybe because my mind was elsewhere. Into the thin light of morning, I waited for the bleeding to come. I knew it would.

Fresh tears for a new loss.

I may have killed one of Abdul Khaliq's children. But he had just killed another.

CHAPTER 62
RAHIMA

"Do you want to go or don't you?"

I sighed and stared at my feet. My arches ached but it was too much effort to rub them.

"It's up to you. I can always find someone else to be my assistant if you don't want to do it anymore. I'm sure the director's office can help me. Someone else can do what you were doing."

This was actually her way of trying to be considerate.

"Look, I don't care either way . . ."

This wasn't true and we both knew it.

"I'm just telling you, you need to make a decision soon because I'm leaving to go back to Kabul in three days and if you're going to go back then we have to let Abdul Khaliq know."

Badriya had grown accustomed to my help. With me, the parliamentary sessions were easier to follow. I read all the briefs to her. I filled out and submitted all her documents. She listened as I went through the newspaper headlines to give her some background for the *jirga* discussions. She finally felt like she was participating in the process, like she was a woman our province should admire for her role in government. As if she were actually serving her constituency.

She was ignoring the fact that it was another man who decided if she should raise the red or green paddle when voting time came. She believed the lie of Badriya the female parliamentarian, and that was all that mattered to her.

As much as I wanted her to shut up and walk away, I knew I had to make a decision.

An escape. I need to find an escape.

I'd been to the cemetery where Jahangir was buried only once, two months after I'd come home from Kabul to find my son cold and gray. Abdul Khaliq finally gave me permission to go with Bibi Gulalai and his driver. The dead can see people naked, superstition said, so he didn't think it was proper for his wife to step foot in the cemetery. I didn't believe it to be true and even if it were, I didn't care. I wanted to see where my son was buried. I asked Jameela to bring it up with him and she did. I knew I was playing on her sympathy when I asked her the favor but I was desperate. I don't know what magical words she used but our husband relented.

My mother-in-law and I stood over Jahangir's grave marker. Her wailing echoed across the emptiness, the same mournful cries that she'd made two months ago. I was quiet for a time. I didn't think I had tears left to shed.

"You sweet innocent child! I can't believe this was your time, your *naseeb*. Dear God, my poor grandson was so young to be taken from us!"

I stood there in disbelief. How could this mound of earth be my little boy? How could this be all that remained of my grinning, curious child?

But it was. And the more I thought of it, the more Bibi Gulalai's wailing tore at my heart. I wanted to dig into the dirt, to plunge my hands into the earth and touch my son's hand, to feel his fingers close around mine again. I wanted to curl up beside him, keep him warm and whisper to him that he wasn't alone, that he shouldn't be afraid.

"What is our family to do? Why did we deserve such tragedy? His smiling face, oh, it dances before my eyes and rips at my heart!"

I started to cry. Silently at first, then louder and louder until I was loud enough that Bibi Gulalai noticed over the sound of her own lamenting.

She turned around and shot me an icy glare.

"Haven't I told you a hundred times to watch how you act? Are you trying to shame our family?"

I sucked in my sobs, feeling my chest tense as I tried to contain it all.

"It's a sin! It's a sin for you to try to draw so much attention. Don't make such a scene here. It's disrespectful to the dead and people are watching!"

No one was watching. We were all alone. Maroof stood back, leaning against the SUV and waiting for us to return to the car. I swallowed my sorrow and looked to the sky. Three gray-brown red-breasted finches flew overhead. They circled three times, swooped down toward us, then floated back to a tree about forty feet away. They cooed and clucked and cocked their heads so purposefully that I almost thought they were talking to me.

Bibi Gulalai pulled a handful of bread crumbs from her dress pocket and scattered them over Jahangir's grave. She tossed another palmful on a grave to the left, skipped one and tossed some more on a grave to the right.

"Shehr-Agha-*jan,*" she said with a sigh. "May the heavens be your place for eternity."

I recognized the name as belonging to Abdul Khaliq's grandfather. Stories about him, the great warrior, were recounted so often that I had to remind myself I'd never seen him. He'd been gone over a decade.

The finches noticed the sprinkle of food and took flight again, swooping in gracefully and pecking here and there at the newly found bounty. Bibi Gulalai spread what was left on the graves that fell further away. Still she skipped the one to the immediate right of Jahangir.

"Eat, eat," she said mournfully. "Eat and pray for my grandson. And for my beloved father-in-law. God rest his soul and may Allah keep him close and peaceful always."

I watched. The finches bobbed their heads, picking at the crumbs and chirping their gratitude. It did look like they were praying, their little heads going up and down as if in supplication. It gave me some solace.

I looked at the grave marker beside Abdul Khaliq's grandfather, Shehr-Agha. This area was where everyone from my husband's family was buried. I wondered why Bibi Gulalai chose to ignore this one grave.

"Who is buried here?" I asked. I usually didn't invite any conversation with my mother-in-law but at this moment I didn't want to feel so alone. At least she had brought the praying finches to my son. Jahangir would have loved to see the birds, their tiny beaks. I could picture him imitating their delicate walk, their flapping wings and their red chests puffed out proudly.

"There?" She pointed hatefully. "That's where Abdul Khaliq's grandmother is buried, Shehr-Agha's wife. My mother-in-law."

Her lips drew tightly together.

"You didn't toss any seeds there."

Bibi Gulalai stared at the earth angrily. She spoke after a moment of thought.

"Abdul Khaliq's grandmother and I did not see eye to eye. She was an awful woman. No one liked her," she explained without looking at me. "I was respectful to her while she was alive but I've no interest in wasting my time praying for her soul now."

This was the first time I'd heard Bibi Gulalai talk about her mother-in-law. And it was the first time I heard her speak ill of anyone from her in-laws' side of the family. I was surprised at how spiteful she was. I shouldn't have been.

"When did she die?"

"Ten years ago," she said, and signaled to Maroof that we were ready to leave. He opened the rear door and turned back to the front to get behind the wheel. "She was an evil woman if there ever was one. She told my husband terrible things about me. None of them true, mind you, just poisoning his mind against me."

I closed my eyes, knelt at my son's grave and said one more prayer, rushing through the verse so fast I slurred the Arabic words in my head, afraid that I would get pulled into the car before I could finish. But Bibi Gulalai paused — as if she were waiting for me.

I lowered my head and kissed the earth, the finches chirping sympathetically and watching me from the safety of their perch.

"I'm sorry, Jahangir," I whispered, my cheek cooled by the feet of dirt between my son and me. "I'm sorry I didn't take better care of you. May Allah watch over you always."

I stood and took a deep breath, my eyes blurred with tears. We got into the car and I realized Bibi Gulalai was still thinking, unaffectionately, about her mother-in-law.

"She made my life miserable," she finally said. "I did everything for that woman. Cooked and cleaned and took care of her son like no other wife would have. I cooked for their whole family, any time she had guests, when she was struck with a craving. But nothing was ever to her liking. She badmouthed me every chance she got."

I listened, seeing a different side of my mother-in-law. And feeling, for the first time, that she and I had something in common. Ironically.

"What happened to her?"

"What happened to her? What happens to everyone! She died." Her tone was sarcastic and annoyed. "She wasn't feeling well one night. Asked me to rub her legs for her, so I did. Greased her dry feet and massaged them so long I thought my hands would never open again. The next morning, she came to check on the soup I was making. Shehr-Agha-*jan,* God rest his soul, he had invited thirty people over for lunch. She stood there, looming over my shoulder like a jailer watches his inmates, complaining that I was taking too long or something like that. She didn't look right though. I remember like it was yesterday. She was a pale yellow color and her forehead was sweaty. I thought it was odd because it was the middle of winter. Before I could say anything, she grabbed my arm and her neck twisted to the side. She fell to the ground and knocked over a bowl of onions I'd just finished peeling for the stew."

I watched her recount the story. She was looking out the window, the cars' tires spinning up clouds of dust that obscured the view. It was as if she wasn't talking to me, just reliving the memory.

"I had to get everyone, let everyone know. What a day. But that's how she died — unappreciative of what I was doing up until her very last breath. That's the kind of hard-hearted woman she was."

In other circumstances, I might have told Bibi Gulalai that I understood, that I could sympathize with her.

"You don't know how lucky you are," she said, suddenly remembering I was sitting beside her.

That was my only visit to my son's grave. I knew Abdul Khaliq opposed my going there. Truthfully, I wasn't even sure I was strong enough to go back. It wasn't easy. I lay awake all that night and the next wondering if Jahangir felt like he was suffocating in there. Shahnaz heard my crying through the thin walls and groaned in frustration. I couldn't get my mind off my little boy.

When Badriya came to me again to ask if I wanted to go back to Kabul, I thought about it and made a decision that I thought Khala Shaima would approve of. I packed my bag, my heart heavy with guilt for leaving my son behind again.

I thought of the cemetery, the rows of headstones, simple and hand carved. Some old, some new. The finches had watched us until we left. I saw them chirping to one another as we drove off and then, one by one, the birds had flown away.

Chapter 63
Rahima

It wasn't easy to stay focused on the work this time. Halfway into a parliamentarian's speech, I would realize I had no idea what he was talking about. My mind had drifted, remembering the last time I'd bathed my son. Or fed him *halva,* his favorite food.

Badriya noticed but her exasperation was tempered by sympathy. Most of the time. She was hardly paying attention herself. She spent most of the session pretending to look at papers in front of her when I could see she was watching the people in the room. For a woman who had spent the greater part of her life confined by the walls of her husband's house, every session was a spectacle.

She was even more lax with me than before, which didn't mean much except that I spent more time with Hamida and Sufia and less time with her or our security guard and driver. The ladies were kind to me. When Badriya had returned to Kabul without me, they'd asked about me several times. She'd made vague excuses until she finally told them about Jahangir.

Sufia's arms around me were more comforting than I could have imagined. Hamida shook her head and told me of the three-year-old son she'd lost to some infection. She and her husband hadn't had the money at the time to pay for medications.

I forced a smile and nodded, appreciative of their warmth but not wanting to talk about what had happened. There was too much there and I still felt a fresh guilt for leaving my dead son behind.

The home Abdul Khaliq was fixing had not yet been finished, so we continued to stay at the hotel. I floated through my daily routine in a perpetual state of misery, wondering from time to time why I bothered to do any of it at all. I think I was driven by fear of my husband. And because I didn't know what else to do.

Badriya was dropping hints here and there about our husband's new prospect. As much as she didn't want to talk to me, there was no one else around and there were things that she could not bottle up.

"I'm not supposed to say anything. I only know because, of course, he thought it was right to share this information with me since I'm the first wife," she said with one hand over her chest as she spoke of her own importance. "The girl's name is Khatol. She's

616

very beautiful, they say. And Abdul Khaliq has known her brother for a long time. Her brother is a well-respected man. He fought alongside Abdul Khaliq but now he owes a lot of money to our husband. He showed him and his family much kindness. Even sent them food when he heard they didn't even have bread."

"But what will happen to . . . to the rest of us?" I didn't want Badriya to know that I'd heard her conversation with Bibi Gulalai.

"The rest of us? Nothing! Why should anything happen to the rest of us?" she said, and busied herself cleaning a grease spot from her dress. "Aren't you going to that silly class with your friends?"

She wouldn't say anything more than that, nothing about my husband's plans to keep in line with the *hadith*. It wasn't in her interests to alert me.

I didn't understand why my husband suddenly found it so important that he follow the *hadith*. He wasn't a man who let rules dictate his decisions. If he wanted to have five wives, or twenty-five for that matter, he would.

Thick, industrial smoke from a million exhaust pipes blackened Kabul's air. Badriya coughed violently. I would ask, only because she would bring it up later if I didn't, if she wanted to join the ladies and me at the

617

resource center. Each time she would wave me off.

"I'm not wasting my time with those busy-bodies."

Maroof and our bodyguard stayed with her because she was the more important wife and because she always claimed to be considering going to visit her cousin across town. As far as I could tell, she never actually left our room. She knew better. She knew word would get back to our husband. Badriya's survival instincts were strong.

I spent my evenings in the training center under Ms. Franklin's tutelage. I was getting better at navigating my way through the computer programs. For practice, I would type letters to my sisters Shahla, Rohila, and Sitara — letters that were never sent. The woman from the shelter, Fakhria, came from time to time and brought with her stories of girls who had fled from home, hungry for a new chance. Their shelter functioned on money raised in the United States and it was becoming obvious that she was trying to garner Hamida and Sufia's sympathy, hoping to secure some funding from the parliament. I wanted to tell her that she was wasting her breath. Even I, the lowly assistant to a parliamentarian, could have told her there was no chance of getting the *jirga* to allocate money to a shelter for women who had run away from their husbands. In fact, I'd heard several people say the shelters were nothing more than brothels. I didn't think it was true, but others did.

Four weeks remained until the parliament's winter break. Four weeks left for me to attend class at the training center, four weeks of Ms. Franklin patting my shoulder in praise, four weeks left of Hamida and Sufia, instead of cooking and cleaning.

I wondered how Khala Shaima was doing. She looked worse each time I saw her. Still, she had outlived both Parwin and Jahangir. Their deaths had taught me that anything was possible, and that death was closer than I wanted to believe.

"I'm an old woman," Khala Shaima had told me before I left for Kabul. "I've cheated the angel Azrael more than once but he'll come and claim my last breath soon enough."

"Khala-*jan*, don't say such a thing," I said, protesting.

"Bah. I've wanted to be around only so I can look after you girls, to tell you the truth. Nothing else matters much. But I can't slip through his fingers forever. It's like the story of that man — did I tell you that one?"

"No, Khala-*jan*. You've only told us about Bibi Shekiba."

"Ah, and I hope you've learned something from her story. You are her legacy, after all. Remember, your great-great-grandmother was Bibi Shekiba, guard to the king's harem.

"*Dokhtar-em,* my dear, I'm not well. You are not a naïve girl anymore. It will give my heart peace if you can tell me that every story I've told, every *mattal* I've shared, that you've gotten some wisdom and courage from it. Remember where you come from. Bibi Shekiba is not a fairy tale. She is your great-great-grandmother. Her blood courses through your veins and gives strength to your spirit. Always walk with your head high. You are the descendant of a *somebody,* not a nobody." She sighed heavily, which turned into a long, exasperated cough. She took a minute to catch her breath before she continued.

"I've tried to tell Rohila and Sitara the same. But Rohila is to be married soon and I think she'll be better off. The family seems reasonable. Sitara will be alone with your parents, left to fend for herself. I can't do much more for her. I wish I could tell you to watch out for her but you could do more for her if a mountain stood between you. These walls hold you tight. Focus on yourself. Everything you've endured in life should have taught you something, made you hungry for something. Remember, Allah has said, 'Start moving, so I may start blessing.'"

I tried to find the words to reassure Khala Shaima, to tell her that I understood what she was telling me and that I was proud to know I was a descendant of Bibi Shekiba, the

620

woman who had guarded the king's harem, who had walked through the royal palace. I may have lived my entire life in a small village but I was connected to Afghanistan's aristocracy.

But I'd never been able to find the right words. As I sat there, I had to admit I could see my aunt fading. She didn't look like the person I remembered. She had spent her adult life trying to guide us, trying to look out for my sisters and me.

And she was right. As much as I might have wanted to do for my sisters, Abdul Khaliq's walls were high and his leash short. I could only pray for them.

Badriya was lying on the bed. She'd spent the day griping about how long it was taking for Abdul Khaliq's men to finish the home he'd bought in Kabul. She was tired of staying in a hotel and having the man in the lobby watch our comings and goings with interest. I wanted to go for a walk, tired of listening to her complaints.

I adjusted my head scarf and opened the door. Badriya looked up, shook her head and turned around to face the wall. I could tell she didn't want me to leave since it would leave her without an audience but I was starting to feel the walls close in. I walked out of our room.

To my right was a staircase leading to the lobby. I could hear Maroof and Hassan on my left, about forty feet down the hall, talk-ing. I could make out Maroof's back, sitting on the chair. As much as I wanted to head directly down to the street level, I knew there would be hell to pay if I were to leave unchap-eroned and unannounced.

I could make out their voices as I neared.

"You told him that?"

"I did. What the hell was I supposed to tell him?" Maroof asked.

"God help her. What did he say?"

"You've heard how he gets. He said a lot of things. I don't know what he's going to do to her but I had no choice. And it's your fault anyway, Maroof. You're the one who told him she was spending a lot of time with those two hags. You didn't stop to think that he would get pissed we weren't guarding her? Maybe you don't think it's your job since you're the driver, but I'm their *guard*. Did you miss that?"

"What was I supposed to tell him? He called when she wasn't around. He wanted to speak to Badriya too. If I hadn't said she wasn't here, she would have told him. He would have had my neck for sure if he thought I was keeping something from him."

"Yeah, yeah. Well, I hope he got that she went without our knowing about it. I don't want to get back to the house and find out it's us he's mad at."

"Just stick to what we said. She snuck out

622

without telling us and went to hang out with those godforsaken women. He'll believe it. You know he doesn't think much of her anyway. You've heard about his plans. He's lost interest. She's not as exciting to him as she was in the beginning. Remember that day he saw her in the market?"

Maroof let out a guffaw.

"He looked like he might pick her up right there. Send a note and a few afghanis to her parents!"

"Would've been a lot easier if he'd done it that way. What a pain her family was. Putting up a show like they come from royalty or something."

"But I remember your face when he made us stop so he could watch her . . . you thought she was a real boy then, you idiot!"

"You did too!" Maroof said in self-defense. "She looked like a boy. How the hell should I have known there was something more interesting under those clothes?"

"You probably liked her better the other way!" Hassan chuckled. "What do you think of her new haircut, eh? Got your appetite going?"

I backed up slowly and as quietly as I could, my mind racing.

They had sold me out to my husband. I trembled at the way they talked about me.

My thoughts tumbled and turned until I finally realized what it was that I had just

623

overheard.

I wasn't safe.

I turned the doorknob, watching the hallway to see if the men had noticed my presence. They hadn't. I closed the door behind me and went straight to the washroom. I couldn't look at Badriya right now, knowing she would be of no help to me. It looked like she was asleep anyway.

My husband was a man of violence and I knew that I'd barely seen a tenth of what he was capable of. He was a man of war, of guns, of power. He demanded respect and obedience, and the guards had just told him that I was out of control. He must have been wild with rage.

I couldn't help but remember he was looking to add a wife and that five was one more than he wanted. I knew what that meant for me.

I thought of the woman in the shelter. She'd disobeyed and her husband had sliced off her ear. I had no doubt Abdul Khaliq could be just as vicious. I leaned against the wall, my heart pounding in fear. I had to think fast.

We were due to return home in three days.

CHAPTER 64
SHEKIBA

Shah's feet pounded against the dirt of the road. Just because he was supposed to accompany his sister home from school didn't mean he couldn't race her to the front door. He panted, turned around and saw Shabnam walking hurriedly to catch up. She looked frustrated.

"Why are you always in such a rush? Don't you know it's not easy to run in a skirt? And anyway, Madar-*jan* would be upset if she saw me chasing after you through the streets!"

"It's not my fault I'm faster than you. I could have been home a long time ago if I didn't have to wait for you!"

It was the same argument every day. They bickered but adored each other, oblivious to the resentment between their mothers. Shabnam had long ago opted to ignore her mother's hand pulling her back and would sit with Shekiba while she washed the clothes, asking her question after question about everything from horses to baking bread. And Shah, who

625

knew no boundaries thanks to his father, loved to torment Gulnaz by pulling at her knitting and running away, his giggles undoing her anger at the work he had unraveled.

Aasif had hoped for more children but Gulnaz and Shekiba seemed to alternate; one would start her womanly illness when the other stopped. He wondered if a curse had been lifted from him for those two years. Or maybe the women had done something . . . but he grew tired of being angry. His mother had not given up hope. Even one week before her death, she'd reminded her son that Allah had wanted men to take on more than two wives.

"And where will I put another wife, Madarjan? In our small home, there is no room for another woman and I have enough trouble feeding the ones I have."

"Marry and Allah will provide a way," his mother had told him, her eyes half closed with fatigue.

He debated her advice, as illogical as it seemed, on his way to and from the Ministry of Foreign Affairs. He had been transferred from the Ministry of Agriculture and given a position working with a higher-ranked vizier two years ago thanks to his relationship with Amanullah.

When Agha Khalil arrived with his wife, it was Shah who met them at the door. His knees were dusty from trying to climb past the second branch of the tree in their court-yard, which made the visitor and his wife smile and think of their own young son at home.

"Good evening, dear boy! Is your father home? I would like to speak with him."

"Yes, he is. Come in! My mother is making dinner. Why don't you stay and be our guest?" he said with a grin, aping his father's hospitality. Agha Khalil's wife could not help but laugh.

"Isn't that kind of you! We wouldn't want to trouble her, my friend," he said just as Aasif entered the courtyard.

"Agha Khalil, how pleasant to see you!"

"And you as well, Agha Baraan. Forgive me for dropping by at this hour but I wanted to bring you those papers since I will not be at the office tomorrow."

"Please, please, come in," Aasif said, motioning to the house door.

"Your son was quite the host and already invited us but my wife and I were just on our way home from visiting relatives. We don't want to be a bother."

Aasif insisted and Shekiba quickly set out cups of tea and dried mulberries. Gulnaz had taken to her room with a headache, so Shekiba was forced to join Aasif in sitting with the guests. Shekiba and Agha Khalil's wife, Mahnaz, were introduced and they sat in one corner of the living room while the men chatted in the other. Shekiba kept her head turned to the side as she always did when she met someone new.

"Your son is such a darling boy, *nam-e-khoda*!" Mahnaz said. Shekiba bowed her head and smiled to hear the kindness in this woman's voice. Mahnaz wore a taupe-colored ankle-length dress with airy sleeves that buttoned at the cuff. She looked elegant and fitting of someone who might be a palace guest.

"May Allah bless you with good health, thank you," she said, not wanting to invite *nazar* by saying any more about her little king.

"Do you have much family in Kabul?"

"No, I came from a small village outside Kabul."

"So did I. This city was quite a surprise for me! So different from where I grew up." Mahnaz was young, probably no more than twenty-four years old, with a bright and cheerful face. "Where was your village?"

"It was called Qala-e-Bulbul. I doubt you ever would have heard of it," Shekiba said. At the age of thirty-six, she hadn't thought of her village, named for the hundreds of songbirds that lived there, in years. And her village made her think of her songbird sister. Aqela's lifted voice and dimpled face flashed across her mind, blurry and vivid all at once as memories are.

Mahnaz's mouth dropped open. She put a

hand on Shekiba's. "Qala-e-Bulbul? Are you really from there? That is my village!"

Shekiba suddenly felt a surge of panic. She did not regret in the least that she had no contact with her family. She looked over at Aasif and saw that the men were deeply engaged in a conversation. He had never cared to ask her anything about her family and she saw no reason for him to learn anything now.

"I left when I was fairly young and I barely remember anyone . . . ," Shekiba said quietly.

"What a remarkable coincidence! What is your family name?"

"Bardari."

"Bardari? The farm that was north of the hill of the shepherd? Oh, my goodness! My uncle was neighbor to the Bardari family. I spent so much time at my uncle's house that I know them well. We lived not too far from there ourselves. How are you related to Khanum Zarmina or Khanum Samina? Their daughters and I used to braid each other's hair and sing songs by the stream that ran behind my uncle's land."

"You did? They are my uncles' wives."

"Oh my! Then it was your cousins that I played with as a girl! Do you write to them often? My letters to my family take so very long to reach home. Do you have the same trouble?"

"I . . . I am not in contact with my family

629

now that I am living in Kabul. It has been a long time," Shekiba said vaguely.

"Really? I understand. I was just there two years ago, you know. For my brother's wedding. The village hasn't changed a bit. But did you . . . Shekiba-*jan,* do you know about your grandmother?" Mahnaz's eyes softened and her voice quieted.

"My grandmother? What is it?"

Mahnaz bit her lip and looked down for a second. She shook her head and held both Shekiba's hands in her own.

"She passed away just two days after the wedding. It was such a sad time. I did not know her personally but I heard that she was a very strong woman. The whole village marveled at how blessed she was to have lived such a long life!"

Shekiba was taken aback. Part of her had expected her grandmother to live on forever, pickled in her own bitter juices. She quickly realized that her guest was expecting some kind of reaction.

"Oh. I had no idea. May she rest peacefully in heaven," she mumbled, lowering her head.

"I am so sorry that I should share such sad news with you, especially in our first meeting. How awful of me!"

"Please, please. My grandmother, as you said, lived many more years than anyone would have expected. Such is life and the same end awaits us all," she said, struggling to sound polite.

"Yes, yes, God bless her. She must have had a good soul to have been blessed with such a long life."

You did not know her, Shekiba thought.

"Mahnaz-*jan*," Shekiba said hesitantly. She wondered how to ask what she really wanted to know. "Do you happen to know how the farms are doing? My father's land . . . my father's land used to produce such a yield of crops. I often wonder . . ."

"Which was your father's land?"

"It was behind my grandmother's house, separated by a row of tall trees . . ."

"Oh, of course! Well," she said. The subject obviously made her uncomfortable. "From what I heard there were some . . . some disagreements about the land. When I was there, Freidun-*jan* and Zarmina-*jan* were living there but they were about to divide it up."

Shekiba could decipher what Mahnaz was too polite to say. Her uncles must have quarreled over the land. She could imagine Kaka Freidun asserting his right as eldest and haughty Khala Zarmina pushing the others aside to get a home of her own. Greed had torn the family and the land apart.

"But they were not having a good yield when I visited. I saw their daughter, your cousin, at the wedding and she told me that they believed there was some kind of curse on the soil."

Shekiba smiled. Mahnaz thought her odd. Shekiba realized but couldn't help it. She could hear her grandmother's cackling voice telling her sons that it was Shekiba who had cursed the earth and condemned their crops.

"How did things go at the wedding? Congratulations to your family," Shekiba said. She had no interest in hearing anything else about her family.

Mahnaz relaxed and broke into a smile. "It was wonderful! Dancing and music and food! It was so lively and I had not seen my family in so long. I could not have had a better time!"

"How nice! I wish the bride and groom a happy life."

"They nearly had to call off the wedding, truthfully."

"Why?"

"Well, the bride's family had asked for a huge sum of money as her bride price, but my father had said it was unreasonable, especially since King Amanullah had outlawed the practice of bride price. The bride's father felt disrespected, so they settled on a lesser sum. I suppose I could understand though. No money at all? I mean, a bride is worth something, isn't she? I know I was!" she laughed.

Shekiba smiled meekly and looked away. "You are right. Amanullah's laws seem so foreign in a village like ours. Kabul is so different. Can you imagine if people in Qala-e-Bulbul knew about the English and German secondary schools here?"

"You are so right, Shekiba-*jan*! Only some of the girls went to school in our area. Do you know that Queen Soraya will be making a speech in two days?"

"No, I didn't."

"Oh, it will be amazing. I can hardly wait to hear what she has to say. Though I worry about her. Many will not welcome so many changes so quickly. Why don't you come with me? We can go and hear her speak!"

Shekiba was taken aback. Queen Soraya? Shekiba had wondered about her so much, she brightened at the thought of actually seeing this revolutionary woman. But Shekiba was not accustomed to attending public events.

"Oh, I couldn't . . . I mean, I have to tend to —"

"Come, just for a day! It'll be great to see!" she said with excitement, and then turned her attention to the men. They were so deeply engaged in conversation that they had not yet touched their tea. "Excuse me, dear Agha Baraan!"

Aasif turned around. He looked startled. "Yes, Khanum?"

"Could I steal your wife tomorrow?"

Steal your wife. I wonder how that sounds to him, Shekiba thought. The talk of Amanullah and Soraya reminded her of the palace. And Benafsha.

"Steal my . . ."

"Yes, I would love to go to the speech and have been looking for someone to join me! We won't be gone long. We can take adorable Shah-*jan* with us too!"

"It will be an important speech. I have no doubt that the Afghan people will be impressed with Queen Soraya the more they get to know her," Agha Khalil said.

"You will be there?" Aasif asked him. Shekiba watched as her afternoon was planned for her.

"Certainly."

"Well, then . . ."

"Wonderful! Hope you don't mind her escaping for a bit!" Mahnaz said contently. Aasif tried not to let his face show his displeasure.

CHAPTER 65
SHEKIBA

"They said around one o'clock. Shouldn't be much longer. Just look at this crowd! All these people here to see our Queen Soraya!"

Shekiba held Shah's hand tightly, her eyes scanning the stage for any sign of Amanullah. She wondered what he looked like now. It had been years since she last saw him.

Stupid, she told herself. *Look at this crowd. How could you have thought you were suited for something like this, that you could be worthy of taking that stage, of appearing before all these people!*

Shekiba adjusted her veil and leaned over to give Shah a handful of nuts to snack on. She'd been unable to stomach much food in the past few weeks and even the woody smell of roasted almonds turned her nose, a smell she'd never before even noticed.

Little Shah was happily entertained by the many faces, the man selling vegetables from his wooden cart, the children holding their mothers' hands. He did not mind that they

635

had been standing around for over an hour, nor did he notice the number of stares his mother's face attracted. Shekiba kept her veil draped over the left half of her face and averted her gaze when she saw curious eyes. Shah was seven years old now and wise enough to detect stares and whispers. She did not want her son to feel embarrassed by her.

Gulnaz and Shabnam were at home. Gulnaz was not happy that Shekiba had been invited for an outing by Agha Khalil's wife and she had only spoken a few words to Shekiba since finding out. But she contented herself with the knowledge that Aasif would be pleased she'd stayed home instead of shamelessly wandering around Kabul in a crowd of people.

Soldiers lined the stage and created a perimeter around it so the crowd couldn't get too close. In the center of the stage was a podium draped in navy blue velvet with gold tassels and embroidered with two crossed swords. Shekiba looked at the soldiers and thought of Arg, the guards, the harem. It seemed like a hundred years ago that she'd walked about the palace grounds with cropped hair and men's slacks. She looked at her son, soon to be a young man, and wondered what he would have thought to see his mother dressed that way.

He wouldn't understand. Only a daughter

could know what it was to cross that line, to feel the freedom of living as the opposite sex. Her fingers touched her belly briefly. She looked at Shah and knew this one was different. She could feel it.

Mahnaz shielded her eyes from the sun.

"Have you seen her before?" she asked.

Shekiba shook her head.

"She looks like a queen. I don't know how else to describe her. You should see the clothes she wears! Straight from Europe! My husband tells me that even the children wear European clothes!"

"Your husband works with them?"

"Yes, he does some calligraphy work for the king and he serves as counsel to the queen when the king is away. He's going to be traveling with them soon."

"He's away often, isn't he?"

Mahnaz nodded, her face showing her disappointment. "He is, but at least I have my mother-in-law and his family around. I would be so lonely otherwise."

"How was your marriage arranged? His family is from Kabul, are they not?"

"Yes, they are. He and his family had traveled through our village on their way to Jalalabad one year. In that time, his father and my father came to know each other and they arranged for us to be married. I had seen him only once, just for a second. It was so unexpected!"

"And you've been living in Kabul since then?"

"Mostly," she said, and leaned in to speak more discreetly. "My husband had some differences of opinion, you could say, with some of the government officials. We went through some difficult times then. They took everything from us. Our furniture, our home, our jewelry. We moved into the countryside for a year and a half until word was sent that we could return. The children were miserable there. We were so happy to come back!"

"That sounds awful," Shekiba said. *But worse could have been done to you,* she thought.

"It was awful. But that's how it is. When you don't agree with powerful people, be prepared to lose everything. I only hope we will not go through such an experience again." She sighed. "It is hard to say, though, since what men will tolerate changes as often as the shape of the moon."

Shekiba nodded.

"There they are!" Mahnaz spotted Amanullah and Soraya being escorted onto the stage. Soldiers were lined up ceremoniously on either side of them and generals stood at their side. They were smiling and waving to faces they recognized in a group of dignitaries just in front of the platform.

A man in a suit took the podium and began to speak. He introduced himself and spoke of

King Amanullah's recent trip to Europe. Afghanistan was in a period of rebirth, he declared, and would grow with the leadership of such a strong-willed and visionary monarch. His speech went on until one of the generals could take no more and whispered something into his ear that brought him to closing remarks rather abruptly.

"Our noble king Amanullah!" he announced, and stepped away from the podium, his arms outstretched dramatically to welcome the country's leader to the stage.

"*As-salaam-alaikum* and thank you! I am pleased to come and speak here with you!"

Shekiba's lips turned up ever so slightly in a half smile. He looked even more dignified than she remembered, his olive-brown military jacket was decorated with medals and stars and cinched at the waist with a leather belt. He took off his hat and placed it on the podium before him. His posture gave an aura of confidence, a self-assurance that seeped through the crowd. Shekiba looked at the faces around her, their eyes focused on the stage, their expressions eager.

We are in good hands, people seemed to be thinking.

Shekiba tried to focus on his speech but her mind wandered. She kept her eyes on Amanullah, wondering if he would remember her, the harem guard with the scarred face. She willed his kind eyes to fall upon her again. She felt a flutter in her stomach and wasn't surprised that even the smallest of spirits could be moved by Amanullah's presence.

Mahnaz looked over at her occasionally, nodding in agreement. Shekiba realized the king must have said something noteworthy. Shah pulled at her hand and she absentmindedly pulled raisins from her purse. He ate them one by one, bored by the speech.

Queen Soraya joined him at the podium. She wore a thin head scarf, plum colored, to match her skirt suit. She wore a fitted jacket with a brooch that caught the sunlight, over a pencil skirt that ended midcalf. Her shoes were smart — black Mary Janes with a modest heel.

This is his wife, the woman he spoke of as thoughtful and dedicated, strong-willed. Indeed, she does walk with her head held high. Then again, why shouldn't she? She is queen to our beloved Amanullah.

Suddenly, Queen Soraya looked at her husband and pulled her head scarf off her head! Shekiba's mouth dropped open. She looked at King Amanullah and was shocked to see him smiling and clapping. Mahnaz grabbed Shekiba by the forearm and broke into a grin. A mix of gasps and applause rippled through the crowd.

"Isn't that amazing?" she said excitedly.

"What just happened? Why did she do that?"

"Weren't you listening? He just said that the *chador* is not required in Islam! The queen is doing away with her head scarf!"

"But . . . how could she . . ."

"It's a new day in Kabul! Aren't you glad I dragged you here?" she said, nudging Shekiba with her elbow.

Amanullah went on to say a few more words with Soraya at his side. He declared her, his wife, to be the minister of education and queen to the Afghan people. He turned the podium over to Soraya. Shekiba looked to Shah, then turned her attention back to the stage. Today's speeches were more interesting than she had anticipated.

Queen Soraya spoke eloquently and with a confidence that complemented her husband's. Shekiba felt humbled and listened to her talk on the importance of independence.

"Do you think, however, that our nation from the outset needs only men to serve it? Women should also take their part as women did in the early years of our nation and Islam. From their examples we must learn that we must all contribute toward the development of our nation and that this cannot be done without being equipped with knowledge. So we should all attempt to acquire as much knowledge as possible, in order that we may render our services to society in the manner of the women of early Islam."

"Imagine. Just imagine, being able to speak like her to a crowd of people this size. She is a remarkable woman. Oh, the people of Qala-e-Bulbul would just faint to see something like this, wouldn't they?" Mahnaz said with a laugh.

Shekiba thought of her own uncles. No doubt they would have sneered and walked out on such a speech. A woman? Telling their wives to acquire knowledge?

It was an exhilarating day. Shekiba was vaguely aware that this day would change something, though she wasn't sure what.

She's a wise woman, Shekiba thought. *A woman like that would have given my father's land to me. She would have told my grand-mother to send me to school instead of the fields.*

Shekiba's lip stiffened with resolve.

She knew Queen Soraya was speaking of changes that wouldn't affect her.

My story ends here, she thought. She now had a better life than she could have imagined. Somehow she had found an escape from a much worse *naseeb.*

But something in Shekiba did shift. She had a glimmer of hope, a feeling that things might get better with this woman Amanullah had chosen over her. Her face flushed knowing it still felt that way to her, as ridiculous as it was.

She thought of the way she was beaten when she took the deed to Hakim-*sahib*. She thought of Benafsha succumbing under the weight of the stones.

But sometimes you have to act out of line, I suppose. Sometimes you have to take a chance if you want something badly enough.

Things would be okay for Shah, Shekiba knew. He was a boy and his well-connected father would make sure he had every opportunity. She thanked God for that.

And may Allah give my daughters, should I be blessed with any, a chance to do what Queen Soraya seems to believe is possible. May Allah give them courage when they are told they are out of line. And may Allah protect them when they seek something better, and give them a chance to prove they deserve more.

This life is difficult. We lose fathers, brothers, mothers, songbirds and pieces of ourselves. Whips strike the innocent, honors go to the guilty, and there is too much loneliness. I would be a fool to pray for my children to escape all of that. Ask for too much and it might actually turn out worse. But I can pray for small things, like fertile fields, a mother's love, a child's smile — a life that's less bitter than sweet.

CHAPTER 66
RAHIMA

I used all my strength to stay focused, to keep my composure. I couldn't let anyone know that I had overheard what I had. Beyond that, I didn't know what to do or who to turn to. Frankly, I didn't think I could turn to anyone.

I sat beside Badriya in the following day's session, ignoring the debate on funding for a roads project when everyone knew the decision was really in the president's hands. And that he'd already made up his mind.

Tonight, Ms. Franklin was going to let us work more on the Internet. It was as important as learning to read and write, she said. The Internet was our gateway to the world.

I could have used a gateway.

While the debate of no consequence went on around me, a more important debate raged in my head. Should I go with Hamida and Sufia to the training center or should I stay with Badriya and the guards?

My hands were clammy and my shoulders stiff. I dreaded the session ending, knowing I would have to make a decision.

What does it matter? I thought. *He already thinks I've snuck away from the guards. How could it get any worse?*

But I was afraid. Maybe he would believe me, take my word that the guards had let me go. That Badriya had said it was all right. That I did nothing inappropriate or shameful at the resource center.

Impossible.

We were outside. I was looking at the three western soldiers on the opposite side of the street. They were leaning against a wall, talking with a crowd of young boys. *Jahangir would have been one of them,* I thought, *if I'd been allowed to bring him with me.* I wondered what the soldiers would do if I ran to them. They were here to help us, weren't they?

We were just past the security check when Hamida called out to me. My heart raced. What would Khala Shaima tell me to do?

"Aren't you going to come with us? Ms. Franklin's expecting you!"

I looked at Badriya. She raised her eyebrows, wondering why I thought she would care where I went. She walked toward the car, which was parked a few meters away. I saw Maroof mumble something to Hassan, who nodded and mumbled something back.

Figuring I was doomed anyway, I took a leap and decided to go with Hamida. I didn't know what I expected to come of my decision.

"I'm going to . . . I'm going to go with them. I'll have her driver drop me off before they go to her apartment. Okay?"

Badriya shrugged her shoulders without bothering to turn around. I knew she didn't want to give a formal answer, an answer she might have to defend to our husband. She got in the car and they drove off, melting into Kabul's congested streets. I was relieved and petrified.

While we walked, Hamida talked and I thought of my husband. Twice, I thought I might vomit on the street. Sufia joined us two blocks from the parliament building. The guards walked a few feet behind us while the drivers stayed with the cars. With the traffic, it would have taken longer to drive to the resource center.

"Rahima-*jan,* what's going on? You're awfully quiet today. Everything all right?" Sufia asked.

I never meant to share it. My story just flowed out. Like the water that once upon a time bubbled over stones in the Kabul River, I told them about my husband, Bibi Gulalai, Jahangir.

We walked slowly, not wanting to draw attention from the security guards who trailed us. This wasn't a story to share with them.

I answered their next questions before they

646

could ask them. I told them about my parents and how they'd given us sisters away, then cloaked themselves in clouds of opium. I told them how Parwin escaped her hell in a flash of flames and that with Rohila about to become a wife, Sitara would be left cowering in the corner of our home, afraid of what fate my father would choose for her. And Khala Shaima, the only family I'd kept over the years, her twisted spine was squeezing the life from her bit by bit.

But my son. That was the worst of it. I said it and then I left it alone. The sore was too raw to touch. Worse than losing the unborn.

While I tried to control the shaking of my voice, I told them about the conversation I'd overheard. About the wife my husband wanted to take without violating the laws he suddenly wanted to follow. I didn't have to tell them what I was afraid he would do to me. They knew.

They listened, unsurprised. I was only confirming what they'd already suspected, that I was one of those stories. My story was not unheard of.

I was broken and battered and didn't care anymore how much I told them or what they thought or even what Abdul Khaliq would do if he found out. I had had enough. I kept thinking of Khala Shaima's face, her soured expression, her disappointment in what had become of her nieces. And then there was

Bibi Shekiba, the man-woman whose story had woven its way through my own.

"Dear God, what a mess you're in, Rahima-*jan*! I don't even know what I can say . . . ," Hamida said. We stood outside the door of the resource center. Ms. Franklin waved us in with a smile.

"There must be something . . . there has to be some way . . . ," Hamida said unconvincingly.

"Let's not stand out here too long," Sufia whispered gravely. "We can chat about this inside. Come on, ladies."

I let Sufia guide me with a hand on my back, thinking of something Khala Shaima had said when I shared the story of the girl from the shelter with her, how she'd escaped her husband only to be found again and beaten, punished for running away.

"Poor girl. She ran out from under a leaking roof and sat in the rain."

Chapter 67
Rahima

"I'm not feeling well at all," I said. I hoped I sounded believable.

Badriya huffed and rested her hands on her hips dramatically. "What is it now? You expect me to go by myself to the session? And who do you suggest should fill out the ballots that are due today?"

"I'm sorry, but it's my stomach. It must have been something I ate last night. My stomach is a terrible mess," I said, wrapping my arms around my abdomen and leaning forward. "I don't want to cause a disturbance sitting next to you. I just feel like I might have to run —"

"Oh, that's enough already! I don't want to hear more. Some assistant you are. Useless!" she said, throwing her hands in the air. She grabbed her handbag and stormed out. When I heard her footsteps moving away, I crept to the door and put my ear against it. I could hear her speaking to Hassan and Maroof, their heavy voices echoing in the hall.

"She's not going?"

"No, she says she's not well. I suppose we should just let her stay here. I'm not staying with her, if that's what you are thinking. I'll hear it from the director if I miss another session."

"Agh. This girl's nothing but trouble," Maroof said.

"Just take her. I'll stay here with this one," Hassan offered reluctantly. "The last thing we need now is for Abdul Khaliq to hear we left her alone in the hotel."

"Fine."

I heard the metal of the chair scraping against the floor. He was going to stay at his post down the hall. My chest felt heavy with anticipation.

I took a deep breath and went back to the bed, pulling my duffel bag out from under it. My hands dug through the dresses until I found what I was looking for. I thanked God I'd brought it along, even if I hadn't anticipated wearing it. I changed quickly, a small thrill running through me. I went back to Badriya's bag and rifled through it until I found the scissors she kept with her sewing supplies. To the bathroom again, where I looked at my reflection and finished what my husband had started. Snip, snip, snip. It was badly uneven but better than what Abdul Khaliq had done.

I put my sandals on and considered my duffel bag for a moment. From the back, it might give me away. I decided against taking it and sat down to calm my breathing.

It took five minutes of intent listening at the door to convince myself no one was approaching, especially Hassan. No thump of his heavy foot or whistle of his raspy breath. I imagined he'd probably gone out for a smoke.

My fingers touched the knob and closed around it slowly. I turned, still keeping my ears perked.

I looked out through the crack, opened the door wider when I was certain I'd seen no one. And wider yet when I worked up the nerve to walk into the hallway. I craned my neck to see where the chair usually sat.

Hassan's back. I took a deep breath and turned to the right, to the stairwell. I closed the door as silently as I could behind me. I moved one foot in front of the other, walking past the four doors between me and the end of the hallway. I was so focused on listening for the sound of Hassan moving that my left sandal caught on the carpeting and I stumbled, catching my balance by grabbing the doorknob of the next room.

I held my breath when I heard the scraping of the metal chair legs.

"Hey!"

I froze, keeping my back to Hassan. I was sure he could see my whole body quivering even from a distance.

"Watch your feet, you klutzy kid!" he called out.

I nodded and grunted something in a voice deeper than my own but barely audible.

"Boys running around in a hotel . . . ," I could hear him muttering as I resumed my trek to the stairwell. With each step I waited, waited for the moment when he would realize that the boy he saw was actually a girl in Hashmat's new clothes, the pants still unhemmed.

I was and then I wasn't. I was Rahima. And then I wasn't.

I walked through the lobby, keeping my eyes lowered. The man from the front desk was nowhere to be seen. I moved quickly. I opened the door and sunlight tickled my eyes. I lifted my hand and blinked. When my sandals hit the dirt road I scanned the street to make sure I recognized no one and that no one recognized me. My eyes fell on a sparrow, nimbly passing between tree branches and chirping as earnestly as the birds over Jahangir's grave. *Pray for me too,* I thought.

Rahim wound in and out of the streets, heading further away from the hotel and in the opposite direction of the parliament building. Rahim, the *bacha posh,* listened for someone yelling behind him, listened for a sign that he'd been spotted, that he was going to be dragged back to Abdul Khaliq's compound and punished.

Rahim, shaking so badly that he thought his legs might collapse, needed a place to hide.

CHAPTER 68
RAHIMA

Taxis honked. One slid past me, skimming my side as I tried to dodge traffic in a busy intersection. I cursed myself for choosing to cross here, in front of so many cars. I felt a million eyes on me, eyes that might notice something was not right about this adolescent boy. Didn't I look frightened — like I was running away from something? Did they see that my chest seemed to swell where a girl's might?

I had done my best to tie down my breasts with a head scarf but it was harder now than it had been a few years ago. Having Jahangir had thickened me with curves that were more difficult to disguise.

"Hey, *bacha*! Watch where you're going!" a man yelled through the driver's-side window of the taxi, a cigarette between his fingers as he waved at me angrily.

Without a pause in my step, I raised an apologetic hand, silently thankful to know my disguise was working. Funny how easily I slipped back into this person, how comfortable I felt even though my nerves were on fire.

My sandals slapped against the dusty road, my legs free in the pants, a loose tunic covering my curved rear.

It had been nearly eleven o'clock when I left the hotel. That felt like a year ago, though it couldn't have been more than twenty or thirty minutes. A bus came up ahead, slowing near a crowd of people and honking an awkward tune. Maybe that was the one. I looked for signs, turning my head and suddenly feeling my legs weaken.

A black SUV slowed as it approached, only half a block away.

I felt exposed even in the crowded street, wondering if I'd been spotted. If I hadn't been, running now might draw attention.

The driver slowly rolled down the tinted window and I let out a soft moan of panic.

But it was a face I didn't recognize. It wasn't Abdul Khaliq's car.

Regrouping quickly, I pushed my way through and reached the crowd of people clamoring to board the white and blue bus.

"Is this the bus to Wazir Akbar Khan?"

No one turned around.

"Agha, is this the bus to Wazir Akbar Khan?" I asked again, louder. I tried to deepen my voice, to hide my feminine tone.

A man turned around, annoyed. He wore a

button-down shirt over slacks and held a briefcase in his hand.

"Yes, it is! Hurry up and get on if you're coming," he said. He and another man tried to squeeze through the bus door at the same time, each hoping to get a square of standing space.

With my head down, I managed to slip onto the bus behind two men. I waited for the bus driver to notice and shout, but he didn't. I wiggled my way to the back of the bus, as far from the driver as possible. Looking around, there was not a single woman on the bus. I felt my face flush at being surrounded, so closely, by so many men. I kept my elbows close to my chest and cringed when the bus's movements pushed a body against mine. I craned my neck to see between the chests and arms. I hoped I would recognize my stop.

The bus will stop on a road lined with shops. Look for a beauty shop between an electronics store and a food vendor. Usually there's a man with a long beard and half an arm standing around there begging for money.

It was a long ride to Wazir Akbar Khan. Beads of sweat slid down my neck. My nerves were just starting to settle as the bus put distance between me and the hotel — between me and Abdul Khaliq's guards.

I was supposed to be there at twelve. I had meant to leave the hotel earlier but Badriya had taken her time that morning, putting the whole plan in jeopardy.

Wazir Akbar Khan was a neighborhood to the north of the city, a suburb that was home to many embassies and foreign workers. The streets were wider than they were in the part of Kabul I had seen. Two-story buildings lined the road. I tried not to look as nervous and lost as I felt.

The bus slowed. *Pharmacy of Wazir Akbar Khan,* read the sign on a building.

This is it, I thought, and snaked through the crowd to get off before the bus resumed its course.

I recognized no one and didn't notice any suspicious stares. I turned my attention to the shops, looking for the landmarks I'd been given. One storefront had crates outside, boxes of detergent, household supplies. There was a butcher shop. There was everything except what I was looking for.

I turned down another street but saw only houses. Beautiful houses that put Abdul Khaliq's estate to shame. They were new buildings with modern façades that I didn't have time to take in. Minutes were ticking by and I might miss this opportunity.

I worked up the nerve to ask someone, steeling my voice an octave below in disguise.

"Agha-sahib? Agha —"

"For God's sake, boy, I don't have any

money to give!" the man said, and kept on moving.

I looked for someone else to ask.

A woman walked by. I wanted to approach her but my tongue froze when I saw the little boy, probably three or four years old, holding her hand tightly. He pointed at a car in the street and looked up to see if his mother noticed. She nodded and said something that made him giggle with delight.

Jahangir, I thought, my chest tight.

The woman was gone before I recovered. I walked further down the street, blinking away tears. I stood in front of a shop window, a clock catching my eye and sending me into a panic.

One o'clock. My pulse quickened. If I was too late, this could all fall apart. I would have risked everything for nothing. What would become of me?

My eyes moved from the clock to a flyer hung on the storefront.

Visit Shekiba's Beauty Shop, Sarai Shahzada. Weddings and all occasions.

That must be it! I thought. *Shekiba.*

I closed my eyes, reenergized by the shop's name. It was as if a hand was holding mine, guiding me. I read the flyer again.

Sarai Shahzada. I was sure I'd seen a sign with that street name and traced my steps back. Two lefts and I was there again, concrete sidewalks and trees giving it a clean, welcoming appeal. Within minutes, I had found the beauty shop, sandwiched between an electronics shop and a store with crates of fruits and vegetables outside.

Shekiba's Beauty Shop.

As I had been instructed, I looked directly across from it and spotted a teahouse.

I hope I'm not too late.

I dodged oncoming cars again and crossed the street, trying to see through the shop's glass front. The door handle rattled in my hand. I took a deep breath and hoped I didn't look too crazed to the people inside.

I spotted her immediately, her soft bangs peeking out from beneath her gray and plum head scarf. Her eyes were on the door and looking just as nervous as mine. When she recognized me, her hand flew to cover her open mouth. She stood up.

I wove through the tables, the Afghans speaking English, the foreigners drinking cardamom-infused green tea.

"You made it!" she whispered when I approached her table.

"Yes, Ms. Franklin," I said, and collapsed into the chair.

CHAPTER 69
RAHIMA

Nine days passed before I saw Hamida and Sufia. They had kept away, afraid that somehow they might lead someone to me. Hamida became tearful when she saw me. Sufia let out a triumphant yelp, with an energy I'd never seen her display in the parliamentary sessions.

Ms. Franklin and I had gone directly from the teahouse to a women's shelter she had located. It wasn't the shelter that we'd heard about. It was another one, one much further from the parliament building and on the western outskirts of the capital.

The shelter was both sad and uplifting. There were stories there, stories that made me cringe, scars that would never heal.

I met a woman who lived there with her three children. When her in-laws learned of her husband's death, they accused her of killing him. About to be jailed, she decided to run rather than risk losing her two daughters and one son.

Another woman had escaped a heavy-handed husband, a husband who was having an affair with her younger sister. One night, while he snored beside her, she crept out softly and walked two days and two nights to reach a police station.

And there was a girl. She was my age and her story made me realize that I wasn't alone. At twelve years old, she'd been married off to a man five times her age. Her family had put her in a white dress and taken her to a party. At the end of the night, they left without her. Four years later, she had run off, escaping the in-laws who treated her as a slave.

I wasn't ready to share my story with them yet. Even here, in this open room with Afghan carpets and the smell of cumin, I felt my husband's reach. If he knew where to look, it would only take him a day to reach me. The thought made me so nervous I could barely eat.

Hamida and Sufia only came once. I missed them but I could expect nothing more, knowing the route was long and that they had obligations to their own families. Visiting a shelter could attract the wrong attention and endanger everyone involved. I would always think of them warmly and with deep gratitude, remembering how they and Ms. Franklin had formulated a plan to help me escape the *naseeb* that awaited me had I returned to my husband. My plan, though, didn't account for what might happen to Badriya. Hamida and Sufia had seen her once the day after my disappearance. She looked furious and suspicious, they said, but she seemed to believe their surprise to hear I was missing. I was sure Abdul Khaliq would never let her return to Kabul and I hated to think what Abdul Khaliq had done to her when she'd returned to the compound. Though she hadn't been kind to me, I wished his wrath on no one.

I had time in the shelter, time to finally sit down and contemplate all that had happened. I felt embarrassed, remembering the day I'd argued with Khala Shaima, snapped at her that all the education she'd pushed me to get hadn't done me one bit of good.

It wasn't true.

It was only because I was literate that I was able to join Badriya in Kabul. It was only because I could hold a pen with purpose that I was able to be her assistant and feel comfortable joining Hamida and Sufia in the resource center. It was my few years of school that allowed me to read the beauty shop flyer in the store window, to locate the street where Ms. Franklin waited nervously to help me make my escape.

I'm sorry, Khala-jan. I'm sorry I never thanked you for fighting for me, for everything you taught me, for the stories you told me, for the escape

662

you gave me.

My only regret was that I hadn't been able to send word to Khala Shaima, to let her know that I had made it out and that I was safe. I hoped she didn't think Abdul Khaliq had killed me. I prayed she would not try to visit me at Abdul Khaliq's compound, knowing she would be met by my very angry husband. But I wanted to send her a message, somehow — I had to try. I would take pen to paper and write my dear aunt a note, a few words, so that she could share in what I'd managed to do, what she'd given me the strength to do.

I finally was able to convince Ms. Franklin to mail her a letter.

The letter, addressed to Khala Shaima, was from her second cousin and it talked of nothing but the smell of fresh air, the delightful sound of birds chirping, and the hope that the family could pay a visit sometime soon.

I had no way of knowing if it had arrived, so I could only hope that the letter found Khala Shaima. It wasn't until many years later, a lifetime really, that I heard it had been discovered in her hand by her older sister, my *khala* Zeba. Khala Zeba couldn't make sense of it anyway, since she'd never gone to school or learned her letters. She was too distraught at finding her sickly sister cold and breathless to give it much thought then anyway. But two weeks later, when the rhythm of her life returned and the birds had prayed all they could over Khala Shaima's grave, she would ask her husband to read it for her and be puzzled, wondering which cousin would write to her crippled sister of things as mundane as birds and the weather.

The letter was signed Bibi Shekiba.

ACKNOWLEDGMENTS

Thank you to my parents who gave me the tools to write about a girl who deserves the world. I am yours, always. To Zoran and Zayla, you made this story important to tell — I love you. Thank you to my husband, Amin, for your ideas, discussions, and faith in me. You've made my dreams come true. To my street-smart, wise-cracking brother, Fawod, my first and forever fan, thank you for your absolute confidence. Fahima, my muse, the spark that ignited this story and my first reader, how grateful I am for your support, every day! I am thankful for the legacy I've inherited, the creativity and traditions from the greats and grands in my own family, and hope to pay tribute to them through this story.

A great big hug to my agent, Helen Heller, who took my draft and ran with it. Thank you for your confidence and guiding ideas through this process. A special thanks to my editor, Rachel Kahan, for taking this story on and never letting go! Your input and feedback has been invaluable and I am so glad to be with you. Much appreciation to the entire team at William Morrow — marketing, design, editing, publicity, everyone!! — for turning a draft into a real thing! No list of thanks would be complete without acknowledging the impact that teachers and coffee shops have on realizing dreams. My gratitude to Tahera Shairzay, who provided invaluable firsthand insight into the workings of the Afghan parliament and for her contribution to progress in Kabul. My appreciation to Louis and Nancy Dupree for their contributions to documenting Afghanistan's culture and history. Their works have been an invaluable resource.

This story is loosely based on historical figures in Afghanistan as well as contemporary citizens. It is a work of fiction and I have taken great liberties, but I have no doubt that more of it is factual than we would hope. A special acknowledgment to the daughters, sisters, mothers, aunts, and teachers of Afghanistan, and to those individuals and groups who work so tirelessly to make that world a better place. To the daughters of Afghanistan, may the sun warm your faces as you forge your paths.

The employees of Thorndike Press hope you have enjoyed this Large Print book. All our Thorndike, Wheeler, and Kennebec Large Print titles are designed for easy reading, and all our books are made to last. Other Thorndike Press Large Print books are available at your library, through selected bookstores, or directly from us.

For information about titles, please call:
    (800) 223-1244

or visit our Web site at:
    http://gale.cengage.com/thorndike

To share your comments, please write:
    Publisher
    Thorndike Press
    10 Water St., Suite 310
    Waterville, ME 04901